D0182326

MAYA

Also by Jostein Gaarder

Sophie's World
The Christmas Mystery
Hello? Is Anybody There?
The Solitaire Mystery
Through a Glass Darkly
Vita Brevis
The Frog Castle

JOSTEIN GAARDER

MAYA

Translated by James Anderson

A PHOENIX HOUSE BOOK
Weidenfeld & Nicolson

Originally published in Norway in 1999 as *Maya*,
copyright © 1999 by H. Aschehoug & Co. (W. Nygaard), Oslo

First published in Great Britain in 2000 by Phoenix House

Copyright © Jostein Gaarder 1999
This English translation copyright © James Anderson, 2000

The right of Jostein Gaarder to be identified as the author
of this work has been asserted by him
in accordance with the Copyright, Designs and Patents Act of 1988.

The right of James Anderson to be identified as the translator
of this work has been asserted by him in accordance
with the Copyright, Designs and Patents Act of 1988.

All rights reserved. No part of this publication may be reproduced,
stored in a retrieval system, or transmitted
in any form or by any means, electronic, mechanical,
photocopying, recording, or otherwise, without the prior
permission of both the copyright owner and the above
publisher of this book.

A CIP catalogue record for this book is available
from the British Library.

ISBN 1 861591 83 7

Typeset by Deltatype Ltd, Birkenhead, Merseyside
Printed by Clays Ltd, St Ives plc

Phoenix House

Weidenfeld & Nicolson
The Orion Publishing Group Ltd
Orion House
5 Upper Saint Martin's Lane
London, WC2H 9EA

To Siri

Contents

Prologue

I will never forget the damp, windswept January morning in 1998 when Frank landed on the tiny Fijian island of Taveuni. Thunder had rumbled all night, and before breakfast the proprietors of the Maravu Plantation Resort were busy trying to repair some damage to the electrical plant. As the entire frozen food store was in jeopardy, I volunteered to drive to Matei to fetch some new guests who were due to arrive on 'date-line' island by the morning plane from Nadi. Angela and Jochen Kiess were profusely grateful for my offer, and Jochen pointed out that in a crisis one could always count on the English.

I noticed the solemn Norwegian as soon as he got into the Land Rover. He was about forty, of medium height, and fair like most Scandinavians, but his eyes were brown and he had a somewhat crestfallen air. He introduced himself as Frank Andersen, and I remember toying with the notion that perhaps he was one of that rare breed who, throughout their lives, feel themselves oppressed by the grief that the lack of spirit and permanence in our existence brings. This assumption was by no means dashed when, that same evening, I learnt that he was an evolutionary biologist. For those predisposed to gloom, evolutionary biology can hardly be a very uplifting science.

On my desk here at home in Croydon is a crumpled picture postcard from Barcelona, dated 26 May 1992. The picture is a view of Gaudí's unfinished sand-castle of a cathedral, La Sagrada Familia, and on the back is written:

Dearest Frank,
    I'm coming to Oslo on Tuesday. But I won't be alone. It's all

going to be different now. You must brace yourself for something. Don't phone me! I want to feel your body before words can interpose themselves between us. Do you remember the magic elixir? Soon you'll be able to savour a few drops of it. I feel so scared sometimes. Is there any step we could both take to reconcile ourselves to the brevity of life?

Your own Vera.

One afternoon, as we sat hunched over our beers in the bar of the Maravu, Frank showed me the postcard with those high spires. I'd been telling him how I'd lost Sheila some years earlier, and he'd sat there a long while before opening his wallet and extricating a folded postcard which he opened out and placed on the table in front of us. The greeting was in Spanish, but the Norwegian translated it word for word. It was as if he needed my help to grasp what he himself had transposed.

'Who is Vera?' I asked. 'Is she your wife?'

He nodded.

'We met in Spain at the end of the eighties. A few month later we were living together in Oslo.'

'But it fell apart?'

He shook his head, but then added, 'Ten years later she moved back to Barcelona. That was last autumn.'

'Vera's not a typically Spanish name,' I put in. 'Or Catalan for that matter.'

'It's the name of a little town in Andalucía,' he said. 'According to her family, Vera was conceived there.'

I gazed down at the postcard.

'And she'd been over in Barcelona visiting her family?'

He shook his head again.

'She'd been there some weeks defending a doctoral thesis.'

'Really?'

'On the migration of humans out of Africa. Vera's a palaeontologist.'

'Who did she bring with her to Oslo?' I enquired.

He peered down into his glass.

'Sonja,' was all he said.

'Sonja?'

'Our daughter. Sonja.'

'So you've got a daughter?'

He pointed at the postcard.

'That was how I learnt Vera was pregnant.'

'Your baby?'

I saw a spasm pass through him.

'Yes, my baby.'

I gathered that things had gone badly wrong at some point and was trying to work out what it might have been. I still had a few clues to investigate.

'And this "magix elixir" you were to taste some drops of? It sounds terribly seductive.'

He hesitated. Then brushed the whole thing aside with an almost bashful smile.

'No, it's too silly,' he said. 'It was just one of Vera's fancies.'

I didn't believe him. I reckoned it was one of Frank and Vera's fancies.

I motioned to the barman and ordered another beer. Frank had hardly touched his.

'Go on,' I said.

He went on.

'We shared some of the same uncompromising thirst for life. Or should I call it "craving for eternity"? I don't know if you understand what I mean by that?'

How well I understood! I felt my heart pounding so hard in my chest that I thought it advisable to calm down a bit. I merely raised the palm of one hand to signify that I needed no explanation of what he meant by a craving for eternity. It was a gesture he obeyed. Clearly, it wasn't the first time Frank had tried to explain the meaning of that precise phrase.

'I'd never encountered the same uncompromising need in a woman. Vera was a warm and practical person. But she also lived in her own world a good deal, or in what I should call the world of palaeontology. She was one of those who inclines more to the vertical than the horizontal.'

'Really?'

'She wasn't much interested in the hustle and bustle of life. Or about what she saw in the mirror, for that matter. She was beautiful, very beautiful in fact. But I never saw her with a glossy magazine.'

He sat dabbling his finger in his beer.

'She once told me that when she was young she'd had these vivid daydreams about a magic potion which would give her eternal life if she drank half of it. Then she'd have unlimited time to search for the man she wanted to give the other half to. So she'd be certain to find the right man one day, if not next week, then in a hundred, or a thousand years' time.'

I pointed at the card again.

'And now she'd found this elixir of life?'

He gave a resigned smile.

'When she arrived back from Barcelona in the early summer of '92, she solemnly announced that we must have swallowed a few drops of that magic drink she'd dreamt about when she was little. She was referring to the child we were going to have. Now, a little bit of each of us had begun to live its own life, she said. Perhaps it might bear fruit in aeons to come.'

'Posterity, you mean?'

'Yes, that's what she was thinking of. As a matter of fact, every human being on the planet is descended from a single female who lived in Africa some hundreds of thousands of years ago.'

He took a sip of his beer and when he stayed silent for a while, I tried to draw him out again.

'Please go on,' I urged.

He looked me deep in the eyes, as if he was weighing up whether I was a man he could trust.

'When she came to Oslo that time, she assured me that she wouldn't have hesitated sharing her magic elixir with me if she'd had it. I didn't get any "magic elixir", of course, but it was still a great moment for me. I glimpsed something noble in her having dared to make a choice that could never be undone.'

I nodded.

'It's rare to promise eternal fidelity these days. People stay together while the going's good. But then, there are the bad times as well. That's when a lot of people just cut and run.'

Now he became more ardent.

'I believe I can recall exactly what she said. "For me there is only one man and one earth," she said. "I feel it this strongly because I only live once." '

'That was a powerful profession of love,' I nodded. 'But what happened?'

He was very succinct. After draining his beer glass he told me they'd lost Sonja when she was four and a half, and after that they could no longer go on living together. Too much sorrow under one roof, he said. Then he just sat there staring out over the palm grove.

The subject wasn't raised again, despite a couple of discreet attempts on my part to breathe new life into it.

Also, our conversation had been somewhat interrupted when a great toad hopped on to the raised floor where we sat. There was a 'glopp!', and it was crouching under the table between our feet.

'A cane toad,' he said.

'A cane toad?'

'Or *Bufo marinus*. They were introduced from Hawaii in 1936 to combat the insect numbers on the sugar plantations. They've thrived here.'

He pointed out into the palm grove and we spotted four or five more. A few minutes later I was able to count ten or twelve toads in the damp grass. I'd spent days on the island and never seen so many toads all at once. Frank almost seemed to be attracting them, and before long over twenty specimens were in view. The sight of all those toads filled me with a kind of disgust.

I lit a cigarette.

'I'm still thinking about that elixir you mentioned,' I said. 'Not everyone would have dared to touch it. I think most people would have left it alone.'

Then I stood my lighter on the table and whispered, 'That is a magic lighter. If you light it now, you'll live for ever.'

He looked into my eyes without a glimmer of a smile. It was as if his pupils were glowing.

'But think carefully,' I stressed. 'This one chance is all you get, and your decision can never be revoked.'

He brushed my caveat aside. 'It makes no difference,' he said, but even then I couldn't be sure which way he'd jump.

'Do you want a normal lifespan?' I asked solemnly. 'Or do you wish to remain here on earth for all eternity?'

Slowly but deliberately, Frank picked up the lighter and lit it.

I was impressed. I had spent almost a week on that Fijian island, but now I no longer felt alone.

'There aren't many of us,' I remarked.

Then, for the first time, he broke into a broad grin. I think he was as amazed at our meeting as I was.

'No, not many, certainly,' he conceded.

With that he half rose from his chair and held out a hand to me over the beer glasses.

It was as if we were members of the same exclusive club. Frank and I weren't the least troubled by the thought of eternal life. We were simply terrified of the opposite.

It wasn't long to dinner, so I hinted we might seal our new-found solidarity with a dram. When I suggested neat gin, he nodded appreciatively.

The toads continued to proliferate in the palm grove, and again I felt a wave of loathing. I admitted to Frank that I still hadn't got used to the presence of geckoes in my room.

The gins came, and while the staff set about laying tables for dinner, we sat on, toasting the angels in heaven. We also drank to that tiny clique that never quite conquers its envy of the angels' everlasting life. Indicating the toads in the palm grove, Frank said that out of common courtesy we ought to raise our glasses to them too.

'They're our blood-brothers after all,' he pointed out. 'We're more closely related to them than to cherubim.'

Frank was like that. His head may have been up in the stars, but he also had his feet firmly on the ground. The previous day he'd confessed to me that he hadn't relished flying in the light aircraft that had brought him from Nadi to Matei. He'd hinted at a lot of tubulence and at his own disquiet at having no co-pilot for the short hop. As we drank, he told me that at the end of April he was going to a conference in the ancient university town of Salamanca, and that a call to the conference centre the previous day had confirmed that Vera, too, had registered for it. The trouble was, he had no idea if she knew they'd meet in Salamanca.

'But you're hoping so?' I hazarded. 'You're hoping she'll be there?'

He didn't answer my question.

That evening all the tables in the Maravu's restaurant were pushed together to form one long board. It was an idea I had helped to promote, because so many of the guests were on their own. Just as Ana and José, the first diners, made their entrance, I took one last glance at the postcard with those eight Promethean spires reaching into the sky, and passed it back to Frank.

'You keep it!' he burst out. 'I know every word anyway.'

I couldn't ignore the bitter undercurrent in his voice and tried to make him change his mind. But he was implacable. He seemed to have come to an important decision.

'If I keep it myself,' he said, 'sooner or later I might rip it up. So it's better if you look after it for me. And, who knows – maybe we'll meet again some day.'

Even so, I was determined to return the postcard to him before he left date-line island. But on the morning of Frank's departure, something happened at the Maravu that distracted my attention.

That I would indeed meet the Norwegian again, almost a year later, was one of those extraordinary coincidences that add spice to life, and periodically foster the hope that secret powers really do watch over our lives, and occasionally tweak the strings of destiny.

Chance has decreed that it's not only an old picture postcard I have in front of me. From today, I also have in my possession a long letter that Frank wrote to Vera after he met her that April. I regard it as a personal triumph that this rare document has finally fallen into my hands – and a most unlikely triumph it would have been had I not, by some fluke, bumped into Frank in Madrid six months later. We even met at the Hotel Palace, the hotel where he'd sat writing to Vera. It was November 1998.

In his letter to Vera, Frank describes several episodes we both witnessed in Fiji. Understandably enough, he rather dwells on Ana and José, but he also refers to a couple of conversations that he and I had on our own.

In setting myself the task of presenting this long letter in full, there was now and again a temptation to supplement Frank's account with some comments of my own. I have, however, chosen to reproduce the letter to Vera in its entirety, before adding my own substantial postscript.

Of course, I'm delighted to have this long epistle before me, if for no other reason than that it has enabled me to study the fifty-two clauses of the manifesto. In this connection, permit me merely to state that it would be wholly misleading to infer that I set out to purloin a personal letter. That's not how things were at all. But this is another matter to which I shall return in the postscript.

In a few short months we'll be entering the twenty-first century. I think time passes quickly. I think time passes more and more quickly.

Ever since I was a young boy – not so very long ago – I've known that I would be fully sixty-seven before I managed to see the next millennium. The thought has always both fascinated and appalled me. I had to bid adieu to Sheila in this century. She was only fifty-nine when she died.

Perhaps I'll return to the island on the date line for the millennium. I'm considering putting the letter to Vera into a time capsule, which will remain sealed for a thousand years. I doubt there'll be any need to make it public before then, and the same is true of the manifesto. A thousand years is no great span, especially when measured against the aeons encompassed by the manifesto. And yet, a thousand years is long enough for most of the traces of us contemporary mortals to be erased, and for the story of Ana María Maya to become, at best, a myth from the distant past.

Exactly when what I have to say gets heard is no longer of such importance at my time of life. The great thing is that it should be said at some point; and not even necessarily by me. Maybe that's why I've begun to dwell on this time capsule. Perhaps, in a thousand years, the world won't be such a noisy place.

After re-reading the letter to Vera, I have at last felt ready to start clearing out Sheila's clothes. The time has come for that. Some people from the Salvation Army are coming tomorrow morning and they've promised to take everything. They'll even take the old stuff they won't get anything for. It feels a bit like pulling down an old swallow's nest which hasn't been home to birds for many years.

Soon I'll be established as a widower. That, too, is a life. I no longer start when my eye lights on the colour photograph of Sheila.

With all the dwelling on the past I've indulged in recently, it may seem paradoxical that even now I wouldn't balk at swallowing Vera's magic elixir. I'd do it without blinking, even if I couldn't be certain of finding someone else to give the other half to. It would be too late for Sheila anyway. All she could do that last year was have chemotherapy.

I've already got something planned for tomorrow. I've invited Chris Batt to dinner. Chris is the chief librarian of our new library in Croydon. I'm one of his regulars. I think it's a tremendous honour for the town to have a modern library complete with escalators. Chris is an enterprising chap. I don't believe he would have lit the lighter in the bar at the Maravu. Or felt sickened by the sight of all those toads.

I've made up my mind to ask Chris if he thinks the foreword to a book is usually written before or after the main work is complete. Personally, I've a theory that the foreword is almost invariably written right at the end. That would be consistent with something else I've noticed, especially after reading the letter from Frank.

Several hundred million years elapsed from the time the first amphibians crawled on land, to the moment when a living creature on this planet was able to describe the event. Only now are we able to write the foreword to the history of human beings – long after that history has been played out. Thus, the essence of a thing bites its own tail. Perhaps this is true of all creative processes. Perhaps it holds good for musical composition, for instance. I imagine that the very last thing written in a symphony is the prelude. I shall ask Chris for his thoughts on this. He's a bit of a wag, but a wise one. I doubt if Chris Batt could point to even so much as a comic opera in which the overture could conceivably have been written before the rest was finished. The synopsis of any plot doesn't see the light of day until it ceases to have any useful purpose. Just as the thunderclap never manages to warn us about the lightning.

I don't know if Chris Batt possesses more than a passing knowledge of astronomy, but I shall ask his opinion of the following brief résumé of the history of this universe:

The applause for the Big Bang was heard only fifteen billion years after the explosion.

Here follows the letter to Vera in its entirety.

Croydon, June 1999
John Spooke

THE LETTER TO VERA

Dear Vera,

A fortnight has passed since we saw each other, and because of the events of that last evening, you may feel it's time you heard from me. I've only waited so that I could tie up all the loose ends.

I stayed on in Salamanca after the conference, because I was convinced, wholly convinced, that it was them I'd seen beneath the bridge over the Tormes. You thought I was joking, you thought I was spinning a yarn just to keep you amused until we got back to the hotel. But it was Ana and José I'd seen, and I couldn't leave the city until I'd spent a day or two trying to find them again. I bumped into them the very next morning in the Plaza Mayor. But I mustn't get ahead of myself. I've made up my mind to tell you everything in chronological order. Let me just outline my reasons for sitting down to write to you today.

A week and a half later – the day before yesterday – I met José here in Madrid at the Prado. It was almost as if he'd been searching for me amongst its vast galleries. This morning we met each other again. I was sitting on a bench in the Retiro Park carefully sifting through everything he'd told me so far, but some of the pieces still hadn't fallen into place. Suddenly, he was standing in front of me – as if someone had told him where I took my daily walk. He sat down, and there we remained for several hours until I accompanied him through the park to Atocha Station. All at once, he pushed a bundle of photographs into my arms and turned to run for the train. When I got back to my hotel, I discovered that something was written on the back of every single picture. It was the manifesto, Vera! I was holding the entire solitaire pack in my hands.

The things José told me in Retiro Park, not to mention what he gave me as he disappeared, have prevented me tearing myself away from this city before I've sent you the full story. It's two in the afternoon now, and there won't be much sleep for me tonight. I'll have coffee and a bite to eat sent to my room, but apart from that

I've nothing to distract me from my sole task of sending you this epistle before I pack up and leave for Seville on Friday morning.

I'm a little troubled by the thought that perhaps you won't log on to the internet straight away, and there's a temptation to produce this report in segments. But you're to have it all at once, all or nothing. It's struck me that maybe I should at least send you an e-mail to warn you that a longer one will be arriving some time tomorrow. But I'm not even sure if you want to hear from me again. Anyway, I've got to exert myself a bit to make you believe this story, and I still haven't written it yet.

It was in Fiji that I got caught up in this spider's web, but I can't remember now how much I managed to tell you. We were only together for a few days, and we both felt it would be more discreet if we maintained a distance from each other. But when I thought I'd caught sight of that extraordinary couple from Fiji, I remember that everything came pouring out. I just can't recall what I got round to telling you and what I didn't, because you kept interrupting me with your peals of laughter – you thought I was making it all up on the spot, as a sort of evening entertainment calculated to keep you down by the river.

You'll naturally be wondering how Ana and José could possibly concern you, or us for that matter. Perhaps I ought to remind you of a greeting you once sent me from Barcelona. You wrote: 'Is there any step we could both take to reconcile ourselves to the brevity of life?' Now I'm putting that question again, and to answer it I must first speak of Ana and José. To understand the full extent of my mission, you must step back with me even deeper into the past, perhaps as far back as the Devonian period when the very first amphibians made their appearance. That's where I think this story begins.

No matter what happens between us, I shall ask you to do me one favour. But for now, simply settle back and read. Just read!

He who sees last, sees best

The final stage of my two-month-long Pacific expedition was the Fijian island of Taveuni. My task was to investigate how introduced plant and animal species had affected the ecological balance. This included stowaways like rats and mice, insects and lizards, but also the more or less planned introduction of species like the opossum and mongoose, for the control of other animals, in particular pests associated with new forms of agriculture. A third group comprised feral domestic animals like cats, goats and pigs, not forgetting the careless introduction of animals for the pot – or game – represented by herbivores like the rabbit and roe deer. As for introduced plants, both ornamental and useful, the list of species is so long and varied for each island that there's little point in reeling off names.

The southern part of the Pacific is an El Dorado for such studies. Not long ago these isolated islands each had their own primeval ecological balance of endemic and richly variegated flora and fauna. Today, Oceania has the world's highest proportion of endangered animals – both in relation to its size and population. This hasn't just been caused by the introduction of new species; in many places the felling of forest and thoughtless plantation management has contributed to a fatal soil erosion, which has ultimately destroyed traditional habitats.

Until only a century ago, several of the islands I visited had had almost no contact with European culture. But then came Europe's last great wave of colonisation. Naturally, every island, each new settlement and each individual landfall has its own story. However, the ecological consequences have followed the same depressing pattern: shipboard animals like rats, mice and insects were virtually an ecological contagion that arrived automatically with the first vessels. To rectify the ravages of these creatures, new animal species were introduced. Cats were brought in to keep down the rats, and toads to hold certain insects in check, particularly on the sugar plantations. Soon these species became a greater pest and nuisance than the rats and insects had been. So another predator would be introduced. Eventually this animal would itself turn into an ecological catastrophe, not just for a number of bird species, but also for many of the unique, indigenous reptiles. So larger predators were needed. And so on, Vera, and so on. Nowadays, we have more faith in poisons, viruses and sterility agents of one kind and another – chemical and biological warfare by any other name. But it's not so easy to cobble together a whole new food-chain, if indeed it's possible to do at all. By contrast, it's terrifyingly easy to destroy an ecological balance that nature has spent millions of years creating. But the world's recklessness no longer knows any national boundaries. I'm thinking of the arrogant folly of shrewdness – a type of blinkered resourcefulness so charmingly underdeveloped in the Aborigine, Maori and Melanesian before he began to be schooled by the white man. I'm thinking of the folly of profit and greed. Now we employ euphemisms like 'globalisation' and 'trade agreements'. This gives the impression that food is no longer something to be eaten, but a commodity. Whereas humans used to be able to supply their wants from the soil, nowadays larger and larger mountains of useless artefacts are being produced that only the most affluent can afford. We no longer live from hand to mouth. The time of paradise is past.

That apart, you're only too well aware of my abiding interest in reptiles. It was a boyish fascination for life on this planet in the distant past that made me a biologist, and that was long before dinosaurs suddenly became so fashionable. I wanted to find out why these highly specialised reptiles suddenly died out. I was also absorbed by questions that have never ceased to preoccupy me: what would have happened had dinosaurs not become extinct? What would have happened to the small, shrew-like mammals that you and I are descended from? Even more crucially: what would have happened to the dinosaurs?

In Oceania I had plenty of opportunity to study several ancient reptilian species. One high point was the archaic tuatara that lives on a few small, isolated islands around New Zealand. At the risk of irritating you a little, I must admit I was filled with an indescribable sense of wonder when I saw one of the oldest living reptiles on earth thriving in the remains of the old forests of Gondwanaland. These primeval reptiles live in underground burrows, which they often share with fulmars. Growing up to 70 centimetres long, and with an optimal body temperature of only 9°C, they can live for more than a century. When you see them at night, it's as if you were back in the Jurassic period at the time when Laurasia was breaking loose from Gondwana and the great dinosaurs had only just begun to evolve. It was at that moment that the Rhynchocephaliae became distinct from other lizard orders, as a small but very persistent class of reptiles. Its only surviving representative, the tuatara, has remained remarkably unchanged for around two hundred million years.

It took my breath away, Vera. The existence of the tuatara is no less amazing than if a prehistoric bird were discovered living on one of these isolated islands. Incidentally, something like that did happen on 22 December 1938 off the east coast of South Africa, when a fishing boat caught a lobed-finned fish in its nets, the so-called coelacanth. This class of lobed-finned fish, which was so crucial for evolution because you and I and every other terrestrial mammal trace our descent from it, was, until Christmas 1938, solely found in fossil form, and was assumed to have died out almost a hundred million years ago. Both the coelacanth and the tuatara deserve the name 'living fossils', and perhaps I should add a 'thus far'. It's not many years since the tuatara was widely distributed in New Zealand.

I have never found using a colleague's description of an animal species very stimulating. My interest has always focused on the development of species, and here one is often dependent on fossil remains to a large extent. The greatest fossil sensation of the past century is undoubtedly the recent discovery of feathered dinosaurs.

This scoop provided conclusive proof that birds are descended from dinosaurs. You might almost say that birds *are* dinosaurs!

I'm not saying I have no interest in old bones and fossils. However, once I'm dealing with living species, I prefer to conduct my own field studies before profiting from the monographs of others and immersing myself in a more systematic analysis. As far as the tuatara is concerned – as with a number of other endemic species of considerable age – it is the habitat itself which has remained so amazingly intact over millions of years. Ah yes, I won't deny there were moments when I felt like some latter-day Darwin as I flew from island to island above the green, turquoise and azure-blue coral reefs.

In Fiji I was specially interested in studying the rare crested iguana which is only found on a couple of islands there and wasn't described until 1979 (by John Gibbons). Fiji has two species of iguana, and this is remarkable in itself as they aren't found anywhere in Asia except in Fiji and – as far as this species is concerned – on Tonga as well. Formerly, it was often supposed that they must, in some miraculous way, have made the crossing from South America on floating plant remains! This is a possibility, of course, for the ability to move from continent to continent on balsa logs and the like is probably not limited to primates. However, Professor Peter Newell of the University of the South Pacific has pointed out that the iguanas of Fiji may have a much older geological history than previously believed. He writes: 'Recent discoveries of sub-fossils of crocodiles – that can swim for thousands of kilometres – would suggest that iguanas have been here a lot longer than we originally thought. They are thought to be relics from Gondwanaland when Fiji – along with countries like New Zealand, Australia and India – was part of one big continental plate that later broke off into fragments.' Iguanas are also found on Madagascar, which was part of Gondwanaland over 150 million years ago.

But I shan't bore you with my studies now. You'll have plenty of opportunity to find out about them when the report is published some time around the turn of the millennium. And, of course, only if you're interested, promise me that.

I was on my way home from Auckland, and a couple of times a week Air New Zealand runs a convenient service via Nadi and Honolulu to Los Angeles with a connecting flight on to Frankfurt. Nobody was waiting for me at home – truly there wasn't – so I decided to stop over in Fiji for a few days, partly to digest all my impressions while I was still within the tropical archipelago, and partly to recuperate and stretch my legs a bit before the long journey home. I had already spent a week in Fiji when I arrived in Oceania at the beginning of November, but I hadn't got round to visiting the jewel of that island kingdom. I'm referring to Taveuni, which is often called 'the Garden Island of Fiji' because of its unparalleled lushness and relative seclusion from the outside world.

The route from Nadi to Taveuni was overbooked that morning – and as a result my baggage travelled in the overbooked aircraft while I and four other passengers squeezed into something they called 'the matchbox-plane'. The name was apposite, I can tell you. We virtually had to crawl into the tiny six-seater and were duly welcomed aboard by the pilot, who blithely announced that unfortunately there would be no refreshments on the forthcoming leg, and requested us not to move about unnecessarily in the central aisle. He succeeded in whipping up a fair mood of gallows humour amongst his passengers, and just for good measure, half of two fingers from the hand that saluted us were missing. The 'central aisle' was six inches wide, and no one on board could have contemplated food, because as soon as the plane took off, it was tossed this way and that by violent turbulence as the engine worked frantically to haul us over the looming peak of Tomaniivi on the island of Viti Levu.

The man was presumably a retired pilot who had moved to Fiji simply because he refused to wave goodbye to joystick and altimeter. But he was a nice enough fellow; I sat there with my knees pressed up against the back of his seat, and he kept turning to us with a broad smile, asking where each of us came from, showing us where we were on the map any time we asked, pointing enthusiastically to coral reefs, dolphins and flying-fish down below, and talking sixteen to the dozen.

As you've probably already guessed, I sat there with my heart in my mouth. I was well used to light aircraft, I'd done virtually nothing but hop from one island to another during the preceding weeks. But I must confess I felt ill at ease in a plane that had only one pilot. You have every right to call this fear irrational, a kind of idiosyncrasy; yes, I seem to hear you saying just that, since a car, too, has only one driver, you say, and more people are killed on the roads than in the air. That may be true, though a sudden indisposition can hardly be discounted, particularly at five thousand feet, and with a pilot in his late sixties. A faint in the tropical heat isn't entirely unlikely, it's simply human, such things happen.

After all that travelling I wasn't concerned about a technical fault, but rather the contrary, I was fearful of organic failure. I sat there nursing the precarious sensation of being a mere mortal, a flesh-filled vertebrate currently strapped to an aircraft seat, and that this applied just as much to the man sitting so boldly in front of me at the joystick, and he was thirty years my senior. An irrefutable symptom of this perception was a pulse more reminiscent of the end of a marathon, and if my heart was pounding two hundred per minute, what, I thought, was the pilot's doing; not to mention his cholesterol level and the state of his coronary arteries. I had no knowledge of this affable fellow, I had never examined him medically, or satisfied myself about what he'd eaten that morning. More treacherous still was the realisation that I had no knowledge of the ageing pilot's existential inner self. Perhaps he believed in eternal life – a hazard which people in his line of work should be screened for – I mean pilots who fly without co-pilots and with paying passengers aboard; there can't be many of them, after all. He might recently have been deceived by a woman. Or he might be sitting there with the horrible knowledge that later that morning he'd have to own up to some massive embezzlement. I could find no pleasure in Mount Tomaniivi, the dolphins or the coral reefs. It was all so terribly far below me, I was shut in, I couldn't get out, I couldn't get away. I was missing my gin bottle, and I wouldn't have felt the slightest shame in lifting it to my lips if only I'd had it. It was just my luck that my bottle of tranquilliser was in the suitcase that had been sent with the scheduled plane.

This has nothing to do with 'fear of flying', Vera, and I hope you realise that my description hitherto hasn't been intended as a travelogue, either. All I'm trying to talk about is my own awareness of life. In a sense, it's always with me, but normally it only surfaces properly in two situations: as soon as I wake up in the mornings and on the few occasions when I get drunk. They say 'in vino veritas', and for my part I'd subscribe to the notion that intoxication may promote a more naked, unadorned and, basically, far sincerer mental state than woollier quotidian consciousness – at least as regards the really big issues – and it's them we're addressing now. I managed to achieve a far abrupter, cooler and more immediate entry to the same layer of psyche by delegating the responsibility for my continued existence, or non-existence, to a retired pilot in a matchbox-plane with a cracked windscreen and clapped-out instruments. The only difference was that my faculties were even more alert than in the two other situations I've described, as I was neither half asleep, nor were my synapses befuddled with alcohol.

Now, this was the first time I'd ever taken off in a plane flown by a single, superannuated pilot with three whole and two half-fingers on the joystick, whereas so far I'd always woken up to a new day, and it wasn't *that* uncommon for me to drink my way to a truer, nobler and, in reality, soberer mental state. So there is some point in plumbing a little deeper into what I thought and felt up there in the clouds during those seventy-five minutes between Nadi and Taveuni. It also fits in well, because I shall soon be describing my meeting with Ana and José, and of course Gordon, whom I may not have mentioned so far, though my many conversations with him were to colour my stay on the island as well.

There is something I've always shrunk from talking to you properly about, although I think I must have touched on it a couple of times. I'm referring to an early childhood experience I had at my home near Oslo. I must have been rising seven or eight at the time, but anyway it was before my eighth birthday because that was when my family moved to Madrid for four years. I remember I was running along a path in the woods with my pockets full of some hazelnuts I'd found and which I wanted to show to my mother right away. Suddenly, I caught sight of a small fawn lying in full view on the damp forest floor and its carpet of autumnal leaves. Those leaves remain branded on my mind, because some of them, I remember, lay on the little fawn too. I thought the fawn was sleeping, and though I can't be quite sure, I think I crept up to the animal either to stroke it or brush off all the yellow and red leaves. But the fawn wasn't asleep. It was dead.

The fact that the fawn was dead, or rather that I was the one who'd found a fawn that was dead, was something that felt shameful, something I could never tell my mother or father, or even my grandmother or grandfather. If the tiny fawn could lie lifeless in the woods, it might just as easily be my turn to drop down dead next, and this insight – that most children are naturally shielded from, though it's obvious enough – has remained with me as a physical sensation for the rest of my life. I've always had great intuition about things like pastoral care and crisis psychiatry, because it was my self-imposed silence that patently turned the episode into a trauma. If I'd run home crying to my mother I would almost certainly have got the help I needed to overcome that unpleasant experience, but I could never reveal it, not to anyone, it was far too humiliating and ignominious. In a blinding flash it showed me that I, too, was a living being of flesh and blood, another animal, who had my time on earth now, but who one day would cease to be here.

That encounter with the dead fawn may well have proved decisive in shaping my interest in nature. At the very least, the revelation in that leafy woodland influenced the direction of my professional studies. I've always felt drawn towards looking at great spans of time. And so, ever since I was an inquisitive twelve-year-old, I've known all about the Big Bang and the vast distances of the universe. Part of my make-up has made me realise with increasing comprehension that the world I inhabit is almost five billion years old, and the universe three or four times older.

The thought that I might completely cease to exist at some time, that I'm here only this once and that I'll never return, strikes me as monstrous. So I've tried to find a crumb of comfort by placing myself and my own brief life within a wider context. I've practised appeasing myself with the thought that I'm only a tiny part of the great adventure of life, a fleeting scrap of something that is both greater and mightier than myself. Thus have I tried to enlarge my own identity, my own self, and always at the expense of that little self, the one that at any moment might meet the same fate as the fawn – that fissiped that still remains buried somewhere deep in my sub-conscious, that never rises to its feet, that doesn't stir. I've practised, I practise the whole time, though I can't say I've made any liberating advances. Each morning it still hits me that I'm the only one who is me, and that I'm here only now, only at this instant are you and I the bearers of the universe's consciousness of itself.

Looking at one's own life from the perspective of eternity may qualify as a respectable moral or intellectual feat, but it doesn't necessarily bring peace of mind. There is no automatic reconciliation to be found in the realisation that I – a monstrous, conscious primate – am capable of encompassing the entire past of our universe in my memory, from the Big Bang right down to Bill Clinton and Monica Lewinsky, to name but two of the most famous primates of our own time. There is no equanimity to be found in embracing greater reaches of time, rather the reverse I think: it has only made bad worse, and maybe it would have been better to get a mind-healer to excise that dead animal from my swollen subconscious – though I believe it's too late for that now.

This said, we can now return to the cramped aircraft cabin where it wasn't just that ephemeral morning lucidity – always jangling my nerve cells and telling me I'm an over-rational vertebrate doomed, by fits and starts, to face the fact that I have only a few short months left to live. No, it was seventy-five minutes of intense scrutiny of those perspectives. And now the situation was even more precarious, for it might only be a matter of seconds before my life on earth came to a full-stop. Heedlessly, the primate at the controls turned and unfolded a large map, which he poked deep into the lap of a female Australian primate who sat on my right, and who'd introduced herself as Laura. I didn't like this degeneration of aircraft navigation to a level that was even more laid-back and verging on the lecherous. What I'm attempting to say mustn't be construed as meaning that I felt my fellow passengers were bad company; quite the opposite, I loved every one of them, and I could have laid my head in the lap of each of them if only to seek solace and protection. I felt like some wretched lizard, some twitchy creature that should have stayed on the ground, a conviction linked to the fact that it really was an old, blasé and half-way cocky descendant of a lizard that was flying the plane. You realise, because you're reading these lines and because you met me in Salamanca some months later, that the plane came down in one piece. The thing about the flight was that it had provoked an inalienable sense of being just a frail vertebrate in the noonday of life, and this feeling proved impossible to expunge in the days that followed.

Taveuni's airport is called Matei and seems to have been specially designed for matchbox-planes. The runway was a narrow grass strip between an alley of windswept coco-palms, and even the airport building looked more like a bus-shelter with a couple of blue-painted benches and a miniature kiosk. I had an hour to kill until my baggage arrived by the scheduled service. The car from the Maravu Plantation Resort, where I was to put up for three days, arrived simultaneously with the plane and baggage.

I'm not going to deviate from my intention of narrating everything in proper order. So, if I attempt to paint, in a few crude brush-strokes, a picture of 'the Garden Island' it's not for the sake of being discursive, but simply to place Ana and José in an environment with which, as far as my memory is concerned, they will always be irrevocably linked.

As for the name 'the Garden Island', the place might just as well have been called 'the Last Paradise'. This would have had the practical advantage that 'last' could easily be changed to 'lost' in a few decades' time. I can assure you, many of its visitors wouldn't notice the minor change.

Our species has a strange fascination for the 'last' and the 'lost'. The thrill of an experience that future generations can enjoy is as nothing compared to the value of seeing something that subsequently was ruined. He who sees last, sees best. Just as grieving relatives will argue about who had the last word with the deceased.

Gradually, as the world gets smaller, and the tourist industry develops further niches and sub-niches, I forecast a bright future for necro-tourism: 'See lifeless Lake Baikal!', 'Only a few years before the Maldives are under water' — or: 'You can be the last to see a live tiger!' Examples will be legion, for paradises are getting fewer and fewer, they are both shrinking and being despoiled, but this won't hinder tourism, quite the opposite.

There are several reasons why Taveuni has so far been luckier in its encounter with the Western world than many of the other islands I visited. The undulating terrain of this volcanic island has been largely responsible for limiting both visitors and the plantation industry. Beaches of black lava also curb tourism, and although the north-eastern corner of the island actually boasts several unspoilt beaches of white coral sand, the problem here is the frequent rainfall. It was just this combination of fertile volcanic soil and high precipitation which, during the middle of the nineteenth century, encouraged European settlers to establish a number of plantations. To begin with, high-grade cotton was the staple, but when the price of cotton went into sharp decline, sugar plantations in the south of the island began to assume some importance. Today, coco-palms are the island's main industry as well as increasing tourism. By tourism I mean so-called eco-tourism, for there is literally nothing else to do here but enjoy the lush environment; there are no shopping centres, nightlife or modern four-storey hotel complexes, the island has no TV link and electricity is in short supply.

The last two factors in particular have helped keep a strong narrative folk tradition alive. Darkness has descended on the island by six o'clock, and then the spoken word takes over. Perhaps someone has been on a fishing trip, someone else has had an experience deep in the forest, a third has come across a straying American by one of the rivers, and each has something to tell. An ancient flora of myths and legends is kept alive too, for on Taveuni there are no entertainments other than those one makes oneself. Divers and snorkellers from all over the world come here to see corals and marine life in an exhilarating kaleidoscope of colours. In addition, the island can still boast one of the world's most exotic bird populations, rare breeds of bat, outings in forest and bush and, of course, bathing on beaches and under the voluptuous waterfalls.

Significantly for the more than one hundred species of varied birdlife, of which several are unique to the locality – like the famous dove with the orange-coloured breast – the Indian mongoose was never introduced here. However, in order to control the insect populations on the plantations, both magpies and toads were brought in. The magpies have occupied their natural habitats, and the toads have pushed the indigenous frogs deeper into the forests, but Taveuni's unique bird population is still amazingly intact. The same holds good for bats, including the giant fruit bat which, with a wingspan of up to five feet, is also called the flying fox or 'beka'. Boiled beka is considered a delicacy amongst the older members of the population.

Taveuni has more than a thousand identified plant species, of which a considerable proportion is endemic. The littoral has plenty of mangrove swamps and coco-palms, while luxuriant, ferny rain forest with countless local trees forms the island's hinterland. Today there is also a wide spectrum of tropical plants such as orchids and hibiscuses. Fiji's national flower, the *Tagimaucia*, is a species found only here and on the neighbouring island of Vanua Levu.

As usual in this part of the world, the submarine fauna shows the most diversity. You don't even need a snorkel to find a gratifying plethora of fish, molluscs, sponges, starfish and corals. It's hard to avoid descriptions like 'a veritable kaleidoscope' and 'every colour of the rainbow' when talking about the marine life of the South Pacific, and around Taveuni I also got the feeling that many of the specimens are even more exquisitely patterned than usual.

Sticking to the island's indigenous terrestrial vertebrates, all classes are represented although, apart from its diverse birdlife, with only a few examples. Before toads were imported from Hawaii in 1936, amphibians were best represented by frogs. Apart from the iguana, the only reptiles were a few species of gecko and snake. The most conspicuous reptile nowadays, however, is the entertaining house gecko Hemidactylus frenatus, though it didn't make its appearance in Fiji until the 1970s. The bat is the only indigenous mammal to boast of and, to make up for it, enjoys a marvellous ecosystem of its own because of its highly distinctive adaptation. Three and a half thousand years ago the first human settlers must have brought with them the Polynesian rat, which may have been introduced as a source of food.

Taveuni's indigenous vertebrates are thus represented by fish, frogs, lizards, birds, bats and Fijians — who at present number twelve thousand souls. The island thus displays an immensely stylised and almost transparent image of vertebrate development. Looking back with hindsight it's not so difficult to see how the vertebrates on this planet evolved in clearly defined stages from fish to amphibians, from amphibians to reptiles and finally from reptiles to birds, bats and Fijians.

Have you ever considered how 'mainstream' the human anatomy is in purely evolutionary terms or, to put it another way, how archaic we are as vertebrates in many ways? Perhaps you've wondered at how similar the human frame is to that of lizards and salamanders. If so, you'll also notice for example that elephants and camels are, by contrast, fairly exotic fruits that have fallen much further from the tree-trunk, if the tree-trunk is taken as being the primeval matrix of backbone, collarbone and the four limbs with five fingers or toes. The real motorway from the squelching life of the Devonian period to man's conquest of the moon has been trafficked by salamander-like amphibians, by mammal-like reptiles and, in the final phase, by primates. There has, of course, been a fascinating network of exits and slip roads, too.

Your protests are becoming almost audible now, I'm being anthropocentric, you cry, evolution is above all non-linear, it's not deliberate; evolution is more reminiscent of bushes and cauliflower heads than lines or trunks. What right have I to name one or two species within a whole class of animals as more typically representative than others? But that's not what I'm saying; I'm only pointing out that somehow I feel greater kinship to a lizard than to a mammal like a fruit bat or a blue whale. I'm descended from neither the bat nor the blue whale, nor from giraffes, nor from orang-utans for that matter, but I am the direct progeny of a lobed-finned fish, of an amphibian and then of a mammal-like reptile.

The sparse assortment of vertebrates on the island made me see it as one great, living chart of life's evolution on earth. I found myself in a Darwinian showroom, and I'm not just thinking of the four limbs of the frog, the lizard, the bat and the Fijian, with their common pentadactyl structure, even though the Fijians' impressively long feet and toes were every bit as ostentatious as the lizard's extremities.

Of the Fijians it may be added that, apart from rats and bats, the only other meat in their diet has been one another. Cannibalism was widely practised right up until the end of the nineteenth century, if we disregard the lone Japanese soldier who was consumed by the Fijian, Viliame Lamasalato, as recently as the end of the Second World War. This has had no small impact on the island's ability to keep its rain forest and environment intact. I'm not thinking here so much of population control by something we might call reciprocal consumption, as of the fact that cannibalism acted as a kind of ecological prophylaxis against the inroads of the white man. Both Abel Tasman (1643) and James Cook (1774) sailed past the islands of Fiji, but rumours of the dangers on these 'cannibal islands' prevented them from risking a landing. After the mutiny on the *Bounty* (1789), Captain Bligh and his officers sailed past several of the islands in an open boat but, hungry and exhausted as they were, they didn't dare filch a single coconut. Early in the nineteenth century the first Europeans arrived in the island kingdom. There are stories told of missionaries who were welcomed cordially and served real native dishes; the term is apposite, for after the meal was eaten it was ceremoniously announced that the hors d'oeuvre had been woman's breast, the main course man's thigh and the dessert brains, for which the natives had developed a handy, four-pronged fork. One of the missionaries – called, ironically enough, Reverend Baker – was turned into food himself in 1867. And so the cannons, shot and powder arrived, and the rest is colonial history. The first thing the Europeans did on Fiji was to eradicate the valuable sandalwood-tree. Later, they imported sixty thousand plantation workers from India, which is why more than half the population of the islands today is Indian. This influx brought with it a series of epidemics and diseases; first cholera, which left several of the islands uninhabited, and in 1890 measles, from which a third of Fiji's population died.

I descry a thought-provoking paradox in all this: the reason the ecological balance has remained relatively intact on some Fijian islands is that the white man didn't dare land because of cannibalism. It is a paradox, even though I have some sympathy with a society which in lean times can consume its own members rather than compete to kill off every other species. I accept that cannibalism must be seen as a breach of what we call 'natural rights', but the Western world's ecological thoughtlessness is an equal breach of human responsibility. Now, the term 'natural rights' has a history more than two thousand years old, and all I ask is: when will we be ready for the term 'natural responsibilities'?

As I've already touched on the two thousand years let me, finally, point to yet another striking paradox associated with 'the Garden Island of Fiji'. Fate has decreed that the island is situated right on the International Date Line, because it happens to be located exactly on the 180th meridian from the Royal Observatory at Greenwich. Strictly speaking, this means that half the island is in today, and the other half in yesterday. Or the opposite of course: one part is in today, and the other in tomorrow. The reason I call this fate is because Taveuni will be the first inhabited place in the world to see the third millennium. It won't pass unnoticed.

I wasn't the only one picked up by the Land Rover. I was joined by two other guests bound for the same destination. We had exchanged a few words at the airport while waiting for our luggage on the scheduled flight. One of them was Laura, who had shown so much enthusiasm for aircraft as she flirted with our ageing pilot, while I had been leafing through the earth's family album – tableau by tableau – from the first cell division in the early Pre-Cambrian period right down to my own allotted time on earth.

Laura was from Adelaide and was a pretty woman in her late twenties. With her golden-brown skin and long, dark braids she was rather reminiscent of a young Native American. One of her peculiarities was that one of her eyes was green and the other was brown. There may have been a small feather of brown in the green eye, and possibly a fibre of green in the brown one, but she had one green and one brown eye all the same, a genetic rarity I couldn't recall having ever seen before. I also noted a World Wildlife Fund badge on her no-nonsense canvas rucksack. Laura was both alluring and eccentric enough to goad me into paying her a little attention, but she obviously wasn't bent on any superficial airport-acquaintanceship, as she buried herself in her 'Lonely Planet' guide, reading busily about the island.

My other fellow passenger was Bill; I think he gave me his surname too, but I've long since forgotten it. He was in his late fifties, came from Monterey in California and was clearly a pensioner of the younger, more affluent and adventure-seeking type. I quickly formed a picture of him as the typical exponent of a peculiarly North American characteristic, namely the uninhibited pleasure of experiencing the world as much as possible at first hand, and without the distracting social relations of a spouse, child or close friend. Bill was a bit of a lad. It occurred to me, I remember, that some people never quite grow up, they just become extremely rich – and often very old.

The man who met us was British and called himself John. He was a powerfully built man in his mid-sixties, at least six foot three in his socks, and with grey hair and short, almost white sideburns. It was only later I realised he wasn't one of the staff at the Maravu, but was a guest there like ourselves, and had offered to fetch us because the proprietors were in a bind. He seemed to take a particular interest in forming an impression of the new guests as quickly as possible.

No sooner had the car turned off the country road and up towards the Maravu Plantation Resort than I was struck by the beauty of the place. The resort comprised ten huts and one main building dotted about an old coconut plantation. The huts – or *bures* as they're called on the islands – were built on a ridge overlooking the sea amongst dense bushes and swaying coco-palms. This made it impossible to view one hut from another, or at least see one door from another. The main building was constructed just like one of the island's traditional community houses with open walls and high gables thatched with palm fronds. Its great timber floor had room for an open-plan reception area, a bar, a restaurant – resoundingly named Wananavu – and a large dance floor.

We were welcomed in the bar and presented with a coconut, complete with elaborately arranged hibiscus flowers and a straw, while check-in formalities were completed. We sat for some minutes chatting while everyone on duty at the Maravu that morning came across and greeted us one by one. 'Bula!' they said, 'bula!' This very local greeting is repeated so often in the Fiji Islands that it almost becomes a mantra. But it has a more flexible meaning than comparable words in most other languages. 'Bula' means anything from 'hi', 'hello' and 'good day' to 'how are you?' 'enjoy your day' and 'farewell'.

Everyone knew that I was 'Frank', that Bill was 'Bill' and that Laura was 'Laura'. It was as if the entire place had had nothing better to do over the past few weeks than prepare for our arrival, to make us feel elite and special. We had come to the Maravu to be purified and reborn as individuals. Bill found out that the Fijian word 'maravu' meant 'quiet and peaceful', while Laura wanted to know the best place to see the island's famous parrots.

I was escorted past a swimming pool and through the palm grove to *bure* 3, where I did the absolute minimum before settling myself on a covered veranda to gaze out across the sea and, in thoughtful awe, to savour a natural resource that is all too rare in our world today. I'm referring to silence – the human race has virtually eradicated that as well.

I was down on the ground once more, although I could hardly say I'd landed, much less put the flight behind me, even after extracting guarantees that I'd got a seat on the scheduled plane for the return flight to Nadi. I was in a mood of restless panic, a mental state I was convinced I would never be able to throw off. It was as if I was enjoying the effervescent, clear-sighted kick of alcohol, but realising that this time I'd drunk of a wine that would never work its way out of my body.

I'd heard of doctors turning into hypochondriacs, of mountain-eers becoming terrified of heights and of priests losing their faith. I was quite as badly off. I was the palaeontologist who'd developed a fear of bones. I was the zoologist who could barely admit he was an animal. I was the evolutionary biologist who found it hard to accept that his time on earth, too, was limited. Half my life had been spent examining the skeletal remains of mammals; with inquisitive zeal I'd thrown myself into the analysis of dead animal remains, and now I'd developed an almost panic-stricken fear because one day I would deposit my own little heap of that same material I'd revelled in. I felt bankrupt, but it didn't seem like an obsession, just an absolute intuitive understanding. Buddha had seen a sick man, an old man and a corpse. As a child I had stumbled over a dead roe deer in the woods, and now – after that hazardous flight from Nadi to Matei – the old wound had reopened.

Again, I reeled through the long film from the time life began on earth four billion years ago. It was my own history I was seeing, my own ancestors. Not my direct lineage back to small, mammal-like reptiles that lived here a couple of hundred million years ago – but further back to a primitive reptile, an amphibian, a lobed-finned fish, an invertebrate, and right back to the world's very first living cell. Not only was I descended from mammal-like reptiles that lived here a couple of hundred million years ago, but each individual cell in my body contained genes that were literally that old. I was the last link in an unbroken chain of cell division, of more or less charted biochemical processes and, in the final analysis, of molecular biology. It dawned on me that I was no different in principle from the simple, single-celled organisms that were my ultimate ancestors. Strictly speaking I was nothing more than a cell colony – with the one important distinction that my cells were more integrated than the cells in a culture of bacteria, they were more differentiated and thus capable of greater radical division of responsibility. But I, too, was made up of individual cells, and each and every one of them was built up around a lowest common denominator, the genetic code, the master plan itself, that was buried in every cell of my body. The DNA code alone represented a microscopic accumulation of many hundreds of millions of years of heedless toying with nucleic acids. And yet, in genetic terms I was nothing more than a monstrous construct of identical twin cells. Just how these hyperclones were able to communicate with each other and, even more, to switch their genes on and off to the best advantage of the whole – this was one of the earth's greatest mysteries.

The real engine of evolution was the simple fact that only a very small proportion of each generation had been able to grow up and reproduce; without selection no evolution would have occurred. A permanent attrition of progeny and an equally eternal battle for survival were the pillars of evolution. But here I sat. Here I sat on a small island in Oceania like some incalculably rare exception to the rule that you don't win the Lottery's main prize a thousand times in a row. I – and by that I mean my lineage, my family tree, my own unbroken line of zygotes and cell divisions – had survived for millions of generations. In each of these generations I had first managed to divide my cells, then breed, fertilise or lay my eggs and, in the final phase, bear live young. If just one of my many millions of ancestors, for example an amphibian living its clammy life in the Devonian or a particular reptile crawling amongst the pteridophytes of the Permian period, if just one single individual had bitten the dust before sexual maturity – just like that poor fawn back home in Norway – I wouldn't have been sitting on the veranda now. And don't tell me I'm taking a view of things that's too long-term, I could go back even further: if there'd been just one fatal mutation in a particular bacterial cell division two or three billion years ago, I would never have seen the light of day. It was from that one particular bacterium that I was descended and exclusively from that very cell – let's call it cell ZYG 31.514.718.120.211.212.091.514 in cell colony KAR 251.521.118.512.391.414.518 on the 180° meridian a few degrees north of the Tropic of Capricorn. I'd never have had another chance, and I'd never get another chance. So I'd survived the most precarious dangers many billions of times already but, there, there, my forebears had always managed – oh yes, oh yes – they'd always managed to hand the genetic baton on, and undamaged too, Vera, always in the same undamaged state, though regularly fine-tuning their inheritance with certain minuscule, advantageous variations. So there was always a new relay, for there were still many millions of relays to run until, against the most incredible odds, it was my turn, but the new relay was run, and the one after that, and perhaps the next generation will grow up, even though we'll hardly credit it, but so it will be, and over and over again, because nobody fell into the trap, everyone was on their guard, the genetic relay baton had been passed from generation to generation hundreds of millions of times. Because here I was.

That was what I was thinking, and in a way it was thanks to the airline, because they'd placed my million-year-old genetic baggage in even greater hazard. I mused that I'd already been well on the way to this morning's reverie when my lobed-finned fish great-great-great grandma and great-great-great grandpa – who just happened to be neighbours in the Devonian period – were still crawling from puddle to puddle so as not to suffocate through lack of oxygen. But — and this was the painful part — this fantastically long but almost pathetically lucid and transparent relay race was now at an end. This endless game of dominoes that had continued without so much as a second's pause for more than three billion years — had now run into the buffers. I'd already begun to pick up the pieces.

I felt myself so rich in background. How many generations could I reckon since the first amphibian? How many cell divisions could I add to my account since the very first zygote? I was the possessor of such an oppressively opulent past. But I had no future. I was nothing after this.

This was the way my mind ran, and perhaps I should add that I was thinking of us both. I also mused, of course, that I no longer had any children. It was an extra rap across the knuckles that, so far, I was the very first childless generation in a long and plentiful stock that had numbered hundreds of millions of generations before me. For, as is well known, childlessness is never handed down; it is one of the laws of evolutionary biology that childlessness is such an unfavourable characteristic that it's immediately excised. Only those who have children of their own can dream of grandchildren, and without grandchildren one will never be a great-grandad or a great-grandma.

And just when everything had been going so well, I thought. And just when I'd been admiring my priceless family silver. I was mega-rich in a way, I had millions of ancient ancestral jewels lining the bottom of my chest. But I was singing the last verse. I was almost forty, and yet I couldn't even glimpse the slightest trace of any progeny. I was so alone in the world, so unutterably thrown back on myself.

Adam's lack of astonishment

I tried to glance at the final notes I'd made in Auckland after all the meetings with the nature conservancy people. I heard a dull thud a couple of times, and at first I thought it was a distant echo of thunder, but then I realised it must be coconuts falling to the ground from the crowns of the tall palm trees.

After the third coconut had thumped down, the sound of approaching voices could suddenly be heard, and I saw a man and a woman walk past the wall of my hut and continue through the palm grove on a little path that led down to the sea and the road. His arm was close about her shoulders, so close in fact that I felt a trifle bashful about sitting there. It made me think of the Lord wandering about Paradise, watching over his creatures. Now I'd taken over that role, though it must have been after the fall, for the two beings were not only closely entwined, they were no longer naked. The Lord had clothed the woman in a poppy-red dress, the man had been given black linen attire. I heard they were speaking Spanish — and cocked my ears.

All at once the man stopped on the path. He raised his arm from Eve's shoulders and pointed down through the garden and out across the sea. And then he spoke loud and clear:

'There's nothing odd about the fact that the Creator is supposed to have recoiled a pace or two after moulding man from dust and breathing life into his nostrils, and turning him into a living being. The surprising thing about the event was Adam's lack of astonishment.'

The weather was hot, it had cleared up after some heavy morning showers, but now I felt a cold shiver pass through my body. Wasn't it almost as if he'd read my thoughts?

The woman laughed. She turned to the man and responded, enunciating clearly:

'There can be no denying that creating an entire world is a highly commendable achievement. Though even more respect must be due to an entire world capable of creating itself. And vice versa: the mere experience of being created is as nothing compared to the overwhelming sensation of conjuring oneself out of zilch and standing completely on one's own two feet.'

Now it was his turn to laugh. He nodded thoughtfully and draped his arm round her shoulder again. As they began moving off, soon to disappear amongst the coco-palms, I heard him say:

'The perspectives are so labyrinthine that several possibilities must be kept open. If there is a Creator, what is he? And if there isn't a Creator, what is this world?'

Not to mention who these two oracles might be. I was stunned.

Had I been witnessing a time-honoured morning ritual? Or had I just caught a couple of chance remarks from a longer conversation? If so, I wished I'd heard it all. I fished out my little diary and tried to note down what they had said.

When, a little later, I set out for a long exploratory walk, I met them again, and this time face to face. I had made my way down to the road which, except in the most precipitous parts of the south-east, hugs the coastline. I followed the road a mile or so and soon arrived at what according to the map was Prince Charles Beach. Rather a pompous name for such a small lagoon, I thought; some days it couldn't have attracted any bathers at all. But perhaps the imperial heir-apparent had once been dragged here because the inhabitants wished to show him Taveuni's most idyllic beach. They couldn't have chosen better.

Through the mangroves I glimpsed Adam and Eve walking barefoot down by the water-line, as if they were gathering shells. I felt myself drawn towards them and decided to walk down to the beach, as though by chance. Just as I came out from amongst the trees, I had an inspiration: why reveal my knowledge of Spanish? It was a trump card that might be useful to hold, at least for the moment.

They heard me coming and met me with watchful eyes. I think

the woman said something to the man about not being alone any more.

She was as beautiful as in the creation myth – with dark hair that hung in rich curls over her red dress, dazzling white teeth and – jet-black eyes. Her sun-tanned body was tall and elegant and proud, and I thought she moved in an unusually graceful way. He was shorter and looked more reserved, almost on guard I thought, although a mischievous smile had played across his thin face as I'd approached. His skin was pale, and he had fair hair and blue eyes. He was about my own age perhaps, and at least ten years her senior.

Even at that first meeting something told me I'd seen this young woman before. Though not addicted to such ideas, it almost seemed as if I'd met her in some previous life, or in another existence. Having flipped rapidly through my own recent past and social contacts, I found I couldn't place her anywhere. But I had met her before, and considering her youth it couldn't have been so long ago.

I greeted them in English, said what nice weather we were having and that I'd just arrived on the island. They introduced themselves as Ana and José, and I told them I was Frank. We quickly discovered we were all staying at the Maravu, there being no other accommodation for miles around. They spoke good English.

'Holiday?' José asked.

I drew breath. This conversation need not be a long one. I told them I was on my way home after many weeks' field studies in the South Pacific. When I went on to add a few words about the threats to the original flora and fauna of the region, they pricked up their ears. They exchanged cryptic glances and generally seemed so tightly wedded that I began to feel uncomfortable again. I realised that in a situation like this there was an inordinate advantage in operating as a pair.

'And you?' I asked. 'On honeymoon?'

Ana shook her head.

'We're in the film business,' she said.

'In the film business?' I echoed.

I tried to use the phrase in one final attempt to discover where I'd met this elegant woman before. Could she be a famous film star, currently enjoying a holiday in the South Seas with her slightly older husband, the well-known director or film cameraman José something-or-other? I needn't have met her in real life, after all, perhaps I'd only seen her on the screen. No, it didn't make sense, I'd never been a keen cinema-goer, and certainly not since Ana had reached maturity.

She looked at her husband and hesitated a moment before turning her eyes on me again. She nodded defiantly.

'We work for a Spanish TV station.'

As if to underline the veracity of her statement, she raised a small compact camera and began snapping away at the beach, José and me. She smiled roguishly, and I suspected her of having fun at my expense. If she was, I wouldn't find it hard to forgive, as I was dazzled by something more than the white coral sand and the noontide sun.

The man asked the woman the time, and I remember that striking me as strange, because I'd already noticed that neither was wearing a watch. I told them it was a quarter past twelve and, with a wave, said I was off to explore the island. Just as I turned my back on them and was beginning to make for the road, I heard the woman whisper something with liturgical emphasis.

'When we die — as when the scenes have been fixed on to celluloid and the scenery is pulled down and burnt — we are phantoms in the memories of our descendants. Then we are ghosts, my dear, then we are myths. But still we are together, still we are the past together, we are a distant past. Beneath a dome of the mysterious past I still hear your voice.'

I tried to carry on down the road as if I'd heard nothing or, at least, nothing I'd understood. As soon as I'd got round a bend, I took out my little notebook and tried to scribble down what she'd said. 'Beneath a dome of the mysterious past I still hear your voice . . .'

I toyed with the idea that Ana had given me a clue to follow.

Perhaps it was in some mysterious past that I must search for the key to her familiarity.

I'd seen her before, of that I was absolutely certain. But at the same time the whole thing didn't seem quite right. I had the unpleasant sensation that at a certain point something must have happened to her.

The encounter with the two Spaniards had got me so agitated that I decided to walk the three miles along the coast to the 180° meridian, where there was meant to be a kind of monument at the line between the two days. It turned into quite a hike, but it did enable me to form some impression of everyday life on the island. I passed a couple of lively villages and was greeted by smiling people in colourful garb. Some of the streams were awash with bathing children, and one or two adults were in the water too. I noticed that it was often the men who went about with toddlers on their arms. The women had work to do.

I was unable to spot even one troubled face, and I had the opportunity to study quite a number of faces that afternoon. Flowers and coconuts, fish and vegetables were everywhere in abundance, but apart from that there was little to be had in Western terms. But hadn't Adam and Eve lived under just such conditions in the Garden of Eden before they ate of the tree of knowledge and were doomed to toil on the earth all their days and eat bread in the sweat of their brows? I couldn't imagine the women of this island requiring either laughing gas or pethidine in childbirth. Life is a game, I thought, it's all a piece of candy.

My feet were sore when I at last neared the village of Waiyevo, only half a mile from the date line. Here, I got into conversation with Libby Lesuma, a friendly Australian woman who'd married a Fijian and ran both the general store and a small souvenir shop. She was surrounded by a gaggle of children, and when one of them went to fetch a ball from under a coco-palm I pointed up at the tree and asked if she wasn't scared that the child might get a coconut on its head. She just laughed and said she'd never thought about it, she was more worried about the sharks. Even so, she couldn't bring herself to stop the children bathing in the sea, but if they had the slightest sign of a cut they had to stay out of the water. Sharks could smell blood over long distances, she said, and I nodded. When I mentioned that I'd walked all the way from the Maravu she asked – apropos of the sharks perhaps – if I was hungry. I said I was famished, but remarked jocularly that I'd not reckoned on passing any fast-food outlets on the road. She smiled in a warm, motherly way and, like the good fairy she was, took me to a little taverna that lay hidden behind the two shops, right down by the sea. I ate a solitary and simple lunch there while trying to motivate myself for the final stretch. The taverna was called 'The Cannibal Café', and a garish sign in large red letters proclaimed: 'We'd love to have you for dinner'.

What a frivolous attitude the great-grandchildren of the cannibals had to their gastronomic past, I thought. How baffling it was that these ever-smiling, happy and considerate people were only a couple of generations away from putting me in a pot. Something in their engaging manner brought with it such associations. I always felt they were fond of strangers, but occasionally I would get the tingling sensation that they liked tourists in roughly the same way that I like the smell of lamb chops. When Fijians greeted me with their ubiquitous 'bula', I sometimes wondered if they were about to start licking their lips. I don't know if the taste for human flesh is something that can eventually find its way into the genes. The question then would be whether those naturally predisposed in that direction are the ones who have survived. Those who felt an aversion to human flesh were possibly more often under-nourished and died out for lack of protein, not to mention those who *got* eaten before they managed to produce children. They, too, had lost their genetic voting card.

The monument at the date line was blatantly advertised. Behind a red standing stone a vertical placard had been erected bearing a three-dimensional map of Taveuni. It gave an impression of 'the Garden Island' from a bird's-eye view, a view I hadn't dared to enjoy as I sat in the matchbox-plane. Right down the modelled island, with its painted roads, lakes and river courses, a line had been drawn from north to south, in reality a fraction of a circle, a segment of the earth's periphery, which continued across the poles where it turned into the prime meridian that cuts through Greenwich. To the right of the line – in the hemisphere I'd walked in from – it was today, to the left it was tomorrow. Beneath the sculpture it said: INTERNATIONAL DATE LINE WHERE EACH NEW DAY BEGINS.

I won't try to make out that standing with one foot in today and the other in tomorrow was exactly an earth-shattering sensation. But it was on this beach, I pondered, that the third millennium would dawn, and now there were only two years to go. Parabolic antennae would sprout up here like toadstools, in one of the very few places in the inhabited world that was still without a normal television link. Reports would come from the last paradise to an outside world that was doomed, and these very reports from the outer frightened fringes of a wounded world would turn the island's utopian innocence upside down. I thought: It's impossible to report from a dream without ending it.

I recalled something I had read about Fiji's plans for the millennium celebrations. I've always considered myself good at noting the essentials, and one sentence in particular had stuck in my mind. The chairman of the Fiji National Millennium Committee, Mr Sitiveni Yaqona, had said: 'Because Fiji sits directly on the $180°$ meridian, it will celebrate the first moment on earth in the year 2000, and we have been exploring ways in which the new Millennium could be celebrated in Fiji.' And in this context Fiji meant Taveuni – 'directly on the $180°$ meridian'. I was worried that the world might steam-roller this vulnerable island in its delirious fêting of precisely when and where the future began. It was all going to happen right here, literally at the sign marking the boundary between the second and third millennia, 'the first moment on earth in the year 2000'.

As well as seeking 'the last' and 'the lost', we all have an unhealthy desire to be 'the first', I thought, though on maturer reflection I realised they were essentially exactly the same. When Roald Amundsen became the first man to reach the South Pole, he was also the last. He was the last person on earth to conquer that pristine wilderness, something Scott was to learn to his cost only a month later. The first shall be the last. It was the same with the conquest of the moon. The last to be first on the moon – which no one would ever be able to repeat – was Neil Armstrong. So wasn't his famous greeting to Houston about it being one small step for a man, one giant leap for mankind a generous gesture towards his own species?

Where I was standing now there would probably be crowds on 1 January 2000. Arrangements for the party were already under way; I'd heard of several TV documentaries and other previews from the date line. Then the 'year 2000 tourists' would come pouring in like the last despairing cry of an already cynical travel industry. I'd seen the posters: 'Celebrate the dawn of the new millennium in three continents!' Every kind of ticket had been sold out long ago, and they would increase in value. Far too many people on the planet were willing to pay a few thousand dollars to escape the social humiliation that might ensue from celebrating the advent of the new millennium only once, and in just a single continent.

I was ready to begin the long march back to the Maravu, but just as I was making some careful calculations about time and distance, a black jeep drove up to the monument, and out jumped Ana and José. I felt my pulse quicken.

Ana greeted me warmly. Camera in hand, she said, 'Libby said we might find you here.'

I was nonplussed. Then I remembered the good fairy from Waiyevo.

Ana explained in more detail.

'We had an errand in the village. When we heard you'd been through, we thought you might like a lift.'

I must have looked rather bewildered, but I thanked her for the offer of a ride back as I'd miscalculated both the time and how many miles my legs could manage on that dusty road. Dinner was only two hours away.

43

Again Ana began clicking away with her camera — at the monument, the jeep, José and me.

José explained that they were assessing conditions on the island, entering agreements and finalising arrangements before returning later that year to film an important documentary about the turn of the millennium. It would form part of a series of programmes on the challenges facing mankind at the dawn of the new millennium.

Ana pointed to the map of the island.

'This is where we are now,' she said. 'And it's where the third millennium will begin, "the only place where you can walk from today to tomorrow without snowshoes".'

I'd heard the slogan before. Apart from a couple of other islands in Fiji, the 180° meridian only crossed the Antarctic and northern Siberia.

'Is there much interest in that kind of documentary?' I enquired.

José nodded reluctantly.

'Yes, far too much.'

I cocked my head a little, and he added, 'We'll be wagging a warning finger.'

I wanted to know just what he meant.

'About what?'

'In one way or another, the turn of the millennium affects the entire planet, and everyone imagines they have a right to be present at that very first moment. But it could be very traumatic for a fragile South Sea island to have the attention of the whole world focused on it. From that point of view, it would have been better for the date line to run through London or Paris. Though in colonial times it was more practical to have it way out in the bush somewhere. If you see what I mean . . .'

I saw only too well. It's easy to tell what someone means when he's aping you. Yet again I felt as if my mind was being read. It made me more outspoken, because if we really could read each other's thoughts, we might as well stop messing about. 'And it doesn't help,' I said, 'when every TV company, in addition to covering the event itself, also decides to make its own spectacular documentary on precisely how and why culture and environment are destroyed. That can have a certain entertainment value in itself, can't it?'

I thought I might be overstepping the mark when I added, 'Is there anything at all that doesn't have entertainment value?'

I said it with a smile of resignation, and Ana laughed. José beamed as well. I think we were on some kind of high-frequency wavelength.

Ana raced to the jeep and returned with a small video camera, about the size of a domestic model. She pointed the camera at me and announced: 'The Norwegian biologist, Frank Andersen, has recently been studying the ecology of various islands in Oceania. What can you tell viewers in Spain?'

I was so startled and confused that I didn't know what to say. How did she know I was Norwegian? And how had she discovered my surname? Could she have taken a peep at the Maravu's guest book? Or did she remember where we'd met before?

She was so spontaneous and childlike that the idea of extricating myself from this game of hers never even crossed my mind. I think I spoke for six or seven minutes, far too long in other words, but I gave a rough outline and touched on environmental destruction in Oceania, biodiversity, and human rights versus human responsibilities.

When I'd finished speaking, Ana laid the camera down on the ground and clapped.

'Bravo!' she shouted. 'That was fantastic.'

In the background I heard José's comment: 'And that was roughly what I meant by wagging a warning finger.'

Once more I let myself be seduced by those dark eyes.

'Did you record it?' I asked.

She nodded cryptically. It never occurred to me that such a modest video camera could have anything to do with the much-vaunted television documentary. Altogether there was something that prevented me taking the TV business very seriously. I'd begun by saying I was here doing research, and then they'd tried to make themselves sound equally interesting. Or possibly they hadn't believed me; yes, that was it, perhaps they'd assumed I was bluffing. It would be quite plausible for a single man travelling alone in the Pacific to feel the need for an aura of more vital objectives for his long journey than a mere holiday in the sun.

There was something else as well. Was it mere chance this Spanish couple had passed my hut and reeled off a few profundities about the existence of God and Adam's lack of astonishment? And was their popping up at the date line equally fortuitous? Or were they playing some sort of game with me?

They were certainly playful. Ana had pretended to be on a journalistic assignment in the Pacific, and I had gone along with it because I'd still not rejected the idea of a honeymoon. 'But still we are together . . .' If they knew I understood what they'd been saying, I would have felt uncomfortable, and the feeling would certainly have been mutual.

José walked down to the sea. As he stood with his back to us, he said something in Spanish. By his intonation he was engaged in a summing up, and again it was as if he was rattling off a thing he'd either said many times before or learnt by heart:

'There exists a world. In terms of probability this borders on the impossible. It would have been far more likely if, by chance, there was nothing at all. Then, at least, no one would have begun asking why there was nothing.'

I tried to take in all he'd said, but it wasn't easy, because the beautiful woman held my gaze fast the whole time, as if seeking a reaction to José's turning away and launching into a language I couldn't understand. There could be no doubt I'd heard him, but had I understood? And if not: would I ask what he'd said?

It was hard looking into Ana's black eyes without divulging that I understood José's admonishment, words which I was simultaneously trying my hardest to comprehend. Though my mind was in tumult, I couldn't take my eyes from Ana's searching gaze.

I think I emerged from the confrontation victorious, for next moment Ana picked up the video camera and replaced it on the front seat of the car. For an instant she stood leaning against the car, as if she felt giddy. Wasn't her face losing colour too? It only lasted a few seconds, then she straightened up again and, forgetting me, ran the few steps down to José and took his right hand in her left. They stood for several moments in the tropical afternoon light, like a living sculpture of Cupid and Psyche. Then Psyche said something in Spanish, a seemingly rehearsed reply to Cupid's words about there being a world though it would have been more likely if there'd chanced to be nothing at all. She said:

'We bear and are borne by a soul we do not know. When the riddle raises itself on two legs without being solved, it is our turn. When the dream picture pinches its own arm without waking, it is us. For we are the riddle no one guesses. We are the fairy-tale trapped in its own image. We are what moves on and on without arriving at understanding . . .'

While they were still standing with their backs to me, I pulled out my little notebook and tried to scribble down what they had formulated with such ease and sensitivity, but also so peremptorily and dogmatically. 'We are what moves on and on without arriving at understanding . . .'

Had they learnt some Spanish verses by heart and were now busily declaiming them to one another as they walked about? But there was something about the almost ceremonial manner in which they recited those curious aphorisms that made me certain their utterances could have no author other than themselves, nor any other addressee.

In the car on the way back to the Maravu we talked about various things, including my natural history studies. The sun was low in the sky, drawn ponderously down to the sea in the west by the day's own inexorable gravity. I knew that in barely an hour it would be completely dark. In the sharp golden light we watched women taking in clothes from washing lines, children still cooling themselves in the rivers, boys trying to win their rugby match.

'For we are the riddle no one guesses . . .'

It struck me how mesmerised I'd always been by a reductionist view of the world in general, and of my own tiny life on this planet. Ana and José had reawoken a slumbering sense of what an adventure life is, and not just here in this South Sea paradise, but life on earth, the life we live in big cities too, even though there we are in danger of not seeing how magical man's world is because we immerse ourselves in activity, in distractions and sensual pleasures.

As we drove past the village of Somosomo, José turned to Ana as he pointed to a small huddle of people in the square outside the Baptist church. Again he said something in Spanish, and this time almost in counterpoint to my own reflections as I sat in the back seat, my head banging on the roof in time to all the potholes in the road.

'The elves are always more vital than sane, more fantastic than reliable, more mysterious than they can conceive with their slight understanding. Like dizzy bumble-bees buzzing from flower to flower on sleepy August afternoons, the season's elves stick to their urban habitats in the heavens. Only Joker has pulled himself free.'

'The season's elves . . .' This strange expression made me start. I may even have clapped a hand over my mouth to stop myself repeating it aloud in the car. Perhaps you're wondering why I didn't do just that. Why couldn't I confront Ana and José with this odd poetic tic of theirs? If I'd asked what they were saying, they would undoubtedly have supplied an English translation and perhaps even have treated me to a more satisfactory interpretation. Phrases like 'the season's elves' could do with a little explanation.

I've asked myself the same question many times, and I'm not sure if I've found a likely answer, but at the time I considered Ana and José's strange mode of communication to be something that, above all, embraced the pair of them. They were a couple, Vera – maybe that's what I'm trying to get across – they were very much a couple, so inextricably entwined in their mental symbiosis. I saw their strange verbal contact principally as an expression of a deep personal bond between two lovers, and one doesn't read other people's love letters without good reason, at least not while they're looking. If I'd gone so far as to admit I could understand what they said, I would also have risked throwing away the possibility of listening to more of the same.

OK, you're thinking now, I needn't have admitted I understood the language, but once in a while I might at least have asked what they were talking about; after all, wasn't it even stranger to listen to it all without reacting to their extraordinary behaviour? But it isn't all that odd for two people who usually speak English when they meet someone who doesn't know their own tongue, to exchange a few words in their own language. It's called private life, the intimate sphere, and after all, I wasn't supposed to understand what they said. For all I knew they might just have been chatting about a stomach ache or being hungry and looking forward to dinner. In addition, I wanted to go on listening, I was determined to intercept as much of it as I could. When the person you share a bed with suddenly starts talking in their sleep, you don't rush to wake them – even though that might be the decent thing to do – no, no, on the contrary, you try and lie dead still so that the sheets don't rustle, to get as much of the sleep-talker's drift as possible – in what will, for once, be an unexpurgated version.

Ana leant across to José, and now he placed his left arm round her shoulders as he gripped the wheel firmly in his right hand. With sparkling eyes she looked up at him as she said:

'The elves are in the fairy-tale now, but they are blind to it. Would the fairy-tale be a real fairy-tale if it could see itself? Would everyday life be a miracle if it went round constantly explaining itself?'

I sat well back and tried to think of all the squashed toads on the highway, I'd spotted more than a hundred as I walked to the date line, and they really were like pancakes. But it wasn't the toads I was thinking of now. The question I was asking myself was whether I'd got lost inside my own science and forfeited the ability to see the fairy-tale magic of each single moment on earth. I saw the extent to which the agenda of natural science had been to explain absolutely everything. In that lay the obvious danger of becoming blind to everything that *couldn't* be explained.

As we drove through the last village, we had to slow down almost to a stop as we came upon some women and children who were milling about in the middle of the road. They waved and smiled, and we waved and smiled back. 'Bula!' they called through the window, 'bula!' One of the women was eight or nine months pregnant.

Ana had raised herself from José's arm and he again had both hands on the wheel. As she turned to look back at the women, she said:

'In the darkness of swelling stomachs there always swim a few million cocoons of brand-new world consciousness. Helpless elves are squeezed out in turn as they become ripe and ready to breathe. As yet they can take no food other than the sweet elfin milk that flows from a pair of soft buds of elf-flesh.'

'Elf-flesh', Vera. I'd assumed that the 'elves' in this Joséana-universe had to be us, terrestrial human beings in general. Now that it was being coined specifically about Fijians, it seemed even more vile to think of the way their forefathers had been able to shove elf-flesh and elf-blood into themselves with total equanimity. Weren't such ethereal filets far too rare to be consumed?

We turned off to the Maravu, and once back at my hut, I stood on my veranda for some minutes watching the sun go down. I felt the day was owed this last honour as my hazardous air-trip had turned out so well. That had been in the morning just after the sun had risen. Now I followed its pale red disc with my eyes until it turned on to its back and rolled over the rim of the sea. The sun was just one of this galaxy's hundreds of billions of stars, and it wasn't even one of the largest. But it was my star.

How many more times would I be a passenger on this earth's journey around its star in the Milky Way? Behind me I'd nearly forty circuits, forty flights round the sun. So at least half my voyage was over.

I unpacked my suitcase, took a shower and changed into a white shirt I'd bought in Auckland. Before I went to dinner I took a wee nip of the gin I'd brought with me and left the bottle on the bedside table. It was a ritual I always observed when away on my travels. I knew I would take another, bigger swig when I was ready to sleep. I used no other sleeping draughts.

I remembered how much I'd missed that bottle as I sat forlornly in the small plane from Nadi. For a few dramatic minutes we'd been separated, and the airline had taken better care of the bottle than its owner that morning.

As I walked out into the palm grove and closed the door behind me, I heard something scuttle across one of the roof beams. I had a feeling I knew what it was, but I didn't go back for a closer look.

Avant-garde amphibians

Outside it was pitch black. The only points of light in the great palm grove were a couple of discreet gas torches which had now been lit, but above the palm crowns glittered thousands of minute downlights from a dense mass of stellar whorls of light. If you leave the city behind, I thought, you find yourself far out in space as soon as darkness falls. But an ever-increasing swathe of humanity has allowed itself to be blanketed in an optical greenhouse effect that makes it forget what it is and where it comes from. Just as, for many people, nature has become synonymous with television pictures, potted plants and caged birds, so the heavens are something best observed in planetaria.

It wasn't easy to find the way to the restaurant, but I floundered towards a dim, distant glimmer from the main building, forced my way through bushes between palm trees and eventually reached the swimming pool, which had all its uplights illuminated. In the pool, three or four cane toads were swimming up and down, up and down. Could they be taking their swimming certificates, I wondered, for one toad was actually sitting on the lip of the pool overseeing the whole show. Everything had its proper place, I thought. All day the primates had the pool to themselves. Toads weren't allowed to show themselves then. At night it was the amphibians' turn to use the facilities.

I went up to the open restaurant, where candles were burning on all ten tables. There were ten huts or *bures* at the Maravu, and the same number of tables in the restaurant.

Ana and José had taken their places. She was still in her red dress, and I noted she'd also donned a pair of black high-heeled shoes. José had the same black linen suit, the only difference being that he now had a red kerchief round his neck. The kerchief exactly matched Ana's dress, perhaps it was from the same material.

I seated myself at the next table, and we exchanged a few brief nods. As a lone traveller I'd learnt the art of not soliciting invitations to join other people at their tables. It was evening, the afternoon's jaunt was over, I no longer had any claim on Ana and José. They belonged exclusively to one another now.

I also nodded to Laura, who was sitting alone at the other end of the restaurant. At another table sat a dark-haired man with a pepper-and-salt striped beard; he might have been ten years older than me. Later that evening I would discover he was an Italian called Mario. A young couple in their early twenties occupied the table next to him. They really were on their honeymoon. Not only did they lean across the table with their hands clasped together, but from time to time their two heads would meet and melt into a passionate kiss. On the following evening I was to exchange a few words with these youngsters as well. They came from Seattle and were called Mark and Evelyn.

A little way off sat John, the Englishman who'd met us at the airport. He was plainly making notes. I remember that especially well because I often found myself doing the same, and would sit scribbling while waiting for lunch or dinner. I'd never had the composure of mind to engross myself in a novel. I was later to learn that he was the British author John Spooke from Croydon, just outside London. When I first realised he was a writer, I automatically assumed he belonged to that small clique of best-selling authors who, in the winter, could enjoy life on a South Sea island for a few months while seeking inspiration for a new novel. But in fact he'd been there only a couple of days, and he'd come to take part in a television programme. Yes, you're right – it was about the turn of the millennium, too, the date line, global challenges, all that sort of thing. All that sort of thing, Vera, all that sort of thing!

I couldn't see Bill. Perhaps he was in his room doing yoga exercises that offered the prospect of another sixty years of life.

Dinner was served by two tall native men in traditional Fijian skirts and with red flowers behind their ears. One man wore the flower behind his left ear — that meant he wasn't yet attached to a woman. The other had the flower behind his right ear, so he was married. Had I been an inhabitant of Taveuni, I'd have undergone the humiliating social experience of shifting my flower from the right to the left ear several months ago.

I ordered a half-bottle of white Bordeaux and a bottle of mineral water. There were always two dishes to choose from at the Maravu, and we'd already selected our first evening's meal whilst checking in. At the time my head had been so full of graphic images of traditional Fijian eating habits that I'd chosen fish as the safer option.

Ana and José were talking so quietly that to begin with I could only pick up little snippets. However, even these were sufficient to arouse my curiosity. It sounded as if they might be having a discussion, or putting the final touches to a joint statement about something or other — yes, something or other.

José said, *'We are unblemished works of art that have taken billions of years to create. But we're cobbled together from far too cheap a material.'* After this I lost a couple of exchanges, but then intercepted a few more of José's words: *'The door out of the fairy-tale stands open wide.'* Ana nodded solemnly: *'We are diamonds of genius in the hourglass.'*

That was roughly how the conversation went, or more accurately, the bits of it that reached my ears clearly enough to be understood.

While they were sitting there conversing back and forth, Bill finally came sauntering in from the palm grove wearing yellow Bermuda shorts and a flowery blue Hawaiian shirt. Laura must have spotted him before I did, because as soon as he made his entrance she clutched at her 'Lonely Planet' again and began reading avidly, so avidly that I'm certain she couldn't have registered a single word. It was no good. Bill stood there for a few moments, greedily savouring the panorama of the evening's dinner placings, and then, without the least reticence, plumped himself down at Laura's table. She collapsed behind her book so completely that I couldn't see her neck any more, and she certainly didn't look up at him. She reminded me of a sulky turtle seeking solace in its shell, and I remember feeling rather sorry for her, but I also felt that things would have been better for her if she hadn't behaved quite so antipathetically towards a field zoologist at the airport. Perhaps the last sentiment was laced with a little malicious pleasure.

The conversation at the next table had taken a more decisive turn. Ana said, '*It takes billions of years to create a human being. And it takes only a few seconds to die.*'

Discreetly, I pulled my notebook from my shirt pocket. I'd forgotten my pen! My vexation grew when José raised his voice a little and clearly articulated the following words of wisdom:

'*To the impartial eye the world not only seems an unlikely one-off phenomenon, but a constant strain on reason. If reason exists, that is, if a neutral reason exists. So speaks the voice from within. So speaks Joker's voice.*'

Ana nodded meaningfully. Then added on her own account:

'*Joker feels himself growing, he feels it in his arms and legs, he feels that he isn't just something he's imagining. He feels his anthropomorphic animal's mouth sprouting enamel and ivory. He feels the lightness of the primate's ribs beneath his dressing gown, feels the steady pulse that beats and beats, pumping the warm fluid into his body now.*'

Without thinking very clearly, I got up and hurried across the room to the Englishman, who'd been writing zealously while waiting to be served. He'd now finished his hors d'oeuvre, but had laid aside both pen and paper. I bowed and said, 'Excuse me . . . I noticed you were making some notes. You couldn't lend me your pen for just a moment, could you?'

He looked up at me with an inquisitive and obliging expression.

'With the greatest of pleasure,' he said. 'Use this!'

With that he pulled out a black Pilot drawing pen from his inner pocket. He toyed demonstratively with the pen for a moment or two before handing it to me.

'I'll make sure you get it back,' I promised him.

But he merely shook his worldly-wise head and declared that if he came well supplied with anything, especially in remote places like this, it was black drawing pens. I thanked him kindly, and we introduced ourselves more properly than we'd done at the airport.

I attempted to give him a brief outline of my field studies, and he listened attentively; very attentively indeed. I'm of an age now when I place an entirely new value on attentiveness. He offered me his hand and introduced himself:

'John Spooke,' he said. 'Writer, from England.'

'Are you writing something here?' I asked.

He shook his head and explained that he'd been sent to the island at the BBC's expense to take part in a television programme about the turn of the millennium. This was where they thought the future would begin, he said with a note of sarcasm, a full twelve hours before the millennium broke out in London. He also mentioned the titles of a couple of his novels, one of which had, apparently, been translated into Norwegian.

When I'd thanked him for the pen once more and was returning to my table, he called out cheerfully, 'Write something beautiful . . .'

I turned quickly, and he added, '. . . and send my compliments!'

Well, I don't know, Vera, perhaps I ought to acknowledge his wish by passing on greetings from an affable Englishman – even though I wasn't really writing to you just then.

But I am writing to you now, and I'm writing about my experiences on my first evening at the Maravu Plantation Resort so you'll have a better idea of what happened in Salamanca some months later.

Bill struggled to part Laura from her 'Lonely Planet'. Her minimal response seemed to hold her dining companion's invasive attempts at conversation in check.

The young nuptial pair sat kissing voraciously across the salad bowls and again made me think of cannibalism. I come from a culture that finds it socially acceptable to lick and suck someone in public, even across the dinner table. The frontiers of taboo begin at the more irreversible culinary activities. I imagine it must have been the opposite in traditional Fijian culture. There, snogging in full public gaze wouldn't have been acceptable, and certainly not during a meal. On the other hand, civil behaviour accepted the ingestion of a corpse's entrails.

The Italian stared disconsolately down into his glass of red wine. Of all those present he was noticeably the most forlorn. The brooding eye he turned on the young American couple put me in mind of an ownerless dog.

I sat down again and heard José make some remark about *'humdrum-exotic happenings'*. There followed much mumbling I couldn't catch, but then José said something that clearly stirred the lady in red, for next moment she smiled brightly, sat up and declaimed the following with great conviction:

'A longing pervades the world. The bigger and mightier a thing is, the keener its lack of redemption is felt. Who hearkens to the sand grain's suffering? Who lends an ear to the louse's longing? If nothing existed, no one would yearn for anything at all.'

She did glance fleetingly out into the room a couple of times, but she turned quickly back and could hardly have noticed that I was jotting down every word she said. She didn't know I spoke Spanish, nor could she be certain I could hear her clearly, and for all she knew I might be engrossed in making notes about the various species of lizard I'd studied in Oceania.

For a long while I had to content myself with the scraps I managed to catch from the low-voiced murmurings between Red and Black. *'The closer the elves come to eternal annihilation, the more meaningless their speech,'* Ana postulated as she gazed at her spouse with a look of enquiry. He said: *'Without the anomaly of that inconsolable jester, the elves' world would be as sightless as a secret garden.'*

I vaguely suspected that the loose fragments I was overhearing must form part of a larger jigsaw puzzle, and that it would undoubtedly be harder to piece together the fewer bits I had. But food was now placed on the table and I laid my notebook aside. The little I'd managed to intercept was too disjointed anyway. It was only towards the end of the meal that José spoke again, his voice a little louder:

'Joker slinks restlessly amongst the elves like a spy in the fairy-tale. He

reaches his conclusions, but has no one to report to. Only Joker is what he sees. Only Joker sees what he is.'

Ana thought for a moment before replying:

'The elves try to think some thoughts that are so hard to think that they can't think them. But they can't. The on-screen images don't leap out into the cinema and attack the projector. Only Joker finds his way down to the rows of seats.'

I won't swear to the exact words. But, truthfully, these really were the kind of things they talked about.

The tables were cleared, and now the Italian approached. He nodded defiantly to Ana and José as he headed for my table, then stretched out his hand and introduced himself. Yes, this was Mario, and for the past fifteen years he'd run charter crossings from Suva in a yacht he'd built himself. This enterprise had not been part of his original plan, when, some two decades earlier, he'd sailed through the Suez Canal to India, Indonesia and Oceania, but he had never saved up enough money to get home to Naples.

He had an errand.

'Do you play bridge?' he asked.

I gave a shrug, for although I was a competent bridge player, I wasn't sure if cards were at the top of my agenda that evening; the tropical night seemed too magical. But when he added that we'd be playing against the Spanish couple, I assented without further hesitation. The previous few evenings they'd made up the numbers with a Dutchman, he explained, but he'd travelled on with the boat to Vanua Levu earlier that day.

So we joined the Spaniards and played a few rubbers. It was always Ana and José who either just made the bidding for the game or landed the Italian and me with the final decisive trick. Not only did they play with impressive precision, but in a manner that was so coy and effortless that during the game they could indulge their insane pastime of Spanish aphorisms. I noted words and phrases like *'that primeval kettledrum'*, *'this shameless cocoon which grows and grows in every direction'*, *'the chic primate'*, *'the Neanderthal's lionised half-brother'*, *'the enchanted sleep of daily life'*, *'a hot current of half-*

digested hallucinations', '*the soul's plasma*', '*the protein festival's air-bag*', '*organic hard disk*' and '*the jelly of cognition*'.

Twice I was the dummy and had the opportunity to steal away from the table and note down the words I'd been able to snap up. These were the only phrases that came out – old, well-tried formulations and sayings like 'the soul's plasma', 'the protein festival's air-bag', 'the jelly of cognition' and 'the Neanderthal's lionised half-brother'. I'd already diagnosed Ana and José as a couple of poets with Tourette's syndrome, and I won't deny I could have played a lot better if I hadn't had to attend to what was being intoned from North to South and back again all the time. It occurred to me that distracting East and West's attention had perhaps been the whole point.

It was Mario who finally decided he'd had enough. To say he flung his cards on the table is to exaggerate, but he laid them aside so demonstratively that it made me jump. He shook his head without a trace of amusement.

'They're clairvoyant!'

Ana looked up at him with an almost malicious satisfaction, and Mario sought an ally in me.

'Five clubs!' he almost screamed. 'But after that bid Frank might just as easily have had the ace. It's as if they always knew what we had in our hands.'

He might have been nearer the mark than he suspected, I mused, for this closely knit pair, who were clearly not on their first honeymoon together, really might be in a position to read one another's minds. And why not, I thought presumptuously. Here we sat, one enchanted tropical night, four intensely observant primates, beneath a sparkling blanket of stars in our own, almost provincial, spiral of the Milky Way. From this earth, on which we had laboriously evolved from primitive vertebrates, from this insignificant lagoon in the galactic archipelago, our fellow creatures were sending out space probes and radio waves in serious attempts to make some kind of cognitive contact with other biological creatures, equally advanced, on another shore in another solar system many light-years away from our own playpen – and all this without any reference to the highly specialised evolution of these creatures, who could easily turn out to be more like starfish than mammals. So why shouldn't two soul-mates, who not only shared the same biosphere, but came from the same species and country and who, in addition, had precious little else to do apart from go about mirroring themselves in each other – why shouldn't they be able to exchange some rudimentary electromagnetic signals to do with the colour and number of fifty-two cards at the bridge table? Ah yes, I'd already been infected with the euphoria of the tropical night, and it wasn't the first time I'd been smitten by that particular kind of inexactitude.

My condition wasn't to improve very rapidly either, because now came a number of related questions. If everyone round the card-table was equally good at bridge, what was the chance of one team winning eight rubbers on the trot? Mario wanted to know. I said it was all to do with getting good cards, but the chance of one team being dealt the best cards eight times in a row had to be so remote that it was easier, all things considered, to accept that Ana and José had been the better players.

Ana was basking. She didn't even try to conceal her satisfaction, and it obviously wasn't the first time she'd won at cards. She even laid a comforting hand on Mario's shoulder – a gesture he shrank sulkily away from.

José now shifted the question of chance and probability to something that touched on my own speciality. I think the first question he asked was whether I considered that the evolution of life on the planet was driven solely by something as unpredictable as a series of chance mutations. Or was there some sort of mechanism the natural sciences had overlooked? Did I believe, for example, that it was unreasonable to pose questions about evolution's purpose or intent?

I think I sighed, not so much because I felt he'd asked a naïve question, but simply that, once again, he'd steered the conversation towards problems I felt acutely sensitive to that day. But I gave the classic textbook answers to the questions he'd raised and imagined that would be the end of it.

He said, 'We've got two arms and two legs. That's reasonable enough when we're sitting round a table playing bridge, and it's not bad for piloting a spaceship to the moon. But is it accidental?'

'It depends what you mean by "accidental",' I pointed out. 'The mutations are accidental. After that it's the environment that always determines which mutations have the right to life.'

He went on, 'So you believe the sum of such flukes has currently provided the universe with a degree of understanding about its own history and extent in time and space?'

José waved an arm as if pointing out into inky space, and that was really where his question was directed.

I was about to say something about mutations and natural selection, but before I could, he said, 'If the aim was to achieve a more or less objective reason, I'm not sure we could have been so very different in appearance.'

Ana smiled slyly. She put her arm around his neck and kissed him quickly on the cheek as if to stop him. Then she turned to me and said teasingly, 'He's mad on the idea that intelligent life on other planets must resemble us a little.'

'Then I think he's wrong,' I exclaimed.

But he didn't give in so easily.

'They must have a nervous system, and an organ to think with too, of course. Those would hardly have developed if they didn't also have two spare forelimbs.'

'Why two?' I countered.

I thought I had him there, but he struck back.

'It's enough!' he said.

For the first time I had the feeling that I was the one in retreat. He certainly had a point which, at that moment, sent me into a slight confusion. Two arms and two legs *were* enough. Though that wasn't the way an empirical science reasoned. Wasn't it half a millennium since philosophy had repudiated Aristotle's doctrine about 'final causes'?

'And in the long run,' he said, 'there's no point in sustaining more limbs than necessary, not over millions of years.'

Just then a toad hopped on to the floor where we were sitting;

perhaps it was one of the bathers. I pointed down at it and said with a note of triumph in my voice, 'We've actually got two arms and legs because we're descended from a tetrapod like that. We can thank them for the basic design of our nervous system too. This specimen is a *Bufo*, or to be more exact a *Bufo marinus*.'

I picked up the toad and pointed out its eyes, nostrils, mouth, tongue, larynx and tympanic membranes. I explained briefly about the animal's heart, lungs, arteries, stomach, gall bladder, pancreas, liver, kidneys, testicles and urethra. I ended with some comments on its skeletal construction, spinal cord, ribs and feet. As I released the animal from my grasp, I added a few scraps of information about evolution from amphibians to reptiles, and on from reptiles to birds and mammals.

But I'd underestimated José.

'So amphibians got an excellent hand,' he said. 'They were to win all the rubbers. And it wasn't just a matter of luck. By comparison with other kinds of animals they were avant-garde. They had everything needed to create a human being.'

'It's easy to be wise after the event,' I said.

'Better late than never,' he insisted. 'There are *two* reasons why we have two arms and legs. One is that we are descended from tetrapods like that. The other is that it's practical.'

'And if the amphibian had six legs?'

'We'd either not be sitting here having this rational debate, or two of the limbs would have withered away. We once had a tail, which can be useful for a number of animal activities, but it would have got in the way of our sitting at a computer or inside a spaceship.'

I think I settled back in my seat a bit. José had done no more than air the questions I'd been asking myself in recent days. After what befell us, Vera, I've done a lot of thinking. Why did we have to lose Sonja? I've lost count of the number of times I've asked myself that question. Why couldn't we keep her? If any of my students had raised such a question in an exam paper, I'd have had to consider failing them. But we are human beings, and human beings have a tendency to seek meaning even where there isn't any.

'You're certainly right in saying that it wasn't an arthropod that ultimately conquered space, or a mollusc for that matter.'

'And', he said, 'the creatures from a distant solar system who one day will send us their cryptic visiting cards through the ether aren't likely to have an anatomy like a squid or a millipede.'

Ana began to laugh.

'What did I tell you?' she cried.

Ana and José – and soon Mario too – began asking me a host of questions about natural science, and maybe the tropical reaction I was experiencing caused me to enjoy the limelight, rattling off several brief lectures on problem areas for contemporary palaeontology and evolutionary biology. But I became increasingly conscious of my opponent. Several times José managed, in a good-humoured way, to put questions that caused me some professional embarrassment. I won't say I learnt anything new during the course of the conversation, but I think I developed a deeper understanding of the many uncertainties in natural science which I'd never acknowledged before.

José's conviction was that the evolution of life on earth wasn't merely a physical process, but one that was consistently shot through with meaning. He pointed out that a characteristic as significant as man's consciousness couldn't merely be one of many arbitrary characteristics in the struggle for survival, but the very object of evolution. It was almost a law of nature that a planet developed an ever more specialised sensory system, and he provided several good examples of this process. The way life on earth had – and without any inner genetic link – evolved eyes and sight, and the way it had more than once taken to the air or developed the ability to walk upright; thus there was in nature too a latent aspiration to an intellectual overview.

What hurt a bit was that, as a boy, I'd had similar ideas for a time, when I'd been influenced by Pierre Teilhard de Chardin. Then I'd begun studying biology and had naturally cast off all such ideas of purposeful evolution. For science's sake I felt I had to provide some resistance to José. I represented an august institution, far too august perhaps.

I agreed with him that the ability to see, to fly, to swim or walk upright had evolved again and again throughout the history of life. The eye, for example, had been invented some forty or fifty times, and insects had evolved wings for flying more than a hundred million years before reptiles. The first vertebrates that took to the air were the pterosaurs. They evolved about two hundred million years ago and died out with the dinosaurs. Pterosaurs flew rather like huge bats, I explained, they had no feathers and couldn't have been the antecedents of modern birds. The oldest bird – *Archaeopteryx* – had been around 150 million years ago, and was really a small dinosaur. The evolution of wings and feathers in birds occurred quite independently of the pterosaurs . . .

'Wings and feathers,' he interrupted. 'Do such things happen overnight? Or does nature "know" where it's going?'

I laughed. Again, he had touched the tiny kernel, the nub itself, of dissent, even though this time I think his question was rhetorical.

'Hardly,' I said. 'It's a question of a whole series of mutations over many thousands of generations. And only one law obtains: the individual with a slight advantage in the fight for survival has a greater chance of passing on their genes.'

'What advantage would an individual get by developing the clumsy rudiment of wings generations before wings could be of any use?' he asked. 'Wouldn't such embryonic wing stumps merely be in the way and make the individual less able to attack and defend itself?'

I tried to paint a picture of a reptile that climbed trees to hunt for insects. Even the tiniest hint of feathers – originally deformed scales – would give an immediate advantage when the animal jumped or scuttled down the tree trunk. The more deformed the creature's scales were, the better it could leap, manoeuvre or flap, and the greater the chance its offspring had of growing up. Even the smallest inclination to webbed feet could also give an animal an important advantage when life was lived, either partially or wholly, in water. I returned to the evolution of feathers and pointed out that feathers gradually also became important for keeping the bird's body at an even temperature – though that hadn't been the original 'intention' of feathers. The primary advantage of becoming feathered was most probably linked to the animal's movements. But the reverse order of events was also plausible. Feathers might originally have given the birds' ancestors the advantage of insulation before they became important for locomotion. The recent find of feathered dinosaurs was clearly an argument in that direction.

'Then came the bats,' he said. 'Eventually even some mammals learnt to fly.'

I think I said something about how territory in the air had been so thoroughly dominated by birds by then that the bat's niche became nocturnal hunting. Bats didn't only develop wings, they evolved what we know as echo location.

'That's a chicken-and-egg situation,' José opined. 'Because which came first, the echo location or the actual ability to fly?'

I didn't have time to answer as at that point Laura came over to our table and joined us. When I'd last been dummy, she'd still not managed to extricate herself from Bill, but she'd sent me a look that could only have been a distress signal – and, as such, a plea for forgiveness for cold-shouldering me at the airport. She stood at the bar for several minutes with a red-coloured drink, and when she at last crossed the restaurant again, and I looked up and offered her a place at the table, I was in my element. Mario reached for a chair from the next table.

'Give me a living planet . . .' José began again.

'This one!' Laura interjected.

She pointed enthusiastically out into the palm grove, even though it was so dark we could see nothing there. I remembered the World Wildlife Fund badge on her rucksack.

José laughed.

'Give me any other living planet. I feel pretty confident that sooner or later it will conjure up what we call consciousness.'

Laura shrugged her shoulders, and José went on.

'To refute that idea we'd have to find a planet swarming with life of every description, but which had never developed a nervous system complex enough to allow the odd individual to get up one fine morning and think "to be or not to be" or "cogito, ergo sum".'

'Isn't that a bit anthropocentric?' Laura asked. 'Nature doesn't exist just for us.'

But now José was in full flow.

'Give me any living planet, and I'll point out a teeming throng of living lenses with the greatest of pleasure. And just wait, before we know it we'll be staring into a conscious soul with the ability to account for itself.'

Once again Ana came to his aid: 'He means that every planet that's capable of it will arrive sooner or later at a form of consciousness. The road from the first living cells to complex organisms like us may take many detours, but the goal is the same. The universe is striving to comprehend itself, and the eye that surveys the universe is the universe's very own eye.'

'It's true,' said Laura, and she repeated what Ana had said: '"The eye that surveys the universe is the universe's very own eye."'

All evening I'd been racking my brains trying to work out where I'd met Ana before, and I wasn't any the wiser. The only way was to get to know her better.

'What's your personal opinion?' I asked. 'You must have your own beliefs.'

She thought about it hard, and I remember her exact words:

'We aren't capable of understanding what we are. We are the riddle no one guesses.'

'The riddle no one guesses?'

She mulled it over.

'I can only answer for myself,' she said.

For an instant she looked into my eyes. Then she said, 'I'm a divine being.'

Apart from José, I was perhaps the only one who noticed that this response was accompanied by an inscrutable smile. Mario clearly hadn't been so observant for, his brown eyes widening, he said, 'So you're God?'

She nodded firmly.

'Yes,' she said. 'That's me.'

She answered with a matter-of-factness more in keeping with an enquiry about whether she'd been born in Spain. And why should she hesitate? Ana was a proud woman, who made no attempt to explain away her aristocratic lineage.

'Good for you,' Mario acquiesced. 'My felicitations!'

So saying he rose and went to the bar. I think he was still brooding over the card game. At least now he knew why he never won.

At this Ana burst out laughing. I couldn't see what she had to laugh at, but the sound was so infectious that soon we were all joining in.

Now John came walking over with a glass of beer in his hand. He had chatted to the young Americans for a while, but he'd been hovering round us all the time and must have heard a good deal of what was said.

We set some more chairs round the table, and soon there were six of us, as Mario quickly returned with a brandy and humming a Puccini aria, Madam Butterfly I think it was. Mario introduced himself to Laura, and she made herself known to Ana and José.

The Englishman said, 'Inadvertently I overheard a bit of your talk about the "meaning" or "purpose" of things. Well, fine, fine! However, I believe it's important to realise that such questions have to be judged retrospectively as a rule.'

No one had the faintest idea what he was talking about, but that didn't seem to deter him in the least.

'The meaning of a specific event often isn't apparent until long after the event itself. Thus the cause of something isn't obvious until later. And this is simply because every process has a time axis.'

Still he couldn't reap so much as one nod of affirmation. He wasn't even asked to try to make himself better understood.

'Just imagine,' he said, 'if we'd been witness to the events here on earth, let's say three hundred million years ago. I feel sure our biologist here can give us an idea of the period.'

I took up the challenge at once. We were at the end of the

Carboniferous period, I said. Then I gave a brief run-down on the plant life, the first flying insects and, most importantly, the very first reptiles, which had gradually evolved as the environment on earth became drier than it had been in the Devonian and Lower Carboniferous periods. But the amphibians were still dominant amongst the terrestrial vertebrates.

John cut in: 'Crawling between the ferns and spool-like creepers are some large, salamanderish amphibians, and also a few reptiles, including those that were to father our own species. Had we been present in that environment, we would almost certainly have considered what we were witnessing as totally absurd. Only now, looking back on it, is the sense apparent.'

'Because without what happened then, we wouldn't be sitting here today?' asked Mario.

The Englishman gave a quick nod, and I interpolated: 'But you're not saying we're the cause of what happened three hundred million years ago?'

José couldn't hide his gratitude for John's intervention. Now he motioned him to continue.

'I'm only saying that three hundred million years ago it would have been premature to conclude that life on this planet was meaningless, much less without object. The object just hadn't had time to bear fruit.'

'And what was the object?' I asked.

'The Devonian period was reason's embryonic state. And I believe it's quite legitimate to speak of an embryo's having a purpose, for I don't automatically subscribe to the idea that the first weeks of a pregnancy have any objective in themselves, not for the embryo. So it's equally premature to believe that today we can adequately answer a question about the meaning of our own existence.'

'You mean we're still on the way?' asked Laura.

He nodded again.

'Today we are the avant-garde, but we haven't passed the winning post. Only in a hundred or a thousand or a billion years will we see what we were aiming for. So, in a way, what happens at some point far in the future will be the cause of what's occurring here and now.'

He went on a bit more, explaining what he meant by 'reason's embryonic stage', and I think the majority of those sitting round that table put a good part of what he said down to a writer's flights of contextual fantasy.

'But let's go further back by all means,' he said. 'Suppose we'd witnessed the creation of the solar system itself. Wouldn't we have felt a tiny bit uncomfortable at having to watch that monstrous display of natural force? Most of us would certainly have sworn that what we were seeing could only be called totally meaningless. I think that reaction would have been premature.'

Both Ana and José sat nodding, and the Englishman went on: 'Or we can take a step further back still. Imagine we were watching the Big Bang, the very foundation of the universe when time and space were created. If I'd witnessed what was happening then, I believe I would have spat with disgust. What was the point of such an extravagant fireworks display? But now I would say that the reason for the Big Bang is that we can sit here and think back on it.'

'We!' exclaimed Laura. 'Why we the whole time? Why not the frog or the giant panda?'

John sat gazing at her as he summed up.

'Those who maintain there isn't any meaning behind the universe may be wrong. Personally, I've a strong feeling that the Big Bang was intentional. Though the aim behind it is hidden, at least for us.'

'I think you're turning everything on its head,' I objected. 'When we speak of causes, we always mean something that points back in time. A cause can never belong to the future.'

He looked at me askance.

'That's maybe where we go wrong. But let's reverse the perspective by all means. Only if life on this planet *hadn't* evolved from the first amphibians could we have stated that life on earth was absurd and meaningless. But who then would have taken it upon themselves to become the frogs' answer to Jean-Paul Sartre?'

Laura had little time for such views. She sent John a blazing look and said, 'Well, frogs would have been frogs. I can't see why that should be any less meaningful than mankind being mankind.'

The Englishman nodded sympathetically.

'Indeed, the frogs would have been frogs. And they would have done what frogs do. But we are human beings, and we do what human beings do. We ask if there is a meaning or a purpose to everything. It is for us I say that life in the Devonian period was speckled with meaning, not for the frogs.'

Laura wasn't impressed.

'I see things totally differently. All life on earth is equally valuable.'

I couldn't tell just how much of what he was saying John really meant, but he still hadn't quite finished.

'There might have been no life on this planet at all. Clearly, then we could have said that the world had no greater object than to live out its bare existence. But who would have pointed that out?'

When no answer was forthcoming, he concluded:

'If there'd never been a Big Bang, everything would have been completely void and meaningless. Only to the void itself, of course, and that would be even less aware of meaninglessness than frogs and salamanders.'

I noticed Ana and José were constantly exchanging glances and privately associated this with the curious Spanish maxims they'd gone round the island proclaiming to each other. Was there a connection? Was it a pre-arranged game? Could the Englishman be the author of those weird aphorisms? Wasn't it a bit strange that almost all the guests at the Maravu went round talking about the same thing?

To continue the introductions, Ana enquired where Laura was from. She said that she was originally from San Francisco and had studied history of art, but that lately she'd worked as a journalist in Adelaide. Recently she'd been given a kind of working grant from an American environmental foundation, and her task, basically, was to chart all the forces that opposed the popular struggle against environmental destruction. More specifically, it was Laura's job to keep an annual record of individuals, institutions and major concerns who, for reasons of profit, publicly minimised the threats to the earth's living environment.

Mario wanted to know why such outing was necessary, and Laura took the opportunity of submitting her own, very generalised, portrait of the earth's condition. She believed that life was threatened, that the planet's arable resources would progressively diminish over the long term, that the rain forests would be burnt down and that biodiversity was steadily being diluted. It was a process that would be completely irreversible, she emphasised.

'Fine,' Mario agreed. 'But what's the point of publishing a list of the culprits in one publication?'

'They have to be brought to account,' she said. 'Up to now the burden of proof has always been with the environmental movement. That's what we're trying to change. We want plain speaking.'

'And then?'

Laura gesticulated.

'Perhaps one day there'll be a legal process. Someone will have to represent the frogs.'

'But you seriously believe that this report of yours is enough to stop the environmental vandals?'

She nodded. 'Many loud-mouths go quiet when they hear why I'm interviewing them, and then do a complete U-turn as soon as they realise the purpose of my interview. That's something to show their grandchildren: look at the time your grandpa stood on the barricades and poured scorn on the problems caused by environmental pollution.'

Mario had got the point at last.

'You want to make them personally responsible,' he said.

I think I must have sat there smiling to myself a little. There was something I rather relished in Laura's audacity.

'I think it's an interesting idea,' I said.

She turned a searching gaze on me. I looked into one green eye and one brown. Like most idealists, she was on her guard.

'Perhaps we need a public pillory,' I said.

John sat nodding in agreement, he nodded so emphatically that he again drew everybody's attention.

'Man,' he declared, 'is possibly the only living creature in the entire universe who has a universal consciousness. So conserving the living environment of this planet isn't just a global responsibility. It's a cosmic one. Darkness may descend again one day. And the spirit of God won't move upon the face of the waters.'

This conclusion drew no dissent. It seemed rather to have united the gathering in quiet contemplation.

Bill came up to the table balancing three bottles of red wine and a glass of whisky. Behind him, with six glasses, trotted the man with the flower behind his left ear. The American put the bottles on the table and fetched himself a chair from a neighbouring table. He sat next to Laura.

Bill gave everyone a glass and pointed to the three bottles.

'On the house!' he said.

Once more I was able to study the way Laura ignored him and I think I glimpsed something misanthropic in her environmental commitment. Beautiful and strange she may have been, but she didn't easily remove her blinkers, or glance up from her 'Lonely Planet' at a friendly remark on a remote airfield.

As the conversation round the table continued in the environmental vein, I gave a short account of my own assignment, prompted, I think, by Ana or José. This time Laura didn't try to hide the fact that she was impressed, and so at last I found myself held in a certain respect. I had the notion she'd somehow taken it for granted that she was the only person in the world – and certainly here on the island – who had a link to the planet's environmental problems.

As I'd imagined, Bill belonged to that substantial group of Americans who are fit and lively pensioners. He'd worked for a big oil company and had been one of those highly specialised experts who fight uncontrolled blow-outs in oil-fields. Not without a note of pride he told us that one of the people he'd worked with was the legendary Red Adair. He'd also been given assignments by

NASA, and could – in all modesty – claim his share of the credit for the fact that Apollo 13 wasn't still orbiting the moon. I mention this because of the following incident:

We had gone on discussing environmental issues for a while before the conversation petered out and the talk turned to more convivial things. Bill – egged on by the rest of us – began to describe some of his feats. He was amusing to listen to, and he'd also bought the wine we were drinking. But just as he was describing a dramatic blow-out, Laura had a violent fit of rage that erupted in her hurling herself at Bill and pummelling him with her fists.

'How about this for an uncontrolled blow-out, you filthy oil pig!' she yelled.

I considered this rather an ill-timed comment, for the man had just related how, at the risk of life and limb, he'd prevented a huge oil disaster.

That the young woman had a bad temper was hardly surprising, nor that she obviously found it difficult to distinguish between commitment and fanaticism. But she pounded away at Bill so furiously that he had to hunch his shoulders several times to parry the blows. In the tumult one of the wine bottles was upset, and the half pint still inside it bled out on to the white damask tablecloth.

Bill now did something quite bizarre. He put his hand on the hollow of Laura's neck and said good-naturedly: 'Hey, now. Take it easy.'

This precipitated the most startling volte-face of the evening, for Laura, who had been seething with anger, calmed down as instantly as she'd flared up. I remember thinking of a tiger and its tamer, and the way they were dependent on each other: the tamer needed the tiger to have something to subdue, and without the tamer the tiger would have nothing to get riled about. The scuffle at least stood as a monument to Bill's mastery when it came to fighting uncontrolled blow-outs. What I understood least was the force behind it.

In a way the event put a natural full-stop to the evening. Laura was the first to get up, and she thanked Bill for the wine and apologised, too, before going off to her hut. I seem to recall that she turned round once and sought eye-contact with me, as if I might possess some salve for the agonies of her soul.

'La donna è mobile,' Mario mumbled gesticulating – it was he who'd drunk most of the wine – and then got to his feet and turned in as well.

The big Englishman looked round and nodded contentedly.

'A very promising start,' he said. 'But how long are you all staying?'

I said I was spending three nights on the island, and so was Bill, before he hastened on to Tonga and Tahiti. The Spaniards were to leave the day after me.

The newly-weds from Seattle had retired to the wedding suite long before, and the staff were busy putting out lights and clearing tables. John drained his beer tankard before ceremoniously taking his leave. Once Bill, too, had thanked us for a pleasant evening, only the Spaniards and I were left to sit on awhile before making our way through the palms. As we did so, we stood watching the toads swimming up and down the pool, I remarked that they did the breaststroke just like us.

'Or the other way round,' José said. 'We learnt it from them.'

Above us the stars flashed like Morse code from a lost past. José pointed into the universal night and said, 'Once this galaxy was teeming with them.'

I didn't get his gist right away, perhaps because my thoughts were still full of Laura and Bill.

'What?' I asked.

Again he pointed down at the pool.

'Toads. But it's doubtful they realise it themselves. I assume they still have a geocentric view of the world.'

We stood there marvelling at the red and white and blue sparks in the heavens.

'What's the chance of something being created from nothing?' José asked. 'Or the opposite, of course: how great are the odds that something could have existed for ever? And is it even possible to calculate the likelihood of cosmic material rubbing the sleep of ages out of its eyes one morning and suddenly awakening to consciousness of itself?'

It was impossible to tell if these questions were directed to me or to Ana, to the universal night, or to himself. I heard the lameness of my reply: 'We all ask those questions. But they have no answer.'

'You mustn't say that,' he parried. 'Just because an answer isn't within reach, it doesn't mean it's not there.'

Now it was Ana's turn to speak. I was taken aback when she suddenly addressed me in Spanish. She looked me straight in the eyes and said:

'In the beginning was the Big Bang, and that was a very long time ago. This is just a reminder of this evening's extra performance. You can still grab a ticket. In brief, the encore revolves around creating its own audience. And in any case, without an audience to applaud, it would be unreasonable to describe the event as a performance. Seats are still available.'

I applauded, realising too late what a gaffe I'd made. To cover up my mistake I said, 'But what did all that mean?'

For answer she gave me a smile which I could just catch in the light from the swimming pool.

José had placed his arm around her, as if to protect her from empty space. We wished each other good night and began to go our separate ways. Before the night had swallowed them, I heard José say:

'If there is a god, he is not only a wizard at leaving clues behind. More than anything, he's a master of concealment. And the world is not something that gives itself away. The heavens still keep their secrets. There is little gossip amongst the stars . . .'

Ana joined in, and they recited the rest of José's message in unison as if it was an old chant:

'But no one has forgotten the Big Bang yet. Since then, silence has reigned supreme, and everything there is moving away. One can still come across a moon. Or a comet. Just don't expect friendly greetings. No visiting cards are printed in space.'

Mosquito-man to a gecko

I had an uneasy feeling as I opened the door to *bure* 3, and the first thing I noticed as I switched on the light was the movement of a gecko on the gin bottle. So, it was as I'd thought. Perhaps this was the one that had flitted across the beam when I went to dinner. The gecko was almost a foot long, with nothing to indicate that it had ever been short of mosquitoes. We both started, then the gecko became motionless, and it was only when I took a step towards it that it wound itself half-way round the bottle and I began to worry that the gin would topple over and fall off the bedside table. There'd been enough spilt this evening already.

I was acquainted with geckoes, and though I knew it was just wishful thinking to imagine they didn't inhabit bedrooms in this part of the world, I disliked seeing too many of these hyperactive creatures scuttling about the room just as I was preparing for bed, and certainly didn't want them darting across the counterpane or lying torpidly on the bedposts.

I took another step towards the bedside table. The gecko sat quite still with most of its weight on the far side of the bottle so that I was able to study its belly and vent, somewhat magnified by the refraction. It moved not a muscle, but its head and tail protruded from behind the bottle, and the little lizard stared intently up at me with the instinctive knowledge that now there were only two possibilities: either to remain totally still and hope that it melted into its surroundings, or to dart quickly up the wall and take refuge on the ceiling, or better still behind a roof beam.

Paradoxically, this meeting with a well-nourished specimen of *Hemidactylus frenatus* made me even more determined to get a decent dram inside me as quickly as possible, and I was now beginning to fear that the reckless creature might actually thwart this, not just tonight, but for the rest of my stay on the island. The bottle was almost full and I'd worked out, with careful consideration of my own best interests, that it would last the three nights before my flight home. I'd inspected the mini-bar on arrival, and it contained nothing but beer and mineral water.

With my left hand ready to rescue the bottle if it fell, I took another pace towards the gecko. But my unbidden guest still sensed that his dogged combination of passive and possessive resistance was a better tactic than taking to his heels. But for my desperate concern about the bottle's contents, I would simply have gone into the bathroom and given the gecko a chance to disappear with his honour intact. Still fresh in my mind, though, were all those times when geckoes had knocked over shampoo bottles and tooth mugs. And now, to crown it all, I noticed the cap wasn't screwed on properly.

One more step and I'd be able to grab the bottle, but then I'd be holding the gecko as well, and I have to admit that my relationship with reptiles has always been somewhat ambivalent. I'm fascinated by them, largely because of their palaeontological associations, but I'm not happy about handling them, and I hate them crawling through my hair – especially when I'm about to turn in for the night.

To most people lizards are a *mysterium tremendum et fascinosum*, and I was no exception to the rule, even though I considered myself an expert on them. It's perfectly possible to nurture a professional interest in bacteria or viruses even though one doesn't exactly long for a close and unprotected encounter with them. Every X-ray enthusiast since Madame Curie has had to take certain precautions in their fascinating game with radioactive isotopes. There's no contradiction in terms between having a rabid fear of spiders and being able to write a rapturous dissertation on the morphology of those carnivorous arthropods.

When it comes to vertebrates like geckoes and iguanas, they must also be regarded as sentient individuals to a much greater extent than bacteria or spiders, for instance. Ever since I found the dead fawn at home in Norway, I'd been alert to the idea that animals too could be little characters, and I couldn't face making a new acquaintance just now, I had no desire to be ogled by a lizard, not at this time of night, and not in what I considered my private domain, bought and paid for, and after I'd expressly pointed out that I wasn't willing to share facilities with other guests. Insects were quite different. I never felt any anxiety about them, I'd never been able to look on a house-fly as a personality. A fly has no face, it possesses no individual expression, but lizards do, and so did the steadfast gecko on the gin bottle.

I could almost certainly have conquered the smidgin of repugnance I felt at coming into close contact with that conscious reptile if I'd first been able to take a few stiff pulls at the gin. But the nicety here lay in the very sequence of events. I had to imbibe some of the bottle's contents *before* I dared to raise it to my mouth. The situation was at deadlock, and this little horror drama was to last much longer than I could have imagined; I was tired, so very tired, and I hadn't the courage to lie down and sleep next to a gecko before I'd had some of my sleeping-draught.

But I couldn't just go on standing there either, my feet ached far too much after the long trek to the date line, and besides, it was embarrassing in front of a gawping reptile that never took its eyes off me for an instant, and was certainly forming its own conclusions. So the first thing I did was to sit down gently on the bed close enough to grab the bottle if things came to a head, something that was well within the bounds of possibility, as this overblown specimen of a 'half-finger' gecko was the fattest I'd ever seen. I was no longer in any doubt that the creature's strength and body weight would be enough to bring the bottle crashing to the floor, at least in a worst-case scenario, and I hadn't the luxury of contemplating any other.

We sat there for a long time staring at each other, I from the edge of my bed and the gecko enthroned like some sphinx over the entrance to my drugstore. A clap of my hands would certainly be enough to make the gecko give up all passive resistance, but either in its undue haste to get away, or from pure devilry, it would also ensure that my bottle headed for the floor only microseconds after the palms of my hands came together, and long before a sluggish primate could save its contents from destruction. There was nothing that impressed me more about these creatures than their almost clairvoyant powers of reaction. And this individual was a particularly alert member of the species.

I christened him Gordon after the label on the bottle. I'd already discovered his sex before seating myself on the bed. Mister Gordon had clearly passed the prime of life; in human terms he might perhaps be a couple of decades older than me, and although he belonged to a species whose oviparous females never laid more than a couple of eggs at a time, he presumably had extensive progeny. Gordon had long since become a grandfather and a great-grandfather, I felt pretty sure of that, and as his species had only been introduced into Fiji in the 1970s, his own grandfather could have arrived on Taveuni as a first-generation immigrant.

I decided that it must be his own experience of life that had taught him to remain on the bottle, for by now he was well aware we were holding each other in check. He must have discovered that primates with clothes and hair on their heads posed no real threat, though he should have realised that retreating would involve no greater risk either. But there was also another possibility: Gordon might possess an inquisitive nature, or even a social disposition.

My desire for a swig was now so acute that I looked into the animal's vertical pupils and whispered forcefully, 'Now you just bugger off!'

I think his repiration rate increased a little, and perhaps his blood pressure rose a tad, but apart from that he kept distinctly calm. He was like those passive protestors the police have to carry away, whether they're demonstrating about road-building or – as in this case – against over-liberal licensing laws. Unlike me, this spontaneous demonstrator didn't even need to blink, and the fact that geckoes don't have mobile eyelids annoyed me intensely, not just because I'd never be able to utilise even a second's lapse in attention on his part, but because for short periods he was able to observe me without me being able to look back at him. An instant is a much shorter interval for a human than for a gecko, so he was able to glare at me for lengthy periods as he registered that I took one slothful nap after the other.

'OK,' I said loudly. 'That's enough now!' Gordon didn't budge. Not only was he getting on, but I was clearly dealing with a cynical and world-weary old fogey, one who may have had no other solace than defrauding higher primates of much needed sedation. Fraud – yes, there was the cue – for hadn't there been someone else who'd had to own up to embezzlement that day, someone who believed in eternal life, who'd recently been deserted by a woman? That was when I recognised the matchbox-plane-pilot. Gordon Gecko had precisely the same expression as the hoary airman, the same piercing glance, the same wrinkled throat with its pendulous flap under the chin, not forgetting the gecko's shovel-shaped hands with their five short fingers. *Hemidactylus* means 'half-fingered', and the pilot, too, had a couple of half fingers. Things were beginning to fall into place. It wasn't the first time that day I had found myself held hostage in a horror film, and once more the tense situation unleashed a rabid thirst which circumstances prevented me from assuaging.

I was so infuriated that I again assessed the possibility of a lightning strike. I ended up rejecting the idea solely on the grounds that though it was clear I could probably save the bottle during a *blitzkrieg* commando operation, the danger of much of its contents being lost was still there, especially if – and I couldn't exclude the possibility – Gordon's reaction was inadequate. I hadn't the reserves to lose even a toothful of the stuff.

'Listen here,' I said, looking into the stern gaze of a distant relative. 'The last thing I want to do is throttle you; and I think, if we're being honest, you know that. I won't even ask you to shove off. All I want is the bottle you're sitting on.'

I was in no doubt that he understood what I said, for it was as if he answered roughly along the lines that he knew all that, and had done for more than a quarter of an hour, but that he'd been sitting on that bottle catching mosquitoes long before I'd turned up. I therefore had no right to demand that he pushed off; on the contrary, I was the one trespassing on his territory. He'd never seen me here before, so if I didn't make tracks immediately, or at least leave him in peace, he'd be forced to ensure there was no bottle left to argue over. And I'd do well to note that he had a brown belt in tail-flicking.

'I didn't mean it like that,' I said. 'If I could just take a few mouthfuls of the distillation, it wouldn't take more than a few seconds, you'd be welcome to get back on the bottle again. I'm a black belt in reptile-squishing myself, and since there isn't one hundred per cent trust on either side, I suggest you climb down on to the bedside table for a moment while I take a drink. I've also got to screw down the cap, otherwise some misunderstanding might leave us both smelling of juniper berries.'

His face was impassive, but then he said, 'I've heard that one before.'

'What?'

'You'll just go off with the bottle.'

'I don't think you realise how thirsty I am.'

'Well, I'm hungry,' he replied. 'And I only eat at this time of day. And mosquitoes like bottles, you see, they land here all the time, and all I do is flick my tongue out, and slurp – end of story.'

He had a point, though the idea that he could teach me anything about geckoes' habits annoyed me a bit. But for the contents of the bottle with the loose cap, we could have shared a bedroom in perfect symbiosis. Gordon could have sat on the bottle and taken care of the mosquitoes and allowed me to sleep undisturbed and awake without itchy lumps the next morning. In the olden days, Fijian chiefs would have a 'mosquito-man' sit by them, naked, while they slept, just to get bitten by mosquitoes, thereby relieving the chief of the same irritation. The demand for mosquito-men must have fallen off when the efficient house gecko spread across the islands. Nowadays they were an almost permanent fixture.

I had an idea.

'I'll fetch another bottle,' I said. 'You can have an ice-cold beer bottle from the fridge. That'll really attract the mosquitoes.'

He sat mulling over the suggestion. Then after a while he said,

'To be honest, I'm getting tired of this squabbling too. I accept the swap.'

'You're a gem!' I cried.

For a few moments I was happy, and remember praising my own resourcefulness.

'Get down off the bottle, then. You'll get a new one in a moment.'

But now the little beast gave a twitch. He said stubbornly:

'First get the beer, then I'll get off the bottle.'

I shook my head.

'In the mean time you might knock over what I want in return for the beer bottle. It's easy to get a bit clumsy, isn't it, especially if one isn't being observed.'

'The bottle only goes over if you don't come up to scratch. But now you can forget the whole exchange.'

'Why?'

'I'm fine where I am.'

I hadn't given up hope of shifting him, so I said, 'If there are any more mosquitoes here, I'm certain they'll prefer a cold beer. All mosquitoes like the condensation from cold beer bottles.'

He just stared up at me derisively.

'Oh yes, and what do you think would happen to me if I sat on something ice-cold? It would be pure suicide for a sensitive chap like me. But perhaps that was what made you come up with the idea in the first place?'

It wasn't, because I hadn't even considered the obvious fact that Gordon was a cold-blooded creature who would lose consciousness if he spent even five minutes on a surface that was only two degrees centigrade.

'Well, I'll warm up a beer for you. I'll be only too pleased to do it.'

'Dummy!'

'Huh?'

'Then it wouldn't be cold any more, so I might as well stay where I am.'

Now I was fuming.

'You realise I could just lash out and squash you with my bare hands?'

I could almost hear him laughing.

'I don't think you dare. Or that you'd manage it. Only just now you were praising the speed of my reactions, weren't you? Almost clairvoyant, you said.'

'That was something I thought, not something I said, don't mix the two up.'

Now he really did laugh.

'If we're clairvoyant, we're clairvoyant, so it makes little difference what I hear you say and what I just guess you're thinking. I expect I'll see your hands coming towards me in slow motion long, long before they reach me. In the mean time I'll have oodles of time to wave goodbye with a hefty swipe of my tail and then make it up to the ceiling all in one piece.'

I knew he was right.

'This isn't funny any more,' I almost shouted. 'I don't usually argue with reptiles, but I could lose my rag quite soon.'

'"Argue with reptiles",' he repeated. 'Spare yourself the sarcasm.'

I sank back on the bed – so far this time that for several seconds I'd have had no chance of saving the bottle if he'd carried out his threat.

'I didn't mean it like that,' I said ingratiatingly. 'I've actually got more respect for creatures like you than you might think.'

'"Creatures like you",' he mocked. 'The most insidious prejudices are often so deeply seated you can't see them yourself.'

'I really don't want an argument,' I assured him. 'But it does sound to me as if you're labouring under a profound inferiority complex.'

'Certainly not. When your species were insignificant animals the size of shrews, my uncles and aunts lorded it over all earthly life, and many of them towered above the landscape like proud ships.'

'OK, OK,' I said. 'I know all about the dinosaurs, and I can tell the difference between synapsid and diapsid. But be warned: I can also distinguish Lepidosauria from Archosauria as well, so don't boast too close a relationship with the dinosaurs, leave that to the doves and parrots further inland.'

I thought I'd dumbfounded him with taxonomic labels; he sat there for a long time not saying a thing. Perhaps he didn't even have any Latin or Greek. After a lengthy pause he said, 'If we go just a little further back still, our lineages meet. So we're related. Have you thought of that?'

Had *I* thought of it! It was such a silly question that I couldn't be bothered to answer. But he wouldn't leave it alone.

'If we go back to the end of the Carboniferous period, you and I both had the same parents. You're my brother, when all is said and done. D'you see?'

All this was becoming a little too intimate for me, but my main concern was still not losing the gin.

'Of course I see,' I said. 'And you only see because I see. Or is there a special university for geckoes on the island?'

I shouldn't have said that, because it put him in a huff. To begin with he just stared at me and his face went flinty; it was as if he was tensing all his muscles. Then, what I'd been fearing right from the start happened. Suddenly, he hurled himself two and a half times round the gin bottle, and I witnessed for myself how it wobbled a couple of inches, but the worst of it was that the disturbance loosened the cap completely and it dropped to the bedside table and rolled on to the floor. I felt the tears well up in my eyes, for now the enraged dragon had demonstrated his hold over me, and it wouldn't take much to make my whole world fall apart at the seams and condemn me to sit up all night drinking Fijian beer. He'd taken against me, I thought, ever since I'd sent him a couple of disapproving glances for unfolding that big chart in Laura's lap when things had been at their worst up there in the thin air above Tomaniivi.

I picked up the cap from the floor, inwardly boiling with rage, but I put a brave face on it and spoke appeasingly. 'That comment about the university for geckoes was a little flippant, I freely admit. Can you accept my apologies?'

He was now on the front of the gin bottle with his back towards me, so he could only see me with one eye.

'And you're right about the proud reptilian epoch in the Jurassic and Cretaceous periods,' I went on. 'You were more advanced than the first, primitive mammals, and towards the end of the Cretaceous even more advanced than either marsupials or placental mammals. I really do understand that. That was why the fatal meteorite that marked the start of the Tertiary period was so incredibly unfair.'

'Why so?'

'You had such a glorious future ahead of you. Many of you had already begun to walk on two legs, some were warm-blooded like us, and I really believe that you were well on the way to establishing an advanced culture with universities and research facilities. Some species were no more than a few million years away from it, and that's not long when you consider that dinosaurs dominated life on dry land for almost two hundred million years. By way of comparison, just consider the enormous advances made by my own kind over barely the past two million years, and by that I mean genetic advances. Cultural achievements are measured in centuries and decades, so they're hardly worth speaking of.'

I heard my own words and again feared that I might have been a little incautious in my choice of perspectives. Wasn't I yet again indulging in an unbridled vaunting of my own species to the specific detriment of the reptiles? I tried pouring oil on troubled waters.

'Like you, I believe that, in the Jurassic and Cretaceous periods, it was your ancestors who were the most advanced. Then everything was wrecked by a mindless collision with another celestial body. It wasn't fair, it simply wasn't fair. It was our planet's very first, and perhaps, to date, most gargantuan effort at gaining intellectual perspective, a notion of its evolutionary history and a view of the universe. And it foundered just because some meteoroid strayed from its course and was relentlessly drawn by the gravity of this planet. That lost you millions of years.'

Gordon's gaze bored into me, and I didn't dare take my eyes off

84

him even for a second. I tried my most honeyed tones, and thought I'd managed to soften him a bit.

'What do you mean we lost millions of years?' he said.

He was more conciliatory now, more like some pouting child who wants his dad to go on with the fairy tale, even though he didn't get his own way with the chocolate.

'You lost the race to be the first on the moon. It was the shrew's progeny that won that competition.'

I bit my lip. I'd gone over the top again.

'Thank you, and you can forget the rest of the insults,' he said, and I realised that was the final ultimatum before some catastrophe on a par with the aforementioned meteorite might strike again, and this very night.

'I'm afraid you've misunderstood again,' I said. 'And that's totally my fault, as I don't always think very clearly in the middle of the night, and particularly when I'm prevented from having . . . well, er, well. But as you so rightly point out, we're blood brothers. In fact, with a whole array of identical genes in our baggage, we're both pentadactyl tetrapods, and I believe we can arrive at a better mutual understanding if we can only learn to view the planet we live on as a common arena or sphere of interest. It was the planet itself, and not you or I – or more accurately it was both of us – that lost millions of years because of this senseless collision with the stray meteoroid. We must understand that even a planet doesn't have unlimited life, and that one day time will run out for planet earth. Had it not been for that capricious lump of rock, you'd now be sitting on the edge of this bed and I'd be scuttling about the room hunting insects. And it can happen again. Perhaps that's what I'm getting at. It can happen again! The balance of power between universal consciousness and a similar universal unconsciousness is a precarious one, a balance of cosmic terrorism which makes our little spat pale into insignificance, and perhaps I should add that in this balance it is reason that is David with his puny catapult, against the massive Goliath of irrationality with its ready arsenal of irascible comets and meteoroids. Intellect is a rare adaptation, whereas there is plenty of ice and fire and rock, a veritable mass of it, for there are still thousands of impulsive asteroids in their highly unstable orbits swarming between Mars and Jupiter, and it would only take one more unlucky conjunction and another will come out of its trajectory and hurtle towards the earth. So just wait, next time the primates may depart this life and perhaps it will be the family Gekkonidae of the sub-order Sauria which will pilot nature's next attempt to gather a tiny crumb more knowledge about the universe. But will it be too late for the world by then, that's the question. For who can tell how long it will be before the sun becomes a red giant; but I shan't pass judgement, only wish you the best of luck. Some day, perhaps, you'll take one small step for a lizard, one giant leap for Nature, and then you must remember that we, too, were part of the journey.'

'You talk too much,' he said.

'Far too much,' I admitted. 'It's known as cosmic angst.'

'Have you no praise for my family as it is now?'

I had considerable sympathy for this objection.

'Oh, yes, in the very highest degree. For example, I'm extremely impressed by the way you've managed to steer clear of intoxicants for so many millions of years. Maybe that's why you live to such a great age. I'm certain being a reptile isn't always easy – the life of a hominid is sometimes a burden, I can tell you. Perhaps we suffer from that little anomaly of having an excess convolution of the brain or two; and I don't speak from self-pity, for who can say that there isn't the odd reptile that goes through life suffering the affliction of some inherited defect or other? But as I was saying, alcohol is so freely available, in various kinds of windfalls for example, but none of you have become dependent on the stuff, and in that I include every order, Rhynchocephaliae, scaly reptiles and crocodiles, to keep to the diapsids. Though the dietary habits of tortoises I'm ashamed to say I know little about, but I assume all species of tortoise can manage without alcohol, at least for long periods, and they live to a ripe old age, certain kinds up to two hundred years. Like the Greek land tortoise for example. The bishop of St Petersburg was said to have had one that lived to the age of 220, and though that might have been a slight exaggeration, the literature does mention a giant tortoise that was captured as a mature specimen on the Seychelles in 1766, and which lived on in captivity and only died on Mauritius as the result of an accident in 1918, though by that time it had been blind for 110 years. But longevity is not the sole preserve of tortoises, I realise that of course, reptiles in general live to be very old, but this doesn't predispose you towards any sort of age-related alcoholism, to which my own species is so sadly prone, at least in the cultures that worship those extra convolutions of the brain, which are excessive, or rather, too much of a good thing, and bring with them so many fears associated with the cosmos, our all too brief life on earth, and the immense spans of time and space.'

'As I said, you talk too much.'

My last tirade had been aimed at making him more tractable, and if it had done the opposite, I had little doubt I'd soon be one gin bottle the poorer. For safety's sake I decided to surrender.

'Mister Gordon. As regards that bottle, I've decided to throw in the towel.'

'That's wise.'

'So we'll say no more about it.'

'I've wanted to do that for a full hour.'

'But, naturally, you don't have anything against me just putting the cap on again. It's a thing one should always learn to do.'

He made no reply.

'It won't affect your hunting, I'm sure. On the contrary, I believe I've heard that mosquitoes can't stand the smell of gin, they say it's pure mosquito repellant. Wasn't that why the British colonials drank so much of the stuff, to protect themselves against malaria?'

At this he altered position slightly, perhaps to bring me within his binocular vision, which is limited to about 25 degrees in geckoes.

'Just try it,' he said.

This pithy answer had two interpretations, so I asked, 'Does that mean yes?'

'No. It also means that you should be more careful how you

phrase things. Because you're right, of course, a bottle without a cap needs to be handled with a lot more care than one which is properly stoppered.'

'Don't you ever get tired?'

'I'm a nocturnal gecko. As you well know.'

I was no longer worried about the next few nights at the Maravu. Maybe I could buy a bottle of gin at the hotel or the store in Somosomo, although I knew nothing of Fiji's laws and regulations concerning the purchase and sale of alcohol. All I knew for sure was that I needed several hefty swigs from Gordon's bottle to make me sleep the rest of the night. I was now prepared to gamble half a litre of its contents just to secure myself the amount I needed, and could contemplate a commando raid on entirely new premises, premises that might lead to heavy spillage, but which indubitably could save quantum satis for tonight. But at worst, the operation would end with the bottle on the floor, and the mere thought of my humiliation if Gordon were to see me crawling about on the ground lapping up the tainted remnants of my tranquillising elixir, before it seeped through the floorboards, made me think again.

In the middle of the room, about a pace and a half from where I sat, was my black cabin bag, and suddenly I remembered that inside it was a carton of juice from one of my flights, with a straw attached – well, there'd been a straw stuck to the carton when the stewardess handed it to me. It might be my last card, and this time I decided not to tell the conceited terrorist what was in my thoughts, whether he was clairvoyant or no.

With my left hand stretched out in the direction of the bedside table and my eyes firmly on the bottle and Gordon, I managed to reach the cabin bag, and seconds later I was sitting on the bed again.

'What are you playing at?' he asked.

'I'm only going to bed,' I lied. 'I'm really a diurnal creature, you know.'

'Those shrews you're descended from weren't,' he said. 'They crept out to hunt at night when the air was cool, because the cold-blooded predators had to keep still then.'

As I opened the cabin bag I said, 'I know that. I know all about that. I did also say that had it not been for that meteorite sixty-five million years ago you might have been the one going to bed, while I scurried about the floor searching for insects. You're quite unable to know any more, or anything different, from what I already know.'

My final flourish was to test his temper, but also to hide the fact that I was fiddling with a juice carton. Soon the straw was in my hands.

I wasn't so stupid as to ask for Gordon's blessing in relieving his perch of some of its wretched liquid. I simply leant across to the bottle and said, 'I'm a bit of a connoisseur of reptiles, you know . . .'

'Yes, I realise that. You're a monomaniac.'

'But perhaps I wasn't emphatic enough in saying that I've always entertained a particular fondness for geckoes. And especially the thirty-five species of "half-finger" geckoes . . .'

Then I put the straw in my mouth and lowered it into the bottle without touching it with my hands, and the extraordinary thing was that Gordon kept still. Perhaps he didn't dare do anything else, I thought, perhaps he was confused.

I'm certain I sucked up the equivalent of a couple of doubles before I had to pause for breath. But I'd managed it, I'd pulled off the rare trick of drinking from a bottle without raising it to my lips. Now Columbus's egg didn't seem such a big deal after all.

'Aaah, lovely,' I said and belched loudly.

It wasn't done to be rude, or to manifest an alcohol-related insolence, it just came out. I must admit, though, that I immediately felt my mood improve and my courage returning. Taking this into account, Gordon had good reason to be so stubborn about letting me have my way with the bottle right from the start.

The next instant, Hemidactylus frenatus began to career round the bottle, and though I steadied it with a finger, I couldn't prevent some valuable drops splashing out and running down on to the bedside table. But I'd reckoned with this, and I let go of the bottle only because I knew he'd scamper up on to me as soon as he got the chance, and my mixed feelings about geckoes hadn't altered on making Gordon's acquaintance.

'I'll be quite frank,' he said. 'If you try that once more, I promise you'll regret it.'

I had some sympathy with this advice, for deep down I knew that if I managed to get another couple of doubles inside me, my Dutch courage would rise to such an extent that I would be able to betray him. Even now the first dose was making my fingers tingle.

'Understood,' I said. 'I didn't realise you had a problem with me testing this clever straw – it really is watertight – and I never for one moment considered crushing you.'

'Perhaps you might put a stopper on that verbal diarrhoea of yours, too.'

True, I had nothing to say to Gordon Gecko just then, in the same way as a police psychologist has nothing to say to a hostage-taker, though he pretends to have, that's the whole point, he needs time, that's why he keeps the conversation going, and it's here there's often common cause between the two, because when the situation reaches deadlock for both, and the hostage-taker knows that he's temporarily surrounded by a superior force, he needs to play for time as well.

He said, 'Or you must talk about something more sensible.'

'You'd like to? You'd like to talk about something sensible?'

'The night is young, the mosquitoes are more likely to come if you're in the vicinity, and maybe they'll also be plumper and more nutritious by the time I swallow them.'

I didn't relish the idea of being a mosquito-man to a gecko, and I thought he was getting close to cheeky when he added, 'I'd rather hoped you wouldn't be so quick to shut the door behind you after you'd turned on the light.'

The truth was that I'd closed the door *before* switching on the light. I'd lived in the tropics for nearly two months, and though I wasn't all that sensitive to mosquitoes, I was still careful not to bring them into the bedroom with me, simply to keep the numbers of geckoes as low as possible.

'We can talk about anything you like,' I said. 'Are you interested in football?'

'Not in the least.'

'What about cricket?'

'Nope.'

'Rare stamps?'

'Stop!'

'Then I suggest we talk about reality.'

'Reality?'

'Yes, why not? Or do you think it's too arbitrary a theme?'

'Well carry on, I shan't be going to bed before the sun comes up, anyway.'

'Above all, it's immensely big and quite incredibly old. Though no one knows precisely where it comes from.'

'The sun?'

'No, reality. That's what we're talking about at the moment. I think we should try to concentrate on one thing at a time, and the solar system is just a microscopic fraction of what we know as reality. In its entirety, reality comprises something like a hundred billion galaxies, one of which is the Milky Way, our own little turning with its milk ramp at the bend in the lane, and within it the sun is only one of more than a hundred billion other stars. That's the one that will rise in a few hours' time, and then an entirely new day will begin on earth, as we're practically on the date line, "where each new day begins".'

'Reality's really huge, then,' Gordon commented, thereby making himself look even stupider than in my opinion he was.

'But we're only here for a brief instant,' I said, 'and then, phht – we're gone for the rest of eternity, which is quite a long time. I, for example, will be gone after only a few years or decades, and then I'll have no way of finding out how things are progressing here. Obviously, I'll be absent in a hundred million years from now too, and then I'll have been out of it for precisely a hundred million years minus a few weeks and months, not forgetting the rest of tonight.'

'I don't think you should plague yourself with such worries,' he said almost consolingly, as if he hadn't been the author of my melancholy.

'What troubles me most is not the shortness of life,' I went on. 'Even I could do with a rest, with a little shut-eye, since to tell the truth I feel rather battered even now. What infuriates me is that I won't ever be allowed back after the rest – back to reality. I wouldn't necessarily insist on returning to this spot, to the Milky Way; I mean, if there was a problem with overcrowding, I'd be willing to think about an entirely different galaxy, at least if there was a pub there, and on condition that I'd be incarnated as one of two sexes – monkish planets where reproduction is an hermaphroditic process have never appealed to me, so I'd give them a wide berth. It's not the leaving that's problematic, but the never being able to come back. For those of us who have these two or three virtually redundant convolutions of the brain – which really are superfluous, or spare if you will – for us, such notions can sometimes destroy the whole enjoyment of life, and not only emotionally. We're not talking merely about an attack on the feelings, but on rationality itself. You may well say that what these two or three superfluous cerebral convolutions affect is precisely the same two or three convolutions: they bite their own tails, and not just playfully, but viciously; in other words, they have a self-destructive character, and it's not easy to get rid of them. Whereas the lizard can easily jettison a tail that's been attacked, no cerebral counterpart of the lizard's autotomy can be found in higher primates. Certainly, the synapses under attack can be anaesthetised for a few hours, with a couple of gins for instance, but that's only an interim suppression of the symptoms and not a solution to the dilemma itself.'

'I know,' was all he said, and now I seriously began to wonder if he was exaggerating, because I don't believe he understood a word of what I was saying.

'The areas of the brain which aren't strictly necessary for the basic functions of life, the superfluous ones in other words, have allowed us to acquire crumbs of understanding regarding the evolution of life on earth, some basic laws of nature and, most importantly of all, the history of the universe itself, from the Big Bang to the present. We don't fill our heads with baubles, you know.'

'I'm impressed.'

'We understand just enough to have a few clear ideas about the history of reality, its geography and the nature of mass itself. But no one knows the essence of what mass really *is*, at least not in our neck of the woods, and distances in the universe are not just enormous, they're grotesque. The question is, would we understand more – about what the world is at its deepest level – if our brains were, let's say, ten per cent bigger or fifteen per cent more effective? What do you think? Do you believe we've gone as far as we can go, no matter what brain we had, regardless of its size? Because there are things that undeniably point to the fact that, in principle, it's impossible to comprehend very much more than we already do. If this really is the case, it's a small miracle in itself that we have a brain that's exactly the right size to understand such things as the theory of relativity, the laws of quantum physics and the human genom. In these spheres there really aren't many missing links. I doubt if even the most advanced chimpanzee has the slightest inkling about the Big Bang, the number of light-years to the nearest galaxy or, for that matter, that the world is round. An interesting factor here is that if the human brain were any larger it would inhibit women from walking upright. Now, I should hasten to point out that without human beings' upright gait, the brain would never have been able to develop to its present size. I'm demonstrating a fine equilibrium, so let me put it another way: the amount we understand about the enigma we're floating around in might be dependent on the female pelvis. I think it's inconceivable that the intellect of this universe should be restricted by such banal anatomical limitations. But isn't it odd that this fleshy equation appears to hold good? It looks as if this equation's x might be precisely quantum satis, and therefore quantum satis for this universe to be, for the time being, conscious of itself. The human pelvis is just large enough to allow us to understand what a light-year is, how many of them there are to the furthest galaxies and how, for example, the smallest particles of matter behave both in the laboratory and during the first seconds after the Big Bang.'

'But why shouldn't there be bigger brains somewhere in outer space?' Gordon interpolated.

I stifled a laugh.

'That's quite possible, of course, and I've no problems envisaging a brain that might, for instance, be able to learn the entire Encyclopaedia Britannica by heart. I don't even find it difficult to imagine a single mind capable of absorbing the whole of man's collected wisdom. What I do doubt is whether, theoretically, it's possible to understand a lot more about the secrets of the universe than humans do already. So every question I'm posing boils down to the problem of whether the universe itself has more secrets to divulge. I mean, if you find a piece of meteorite, you can start calculating how much it weighs, its specific gravity and, most importantly, its chemical composition. But when that's all done, it's impossible to wring further secrets from the rock. After that, it's just what it is, and what it's always been. So it can be put aside, perhaps to gather dust in a museum. But we're no wiser. For what is a stone?'

'I don't think I quite follow,' Gordon sighed. He seemed almost exhausted now.

'Well, there you are, you see. I'm merely saying that perhaps the age of science is beginning to draw to its close. We've already reached the objective; the goal is the awareness of the long road towards the goal. We have introduced ourselves to the universe, and the universe has forcibly presented itself to us. Perhaps science is at an end, is what I mean, perhaps we know everything worth knowing. And when I say "we", please understand that I don't just mean we two, I'm including all the other potential brains in the entire universe. If this were the case – and it's the theory I incline towards at the moment – if this were the case, reality is suffering from an irremediable anonymity. Who am I?

94

asks reality. But no one answers. No one sees or hears us. We only see ourselves.'

'I wish I could be more help,' Gordon muttered, non-plussed, and he undoubtedly could have been if he'd had the wit to remove himself from the bottle he was sitting on.

'But you said you believed in eternal life,' I put in. 'So you shouldn't take passengers when you're flying without a co-pilot; but OK, we can leave that to one side.

'Is it normal for individuals like you to believe in eternal life?' I asked.

'I've never met any geckoes with a compelling argument to the contrary.'

'Can you be a bit more precise?'

'There are absolutely no geckoes who deny the existence of an eternal life. I don't think it's occurred to a single reptile that life could end some time. The thought has simply never struck us.'

And as he continued, it was as if he were trying to mimic the way I spoke.

'And by that I mean all species in every genera and family in all four orders of the vertebrate class Reptilia. Not one of us has the least inkling that life ends at some point.'

It struck me that if I delved back a few generations in man's history, the same could be said of the primates. The chilling draught from the great void was a new phenomenon. And who could tell, maybe the fear of death was unknown on any other planet in the entire universe. He said:

There exists a world. In terms of probability this borders on the impossible. It would have been far more likely if, by chance, there was nothing at all. Then, at least, no one would have begun asking why there was nothing.'

When I didn't answer, he added, 'Did you hear what I said?'

'Yes, of course, and now perhaps you can tell me if this is something all of you here on this island just go round making up or if you found it in a book of old maxims.'

He didn't reply, so I tried to get him talking.

'Have you been thinking about that for a long time? Or are you all itinerant poets of some sort?'

But he was just going into his wind-up, for now he proclaimed:

'We bear and are borne by a soul we do not know. When the riddle raises itself on two legs without being solved, it is our turn. When the dream picture pinches its own arm without waking, it is us. For we are the riddle no one guesses. We are the fairy-tale trapped in its own image. We are what moves on and on without achieving clarity.'

'Perhaps it's your turn to pack it in,' I said. 'I'm getting rather impatient.'

'You can go to bed whenever you like,' he said dismissively. 'I'll take care of the bottle.'

'Over my dead body!' I screamed, for the moment had now arrived. My synapses just had to be anaesthetised.

With that, I leapt on both him and the bottle.

Gordon clambered angrily across my hand, then rushed full pelt up the wall as the bottle toppled and fell on the floor, allowing the vital sedative to pour out and disappear through the gaping chinks of the floorboards. By the time I'd managed to retrieve it and hold it up to the light, there were only about two doubles left, or at best three. I put the bottle to my mouth and emptied it at one go.

'You swine!' he mouthed from the wall. 'But we'll meet again!'

The last thing I remember before falling asleep was Gordon reciting these sentences in Spanish, filched from Ana and José's many descriptions of reality:

'If there is a god, he is not only a wizard at leaving clues behind him. More than anything, he's a master of concealment. And the world is not something that gives itself away. The heavens still keep their secrets. There is little gossip amongst the stars. But no one has forgotten the Big Bang yet. Since then, silence has reigned supreme, and everything there is moving away. One can still come across a moon. Or a comet. Just don't expect friendly greetings. No visiting cards are printed in space.'

I've only vague, and often indistinct memories of the things Gordon said to try to keep me awake the rest of the night, but I

think he woke me some time around five o'clock with the
following aphorism:

'It takes billions of years to create a human being. And it takes only a
few seconds to die.'

The Neanderthal's lionised half-brother

That was how my first day on the Fijian island went, and I needn't go on in detail. I've described it just so you'd understand why I reacted that way in Salamanca.

I was just going to start talking about us, when suddenly I caught sight of Ana and José down by the banks of the Tormes, and all at once it was as if I was back at Prince Charles Beach. So I never got round to us, or what happened to Sonja, simply because you laughed so uproariously at what you assumed was me telling tall stories just to keep you there. But it *was* good to hear you laugh again. I'd have come out with a lot more nonsense just for that. It was Ana and José I'd seen, however, I was quite certain of that, and the proof was there next morning. Only ten days were to pass before I again met José, this time in Madrid. When he'd narrated the whole incredible tale of El Planeta and the two portraits in the Prado, it became crystal clear to me that we have a serious lesson to teach each other and that the only possible opening for a new dialogue between us is that I write to you.

Vera – I'm going to ask you to do me a favour, even if it's the very last thing you ever do for me. I'll try to send everything I've written some time on Thursday afternoon, and on Friday you must come with me to Seville. I owe it to Ana and José to go to Seville that day, and I'm almost sure you'll think so too when you've read the story of Ana and the magic picture.

You've surely not forgotten the card you sent me from Barcelona all those years ago. 'Do you remember the magic elixir?' you wrote. When you arrived home you announced that if you'd found that drink, you wouldn't have hesitated to give me half of it. You wished so fervently for us to be together always. 'For me there is only one man and one earth,' you said. Do you remember that? And you went on: 'I feel it this strongly because I only live once.' Then fate intervened and decreed otherwise.

For the moment all I ask is that you set aside one day of your life for my sake. I can't travel to Seville without you. I just can't.

After reliving that first, fractious meeting with Gordon, I went down to the Rotunda and read *El País* and had a cup of tea and some little cakes. It felt good to unwind completely after all that concentrated writing and just listen to harp music accompanied by the buzz of all the mini-conferences beneath the dome. I know I'm running up a stiff hotel bill, but I've made up my mind not to leave Madrid until I've told you everything. As you can see, I've treated myself to a stay at the Palace again. The staff here know me, and it's only a stone's throw from the Prado, two from the Botanical Gardens, and no more than five minutes' walk to the Retiro or Puerta del Sol.

But to return to Fiji. When I woke up the next morning, I was immediately gripped by a morning-after angst for revealing myself so candidly the previous night to someone I didn't know and with whom I had no wish to become acquainted. Such contriteness is always double-edged, because although one may have been a little careless, something about a hangover magnifies the aspect of such slight, occasional indiscretions. In the throes of remorse you never quite know what you've said and what you've kept back. The whole of the following morning you're nagged by a conviction that you've made an enemy for life – or worse still, a friend – and by that I mean a best friend, ergo someone who knows your innermost secrets. I knew he was in the room somewhere, but as a geckologist I also knew that at this time of day he'd be considerably less bumptious than he could be at night.

I was soon facing the bathroom mirror, and though I wouldn't say I belong to that category of people who like to start the day by pulling faces at themselves, the older I get – and the nearer I get to my own end – the clearer I see the reflected animal expression that greets me in the morning. I see a metamorphosed frog, an upright lizard, a grieving primate. But I see something else too, and it's that that troubles me most. I see an angel trapped by an acute shortage of time, and if he can't find his way back to heaven now, his biological clock will start ticking faster and faster, and it'll be too late to return to eternity. It was all a fatal mistake made a very long time ago, when the panic-stricken angel was to assume a body of flesh and blood, but if he can't get deliverance now, he'll no longer be redeemable.

On my way to breakfast I bumped into John in the palm grove. He was standing beneath a coco-palm studying a notice that read: BEWARE OF FALLING NUTS. Possibly he was short-sighted, for he stood close to the trunk and directly under the palm crown.

'Are you playing Russian roulette?' I enquired.

He walked towards me.

'What did you say?'

But I didn't need to explain further, because just then a large coconut hit the ground exactly where he'd been standing a few seconds earlier.

He turned to look.

'I think you saved my life,' he said.

'Don't mention it.'

I wasn't quite sure what to say next, but I knew I needed someone to talk to – someone to talk to about Ana and José. From the moment I'd looked in the mirror I'd made up my mind that today I'd do some detective work. Though the chances were slim, I couldn't afford to dismiss the idea that the Spanish couple might be able to assist a greatly over-incarnated angel in distress.

'Have you seen anything of the Spaniards?' I asked.

He shook his head.

'You met them at the date line yesterday, didn't you?'

Again I got the feeling that he had something to do with Ana and José. Who'd told him I'd met them at the date line? Was it the sort of thing people talked about?

I nodded.

'They're a charming couple,' I said. 'Do you speak Spanish?'

Did I glimpse the slight play of a smile? At all events I had an inkling he knew why I was asking. But he merely shook his head.

'Very little. But they speak excellent English.'

'Oh yes. But they do talk to each other from time to time.'

He listened intently; his alertness was almost frightening. It was as if he nurtured some special interest in my observations. Did this interest embrace the Spaniards in some way?

'And you understand what they're saying?'

Now I was faced with a problem. I didn't want to tell John that I went about the island eavesdropping on Ana and José.

'Well, they don't chat about football or cricket, I've gathered that much,' I said. 'They talk to each other about some fairly strange things.'

He stood scenting the air.

'She's supposed to be one of Seville's most famous flamenco dancers,' he said.

Flamenco! Again my mind had the chance to search a key word that might help it home in on some earlier meeting with Ana. I'd visited a flamenco bar in Madrid a couple of times, but that had been several years ago, and if I'd seen Ana there my memory certainly wouldn't be able to single her out among all the passionate rhythm, swirling costume and sensual song. Also, at the back of my mind I had a mental picture of Ana that must have extended over a much longer period than just one flamenco show. But the news about flamenco was useful all the same.

'I have a feeling that I've met Ana before,' I said.

He started.

'Where?'

'That's just the problem. I can't work out where she fits in.'

'Interesting,' he said. 'Not to mention extraordinary. I'm having exactly the same problem myself. There's something almost irritatingly familiar about her . . .'

So now there were two of us, and I could forget the idea that I'd dreamt Ana up, or that I'd been married to her in a former life. Now, perhaps, I also knew why John was determined to discover if I had, or had not, met the Spaniards at the date line.

'It isn't a face one forgets,' I said.

I thought my rejoinder might have sounded flippant. He stood deep in thought before replying, 'Possibly. But it's evidently not a face one remembers, either. There remains a third possibility . . .'

I was on tenterhooks to hear what he'd got to say.

'We've both seen this woman before. So possibly she's undergone some kind of . . . metamorphosis.'

I'd been thinking along the same lines myself and was beginning to feel light-headed. The heat and humidity didn't help. But now we were interrupted by the sound of an angry woman's voice coming from the area by the swimming pool. It was Laura, who was practically yelling out in the palm grove. 'I'm just saying you don't have to follow me about the whole time!'

The next second we heard a splash from the water, and I realised that Laura had pushed Bill in. I nodded to John and said that I'd have to hurry in to breakfast before it was too late.

As I passed the lip of the pool, I took in the scattered aftermath of a drama. Bill was clambering out of the water after an unplanned belly-flop with familiar, Buster Keatonish looks of rage, but impeccably dressed for his ducking in yellow shorts and a light blue T-shirt with a motif of coco-palms on it. Laura was busy settling down in a sun-lounger, and she too was expressing a silent-screen shorthand for malicious satisfaction. When she looked up and noticed I was on my way to the restaurant, she covered herself with a towel and asked if I was having breakfast. I nodded.

'I'll have a cup of tea with you,' she announced. She's obviously finished reading 'Lonely Planet'.

She put the towel back on the chair, pulled a red dress over her black bikini and pushed her feet into a pair of sandals. I stood waiting for her. Then we went up to the restaurant.

The staff dispensed coffee and tea. I'd just managed to help myself to bread and jam when they began clearing the buffet. I looked into one green eye and one brown one.

'Is he annoying you?' I asked.

She just shrugged her shoulders.

'Oh no, not really.'

'But you pushed him into the pool?'

'Tell me about your studies,' she entreated.

And I had nothing against changing the subject. I quickly explained about my fieldwork, and realised that she was no amateur on the subject herself. She was also from the region and could tell me things I didn't know about similar problems on the Australian continent.

I asked her some questions about the environmental foundation that supplied the money for the annual situation report she'd told us about the evening before. At first Laura was a bit evasive, but eventually she volunteered the fact that the foundation was virtually an endowment, as all the money had been donated by a single American.

'An idealist?' I asked.

'A rich guy,' she corrected. 'He's rolling in money.'

I asked if she were an optimist or a pessimist when it came to the long-term future of the earth and humankind.

'I'm a pessimist as regards the future of humans, but an optimist about the earth.'

I began to understand her point of view, and soon she'd explained everything. Laura's environmental interest was founded on deeper ideological bedrock than I'd imagined. She believed the earth was an organism, which for the moment was suffering an acute attack of fever, but it was a purifying fever and would ensure that she'd soon get better.

'She?'

'Gaia. Unless something extraordinary happens, she'll ultimately destroy the microbes that have made her sick.'

'Gaia?' I repeated with a gentle sigh.

'It's just a name we've given "Mother Earth"; of course we could just as easily have called her Eartha. But it's important to realise that the world is a living person.'

'Who will destroy the microbes.'

'Many millions of years ago it was the dinosaurs that were eliminated,' she began. 'And it may not have been due to a meteorite strike. Maybe they gave the world a disease and exterminated themselves. I've heard a theory that it was something to do with the dinosaurs' intestinal gases. But the earth recovered, it was really reborn. Now human beings are threatening life on earth. We're ruining our own habitat, and Gaia wants to be rid of us.'

'And then . . . then the world will revive again?'

Laura nodded. I looked into her brown eye and said, 'Don't you think humanity has intrinsic value too?'

She merely shrugged her shoulders, and I understood that she had no great regard for human worth. Personally, I'd always had difficulty seeing the value of a world that brought forth no life apart from lower organisms. But I had more sympathy for the idea of a rebirth. Though, as I'd confided to Gordon the night before, it was late for the world and there was no certainty that reason would get another chance, not on this planet at any rate, because that might take a very long time indeed.

'I've always considered each individual to be priceless,' I said.

'So is every panda.'

I was looking into the green eye.

'So what about you?' I said. 'Aren't you afraid of dying?'

She shook her head.

'I'll only die in my present form.'

I remember thinking how particularly beautiful that form was.

'But I'm also this living planet,' she went on. 'I'm more worried that she'll die. Because I've a deeper and more permanent identity in her.'

'"A deeper and more permanent identity",' I repeated.

She smiled defiantly.

'You must have seen photographs of Gaia taken from space . . .'

'Naturally.'

'Isn't she beautiful?'

I didn't believe a word of it. In any case, I'd never had much time for that type of extreme monism combined with a somewhat misanthropic environmental concern, and though this disgruntled me a little, I have to admit that I liked Laura all the same. She was a wary, engaging and, in some ways, wounded being.

I tried to plumb her rhetoric. All right, I thought, we live our brief lives on earth, but it doesn't end there, because we return, we return as lilies and coco-palms, as pandas and rhinoceroses, and all this is Gaia, our innermost and truest identity.

She sat flicking her sandals. Through the red material of her dress I glimpsed the black bikini-top.

'How did life on earth begin?' she asked.

I took this as a rhetorical question, but gave the traditional answer that all life on earth could have originated from one single macromolecule since all genetic material displays an incontrovertible relationship.

'So the earth is a single living organism,' she concluded. 'And that's not just a metaphor. I really am related to that hibiscus.'

She was pointing out into the garden, and I noticed that Bill had taken the towel she'd left on her sun-lounger, something I thought it better not to mention.

'In fact,' she went on, 'I'm more closely related to that hibiscus than one drop of water is to another. And if all life really does spring from one and the same macromolecule . . .'

She hesitated a moment, and again I was looking into her green eye.

'Yes?'

'. . . then it was a fantastic molecule. I wouldn't hesitate to call it divine. It was a divine seed. And so I wouldn't hesitate to call Gaia a goddess, either.'

'And Gaia is you?'

'And you. And the hibiscus.'

I'd heard it all before, and as I said, I didn't believe she meant half of what she said.

'But the earth has a limited lifespan, too,' I interjected. 'It's just a "lonely planet" in the great nothing.'

'Or in the Great All!'

With these words she took me by the hands, and made me feel so flustered I didn't know what to do. I didn't even know if I could tell the difference between 'all' and 'nothing'. Weren't they virtually synonymous?

She squeezed my hands tenderly. Then she said, 'Together we're one.'

I felt stunned by the sudden shock of twosomeness. But having talked about the great all – or the great nothing – it was good to have a warm hand to hold. If all was not one, we at least were two. I wasn't close to being converted on any ideological grounds, I'm not saying that, because I also knew that if the night is black enough, all contours vanish.

We sat there for some moments holding hands. Laura was a captivating woman and a wrong-headed idealist at one and the same time. Although, on a certain level, what she'd said was quite irrefutable, as irrefutable as my own spiritless individualism. And together we were one.

'Does that apply to the oil engineer, too?' I asked, and only then did she withdraw her hands.

She shook her head and said with a warm smile, 'He belongs in a different universe.'

Nevertheless, she rose soon after and went down to the sun-lounger by the pool, there perhaps to give the American a thorough ticking-off for taking her towel.

I'd decided to order a car and drive to Tavoro National Park on the east side of the island to try to catch a glimpse of the famous parrots, and to see the mighty waterfalls. I also had another chore to attend to, one that carried more of a health warning.

Jochen Kiess, the proprietor of the Maravu Plantation Resort, had originally come out from Germany. He was very helpful about ordering the car, but my other mission wasn't so easily discharged. The place had a bar, and a fully licensed one of course, but national law forbade him to sell a whole bottle of spirits. I said I quite understood this, that we had precisely the same rule in Norway, but that this wasn't a normal sale, more a legitimate compensation for damage caused by one of the establishment's many geckoes. However, I made it clear that I would be willing to pay for the bottle, and per measure too – at the same price per shot as at the bar. I don't think he was convinced by my arguments, but in the end his good nature allowed me to go whistling back to *bure* 3 with an unopened bottle of Gordon's Dry Gin. On the way, I broke off a small sprig from the hibiscus Laura had pointed out, the one she was more closely related to than two drops of water are to each other. Of course she was right about the drops of water, but that was only because two drops of water aren't related at all. They're just extremely similar.

I filled the empty gin bottle with water, stuck the hibiscus spray in it and placed the bottle on a little table in front of the window looking out over the palm grove. Next, I unscrewed the cap of the new bottle and put it to my lips. I took a little nip, only to lay my own claim to the bottle, and to make sure it couldn't be taken back to the bar. I opened my cabin bag, laid the bottle carefully inside and locked it.

Just then I caught sight of him again. Gordon was taking his daily doze on the pelmet above the curtains. I thought he was asleep, though it's hard to tell with reptiles that are born with a pair of coalesced spectacles for eyelids. Perhaps he'd seen me enter with a new gin bottle. At all events, I was now looking straight into his open gaze.

'Hair of the dog?' he asked.

Damn! He was off again.

'I was just rinsing my mouth out,' I assured him. 'Anyway, what I do in the privacy of my own room has nothing to do with you.'

'You don't mean you want to carry on where we left off last night?'

'Definitely not. I'm just saying that you mustn't get above your station. You're just a gecko.'

'Well, yes and no, mister.'

'What do you mean by that?'

'That's maybe how I seem here and now, but in reality . . .'

I had an inkling of what he was driving at.

'Go on!' I said. 'I won't place any bar on freedom of speech.'

'I'm really the world spirit. It's taken up residence inside a gecko. So, if there's anything you want to know, all you have to do is ask.'

'I don't think I can be bothered,' I said. 'Whatever you say, I know it all already.'

'I doubt that. I'm an omniscient world spirit.'

'Well, spit it out then. What do you know?'

'You've had breakfast with an Australian she-primate.'

'OK. Well, let's say you've passed the test. Now can you tell me if I'm in love with her?'

He laughed.

'No, that would be ridiculous in such a short time, even for a he-primate like you. But if you don't manage to tame your animal instincts, you could be lost.'

'She's a world spirit too.'

'That's right, mister. I'm everywhere around you. You live and move and have your existence within me.'

There are still a few isolated enclaves of people who aren't tempted to sell their souls for money. The inhabitants of the tiny village of Bouma on the eastern side of Taveuni knew that they'd been handed one of the world's loveliest rain forests as a birthright; it had acted as a magnet to nature lovers and the makers of such paradise films as *Return to the Blue Lagoon*. So when the villagers were offered large sums of money to sell their outlying forest for logging, it sparked off a good deal of discussion, because capital in cash form isn't what Bouma, or Fiji, is richest in. But in the end they said no to logging and yes to the flexible idea of turning their lush surroundings into a nature park, which would also provide the poor village with a source of income – a renewable source of income that would last much longer than the cash incentive the village had been offered for clear-felling. Today twelve and a half thousand acres of protected park have been developed to receive the eco-tourists who make their way here, and the villagers themselves plant the paths and fence the most precipitous parts, as well as providing toilets and facilities for picnics and camping. And their example has spread. Several similar projects are now being planned in other parts of the island.

Once I'd passed through the village and crossed the delightful Bouma river, it was with a light heart that I paid my five Fijian dollars for admission to this protected paradise. In a small shack I was given useful information about the five miles of prepared paths, and purchased a packet of biscuits and a bottle of water. I also assured them that I was aware any use of fire could have catastrophic consequences.

I strolled up the Bouma river for about half a mile. The path I was following was so lavishly planted that it was nothing but one long alley of palms and flowering shrubs. That's what I call a cultural landscape, Vera. You should have been there!

Soon I heard the rush of the first substantial cascade. I'd read that it had a sheer fall of sixty-five feet and had carved out a gigantic bubble-bath. I'd been told that the place wasn't much frequented, and so I had abandoned my swimming trunks and decided I'd leap naked into the natural pool if I was alone, and if not, I'd go on to the other waterfall half an hour further up, where the fall was almost 170 feet, although the pool itself wasn't as large.

No sooner had I seen the waterfall — its soft rush is with me still — than the sound of familiar voices greeted me, and shortly afterwards I caught sight of Ana and José in the pool. I don't know whether I was disappointed at no longer being alone or simply surprised at who I'd stumbled on. All the same, it presented an unforeseen obstacle, because although it would doubtless be pleasant to meet them again. I had to contend with the fact that they'd had exactly the same idea as me and were swimming naked. Again they put me in mind of Adam and Eve, God's first-created man and woman, the primeval matrix of contentment — at least prior to the pathos of the apple and the ensuing banishment from the garden. But banishment would only come in the next chapter, for now they were still cooling themselves *au naturel*. Before I turned away, I noticed that Ana had a large birthmark on her stomach.

Going about pretending that I didn't understand what Ana and José said to each other was one thing, but I hadn't yet sunk so low as to spy on their nudity. Such base behaviour could be left to God alone — he was the perfect prototype of the Peeping Tom. The problem was that I couldn't continue to the next waterfall without showing myself, because there was no alternative to the official path, and that ran right past the bathing pool. So I'd have to retrace my steps.

I didn't turn back, however, for just at that moment I heard José say something to his naked partner, and although I didn't catch it all, I was to hear it repeated in its entirety at a later date:

'*Joker awakes from unfettered dreams to skin and bone. He hurries to pluck the berries of the night before the day over-ripens them. It's now or never. It's now, or never again. Joker realises that he can never get out of the same bed twice.*'

Perhaps, I thought, perhaps I might hear what Ana wanted to get off her chest this morning if I stayed where I was on the path and didn't either advance or retreat. She said:

'*What do the elves think as they are released from the secret of sleep and arrive fully formed at a brand-new day? What do the statistics say? It is Joker asking. He gives the same start of amazement each time the small miracle occurs. He is caught out by it just like one of his own pieces of hocus-pocus. This is how he celebrates the dawn of creation. This is how he greets the creation of today's dawn.*'

I'd often wondered who this 'Joker' could be, and now I was given a sort of explanation, as José said:

'*Joker moves amongst the elves in a primate's guise. He peers down at a pair of strange hands, strokes a cheek he doesn't know, clasps his brow and knows that within lies the haunting riddle of the self, the soul's plasma, the jelly of cognition. Closer to the essence of things he will never come. He has a vague notion he must be a transplanted brain. Therefore he is no longer himself.*'

Or a biochemical angel, I thought, a representative of eternity who'd been so curious about the teeming life of the realms of the flesh that, in his arrogance, he'd forgotten to arrange for his retreat. It wasn't only the primate who had to beware of donning wings of wax and drawing the over-hasty conclusion that he could fly up to the heavens like an angel. The reverse was just as foolhardy. It was equally unwise for an angel to believe that he could share a primate's lot, without foregoing his status as an angel. The angel had infinitely more to lose than the primate, although in a sense they would both lose the same: themselves. The difference lay in the fact that the angel had taken it for granted that his life would be eternal.

Perhaps I'd assumed that Ana and José must have spotted me and had again begun to display their little basket of philosophical crumbs. If so, it would be silly to retreat. But whether I made such calculations or not, I only remember revealing my presence on the path, one hand over my eyes, and with a reminder to myself that I hadn't heard a word of what had passed, naturally.

'Is there room for a stranger?' I asked. 'I've paid my five dollars for a visa to paradise.'

They laughed, and began to get out of the pool while I stood with my hand pointedly covering my eyes. Although a couple of my fingers did, for an instant, part an iota, just enough to give me a glimpse of their naked bodies before they managed to pull on a pair of black trousers and a red summer frock.

I had a revelation as soon as I saw Ana in the guise of Eve. Her head was the only part of her I'd seen before. Eve's body had nothing familiar about it – though it suited her perfectly, no question about it. But surely it wasn't possible to move a head from one body to another? I'd never heard of anything like a head transplant.

They had dressed, and we sat on a bench in the shade eating biscuits and trying to outdo each other with superlatives about the nature reserve, and Bouma's inhabitants as well, for we were their guests. Ana began padding about with her camera again, and I had to take several pictures of them. While she snapped away, José again began to pick my brains about various evolutionary hypotheses. He was extremely well informed about the topic for a layman, a fact I'd registered the previous evening. He used technical terms like gradualism and punctualism without batting an eyelid.

They'd made an arrangement with a driver who was waiting for them down by the reception cabin, and we agreed it was my turn to have paradise to myself. After taking a dip I walked up to the other waterfalls.

The next time I crossed Ana and José's path was in the palm grove at the Maravu several hours later. And here, too, Ana continued to take photographs. I mention the fact specifically because it seemed that photography was as much a part of the ritual as the volley of more or less cryptic sentences which constantly passed from one to the other.

I was alone in the grove, when all of a sudden I heard familiar voices. I found I was near Ana and José's hut and realised they must be sitting out on their veranda. It was improbable that they'd seen me, and I was certainly hidden from view where I stood just then, though I was now as close to them as they'd been yesterday when I'd been sitting on my veranda and they'd been in the grove. I would have moved away had it not been for the veritable cascade of piquant aphorisms that now began to pour forth.

It was José who initiated the recitation.

'*Who could enjoy the cosmic fireworks display when the rows of seats in the heavens were filled with nothing but ice and fire? Who could have guessed that the first bold amphibian was not only crawling one small step up the shore, but also taking a giant leap on the long road to the point where the primates could see a panorama of their proud evolution from the start of that selfsame road? The applause for the Big Bang was heard only fifteen billion years after the explosion.*'

'Or should we do this one first,' Ana said. '*Something cocks an ear and opens an eye: up from the tongues of flame, up from the thick primeval soup, up through the labyrinth of caves, and up, up across the horizon of the steppes.*'

'Fine by me. But should we call it "the leaden primeval soup"?'

'Why? A soup is never like lead.'

'I mean it was heavy metaphorically. The odds were minimal that any living creature would crawl up on land one day.'

'Doesn't it spoil the rhythm?'

'Quite the opposite: "up from the leaden primeval soup . . ."'

'Well, we'll see.'

Now it was José's turn. It was obvious he was pausing for thought for a moment before making up his mind, but then it came:

'*Like enchanted mist the panorama rises, through the mist, above the mist. The Neanderthal's lionised half-brother clasps his brow knowing that behind his primate's forehead swims the soft cerebral matter, evolution's auto-pilot, the protein festival's air-bag between mind and matter.*'

And this time Ana didn't need to ponder a reply, it was already built into the dramaturgy of the rite.

'*The breakthrough comes in the tetrapod's cerebral circus ring. This is where the newest triumphs of the species are announced. In the warm vertebrate's nerve cells the first champagne corks fly. Post-modern primates finally achieve the great overview. And are not afraid: the universe is viewing itself in wide-angle.*'

A short pause ensued and I thought the recital was at an end, especially as there was the sound of a bottle of wine being opened. But then José said:

'*The vertebrate suddenly looks back and sees the enigmatic tail of its kin in the retrospective reflection of the light-years' night. Only now has the secret path reached its end, and that end was the consciousness of the long journey towards the end itself. All one can do is clap one's hands, extremities one places on deposit for the heirs of the species.*'

'"The retrospective reflection of the light-years' night",' Ana repeated. 'Isn't that a bit heavy?'

'But looking out into the universe is the same as looking back over its history.'

'We can come back to that. Then, perhaps, we can take this one: *From fish and reptiles and small, sugar-sweet shrews, the chic primate has inherited a pair of becoming eyes with binocular vision. The distant heirs of the lobed-finned fish study the flight of the galaxies through space, knowing it's taken a few billion years to perfect their sight. The lenses are polished by macromolecules. The gaze is focused by hyperintegrated proteins and amino acids.*'

It was José's turn again:

'*In the eyeball there is a clash between creation and reflection. The two-way globes of sight are magical revolving doors where the creative spirit meets itself in the created spirit. The eye that surveys the universe is the universe's own eye.*'

There was silence for a few seconds. Then he said, 'Clubs or diamonds?'

'Diamonds! It's obvious.'

Two glasses were filled, and I stood there for a while. When there wasn't any more, I withdrew as quietly as I could.

I was in shock, but I'd also found the answers to many questions, because now it was clear that the odd maxims were something Ana and José pieced together at home on their veranda. They also had to be possessed of an extraordinary cheek, for I felt certain that the long tirade I'd just overheard also demonstrated something I wouldn't hesitate to call intellectual kleptomania, not to mention mental hacking. The fact that Ana and José's aphorisms began, more and more, to resemble my own perspective on evolution could hardly be a coincidence – not after yesterday's conversations, or the short talk I'd had with José only a few hours ago. Ever since our first meeting they'd cross-examined me and teased out practically every idea I had.

Several questions, though, were still outstanding. 'Diamonds! It's obvious.' And diamonds it obviously was, Vera, not clubs or spades, most definitely not. But what did it mean? What was the connection with cards? And who were 'Joker' and 'the elves'?

I wasn't sure either if the afternoon's workshop might not have been intended as a regular show for any lone tourists sneaking round the coconut grove. I couldn't be certain they hadn't seen me, for example, in the minutes before I found myself at the back of their veranda. Then there was Ana. Return from the oblivion within me, Ana!

I was determined to take action. First I went back to my own hut, got out pen and paper, then seated myself on the edge of the bed. I wrote: 'The closer Joker comes to eternal annihilation, the clearer he sees the animal that meets him in the mirror when he awakes to a new day. He finds no reconciliation in the inconsolable gaze of a grieving primate. He sees a bewitched fish, a metamorphosed frog, a deformed lizard. This is the end of the world, he thinks. This is where the long journey of evolution comes to an abrupt end.'

I read it aloud, and suddenly a reply came back from the pelmet.

'I liked the bit about the "deformed lizard",' said Gordon.

'Why?'

'It somehow emphasises that we're the ones who are genuine.'

'Rubbish! You're a bewitched fish as well.'

'But I'm not deformed. I haven't a single cerebral convolution too many. I've got a nervous system that's just right for the job, no more and no less.'

'Well, I'll put "an upright lizard" in that case.'

'I think you should stick to "deformed", and not only because of those excessive convolutions of the brain, but also with regard to the rhythm of the language. Not to mention good neighbourliness.'

'I've got another, too,' I said, and I read it out as I wrote:

'"Joker is an angel in distress. It was a fatal misunderstanding that led him to assume a body of flesh and blood. He only wanted to share the primate's lot for a few cosmic seconds, but he pulled down the celestial ladder behind him. If no one fetches him now, the biological clock will tick faster and faster, and it will be too late to return to heaven."'

I looked up.

'Romantic nonsense, if you ask me.'

'I haven't asked you anything.'

'What if there isn't any eternity?'

'That's precisely what's making me so exasperated. But sad, too. I'm a grieving primate.'

'But you're postulating that there's a heaven from which angels can be incarnated, only to find out one day that they're so stuck in the mire of the temporal world that they can't drag themselves home again.'

'Shall I put that in? ". . . so stuck in the mire of the temporal world that they can't drag themselves home again"?'

'Definitely not. There's unlikely to be any other world than this one, and it's this one that unfolds in time and space.'

'I know that!' I almost screamed. 'And that's the only reason you're saying it. But my simile had an implicit "if" in it, you see. I am *like* an angel in distress — and only *if* angels existed. You must just try to imagine a distressed angel who's gone astray in the quaking bog of the flesh and who suddenly realises that he's done something ominous and inevitable because he can't find his way back to heaven again. Can't you see how fatal this must be for the angel? He has assumed, in the natural order of creation, that his existence will never end. He has always existed, and is practically under divine contract that this is how it'll be, world without end. But now there's a flaw, a hamartia — just as that apple in the Garden of Eden caused a flaw — now finally the angel realises that his status has been severely reduced because, at a stroke, he's been down-graded to a biochemical angel, i.e. a man, and therefore a protein-based mortality machine much like a fish or a frog. He stands in front of the mirror and realises that because of a stupid mistake he's worth no more than a gecko.'

'As I said, we've never complained about our ontological status.'

'But I do!'

'Because you've got a convolution too many.'

'Yes, yes. And the angel hasn't. Perhaps he has exactly the same understanding as a human being, enough, I mean, to encompass certain concepts about the universe, where he, in stark contrast to humans, will remain for all eternity. It's there that the great difference lies, just there. Viewed from this perspective the angel has an adequate understanding, tailored to his cosmic status. Personally, I know far too much considering I'm only here on a flying visit.'

'I don't see the need to discuss an angel's understanding when you've just admitted you don't believe in them.'

I simply ignored him.

'I am of the house of the salamander,' I went on. 'And it's against the background of how short a time I'm here that I have a redundant cerebral convolution or two. So it's not an intellectual point I'm discussing, but an emotional question, not to mention a moral one. I find it both provoking and sad to be faced with how short life is and how much I already have to leave behind. It's not fair.'

'Perhaps you should use your allotted time doing something other than bewailing the fact that it's so short.'

'Imagine you're on a long journey,' I said. 'Suddenly, you're invited to the house of some nice people you've met, but only for a quick visit. At the same time, you also know that you'll never return to that house or, for that matter, to that country or town.'

'Well, you can still sit down and have a pleasant chat.'

'Of course. But I don't need to know everything about how the house functions. I don't need to know where all the ladles and saucepans, garden shears and bed linen are kept. I don't need to know how the two kids are doing at school or what mum and dad gave the guests to eat on their silver wedding anniversary last year. It might be nice to be shown round a bit, and I'm not trying to denigrate that kind of hospitality, but to have everything in the entire house, from cellar to attic, explained when you've only come for coffee is overdoing it.'

'Just like those two or three convolutions.'

I didn't let myself get sidetracked.

'For a stay of several months it would have been quite different, because undoubtedly they're nice people to know – if they weren't I'd hardly have dropped in on them, even though I didn't realise they were going to use so much of my brief visit to expand on their perfect life, and ditto house, with its under-floor heating and brand-new jacuzzi. I have to catch a plane, I'm leaving for another hemisphere. I'm on tenterhooks, because shortly I'll be getting up to leave, the taxi may be here at any moment, and I will never ever return . . . Do you really not understand what I'm getting at?'

'I'm definitely beginning to understand that you understand too much.'

'Too much, exactly, that's what I've been saying all along. I share almost ninety-nine per cent of my genes with a chimpanzee – and our longevity is virtually the same – but I don't think you have an inkling of how much more I comprehend, and yet I know I must tear myself away from it. For example, I have a good grasp of just how infinitely great outer space is and how it's divided into galaxies and clusters of galaxies, spirals and lone stars, and that there are healthy stars and febrile red giants, white dwarfs and neutron stars, planets and asteroids. I know everything about the sun and moon, about the evolution of life on earth, about the Pharaohs and the Chinese dynasties, the countries of the world and their peoples as presently constituted, not to mention all the studying I've done on plants and animals, canals and lakes, rivers and mountain passes. Without even a pause for thought I can tell you the names of several hundred cities, I can tell you the names of nearly all the countries in the world, and I know the approximate populations of every one. I have a knowledge of the historical background of the different cultures, their religion and mythology, and to a certain extent also the history of their languages, in particular etymological relationships, especially within the Indo-European family of languages, but I can certainly reel off a goodly number of expressions from the Semitic languages too, and some from Chinese and Japanese, not to mention all the topographical and personal names I know. In addition, I'm acquainted with several hundred individuals personally, and just from my own small country I could, at the drop of a hat, supply you with several thousand names of living fellow countrymen whom I know something about – fairly extensive biographical knowledge in some cases. And I needn't confine myself to Norwegians, we're living more and more in a global village, and soon the village square will cover the entire galaxy. On another level, there are all the people I'm genuinely fond of, although it isn't just people one gets attached to, but places as well, just think of all the places I know like the back of my hand, and where I can tell if someone's gone and chopped down a bush or moved a stone. Then there are books, especially all those that have taught me so much about the biosphere and outer space, but also literary works, and through them all the imaginary people whose lives I've come to know and who, at times, have meant a great deal to me. And then I couldn't live without music, and I'm very eclectic, everything from folk music and Renaissance music to Schönberg and Penderecki, but I have to admit, and this has a bearing on the very perspective we're trying to gain, I have to admit to having a particular penchant for romantic music, and this, don't forget, can also be found amongst the works of Bach and Gluck, not to mention Albinoni. But romantic music has existed in every age, and even Plato warned against it because he believed that melancholy could actually weaken the state, and it's patently clear when you get to Puccini and Mahler that music has become a direct expression of what I'm trying to get you to comprehend, that life is too short and that the way human beings are fashioned means they must take leave of far too much. If you've heard Mahler's *Abschied* from *Das Lied von der Erde* you'll know what I mean. Hopefully you'll have understood that it's the farewell itself I'm referring to, the actual leave-taking, and that this takes place in the self-same organ where everything I'm saying goodbye to is stored.'

I went to my cabin bag and opened it, pulled out the gin bottle and put it to my mouth. It was hardly worthy of comment as I only drank a little drop, and it wouldn't be long to dinner.

'Are you starting already?' he said.

'Starting? I think your use of the word is thoroughly tendentious. I'm having a nip because I'm thirsty, for the purpose of quenching in other words, and you say I'm starting something.'

'I was just worried that this drinking habit of yours might shorten your life even further, if the worst came to the worst.'

'Possibly, and I can see the paradox, but I'm not talking about getting old, I'm talking about eternity, and where that's concerned a couple of years is a mere bagatelle.'

'Luckily I'm spared the worry of eternity.'

'Well, I'm not!' I said. I snatched up the note I'd written, rushed out of the room and slammed the door hard behind me.

I walked purposefully towards Ana and José's hut, though as I drew near I slackened my pace considerably, so that when I passed the veranda it might, with a bit of luck, seem totally fortuitous. I'd folded the paper and stuffed it in my back pocket.

'Would you like a glass of white wine?' Ana sang out.

'Yes, thank you.'

She fetched a chair and a glass from inside, and when we'd sat down and the glasses had been filled, I pretended to gaze thoughtfully out into the palm grove while mumbling something to myself, like an old adage one was digesting:

'The closer Joker comes to eternal annihilation, the clearer he sees the animal that meets him in the mirror when he awakens to a new day. He finds no reconciliation in the inconsolable gaze of a grieving primate. He sees a bewitched fish, a metamorphosed frog, a deformed lizard. This is the end of the world, he thinks. This is where the long journey of evolution comes to an abrupt end.'

You could have heard a pin drop, it was so quiet on the veranda it scared me. I believe Ana and José exchanged glances, but not a word was spoken until Ana finally asked me what I thought of the wine.

I'd taken it for granted that some kind of response would be forthcoming, for what I'd said could only be interpreted as a reaction to their own oral extravaganza of the past couple of days. But we merely sat for a quarter of an hour discussing Fiji and various other topics of general interest.

I remember being struck by the dreadful possibility that everything I'd heard Ana and José reel off to one another might theoretically be the same kind of communication as the conversations I'd had with Gordon. But in that case the problem would be turned on its head, because why didn't Ana and José make any comment on my sudden pronouncement about the bewitched fish and the grieving primate? Our roles had been suddenly and completely reversed.

Or did they feel themselves the victims of eavesdropping and spying because they'd never intended me to understand any of their recitations? The confidences of a pair of lovers bathing naked beneath a tropical waterfall were perhaps not intended for the ears of third parties, and certainly didn't warrant a response. In addition, I had no reason to feel insulted that they were inspired to treat the subjects we'd discussed in a more lyrical vein.

I had to make quite certain. After I'd thanked them for the wine a coconut fell from one of the palms, and again I spoke to myself – loudly enough to ensure they could hear it:

'Joker is an angel in distress. It was a fatal misunderstanding that led him to assume a body of flesh and blood. He only wanted to share the primate's lot for a few cosmic seconds, but he pulled down the celestial ladder behind him. If no one fetches him now, the biological clock will tick faster and faster, and it will be too late to return to heaven.'

Again it went totally quiet, and I felt that an atmosphere of embarrassment reigned on the veranda. I received not the slightest response, Vera, not even of the non-verbal kind. And I should add that from that afternoon on there was nothing more. Not once after that did Ana and José hold forth to each other in my presence. Something had died, died as irrevocably as that angel who'd lost the key to eternity.

We walked out into the palm grove together. Ana took her camera along and began taking pictures again. I had to photograph them here, too, for example standing beneath the palm tree with the notice warning about falling coconuts.

Apart from angels in despair, there was something about heads and falling coconuts that put me in mind of how easy it was to touch up photos and forge nude pictures of acquaintances on the internet. But it wasn't in a photograph that I'd seen Ana's face before. I was absolutely sure of that, so sure indeed that I had to ask myself why I was so certain about something I couldn't remember.

Tropical Summit

When we arrived for dinner, the small tables had been pushed together to form one big one. On the previous evening the guests had begun mixing as soon as the meal was finished, and I assumed our hosts wanted to help bring us together from the very beginning of the meal. Only later did I glean that the initiative for this unusual place setting had come from Mr Spooke because, as Jochen Kiess expressed it, the Maravu Plantation Resort wished to stand out as a beacon of refuge for individualists.

I'd arrived early and was in time to take a beer in the bar with the Englishman. We talked about the reptiles of Oceania, and especially house geckoes, because John had a number of them in his room too. I said nothing about the bottle of gin. That could remain a secret between the proprietor and me. Instead I must confess I told him a bit about Oslo, including of course a few words about us. I told him about that as well. I said we'd lost a child in a road accident.

Early that morning I'd made a telephone call to the conference centre in Salamanca to confirm that I was on the list of participants, and I couldn't help blurting out to John that I'd been told you were expected there, as well. What I couldn't know was whether you actually realised I was coming. John responded by saying that he'd lost his wife some years before after a long illness. Her name was Sheila, and I gathered he'd been deeply attached to her. We agreed that life wasn't easy. After many years of literary inactivity the Englishman had begun to make notes for a new novel. That led us to exchange a few words about art and culture generally, and I confided that I had a love of the Spanish masters, especially that sumptuous collection in the Prado. At that, his eyes widened as if something specific had struck him.

As we sat talking, the guests began to arrive. At dinner I had Laura on my right and Evelyn on my left. Mark, who was already a qualified lawyer, was on the other side of Evelyn, and at the head of the table, to the left of him, sat Bill. John had placed himself opposite me, and to his left, opposite Laura, was Mario, on the Englishman's other side sat Ana and next to her José.

I'll try to stick to the main points of the evening, and go right to the essentials. Before pudding arrived, John tapped his glass and made a few discursive remarks about the setting in which we found ourselves, the rare intellectual inspiration such tropical nights so often afforded – man was, after all, a tropical creature – and more particularly, how nice it had been to meet all of us, whether we hailed from far-away Europe, America or Australia. Our hostess at the Maravu, Mrs Angela Kiess, had also told him in passing that it was the first time for many months that exactly the same guests sat down to dinner two nights running; usually someone came or went during the day. Furthermore – and this was the Englishman's intention for this evening – he believed that everyone at the table, all incidental differences apart, had something in common, yes, a least common multiple, if he might borrow a mathematical expression. In short: he'd already managed to have a few words with each one of us, and had become aware that in our own separate ways we all had a special interest in what he chose to call the dilemma of modern man, as evinced the previous evening, though the conversations then had been more diffuse than he hoped they'd be tonight, as even an informal gathering could find a chairman useful. He then listed us all by name as he tried, not without some difficulty, to shape us into a sort of cross-section of humanity that had arrived at its tryst beneath a vast, starry sky.

The evening's meeting was thereby called to order, and John christened it a 'tropical summit'. Then he made the following speech. It must have been something he'd been mulling over for a long time:

'When we meet other people, whether it's at a professional conference or on a South Sea island, part of the form is to give your name and say where you live, and maybe provide other information too, especially if the acquaintance is to last for several days. Perhaps you might supply details of your marital status, work, and the country or city you hail from. And it could be you discover you have mutual acquaintances, a shared interest or, for that matter, some common problems, like an over-jealous spouse, or a physical handicap, a rare phobia or recently deceased parents. Good!'

I glanced round the table, and most of the guests looked like living question marks. Laura — who that evening was dressed in a black blouse and cut-down jeans with long frays — put a hand on my arm and whispered, 'He's a real clown.'

'Good!' the Englishman repeated. 'A virtual requisite for such introductions is the desire to show oneself off to the best possible advantage, whether in matters of sex, status, financial affairs, social connections or special achievements and skills. The art is not merely to reveal one's most advantageous facets, but to do it in the most casual, disguised or unintentional way possible. For man is not merely a social animal. He is above all a vain creature, vainer, I assume, than any other vertebrate. Look how wonderful and clever I am, we say. I hope you realise I'm not just one of the crowd. I've got two grown-up sons, you know, both at college, and a teenage daughter who wants to be an actress or an artist. Oh, really, well our daughter recently married the mayor of Liverpool's son, he was absolutely crazy about her. You can also see that I'm pretty well off. Oh, yes, our name's the same as the steel company, that was my great-grandfather, you know. Well, I've dipped into Derrida naturally, and for the past few days I've had a book by Baudrillard on my bedside table. And then there's art; actually we have a small Monet in the bedroom, and a Miró in the sitting room, and as a matter of fact, we've just hung a baroque mirror over the fireplace . . .'

He interrupted himself by exclaiming: 'Well, fine! Good!'

I looked round again, and found several other people doing the same, for at that moment no one quite knew what he was driving at. At least that was what I thought, though subsequently I've wondered if he didn't have an accomplice.

124

'It's hot,' Bill declared. 'Maybe we should order a couple of bottles of white wine? Or should I crack open some champagne?'

But John just carried on.

'Apart from all this, apart from all the dresses and dinners, powder and tie-pins, the bank drafts and baroque mirrors above the fireplace – apart from all these social frills – we may have two years or ten or, at best, a few decades of life left on this planet. And because of this, yes, because of this, certain existential viewpoints commonly impinge on us all, though we rarely speak of them. I therefore suggest that this evening we try to leave our arbitrary interests and activities behind, and instead concentrate on something that affects us all.'

Just then, because I was recalling something I'd been talking to Gordon about the night before, I suddenly came out with, 'The universe, for example.'

I'd only muttered it to myself, but John enquired, 'What did that gentleman say?'

'The universe, for example,' I said.

'Excellent, absolutely excellent. So now we have the suggestion that we try to concentrate the evening's conversation on the universe. We'll therefore put party politics to one side, Linda Tripp and Monica Lewinsky too, though I've never understood how such a huge scandal could have been generated out of the erotic potential of a Havana cigar – but that's enough of that, more than enough of that. We, and by that I mean each and every one of us, are not merely products of a man-made sociality. We also live beneath a deeply mysterious sky, full of stars and galaxies, and even our own satellites find it almost impossible to tell a prohibited Cuban cigar from a harmless Brazilian one.'

I felt the stirrings of a nervous atmosphere round the table. Ana and José had completely entered into the spirit of the thing, although they might well have been on the organising committee. I think Laura now began to be drawn in, even though she'd labelled John a clown only a few minutes earlier. Mark and Mario, on the other hand, were only playing the game on sufferance I think, and Evelyn, who was studying pharmacy in Seattle, said straight away that she knew nothing about astronomy and might as well withdraw. Bill seemed totally apathetic; even as John was speaking he'd beckoned the man with the flower behind his left ear and placed an order of some sort. As for me, I threw myself into the situation, and into the Maravu Plantation Resort as a refuge for the big questions as well as for the individualist.

John began trying to thaw out the gathering by asking how many of us believed there was life on other planets. As Evelyn wouldn't be drawn either way on the question, the company split into two equal factions, and John was ready to sum up for the first time that evening.

'Astonishing! I must say I'm impressed with the judgement of this assembly. I posed a most fundamental question about the nature of the universe and can declare that, after only a few minutes, I've been given four completely correct answers to that question. Although the other four are totally and utterly wrong.'

'You know the answers then, do you?' was Mario's comment.

The chairman ignored him. He went on:

'Because either there is life in the universe – or there isn't. *Tertium non datur!* Of course, the mere thought that it's crawling with life out there can make our heads spin. But it's also possible that life is limited to our own planet, though that doesn't make the thing any easier to accept; the thought of that, too, can be perplexing. So it's obvious that four of those present have given an exact and correct answer to the question we put. In other words, the answers to conundrums aren't necessarily that complicated.'

'You haven't said *which* of us gave the right answer,' Mario sulked.

'That doesn't matter in the least,' John emphasised. 'As far as I'm concerned, it's a tremendous achievement that there are four people actually sitting round this table who've given the correct answer about the presence of life out there.'

It was then I jumped the gun so shamefully.

'It's obvious there's life out there,' I said. 'There are maybe a hundred billion galaxies in the universe, and each galaxy has a hundred billion stars. It would be an incredible waste of space if we were all alone.'

'That's an interesting comment,' José replied.

'Why?'

'Yesterday evening you were most emphatic that no intent lay behind natural processes.'

'I still am,' I affirmed.

He swept me aside: 'And today it would be an incredible waste of space if we were all alone here . . .'

I nodded, because I still hadn't realised my own loose thinking. But the trap was sprung, Vera, for now he had me: 'Then perhaps you could tell us who is, or is not, wasting space?'

All I could do was eat humble pie and admit he'd caught me in an inconsistency. At the same time, it occurred to me that the first people to use the 'waste of space' argument in support of a universe full of life were often those who most vehemently denied the existence of a deeper meaning to natural processes. But if the creation of life on earth is no more than a crazy coincidence, it's all the more unreasonable to hold up that same crazy coincidence as a cosmic principle.

John went on to clarify a number of other cosmological questions, and always by posing a question that divided the participants into two camps. He wanted to know if cosmic energy had always existed, and if not, we had to decide if it had evolved completely by itself or from some internal or external creative force. Then he wanted to find out if the universe would continue to expand, or if its mass was so great that it would be drawn back together again and thus cause an infinite number of new Big Bangs and their attendant universes. He tried to discover if there was any transcendental consciousness or if the physical universe was the only thing that existed. Then he was interested to hear our thoughts on whether human beings had a soul that in some way survived brain death, or if everything in nature was equally ephemeral. Were there any extrasensory phenomena, he demanded, or was every sort of so-called extrasensory phenom- enon complete and utter fantasy, nothing more than modern man's vestigial remnant of a mythical or even animistic outlook on the world? All the time he was careful to note just how the meeting divided into two diametrically opposed camps, and was punctilious in reminding us that at least some of those present had given the right answers to the questions he'd asked, for never once did we all share the same point of view.

'Either-or!' John Spooke snapped in his clipped Oxford English voice before duly sealing his ontological quadratic equations with a Latin tag: *Tertium non datur!*

Not long after, the man with the flower behind his left ear put two bottles of champagne on the table in fulfilment of Bill's order, and now the conversation entered an entirely new phase. John wanted to go round the table so that each in turn could give a quick summary of his or her philosophy of life. We were all interested by now; even Evelyn had warmed to it.

José led off, and took the opportunity to argue for what I could safely call an anthropocentric viewpoint. He simply believed that the universe couldn't have been much smaller than it was, or been very differently constituted, if it was to create mankind. The conclusions he drew were always far in excess of the arguments he produced, but he reminded us that the human brain is possibly the most complex material in the entire universe, and basically much harder to understand than neutron stars and black holes. Furthermore, the brain is composed of atoms that have once simmered in long burnt-out stars, and had the universe not been the size it is, it wouldn't have been capable of creating stars and planets, or even so much as a micro-organism. Even an 'unintelligent' planet like Jupiter for instance had a vital role in enabling us to sit here talking so rationally. Were it not for that gigantic planet's vast gravitational field, the earth would have been continually bombarded by meteoroids and asteroids; but Father Jove acted like a vacuum cleaner against the forces of chaos that would otherwise have made it impossible for planet Tellus to foster a biosphere and eventually human consciousness. He described it all in a manner that put me in mind of the ways the chiefs in erstwhile Fijian society had kept close to a mosquito-man. If the earth was the chief and the meteoroids were the swarms of mosquitoes, Jupiter was the one doing service as the mosquito-man. Nor should we forget that over the years Jupiter had drawn some severe mosquito bites, just one of which, according to José, would have been enough to finish off virtually all life on earth.

'Give me a living planet!' he exclaimed by way of peroration. 'And the earth can be the only one as far as I'm concerned, provided, of course, there isn't a force that's decided not to waste space. Though it's conceivable that the universal mass is only just sufficient to create a consciousness capable of postulating theories like these. It takes time, too, to create anything as complicated as the human mind, it's not just a matter of seven days. The applause for the Big Bang was heard only fifteen billion years after the explosion.'

Bill argued that it was only a matter of time before science would reveal all the secrets of matter and the universe, Mark intimated that more and more of the basic research would be funded by multi-national corporations, while Evelyn had an unshakeable faith in Jesus as the saviour of mankind and the universe.

Then it was Laura's turn. Laura made no secret of the fact that she'd derived much of the inspiration for her view of life from Indian philosophy, especially *vedanta*, one of the six orthodox schools, or more accurately *keval-advaita*, a term that derived from the philosopher Shankara, who lived in India early in the nineteenth century. 'Keval-advaita' meant 'absolute non-dualism' Laura told us. She went on to declare that there was only one reality, which the Indians called *brahman* or *mahatman*, meaning world soul or more literally, 'the great soul'. *Brahman* was eternal, indivisible and non-material. So all of John's questions had one answer, and only one answer, because *brahman* was the answer to all the questions he'd posed.

'Oh hell, Laura,' sighed Bill, the man who'd expressed an almost naïve scientific optimism.

But Laura wouldn't let herself be deflected. She explained that all variety was merely an illusion. An illusion that causes our daily lives to reveal the world as multi-faceted, she said – an illusion the Indians have for thousands of years called *maya*. Because the real world is not the outward, visible or material one. That's only a dreamlike delusion, and real enough for those in its thrall, but to the wise only *brahman*, or the world soul, is real. The human soul is identical to *brahman*, she went on, and only when we realise this does the illusion of the external reality vanish. The soul then becomes *brahman*, which it's been all the time, but without realising it.

'I expect we asked for that,' John remarked. 'The external world doesn't exist, and all diversity is just an illusion.'

Laura wouldn't rise to the bait. She fingered her dark plaits and smiled impishly round the table as she explained in more detail.

'When you have a dream, you think you're part of a multifarious reality and that you're in an external world. But everything in the illusory world of dreams is the product of your own soul, it *is* your own soul and nothing more. The problem is that you don't realise this until you wake up, and then the dream no longer exists. Now it's been stripped of all its false masks and emerges as what it's been all along, just yourself.'

'I'm not familiar with that theory,' our chairman admitted. 'Although it's both beguiling and radical. It's certainly almost impossible to disprove . . .'

He considered a moment, then said, 'Did you really say "maya"?'

She nodded, and the Englishman then turned his glance on Ana, who sat on his right. I noticed she looked down, and at the same time José put his arm round her and drew her closer to him.

'We believe that we are nine souls sitting round this table,' Laura pointed out. 'And that's because of *maya*. In reality we're aspects of one and the same soul. It's the *maya* illusion that makes us think the others are something different from ourselves. That's why we don't need to worry about death. Nothing can die. The only thing that disappears when we die is the actual chimera of being separate from the rest of the world – just as we believe that our dreams are not part of our own soul.'

John thanked Laura for her contribution, and now it was Mario's turn.

'I'm a Catholic,' was all he said, and waved his hand to indicate that he'd no more to add.

But John wouldn't let him off so lightly, and eventually the lone yachtsman elaborated.

'You've all sat there talking so blithely about all you can see, when in reality you're blind in both eyes. You say you see all the stars and galaxies, you see the evolution of life on earth, and you say that you can see the genetic material itself. You see order rising out of chaos, and you even brag about being able to see right back to the moment of creation. And then you end up by announcing that you have disproved the existence of God! Bravo!'

When he didn't offer any more, John tried to get him going again, and after a short pause Mario said, 'We've been almost everywhere now, and we haven't so much as glimpsed a divinity. No God was waiting for us up Mount Everest. No table was prepared for us on the surface of the moon. We haven't even made radio contact with the Holy Ghost. But if we play hide-and-seek, hide-and-seek is what we get. What I'm saying is: who has the most naïve world philosophy? The theologians? Or the reduction-ists?'

When Evelyn briefly applauded, he went on, and had soon warmed to his subject. He let fall that in his younger years he'd been a physics teacher, and that he still kept abreast of things by reading periodicals and books on the subject.

'We saw through the biosphere long ago. It was all just macromolecules, it was proteins, and not even that, it was nothing but a cocktail of animo-acids. Space isn't much to write home about, either. It was just a Big Bang that set the whole thing off. There's nothing mysterious about any of it, about the Doppler effect, about cosmic background radiation, about curved space, or about anything at all up there. It's called physics, or theoretical physics. Then there is only consciousness left, although when you boil it down, it's no more to wonder about than the rest of creation. That, too, has just been cobbled together for the occasion from atoms and molecules. That too. Philosophy might as well take a long holiday. Because there aren't any more riddles left to guess. Or is it science that could do with a pause for thought? Perhaps it's science that's on its last legs. The only thing worrying us now – and when I say "us", I should add that we are very much in the minority – is the world itself. But just give us a couple of sophisticated arguments, and we won't ask any more questions.'

Evelyn clapped again, and José and Bill sat nodding.

After Mario it was John's turn.

'I've already taken the opportunity to demonstrate that I believe there are simple answers to many of the big problems we pose. The difficulty is that it's not easy to choose between them. I've also tried to indicate that cosmological questions are perhaps better suited to party games than to scientific analysis. Science has given us the theory of evolution, the theory of relativity, quantum physics and, last but not least, the alluring theory of the Big Bang. Well, fine! That's all fine. The question then is whether natural science has begun to draw near its end. Though we'll soon have mapped the human genom – with all its hundreds of thousands of genes – it's unlikely to leave us any the wiser. The map itself will almost certainly strengthen biotechnology and maybe help cure a number of diseases, but it's no more likely to show what consciousness is than to say why it exists. And we could just go on like that. The answer to whether there's life in a galaxy several hundred million light-years away from us is something we'll never know, as the distances are just too great. And though we constantly broaden our understanding of the evolution of the universe, we'll never be in a position to give a scientific explanation of what the universe *is*. But let me borrow an image from Laura, who compared the external world to a dream. This can be a superb allegory. If the world is a dream, science attempts to analyse what the actual material of the dream is. It tries to measure the distance from one end of the dream to the other, but everyone also agrees that time and space collapse when we peer towards the outer edges of the universe and when we look back to the Big Bang, even though we're talking about two sides of the same coin, for the further we look out into the universe, the further we look back into its history. So we try, as best we can, to find our way through the dream. And good, all this is perfectly fine. But we can't get outside the dream. We can never see it from the outside. We're banging our heads on the furthest limits of the dream in much the same way as an autistic person may bang his head against a wall.'

I poured more champagne into Laura's glass.

'Do you completely exclude the possibility of us understanding a lot more about the world we live in one day?' I asked.

He shook his head.

'Quite the contrary. I've complete faith in human intuition. But if we want to solve the riddle of the universe, perhaps we should tackle it mentally, and for all we know the riddle may already have been solved. I wouldn't be at all surprised if the solution to the universal enigma already lay in some ancient Greek, Latin or Indian tract. And the answer needn't be all that complicated, it might be between ten and twenty words long. Just as I'm sure that Laura's *maya* theory can be condensed into a couple of sentences. This evening we've had explicit answers to a whole series of questions that don't have more than two alternatives. I'm certain no scientific instrument could assess which of the answers we've given were the right ones and which were hopelessly and completely wrong. But what's your opinion, Ana?'

It was her turn now. For a few moments she gazed out into the tropical night. Then she sat up and said resolutely, 'There is a reality beyond this one. When I die, I won't die. You'll all believe I'm dead, but I won't be. Soon we'll meet again in another place.'

These words heralded the end of the party. The tenor of the conversation had shifted completely. There was an eerie sensation around the table, and I don't think I was alone in seeing a tear fall from José's eye. Ana went on, 'You'll all think you're at a funeral, but in reality you'll be witnessing a new birth . . .'

Now Ana looked me in the eye.

'There is something beyond this,' she insisted. 'Here we are merely fleeting spirits in transition.'

'No more, now,' José whispered in Spanish. 'You don't have to say any more.'

Everyone's eyes had been riveted on Ana while she spoke. That's when it happened, Vera, the thing that's made me report so much of what occurred at that tropical summit at the Maravu Plantation Resort.

'We are merely fleeting spirits in transition,' the chairman repeated.

With that he placed a finger on Ana's forehead and said, 'And this spirit's name is Maya!'

José shook his head anxiously and placed a protective arm around Ana. It was obvious the last comment had displeased him. Or was it simply that he didn't like the way the Englishman had touched Ana with his forefinger? I found his reaction difficult to fathom.

'I think that's enough,' he said.

John chewed his lip as if he suddenly realised he'd acted thoughtlessly. Even so, he said half to himself as he again cast a brief glance at Ana, 'And there's a masterpiece involved here, too.'

José responded by drawing Ana up from her chair.

'Thank you!' he said. 'That's quite enough!'

'Let's go!' he said to Ana in Spanish.

And with that they disappeared into the palm grove. That was the last we saw of the Spaniards that evening, but by now it was past midnight.

I think it was a full minute before anyone spoke. We just sat there pondering on what had passed between John and José. Bill was the first to break the silence.

'You know what I think?' he said with a broad grin. 'I think there's something like six billion garrulous people on this planet, and we're only here for eighty to ninety years at best. And you can find a whole lot of amusing things to say, and a whole lot of bullshit.'

Laura rose slowly from her seat and walked away from the group. On a side table stood a jug of ice-cold water. She picked it up and walked up behind the American. Then she tipped its entire contents, water and ice cubes, over his head.

He sat stock still for at least two seconds, without moving a muscle. Then he jumped up from his chair, grabbed hold of Laura's left arm, drew her towards him and hit her.

I'd had some sympathy with him until that moment, and though it wasn't a sharp blow, more a slap with the flat of the hand, a line had to be drawn somewhere. It was clear the American had incurred everyone's disapproval, and even looking at the two empty bottles of Veuve Clicquot didn't help. Laura just walked calmly back to the table and seated herself beside me without a word.

John began thanking us for another pleasant evening. He added, 'We don't have to be quite so high-flown tomorrow.'

Bill left the table, and Mark and Evelyn did the same – I think the young Americans almost fled at the thought of more fisticuffs to come. Mario had taken his leave even before Laura had emptied her jug of iced water.

I laid my hand on Laura's left cheek.

'Is it painful?' I asked.

She shook her head.

'It didn't look very pleasant.'

She said, 'You must learn to lose yourself, Frank.'

'What?'

'But what you lose is nothing compared to what you gain.'

In the candlelight from the table I looked into a brown eye. Deep in the dark pigment a narrow stripe of green struggled not to be overwhelmed by the brown.

'And what do I gain?'

'You'll gain the whole world.'

'The whole world,' I repeated.

She nodded.

'What you lose may seem big and important. But it's no more than an enforced illusion.'

'The self, you mean. Is that what's an illusion?'

'Only the smaller self. Only the illusory self. That's as good as lost already anyway. But you have a greater self.'

I heard someone approaching in the darkness, and next moment a jug of water was emptied over our heads. I don't believe it was pure accident that most of it landed on me, even though we were sitting extremely close when it happened. Before we'd had time to think, whoever had done it had vanished.

'The idiot,' said Laura, oozing contempt.

I stood up and shook my head. My shirt was soaking wet. So was Laura's blouse, and I felt close to confusion when I saw how it clung to her skin.

'Well, perhaps we should turn in,' I said.

She looked up at me with her green eye. 'Are you sure of that?'

'Quite sure,' I said.

It was only when we'd gone our separate ways that I realised her question could only have been an invitation.

That evening I was almost looking forward to getting back to Gordon. He was a splendid chap at heart, and perhaps he'd been right to say there wasn't much point in dosing myself with all that gin just as I was settling down for the night.

He'd taken up his position on the large mirror to the right of my bedside table, and no sooner had I closed the door behind me than I heard him swish from one end of it to the other. Of course I couldn't be completely certain it was Gordon, as there were sure to be several geckoes in my room, and I hadn't much enthusiasm for starting from scratch and introducing myself to a new gecko. But as soon as I turned on the light I saw it was him. I've always had a talent for spotting the individual characteristics of verte- brates, and of course geckoes are as individual as human beings, I thought. They have exactly the same degree of individuality as we do. That, at least, was a sentiment I felt certain the WWF's representative here on the island could have supported. And besides, Gordon was a jumbo gecko, he must have been the biggest in the class.

'Well, I'm going straight to bed,' I announced. 'I only say that so you won't take it personally if I don't sit around talking into the small hours.'

I'd opened my cabin bag and unscrewed the top of the gin bottle. I took one copious swig, a single shot big enough to ensure I fell asleep.

'I find that hard to believe, to be honest,' said Gordon.

'Huh?'

'That you're turning in. I bet you'll drink more from that bottle, too.'

'I have absolutely no plans in that direction.'

'Had a nice evening?'

'Don't want to talk about it. If I start talking now I don't know if I'll be able to switch off, and then it'll be just like yesterday. If you know what I mean.'

'I only asked if you'd had a nice evening.'

'Laura's a pantheist,' I said. 'She's such an extreme monist, I'd almost call her a vulgar monist.'

'A bright lady, in other words. She doesn't crash around half asleep like some others I could mention. And I'm sure she doesn't clean her teeth with gin, either.'

'Then she talked about *maya*. I've heard of it before, so I don't need any lectures.'

'*Maya* is the illusion of the world,' said Gordon. 'It's what conjures the bitter illusion of being only a poor ego, divorced from the Great Self and with only a few months or years to live. It's also the name of a people in Central America, but that's something completely different . . .'

'I said I didn't need any explanations. But José reacted so oddly when the Englishman put his finger on Ana's forehead and seemed to reveal her true self. "This spirit's name is Maya," he said, and then mumbled something about a "masterpiece". What he said was strange, very strange. But she reacted curiously, too. It was as if she couldn't bear being told straight out.'

'*Maya* has some people so firmly in its grip that it can be painful to wake up. It's rather like waking from a nightmare.'

'Rubbish. You don't know what I'm talking about. You weren't even there.'

'I'm everywhere, Frankie. There is only one me.'

'Can't you just drop that nonsense, please.'

'I'm only expressing the universe's simplest and most obvious statement.'

'And that is?'

'There is only one world.'

'All right, I've got it. There is only one world.'

'And that is you.'

'Oh, do be quiet.'

'You must break the bonds of the self, mister. Just try looking up from your own navel – and out, out at the works of nature about you, out into one unbroken cascade of magical reality.'

'I'm trying.'

'And what do you see?'

'I see a palm grove in the southern hemisphere.'

'It is you.'

'Now I see Ana rising naked from the bubble-bath beneath Bouma Falls.'

'It is you.'

'I know her head, but not her body.'

'Concentrate, now.'

'I see a living planet.'

'It is you.'

'And I see an awesome universe with billions of galaxies and clusters of galaxies.'

'It is all you.'

'But when I look out into the universe, I'm also looking back into its history. I'm really studying events that could be several billion years old. Many of the stars I see – right now at this moment – have long ago turned into red giants or supernovas. Some have already become white dwarfs, furious neutron stars and black holes.'

'You're looking back on your own past. It's what's called

memory. You're trying to remember something you've forgotten. But it's you, all of it.'

'I see a chaotic system of moons and planets, asteroids and comets.'

'It's all you. For there is only one reality.'

'Yes, I've already said I agreed with that.'

'There is only one world material, only one matter.'

'And that's me?'

'It is you.'

'Then I'm no weakling, am I?'

'If only you realise it. If only you can abandon yourself.'

'Yes, exactly. And why is that so bloody difficult?'

'Because you won't let go of your own little self. It's as simple as that.'

'Even simple solutions can be difficult to put into practice. For example, it's very easy to take your own life.'

'You're not that primitive.'

'Primitive?'

'It also presupposes you have an ego to lose.'

'True enough, and the paradox is that I might commit suicide out of pure fear of the slowness of death. Sometimes a child eats a chocolate simply because it's worried someone else may eat it. But we've been through this before. You can simply jettison your tail if it's attacked. I can't do an autotomy on two or three of my cerebral convolutions. I can't just admit myself to a clinic and demand to be lobotomised for cosmic angst.'

'That wouldn't solve the problems anyway. It would just set you right back and you would never get the chance to reawaken again. I think you need the whole of your cerebral cortex for this process.'

'Isn't that a bit rich coming from you?'

'In a sense you have to die. You have to commit that daring deed.'

'I thought you just said that wouldn't be a solution?'

'But you only have to die in a figurative sense. It's not you that has to die. It's that overblown notion of an "I" that much perish.'

'I'm getting a little confused by your use of pronouns.'

'Very likely. Maybe we need a new pronoun.'

'Have you any suggestions?'

'You must have heard of the pronoun called "pluralis majestatis".'

'Of course, it's when a king or an emperor refers to his own noble person as "we". It's called the royal we.'

'I think we also need a royal I.'

'And what use would that be?'

'When you say "I", you're just clinging to a notion of ego, which is false anyway.'

'Now you're beginning to go in circles.'

'But try thinking of the planet as a whole, and the entire universe as well, of which this planet is an organic part.'

'I'm trying.'

'You're thinking of everything that exists.'

'I'm thinking of everything that exists.'

'And of all the galaxies, of everything that exploded fifteen billion years ago.'

'Everything, yes.'

'Now say "I".'

'"I".'

'Was that hard?'

'A tiny bit. But also rather amusing.'

'Think of everything in existence. Then say out loud to yourself: "This is me!"'

'"This is me" . . .'

'Wasn't that liberating?'

'A bit.'

'That was because you used the new pronoun "singularis majestatis".'

'Was it?'

'I think you're getting there, Frank.'

'How so? I'm just grateful for the lesson, that's all.'

'I think you can be like me. Saved in other words, and totally free from all ontological neuroses.'

'No, not likely. You were a bit clumsy there.'

I opened the cabin bag again and took a healthy pull at the gin bottle. I knew he was going to make some snide remark, and a moment later he said, 'You have to admit you don't know yourself very well.'

'That depends which mode of the pronoun you're using right now.'

'It's not long since you announced you were going to bed and definitely weren't going to touch any more drink.'

'Then you started talking. And you almost took me in, too. You almost made me wish I was a gecko.'

'Can you hear what you're saying?'

'I said that you started talking.'

'I mean, can you hear which pronoun you're using. Who was it who began talking?'

That was cunning. He'd wrong-footed me again. In truth I was the one who'd kept the conversation going.

'So you've too little self-knowledge,' he said. 'And you've also got real problems deciding what you want.'

'I acknowledge some trifling weakness,' I confessed.

I felt I wasn't risking anything by this admission. When all is said and done, one doesn't need to hide all that much from a gecko.

'But there's something else as well.'

'Out with it!'

'You talk to yourself.'

'Must you remind me?'

'You're biting your own tail now, Frank. I recommend instant autotomy.'

'Well, shut up then!'

'You're talking to yourself.'

'What?'

'The world spirit does as well.'

'What?'

'The world spirit talks to itself. Because there is only one world spirit.'

'And the name of this world spirit?'

'Yourself.'

I sat mulling over what he'd said.

'In my next life I think I'll study grammar,' I said. 'What about this as the title for a doctoral thesis: "Identity and ontological status. A tentative analysis of the brand-new pronoun singularis majestatis".'

'Excellent, in my opinion. Only then will linguistics have reached its positive stage. All other pronouns being purely *maya*.'

'And Ana is *maya*.'

'Yes, her too.'

'Because she talks to herself.'

'And who, for example, was talking in the fourth century BC?'

'Right at the beginning it was Socrates and his disciples,' I said. 'Then came Plato and his students, then Aristotle and Theophrastus – who doubtless had some lively conversations about the "half-finger" geckoes on the Greek island of Lesbos . . .'

'Do you believe that?'

'Surely you're not going to insist that history's an illusion as well?'

'History is the world spirit talking to itself. It did so in antiquity, too, though then it was befuddled. It had only just begun to wake up.'

'They walked about the market place in Athens. Socrates was a man of flesh and blood, a man who was sentenced to death simply because he searched for the truth. His friends stood round him and wept. Have you no empathy at all?'

'I never said the world spirit has always been fully at peace with itself. I didn't say it was always that happy, either.'

'What rubbish.'

'Go further back, then. Who was it who gathered in the market place a hundred million years ago?'

'You know perfectly well. It was the dinosaurs.'

'Can you give me any of their names?'

'Certainly. Yes, lots of names.'

'Let's hear them!'

'You mean the names of species, genuses or families?'

'No, are you mad? I mean can you supply any names of individuals.'

'Nope. This was in prehistoric times.'

'But it's irrelevant anyway, as they were only a progressive niche of the world spirit. This was before the *maya* concept came fully into play, before these two or three superfluous convolutions, and therefore it pre-dates man's mental delusion that there was a you and an I. In those days the world spirit was whole and undivided, and everything was *brahman*.'

'The dinosaurs were *brahman*. Weren't they dazzled by *maya*?'

'Yes, that's what I meant.'

'Today they're Shell and Texaco. Those nameless tetrapods have gone the full cycle, they are the black blood of the world spirit. Have you thought of that? Have you considered that the cars we drive round in have the blood of the Cretaceous period in their tanks?'

'You're an incorrigible reductionist, Frank. But you've got a point all the same.'

'Come on! I want to get to the bottom of this too.'

'If you'd been on the planet a hundred million years ago, you'd have suffered from the false illusion – on account of your extra cerebral convolutions – that the reptiles were a bunch of individuals. You would have regarded the largest of them as immense ego-beasts.'

'I've an eye for the individual, it's true. The beast bit is your own term.'

'But now they've been rendered down into one huge oil lake. Now they're Shell and Texaco. Seventy pence a litre, sir!'

'That was my line.'

'And precisely the same fate is awaiting you. Seventy pence a litre!'

'I know. If I don't come to my senses and see things in a different way.'

'Yes, if you don't.'

'And I'm beginning to run short of time. I don't belong here. I'm an over-incarnated angel in distress.'

Again I made my way to my black cabin bag.

'But hopefully,' I said, 'tomorrow will be a new day.'

I put the bottle to my lips and took one or two copious gulps. This time I was both generous and bereft of bad conscience. I no longer had any choice given the panoramas Gordon had opened up. In any case, what was a tiny hangover next morning compared with perspectives that stretched over millions and billions of years? The only possible bolt-hole from the night's complex vistas was sleep. Then a new day would dawn, with or without a hangover.

I was prepared for a proper dressing-down. But he only said, 'I'm disappointed, Frank. I mean, you're disappointed. You're disappointed with yourself.'

'So we'll just have to be a bit disappointed. And divide the responsibility.'

'I'm going straight to bed, you said. Then you said you weren't going to touch the bottle again.'

'Yes, true enough. And you said you didn't have a lot of faith in what I said.'

'Still, I'm disappointed.'

'Well, that's easy for you to say. It's so damned easy to be a puritan if you're not tempted by over-indulgences, and don't have any access to them, either. You weren't the one who got given the Big Bang as a christening present. You're not the one doomed to measure the universe's light-years with an overgrown tuber of neurones. You're not the one who feels the universal distances pressing on your cerebrum like a camel squeezing through the eye of a needle.'

I pulled off my shirt and lay on the bed. Then I said, 'Do you think I'll get riches in heaven if I sell all the galaxies and share the proceeds with the poor?'

'I don't know,' he said. 'But perhaps it's no easier for a postmodern primate to take his farewell of this world than it once was for a Jewish rabbi to save it.'

'OK, then. Rhubarb. rhubarb, rhubarb . . . Now I'm going to bed.'

'But you're never completely asleep.'

'I think I will be. I aim to manage on about four doubles. But tonight I had a good eight. That should do it.'

'I mean that I'm awake even when you're asleep.'

'Feel free.'

'And so not all of you sleeps.'

'Pah!'

'Because there is no "me" and "you". There's only one of us.'

'Wake me at breakfast-time, will you.'

'Very good, sir. But in reality you'll be woken by yourself.'

With these words he darted across the mirror, up the wall, and on to the ceiling above my pillow.

'What's the matter now?' I asked.

'Wasn't I to wake you for breakfast?'

I just turned over and thought what a long day it had been. But I didn't relish the possibility of the world spirit shitting on me.

The orange dove

I must confess it's still hard for me to rake over those tussles I had with Gordon Gecko, though, in a manner of speaking, I've still not lost touch with him completely; even here in Madrid I've had the mixed pleasure of holding long, late-night conversations with him. That's often the way with acquaintances who once challenged something within you. They can return many years after the physical connection has been severed.

I've sat up writing all night. After a couple of hours' sleep I went for a quick walk past the Ritz and up to the Retiro Park before taking breakfast down in the Rotunda. I only need to appear at the hatch of the omelette-kitchen now, and a few minutes later I get two fried eggs, cooked on both sides, a couple of slices of bacon and a ladleful of baked beans.

I spent part of my last day on Taveuni in a cordial meeting with the village elders of Somosomo. I hadn't totally abandoned my studies, and needed an up-date on the measures taken over the past few years to preserve old habitats on the island, and with them, various species of flora and fauna. I now learnt that the first British governor of Fiji was the legendary Sir Arthur Gordon, whose administration lasted from 1875 until 1880. Possibly I'd heard his name mentioned before, but the reminder was unwelcome now that 'the Garden Island' was fast becoming 'the Gordon Island'. As you know, my slight penchant for Gordon's London Dry Gin considerably pre-dated my visit. Yes, Vera, I'm well aware of it, and I'm sure you won't believe me when I say that I hardly ever touch the stuff unless I'm on my travels. I'm not very good at being alone. You made sure you'd delegated some of your functions to Gordon. It was almost like hearing your voice.

I was reeling a little by the time I dived into the village store to find out if they sold vitamins. But I almost lost my footing completely when I bumped into Ana and José in the tiny shop, a small country store crammed to bursting with locals. Together we battled our way out and, as this was possibly the last time the three of us would be alone together, I summoned up courage for one final confrontation. They were both noticeably subdued that afternoon, clearly a result of the Englishman's baffling behaviour the evening before, but I felt I had little choice. I was leaving the following morning, and presumably I'd never meet Ana and José again.

Outside the shop José lit a cigarette, while Ana twisted the top off a plastic bottle of water. I took this as an invitation to one brief chat before we went our separate ways. I went straight to it. I looked into Ana's dark eyes and said casually, 'It may sound a little odd, but I keep feeling I've met you somewhere before.'

José's first reaction was to draw her close to him. It reminded me of the scene I'd witnessed at the dinner table the evening before. She looked at him, almost as if seeking his permission to answer for herself.

'But you don't remember where?' she said.

'I've lived in Spain on and off.'

'Spain has fifty-two provinces.'

'Precisely the number of constituencies in the Fijian parliament,' I remarked.

'I suppose you make for the Canary Islands,' she said teasingly. I shook my head.

'I've lived mainly in Madrid. Might I have seen you there?'

José clearly thought this brief exchange had taken on the character of an interrogation.

'There are lots of dark-haired women in Spain,' he said. 'It's just a fact, Frank. Even in Madrid.'

I didn't relinquish Ana's gaze. Was there a hint of a reaction? Did a tiny dilation of the iris indicate that my memory hadn't failed me after all?'

'Do people often recognise you?' I asked.

Again she looked at José. It was as if she was begging for

permission to include me in a secret, and he, without moving a muscle, refused it. But she sent me a friendly smile as she answered, 'Then perhaps you've seen me in Madrid. I'm sorry I can't return the compliment.'

I took this as being a diplomatic reply. She knew perfectly well why I'd asked.

They had a car and were going all the way to Vuna Point on the south-west tip of the island. They offered me a lift back to the Maravu. I thanked them for the offer but said I'd prefer to walk the two-and-a-half miles.

After passing through the village of Niusawa I caught up with a sportily clad woman with dark plaits and a canvas rucksack. Laura was wearing baggy khaki trousers, a tight-fitting sweater and a kind of sun helmet. She was damp and grubby, but then she'd been all the way to the top of Des Voeux Peak, Taveuni's second highest mountain, at over 3,800 feet. She was clearly exhausted. But despite that she gave me a broad smile when I caught up with her, and her first comment was, 'I've seen it!'

She hopped, childlike, from one foot to the other, her face shining like a new convert's. I wondered secretly if she'd seen the light itself. Or maybe a burning bush?

'It's quite amazing,' she said. 'I saw it up there on the mountain just after sunrise.'

I still didn't even know where she'd been, but she went on, 'I've seen the orange dove!'

'Are you sure?'

'Quite sure.'

'On Des Voeux Peak?'

She nodded, almost gasping as she spoke.

'And I . . . shot it . . . with my telephoto.'

Now all became clear, and if what she said was true, it was a tremendous achievement. The myth-enshrouded orange dove was not only very rare, but I'd also heard that it had never been photographed.

'You might well be the first, in that case,' I said.

'I know.'

'Perhaps you'll be the last as well.'

'I know.'

'Well, you must send me a copy,' I said enviously.

Her response was to shake my hand, which I construed as a promise. This meant I'd have to give her my address later on, a thing I've always been wary about doing when abroad.

We began walking again.

'You could have asked me if I wanted to come too,' I said.

She laughed.

'I never got that far! You were pretty quick to leave the table and hit the hay.'

Laura explained how she'd got up at the crack of dawn that morning while it was still dark. A car to the village of Wairiki had been arranged the day before, so she'd set out on the four-mile climb a full hour before daybreak, armed with a jungle-knife and a head-torch. She'd come to the island to see the orange dove, and that was what she was going to do.

From Des Voeux Peak she'd surveyed Lake Tagimaucia, lying in its extinct crater in the middle of the island. The lake is largely filled with floating vegetation, and it's the only site where Fiji's national flower, the tagimaucia or *Medinilla waterhousei*, a bright red flower with white petals, grows.

'Do you know how the tagimaucia flower came into existence?' she asked as we followed the dusty road, forever side-stepping the flattened cane toads.

I shook my head, and she told me the myth of Tagimaucia. Long ago there lived a princess on Taveuni. Her father, the chief, had decided she was to marry a man he'd picked out for her. But the princess loved someone else, and in desperation, fled from her village up into the mountains. Thoroughly exhausted, she finally fell asleep by the shores of the great lake. While she slept, she wept bitterly, and while she dreamt, her tears rolled down her cheeks and turned into beautiful red flowers. They were the first tagimaucia blooms, and tagimaucia means 'to cry in one's sleep'.

I thought she'd just told me a romantic story, but she said, 'I've had exactly the same happen to me.'

'Crying in your sleep?'

She shook her head.

'Arranged marriage.'

'You've been married?'

She gave a quick nod.

'But there's another version of the myth about the tagimaucia too.'

And now she told the other story. Once there was a girl on Taveuni who disobeyed her mother by playing when she should have been working. Suddenly, the mother lost patience with her daughter and began beating her with a sheaf of palm leaves. She told her daughter to clear out and not show her face again. The girl ran away weeping and heartbroken and as far from home as she could. Deep in the forest she came to an *ivi* tree covered in vines. She clambered up the vines, but they ensnared her and in the end she couldn't move. She cried and cried, and the tears that streamed down her face turned into blood which fell on the vines and formed the most beautiful flowers. Eventually she managed to free herself and run home again. Her mother had calmed down by then, and the story had a happy ending. But the people of Taveuni believe that this rare flower comes from the young girl's tears.

'Has that happened to you too?' I asked playfully.

She nodded earnestly, and without a trace of irony.

'Getting caught up in vines?'

She shook her head.

'Being rejected by my mother.'

She stopped then and turned to me.

'I'll let you into a secret, Frank.'

'Yes?'

'I was an unwanted child.'

You and at least half the world's population, I thought.

I couldn't help noticing that a tear had welled up in the green eye. So I went up close to her and laid her head in the crook of my neck. We stood like that for several moments and then she lifted her head and looked into my eyes. I ran my finger across her lips, and when she touched my finger with her tongue, I bent down and kissed her. I held her tightly and didn't let go until my natural instincts told me I ought to release her.

We went on along the road, and now it was my turn to relate some of the myths I'd heard on the islands of Oceania. There were, for example, countless cautionary tales on the theme that a woman should never get too close to a gecko, because if she did, she might give birth to one. I also told her the tragic legend of Verana.

Verana was a beautiful woman who was so spoilt for suitors that she couldn't choose between them. As a result, she was forever bewailing the fact that she hadn't time enough to decide. One day she was given a magic elixir by a sorcerer. If she drank half of it, the sorcerer explained, she would live for ever. Then she'd have ample time to find the man she wanted to live with. Once she'd met Mr Right, all she needed to do was give him the rest of the potion, and her husband would then have eternal life as well. Verana drank her part of the elixir and lived for many years without being able to settle on any particular man. A hundred years passed, and Verana was still as young and beautiful as ever, but as time went by it got more and more difficult for her to choose who she'd give herself to. She realised that the magic elixir had made it even harder for her to make up her mind. It wasn't just that there were too many men to pick from now, but she'd also got so much time to make her selection, and the decision wasn't made any easier by the knowledge that her ultimate choice would remain by her side, not just for a lifetime, but for all eternity. After two hundred years Verana had met so many admirers that she could no longer love any man. Nevertheless, she'd been condemned to live on earth for all eternity. She still roams the world to this day. When a man falls in love with a woman who can't make up her mind, he should be on his guard, because it may be cold, unappeasable Verana he's fallen for. Many a man has lost his heart and his youth to Verana, but none will ever win her.

Laura looked up at me.

'Oh, what a sad story!'

'Yes, what a sad story,' I echoed.

When we arrived at Prince Charles Beach, we strolled down on to the sand, took off our shoes, gathered shells to give to each other and stood admiring a deep blue starfish. Laura thought it must belong to the species that had given its name to the class *Asteroidea*, because it really did resemble a star. Perhaps, she thought, there was a legend about a star that had fallen out of the sky and been turned into a starfish. If not, we could always invent one, it was never too late to invent myths.

Today there wasn't much of the *maya* or world illusion about her. The parts of her mind seemed as different as the colour of her eyes, and I fancied it was the green eye that had seen the dove with the orange breast and the brown one that read Indian philosophy. Or, it must have been the green eye that discovered the blue starfish and the brown eye that wasn't concerned with the worth of the human individual.

As we climbed the steep slope to the palm grove, Laura explained there was to be a large party at the Maravu that evening with over a hundred guests from the island. It was to be what they called a *gunusede* – a Dutch treat the profit from which went to a social cause, and on this occasion it was to assist poor village childen with their school fees. The guests from the Maravu had naturally been invited.

'You must sit next to me,' Laura said.

Some hours later I found myself sharing a table with Laura, John and Mario. All the little tables were occupied, and many more revellers were expected later on.

Bill, the merry American, had arrived at the restaurant just as Laura hastened to offer our one vacant place to the Italian sailor. So he not only had to put up with discovering our table was full, but then found himself seated amongst people he hadn't even met. This reverse was quickly turned to advantage when he found that he was sharing a table with the renowned Kapena, originally a native of Hawaii, his wife Roberta, and an amusing guy called Harvey Stolz.

Kapena, a powerfully built man with a muscular, sun-tanned

face, high cheek bones and large white teeth, was one of the focal points of the evening. He was a famous deep-sea fisherman who, at the age of twenty-three, had won first prize at the Lahaina Jackpot Tournament where he'd dragged a huge, 1,202 lb marlin aboard his boat. He was now in his mid-forties, retired from his career as a deep-sea fisherman, and had moved to Taveuni where he took tourists fishing in the Somosomo Straits on his high-tech boat, *Makaira*. That morning he'd been out catching all the fish we were to eat during the evening; it was his contribution to the *gunusede*. The Maravu's cook, Kai, had also been aboard and he'd made sure the fish was cleaned and prepared just right. During the meal Bill introduced us to Kapena, Roberta and Harvey, the boatswain on the *Makaira*, and we found ourselves drawn, rather reluctantly, into the kind of technical discussions that might fascinate an oil engineer and a deep-sea fisherman.

Ana and José sat at the far end of the restaurant with Mark and Evelyn. The Spaniards had seemed eager to share a table with the young American couple. Perhaps it was their way of escaping.

After the meal itself a small choir and orchestra assembled. Some of the performers worked at the Maravu – like the gardeners Sepo, Sai and Steni, the barman Enesi and the domestic staff Kay and Vere – but there were also musicians from the villages. To the accompaniment of guitars and ukuleles they sang seductive, polyphonic songs about Tagimaucia, the Maravu and everyone who'd travelled over the clouds from far-flung places to visit the island. Several *mekes* were also performed. A *meke* is a traditional folk dance in which ancient Fijian legends are told sitting, using a mixture of song, exaggerated mimicry and vigorous arm movements.

After the folk dances, Jochen Kiess came to our table and invited us to the *kava* ceremony. *Kava* – or *yaqona* – is an intoxicating drink made from the root of a mildly narcotic member of the pepper family *Piper methysticum*. It was served in a large wooden bowl and drunk from half coconut shells. John had tried *kava* before and declined the invitation, but Laura had read in 'Lonely Planet' that it would be rude to refuse an invitation to the *kava* ceremony — it wasn't done. Soon, Laura, Mario and I were sitting on the ground before the *kava* bowl. Each time someone was offered half a coconut of the stuff, there was a clapping of hands and the cry went up: 'Bula!'

Kava wasn't pleasant. It looked like muddy water, and that was pretty much how it tasted. After a couple of cups I felt slightly numb around the lips, after three I felt a little more relaxed than before, but also rather sleepy. I remember noticing how Bill stomped disrespectfully around the *kava* gathering, once actually informing Laura that *kava* was just a load of bullshit, and something nice girls should keep away from.

Laura gazed into my eyes, and now I think she was looking with her brown eye.

'How does it taste?' she asked.

I was about to say that it tasted like five milligrams of valium and not much else.

'Can you feel the illusion crumbling?' she said.

'A smidgin perhaps,' I said jocularly. 'There is only one world.'

'There is only one consciousness, *purusha* . . .'

'This is biochemistry,' I said. 'This is "instant religion".'

I don't know if she understood what I meant, but she said, 'So is everyday consciousness as well. Pure biochemistry. And it makes us believe in the material illusion, in *prakriti*.'

'That's a funny word.'

'It means about the same as *maya*. Luckily, some chemical substances can anaesthetise the parts of the brain that make us believe in the world illusion.'

Those must be the two or three superfluous cerebral convolutions, I thought, but I don't think I said it out loud.

Laura talked a great deal more, though I can't recall the content line for line, but I remember her confiding to me that after *vedanta*, the *samkhya* philosophy was closest to her heart.

I noticed that *kava* also had a powerful diuretic effect, and it acted equally on both sexes, because Laura was the first to say that she needed to visit the loo. We both found it rather comic to think that the world spirit needed to pee as soon as it had found the way back to itself.

A little later we were back at the table where John was sitting with his beer. He thought it would be nice if some of the guests at the Maravu could contribute to the entertainment.

'Ana is a famous flamenco dancer, you know,' he said. 'I've been on the internet, and although my Spanish isn't too hot, I can see that she's Seville's great star of the moment, "La Estrella de Sevilla".'

I don't know if the *kava* had distorted my sense of time, but it seemed only an instant before we were standing at the Spanish couple's table. Laura was the one who put our request: would Ana consider contributing a flamenco number? Not only would it be an experience for us all, but a sort of thank you to the Fijian dancers for our evening, too.

'The answer is no,' José said.

'La Estrella de Sevilla . . .' John ventured.

But José wasn't swayed by the Spanish.

'I said the answer is no,' he barked.

Ana, for her part, had now assumed a wounded and distressed look. But what for? Why was she so troubled by a friendly request to dance the flamenco? Or had José upset her with his curt refusal — on her behalf? I was not to discover the answer to these questions until several months later.

We smoothed ruffled feathers and returned to our own table.

Soon couples began to dance. It wasn't vastly different to the dancing at country hotels back in Norway, with a solo singer performing cover versions of international hits — basically just a Western karaoke. Many of the villagers were on the dance floor, so there couldn't be any doubt that the evening's *gunusede* had been a great success. And with incipient signs of punch-ups and fighting amongst the men as well, it was almost like being back in Tønsberg on a lively summer's evening. The difference was that it would have been light all evening there. On Taveuni it was pitch black.

Around our table were gathered John and Mario, Laura and I. Then Mark and Evelyn brought their chairs up as their own table had been cleared away to make more room for the dancing. Ana and José had taken their places on the floor in front of the *kava* bowl. Soon Bill arrived with his bottles of red wine.

'On the house!' he said.

It was close to midnight, and Laura turned to me.

'Let's go!' she said.

I had nothing against the suggestion. I was still a bit woozy from the effects of the soporific puddle water, I'd had a very active day and there was no reason to drag out the time in that noisy heap of humanity. Furthermore, I was to begin my homeward journey to the opposite corner of the globe next morning. We rose and thanked everyone for a pleasant evening.

'Are you going?' Bill asked.

'Yupp,' said Laura. 'We're going.'

'Where?'

What an odd question, I thought. And not even one that had an answer yet. Sometimes you only know you're going, without any idea where you're headed. Would we take a stroll in the palm grove? Or a midnight dip at Prince Charles Beach? Or content ourselves with a nightcap at Laura's hut or mine? Whichever, it wasn't Bill's concern. It was considerate of him to keep buying us wine, although a man who'd worked with Red Adair and saved the Apollo 13 from disaster in space must have been able to afford it. But he shouldn't succumb to the belief that he could buy himself friends, I thought, let alone Laura.

'We're going to look at Frank's herbarium,' she said.

'Well, I don't think you should,' Bill countered.

'Well, I don't think it's anything to do with you,' Laura riposted.

She said this more by way of comradely chaff than criticism.

'You can go on talking here,' he insisted.

'We'll talk where we want to,' Laura declared – and just then I thought she was about to burst out laughing at the audacity of the man.

'The wine's here,' continued the American. 'It's an excellent Rioja, by the way.'

'We only need one bottle,' said Laura, and with that she snatched one up and walked off into the palm grove.

'Put it on my bill,' I said running after her.

A little later we found ourselves seated on my veranda, and Bill was right about it being a fine Rioja. The sultry tropical air was like the caress of some diaphanous material.

'He's a real character, that one,' I began.

She shook her head.

'It's just typical, absolutely typical.'

'You met at Nadi airport?'

'Let's not bother with that guy, Frank. He's not that interesting.'

'He's certainly very outspoken.'

She considered for a moment, then said, 'Bill's my dad.'

I put down my glass and whistled.

'Of course he is,' I exclaimed. 'What an idiot I've been.'

She made no answer, but quickly turned her head and I found myself staring into a green eye. Something made me imagine she'd been born with two green eyes, but that one had gradually become browner and browner as she'd grown up. Maybe the other eye was risking a similar fate.

It irritated me that I hadn't grasped that Bill and Laura were father and daughter on holiday together in Oceania. That was why she'd sat so intently reading 'Lonely Planet', and why he'd seated himself at her table on the first evening, it explained his generosity with the wine, how he'd managed to calm her just by placing his hand on the hollow of her neck, why she'd shoved him into the pool, why he'd seated himself in the chair with her towel and why she'd poured a jug of water over him when he couldn't hide his impatience at listening to her lecture about *maya* and the world spirit yet again. It was also the reason he'd warned her about the *kava* and clearly why he'd tried to prevent her going off with me.

'Was he the one who married you off?'

'He arranged the entire thing. He's organised my whole life ever since I was a small girl. Then he found me a real great business-man, one of his associates in fact, an oil man. For me, he found him for me. And I was a good girl. White wedding and two hundred and sixty guests, mostly from his firm.'

'I didn't think that sort of thing went on any longer.'

'I was a good girl, though. I didn't want to disappoint my daddy.'

'Even though you were an unwanted child?'

'I've never had a mother. Only a father.'

'Didn't you say you'd been rejected by your mother – just like Tagimaucia?'

'That's why I've never had one.'

'But she's alive?'

She nodded.

'Living with your father?'

She nodded again.

'How long since you were separated?'

'Two weeks.'

'Since you were separated?'

'Since I left him. I moved to Australia. Then Pop came to Adelaide. He thought we should take a trip together.'

'He wants you to get back with your husband again?'

'Sure. He sold me to him.'

'And it was your father who gave you the grant? He's the foundation?'

She nodded.

'Are you fond of him?'

She raised her glass and drank a sip of the wine. Then she said emphatically, 'Extremely.'

She took another sip, and then, with a tiny smile, added something which made me realise just how much she loved her father.

'But he's such a fool. He's a real ass.'

I had gathered that Bill and Laura formed a serious case of over-protectiveness, father fixation and a refined Electra complex. The image of the animal tamer and the tiger hadn't been so far off the mark after all.

As we sat finishing the Rioja, we talked about the world soul.

She fixed me all the while with her brown eye. I'd surmised that neither her environmental commitment nor her holistic philosophical concepts were that deep-seated. But then she was one-eyed. She was a monocular philosophical absolutist. And she was a monocularly cheerful, sensual girl who was fascinated by rare birds, ancient legends and blue starfish. Both the brown eye and the green eye had, in their own ways, challenged me and set my own thoughts racing.

When the bottle was empty, we went into the hut. And, well – Laura spent the night with me.

Earlier, when I'd gone to fetch some glasses from the fridge, I'd spied Gordon on the wall. While Laura was in the bathroom I went up to him, looked him sternly in the eyes and said, 'And tonight, you keep your mouth shut! Understand? Tonight I'm taking a holiday from you.'

I didn't touch the gin bottle, and that wasn't only to avoid provoking Gordon.

Perhaps you wonder why I'm telling you all this about Laura. Well don't forget, it was you who said we weren't to be tied to each other any more. I was the one who thought we should allow our year of separation to pass before embarking on any new relationships.

After the profound perspectives that Gordon had constantly forced on me, it was wonderful to be able to surrender myself to another human being. I couldn't bear the thought of another night in Gordon's company, and in fact I was just going to talk to you about something to do with this in Salamanca, when you suddenly began that unbridled laughter as I pointed out Ana and José and told you I'd been with them in Fiji.

When I awoke next morning, Laura had gone, and I never saw her again. At breakfast I heard that early the same morning she and Bill had left for Tonga. I'd already given her my postal and e-mail address however, and a few days before I left for Salamanca, I received a beautifully sharp photo of the rare dove with its orange breast. I have to admit I keep it on my desk, even here at the

Palace. The covering letter told me that Laura had returned to her businessman, reportedly because he'd become a totally new person. He'd even made a start on the *Bhagavadgita*.

I was leaving at two o'clock on the plane from Matei to Nadi, and then on with Air New Zealand to Los Angeles at eight-thirty that evening. I began packing before I went to breakfast. Of course, Gordon just had to appear again; well, maybe that was because I'd allowed myself a tiny nip of gin as I'd abstained the evening before. He was sitting in exactly the same spot as I'd seen him when we went to bed.

'There, you see,' he began.

I knew exactly what he was thinking, and I heartily disliked the notion that he'd probably been sitting on the wall watching us with his open gaze all night long. Not only was he possessed of a phenomenal night vision, he was congenitally unable to shut his eyes to anything. In spite of all this I said, 'Could you be a bit more precise?'

'You're all just like us.'

'I never said we weren't. I've kept my cards on the table all the time and emphasised that I'm nothing more than a vertebrate. I've been absolutely transparent on the issue. I'm an ageing primate.'

'I mean, how well did you actually know her?'

'I *got* to know her.'

'Wasn't she married?'

'But that was a sad mess.'

He said, 'Your species is good at making excuses.'

'Nonsense.'

'Your species is good at covering up generally.'

'I thought we were talking about the opposite.'

'But you know what I'm saying.'

'I know everything you say.'

'What really sets you apart from us is that nearly all you do is a kind of masquerade.'

'If this is to be a proper conversation, I suggest you be a bit more specific.'

'But this outer disguise is merely an attempt at camouflaging your primitiveness. You're born naked just like us, and you're not on this earth a lot longer either, before you're gathered in again.'

'You don't have to be so graphic.'

'You're kneaded back into Gaia's womb to become manure for worms and cockroaches.'

'I think I'm the last person who needs that kind of reminder.'

'But you people do nothing but try to talk yourselves out of it.'

'That doesn't apply to me.'

'Isn't it crazy the way you call yourselves "naked apes"?'

'Yes.'

'I mean, the world's most accoutred animal, with everything from evening gowns and white suits to amusing titles and pretentious mirrors over the fireplace. Not to mention all the diplomas and distinctions, ethics and etiquette, rites and rituals. I'm talking about all the veneer, this over-thick veneer of culture, of "civilisation", of un-naturalness.'

'You've got a point.'

'I suppose you've heard about the emperor's new clothes?'

'Don't try to be funny.'

'Even a gecko can see the whole thing's humbug. We say: But of course you're naked! You're just as naked as us. But you just talk and put on airs, mister! Even though, under all that rigmarole, the biological clock ticks remorselessly on until the whole world comes to a sudden stop.'

'You're pretty loquacious yourself.'

'Under the prevailing circumstances, you say, and at all events at this point in time, you add, it's always been important for us to emphasise that although many of the young Picasso's lines are found in the more mature one too, there is much here that is reminiscent of Schönberg, and wasn't it a shame that Puccini never managed to finish his *Turandot*, it really is the best opera he composed, and did you know, by the way, that Verdi wrote *La Traviata* in only a few weeks, compared to Puccini I would almost characterise it as light music . . .'

He had managed to wind me up.

'We are born into a culture,' I interrupted, 'and we are

excluded from it. We aren't simply guests on earth. We're also guests in the rooms called Bach and Mozart, Shakespeare and Dostoyevsky, Dante and Shankara. We enter and are excluded from Antiquity and the Middle Ages, the Renaissance and rococo, the romantic and modern eras. In that we are clearly different from geckoes, because I seem to recall there still aren't any gecko universities, and certainly no distinct faculty of geckoniora.'

'Don't be perfidious.'

'When we pass away, we not only lose the entire cosmos, though that in itself can be a painful loss, we also say goodbye to thousands of human souls we've got to know. If there are a thousand human souls, that is, maybe we are facets of one and the same world spirit . . .'

'Thanks, I sincerely hope that you haven't turned into one of those vulgar monists yourself. It's not catching, is it? I mean, sexually transmittable. I'm merely trying to point out that we're more in harmony with our surroundings, we're content with being what we are, natural, completely natural. We eat mosquitoes, crap and reproduce. And we do it all with consummate pleasure. We're not led on by fool's gold and intellectual drivel. We don't start preaching about art treasures or musical counterpoint just because we're getting close to pensionable age and haven't any grand-children.'

'As I said, you're pretty verbose. Sometimes you're almost lyrical.'

'Everything you say about me rebounds back on to you, mister.'

'I've been wondering if poets drink because they're poets, or if they become poets because they drink.'

'The main thing is they think too much. Isn't it possible to stop thinking? I mean can't you just switch it off?'

'No, it's not that easy. A human being is condemned to think about something all its life. We can control our thoughts to a limited extent perhaps, but we can't shut down the thought process itself. To do that we must cloister ourselves in some school of meditation with all its trappings of idiotic, pseudo-religious structures. We can't even find peace at night. We're subjected to whatever might come in the way of dreams. Not only do we live in a raucous, pleasure-seeking society, but nature has also fashioned us an arena for psychodrama while we sleep.'

'You fell asleep eventually, but not the she-primate. I regret having to put it so bluntly, but she made tracks as soon as you'd dozed off.'

'I'm not blaming her.'

'Can you remember what you dreamt last night?'

'Yes, as a matter of fact I can. I dreamt that I couldn't remember if my age was sixteen or twenty-four, and that worried me, it worried me that I couldn't remember how old I was. In the end, I decided it didn't make any real difference whether I was sixteen or twenty-four, because I still had my whole life in front of me. Then I suddenly woke up and found that I was nearer forty.'

'And so you'd mislaid either sixteen or twenty-four years? Is that what you mean?'

'That's quite enough,' was all I said.

I was riven by remorse because I'd been caught out yet again. I should have left such gecko thoughts alone after the night I'd shared with Laura. I could well have done without that drink.

'Don't you think there might be an element of reconciliation in a lovers' meeting?' I asked.

'In a what?'

'It's a bit hard to explain. I doubt if geckoes have much of a love-life. Perhaps it's something quite unique to human beings, or at least higher primates.'

'I don't know if what I witnessed last night deserves to be called "higher" anything.'

'I mean that the only thing capable of overcoming the two or three surplus convolutions – and therefore suppressing the consciousness of death – is love. Maybe it has the same sympathetic effect as gin and *kava*, only much more powerful and long-lasting.'

'You may be on to something there. Love is the opium of the people.'

'I mean the simple fact of being two is quite different from being one.'

'You don't say? Is that some kind of subtle arithmetic?'

'No.'

'We also agreed that she was married. So we're already up to three.'

'Laura is separated.'

'Aren't you separated, too?'

'Yes, I am.'

'So we've got four now. Are there any more involved in this twosome?'

'Vera and I don't live together any more.'

'So, you're through with her at last? You said you'd be completely finished with her once you'd returned from your extended Pacific travels. You haven't forgotten that deal you made with yourself?'

'No, no.'

'But now it's over with Vera.'

'That's not what I said.'

'You didn't? You didn't say that from now on there's only room in your head for a father-fixated vulgar monist with dark plaits and one eye that's green and one eye that's brown?'

'No.'

'Then it's just as I suspected.'

'What is?'

'You're just as promiscuous as we are.'

'Nonsense. You're much too quick to draw conclusions.'

'You must know in yourself if you want to go back to Vera.'

'It's not that simple. Human emotions are a tiny bit more elevated than reptilian instincts. They can't be controlled by binary logic.'

'So let me try to help you. It's great to have someone to talk to, don't you think?'

'I'd rather not answer that.'

'If you could choose between Vera and Laura now, who would you pick?'

'For the rest of my life you mean?'

'For the rest of your life. Or have these ideal demands of yours already begun to fray at the edges?'

'Vera or Laura?'

'Yes, go ahead! The choice is yours, mister!'

'Laura was a holiday romance.'

'And Vera?'

'I will see Vera at a conference in Salamanca.'

'Maybe she'll be a conference romance. Which is the more prestigious of the two?'

I'd been moving about the room packing as I talked to Gordon. Now I banged a fist into the suitcase I'd just closed. I hated myself for taking that swig of gin. I'd known perfectly well where it might lead.

'Enough!' I said. 'Now I'm going to breakfast.'

'And I'll sit here and wait. I've got plenty of time.'

'I'm leaving in a couple of hours.'

'What fun. So now the man's trying to get away from himself?'

'I'm leaving for home, at any rate.'

'And I'll be in your baggage. I don't actually remember if I got round to introducing myself. Didn't I tell you I'm your sense of propriety's twin?'

'I'm sure you didn't.'

'Twin brothers like me are extremely mobile, mister. They're as mobile as the shadow of a man who's trying to run away from himself.'

At breakfast I met the Englishman and the two Spaniards. John told me that Laura and Bill had gone, and I simply said that I knew already. Undoubtedly John had sussed they were father and daughter, particularly after Bill's behaviour when Laura and I withdrew. But no one referred to that now, and fortunately he spared us any British public-school banter about how Laura and I had shared a bottle of Rioja on my veranda.

The Spaniards were in a much better humour than the day before, and perhaps that had something to do with my leaving. They laughed and joked, and soon began to recount amusing anecdotes from the party, which they hadn't left until about 2 a.m. I decided to try having a serious talk with them one last time before my departure, and this time in Spanish. Come what might.

But it wasn't to be. While José's attention was distracted for a moment, I suddenly noticed Ana's face begin to lose colour. She put her egg-cup down on her plate, her skin now pale and ashen, and then slumped forward on to the table, upsetting a cup of coffee.

José jumped to his feet.

'Ana!' he cried, in the same heart-rending tones as Rodolfo calls out to Mimi in the last scene of *La Bohème*.

He sat her up in her chair and first gave her a gentle slap. Then he hit her again.

'Ana! Ana!'

After a few moments her colour returned, and then she began to cry. She leant against José, and he supported her as she tottered into the palm grove. Then, as if in slow motion, they sailed between the coconut palms on course for their hut.

That was the last time I saw them in Fiji. When, a few hours later, I was back at reception checking out, John was writing at one of the tables. I asked if he'd had any news of the Spaniards, and he was able to tell me that a doctor had been, and that she was clearly much better.

'Too much *kava*?' I suggested.

'Perhaps,' was all he said.

Someone came to tell me my car was waiting.

'Where are you off to?' John asked.

'Home,' I said.

I described all the connections from Nadi to Oslo.

'But then, aren't you going to that conference in Salamanca in a few months' time?'

'So?'

I couldn't understand why he was asking.

'What about Vera?'

I simply shrugged my shoulders. He said:

'You'll be going via Madrid, of course?'

'Certainly, certainly.'

His sudden persistence was extraordinary.

'And if you're in Madrid, you'll probably take a turn round the Prado?'

With this last question the conversation seemed to take a strange twist. Then I remembered that I'd mentioned I was fond of art, that Madrid has some of the world's largest art collections, and that I was especially fond of the Prado.

'I might do,' I said.

'You must,' he insisted. 'You can't go to Madrid without visiting the Prado.'

'I didn't realise we shared a passion,' I observed. 'Why didn't you mention this before?'

'Tell me, do you prefer El Greco or Bosch, Velázquez or Goya?'

I felt remote from this almost manic conversation during our final parting moments, after which we'd presumably never see each other again. I had two inter-continental flights ahead of me and the driver was already picking up my bag. I thought of the short exchange I'd had with Gordon earlier that morning. I thought of the emperor's new clothes. I thought, too, of Ana's little turn and José's ruthless first aid.

'I like the whole place,' I said.

'Then I think you should make time to view the entire collection carefully.'

The driver pointed at the clock. The plane would be taking off in just half an hour's time.

'Promise me you'll pass my best wishes on to Ana and José,' I asked.

'With great pleasure, sir. And if you're ever in London . . .'

'Likewise. You'll find my name in the phone book. But promise me you'll send them my warmest greetings. And a speedy recovery to the patient!'

The driver was now tooting his horn, and only a few hours later I found myself seated on the upper deck of a jumbo jet bound for Honolulu and Los Angeles.

You chose to split our sorrow in two

As soon as I was back at home in Oslo I threw myself into the work on my report, and a fortnight ago I arrived in Salamanca. I was on tenterhooks to see if you'd really turn up, but even more to find out if you realised that I was expected at the conference too. I still don't know which of us registered first, but I'd sent in a kind of provisional application before travelling to the Pacific, and when I rang from Taveuni to confirm my attendance, your name was already on the list of participants. It was only after my return to Oslo that I was asked if I could read a paper on migration and biodiversity.

Was it possible you'd put your name down for the conference because it would give us a chance to see each other as well? Or had you decided to go for professional reasons, even though you'd probably bump into me? If nothing else, you had the chance to cancel if you really didn't want us to meet.

I don't know if I'm explaining myself very clearly, but as you'll probably understand, I hadn't dared take it for granted that we really would see one another. The short letter you wrote to me in November was still fresh in my mind, and I remember the subsequent telephone conversation. That was the last time we made contact.

But you came, and you hadn't known you'd meet me before you saw the final programme. Then you'd thought just as I did. Even if we couldn't live together any more, we did at least share a deep sorrow, and it was something we were doomed to go on sharing for ever. Doomed, you said, but to share. Eight months had passed since we lost Sonja, and half a year since you'd packed your things and left Sognsveien to go back to your family in Barcelona.

It must have struck you too that, yet again, we were to meet at a scientific conference. Things had come full circle. It had been almost ten years since we'd first met at the big congress in Madrid, and only a few months after that we were living together in Oslo.

When I caught sight of you in the lobby of the Gran Hotel, I thought you looked more radiant than ever. You were certainly a different person from the one I remembered from those final, dismal weeks in Oslo. That first moment we just stood looking at one another, and then as usual you pointed out that I hadn't shaved properly. Afterwards you drew me into a corner, and we put our arms around one another and cried. I don't believe those tears were just for Sonja.

You explained that you'd been given a research grant, and either because of this grant, or just because I found you so beautiful, I assumed you had another man. You also said something that very first moment we saw each other, something you were determined to make clear from the start. You said it was good to see me again, but that we shouldn't take up the subject of a possible reconciliation, as you were quite certain we couldn't live together as man and wife again. And I remember I just went along with what you said, because I was so happy to see you again. I, too, had realised there wasn't any way back for us, I lied.

I don't know if I should describe it as deadlock, for what can be less deadlocked than when two people are in full agreement not to take a certain route? The only reservation might have been just how sincere each of us was in our intentions. Would the situation have been different if one of us had dared to hold out something else? If we two share one common characteristic, it has to be pride.

I needn't say much about the conference itself, although I've never thanked you properly for the support you gave me when that American bio-liberal began to argue that there was no further point in trying to prevent the migration of plant and animals species. Let nature sort it out! he said. It always has. Then you waded in. Human beings are part of nature, you remarked, and you *were* going to sort it out. You said that Dr Gibbons hadn't understood my paper. Perhaps, you suggested, it might be an idea for him to repeat his high-school ecology curriculum. You emphasised that man has suspended natural selection. And that there were no inter-continental flights in the Jurassic or Cretaceous periods, there wasn't even boat traffic between Gondwana and Laurasia. Do you remember his reply? Laissez faire, he said. Lassez passer!

Many of the conference participants knew that we'd been married, and also what had caused our split-up. But the number must have soared after your stout defence of my paper. We both felt we shouldn't be seen together too much so soon after our separation. It might lead to the sort of conference tittle-tattle we wanted to avoid. The more we were seen together, the more talk there'd be, and the more the speculation surrounding the circumstances of the accident would grow. I think we were sensible to act discreetly just then, and now I only want to say a few words about how I experienced our last afternoon and evening.

I'd visited Salamanca a couple of times before, but it was completely new to you, and so before dinner you insisted I show you round the old university town. I stayed on in the city longer than you, and I confess I walked the same route again next afternoon. We began at the Plaza Mayor, which you said must be Spain's oldest and loveliest Plaza Mayor, and walked down to the Palacio Monterrey, which now belongs to the Duchess of Alba. Even as we passed through the little square between the Renaissance palace and Iglesia de la Purisima we began to talk about small events in Sonja's life. We didn't say a lot about the old buildings of rust-coloured sandstone which had now taken on a mellow, roseate glow in the golden afternoon light. Those ancient palaces of culture were no more that afternoon than a backdrop for a muted conversation about a daughter who was no longer of this world.

I remember thinking that if it hadn't been for the accident, you and I might have been walking about Salamanca with a five-year-old girl between us. The conference would have attracted our attention even with a small child to think of – and why shouldn't Sonja have come too?

Then we would have walked on from the square between the church and the Renaissance palace up to Casa de las Conchas with its huge façade of five hundred carved scallop shells, and of course Sonja would have raced into the picturesque courtyard and begun clambering all over the well while you and I looked in at the library and reading-room. A little later she might have run across the street and up the steps of the Jesuit monastery of La Clericía, and as we crossed the Plaza de San Isodoro, she might have tilted back her head and pointed up at the high spires before we set about trying to coax her into the narrow Calle de los Liberos on our way to the old university. She would doubtless have enjoyed the Patio de las Escuelas and maybe asked who the statue in the square was of. You would have said it was Fray Luis de León, and that long ago he'd been a teacher at the university, but that he'd been put in prison for five years because he believed something different to what the church taught. When he was released from prison and started teaching again, he began his first lecture with: 'As we were saying yesterday . . .' When Sonja heard this, she would have screamed with laughter, because it was five years since he'd said anything at all to his pupils, it wasn't yesterday, five years was as long as Sonja had been alive, and that was a very, very long time indeed, almost for ever, but that was how long the man had been in prison. And you, Vera, might have responded by asking Sonja another question, that was what you usually did when there was something she didn't understand. Perhaps you might have asked: Why do you think he started with the words 'as we were saying yesterday' when he'd been in prison for five years? And Sonja might have replied that he was trying to forget all the sad years spent in prison, or she might have asked a new question, if she hadn't already begun to point up at all the medallions, shields and animal figures on the imposing university façade. She'd have caught sight of the skull with the frog on it long before we did, but you probably wouldn't have told her that the motif was a symbolic analogy between death and sexual craving, nor would you have said that the piece was there to warn young students against sexual debauchery, but rather that frogs are so playful and lively, just like some people, but that one day all games must end. Before you and I had completely finished admiring its sumptuous Plateresque façade, Sonja would have sprinted off ahead to the typical fifteenth-century courtyard of La Escuelas Menores. You and I might have walked and talked, while she, quite on her own initiative, would have entered the Museo de las Universidad and stood reverently beneath its azure blue vault showing all the constellations. She might not have let herself be coaxed into Luis de León's lecture theatre, and so we'd have missed the Paraninfo room with its Belgian Gobelins and Goya's portrait of Carlos V, not forgetting the famous library with all its valuable incunabula. But I think she'd have led us loftily into the two cathedrals, and then demanded an ice-cream, so the family would have had to wait until the day after to visit the Convento de San Esteban with great birds' nests high on its façade, the Convento de las Dueñas with its beautiful cloisters and the Renaissance Fonseca Palace which surrounds the stylistically flawless patio once used for bullfighting.

We agreed it had done us good to talk about Sonja so much that afternoon in Salamanca, and I think we could indulge so uninhibitedly because we were surrounded by the past life of many centuries. You insisted on being shown round the old university town, even though we spoke only of Sonja, but you wanted me to do it. So, in a way, Sonja did come with us to Salamanca. No, she's no longer alive, Vera, that's not what I'm saying, I'm not even saying it's something we must learn to accept, but if our many memories of that little girl are to have a living space, a sphere of resonance, an element of something preserved, you and I are the only ones that can create it.

You told me several little stories about my own daughter I'd never heard before, and that was painful, because I regretted not being with her every moment of her time on earth, although it also held out the hope of learning to know her better. You turned away and wiped your eyes a lot, Vera, I saw it, and perhaps you realised that I wasn't taking a closer look at the reliefs when I turned my face to the ancient university façade where you'd just pointed out the frog and skull. But it struck me several times on our long stroll that you were still Sonja's mother. Perhaps it hurts reminding you like this, but it was a little girl's mother I walked with that afternoon. The girl never lived to be more than four and a half, only her mother and father will grow relentlessly older, they will turn forty and fifty and sixty, but it's a four-and-a-half-year-old Sonja they'll live with for the rest of their lives. You were still her mother, Vera, and I was still the father of your child.

After the formal, end-of-conference dinner we abandoned the festivities, and again you were the one who wanted to go out for a walk, and you can't have forgotten how you insisted on showing me the river? You said you'd strolled alone by the banks of the Tormes the afternoon you'd arrived. From the old Roman bridge you'd watched the birds, all the swans and geese, and you were suddenly struck by the intense beauty of it all when you heard the nightingale sing as the sun went down, and Salamanca lay behind you like a rubicund gem.

It was completely dark as we left the hotel and started walking down towards the river, and Sonja was no longer the subject of conversation. Our chat wasn't very lively to begin with, but soon I began to talk about you and your affairs, and you about me and mine. You asked me lots of questions about my long sojourn in Oceania, and I may have got round to telling you something about the events on Taveuni. I think I did at least relate – and not without a certain self-deprecation – the story of how I hadn't dared chase a gecko off a bottle of gin because I was so scared the creature might upset it. I quizzed you about your research project and wound up, I recall, by saying that you were arguably Spain's foremost expert in the field of palaeanthropology, at least as regards prehistoric migrations. You smiled at that, Vera, you didn't demur, at all events. You were so proud of being awarded that grant.

When we were down by the river, we walked out on to the two-thousand-year-old bridge. Perhaps it was the swans that made you think of Sonja again. Anyway, you began recalling family life at home in Oslo, and now it almost seemed like something mystical. You spoke of all the trips to Lake Sognsvann and Ullevålseter, about the first time Sonja had taken water-wings to the beach at Huk and about the time she spent almost a whole hour negotiating the big maze in Vigeland Park. She'd demanded a prize for that, and she got a big ice-cream at the café there.

I let you go on, but I stood there thinking of the compact we'd made with each other about not mentioning a possible reunification of the two thirds of the family that was left. I realised that perhaps there wasn't any way back for us. Still, I thought it craven of us not to try something new. I was in two minds myself, and the idea of restarting our life together wasn't a wholly tempting one for me either. But, while you related how Sonja had got out of the maze, I thought that we had to try to talk some sense into each other.

You must have noticed my silence, because at one point you asked what I was thinking about, and you knew from experience that if my silences were pensive, it meant I was dwelling on something sad. I said I was thinking about us, and you said something about how you thought I shouldn't. You pointed out that the only reason things had gone smoothly so far in Salamanca was because of Sonja. I replied that it was because of Sonja I was thinking of us, but soon you were engrossed in a long tale about how they almost got Sonja mixed up with another baby when you were discharged from the maternity clinic. You ended up by saying: then it wouldn't have been my own child that died. She would still be here.

I remembered how, time and again, you'd told me about what had happened in Sognesveien, and always in painstaking detail – although it really happened very quickly. You'd had to make two or three statements to the police, as well. Ever since then, the actual train of events had been a taboo subject, an 'it' or a 'what happened', and I feel we were both frightened that we might revisit those terrible scenes there in Salamanca. It would have been like opening old wounds, and I'm not just thinking here of the rending loss Sonja had been to us, but also of the wounds we'd inflicted on one another.

'What happened' was so ordinary and commonplace that it made everything even more horrible. You had collected Sonja from play school, you'd put her in the car, and you'd started the engine, but then you remembered you'd left her slippers in the cloakroom. You turned off the ignition and took out the key, but forgot to apply the handbrake or put it in gear. You were soon back with the slippers. It was only then that the car began to roll, because, as you kept on pointing out, fate had enjoyed that cruel twist of making you *see* it all unfold, and then only to realise you were powerless to do anything. And we know what happened at the bend three hundred yards down the road. We know what happened three days later. And we know that regardless of anything else that may befall us, that chain of events is something we two will never speak of again.

I've said it many times, but I have to say it once more, and this time in writing, so you can keep it for ever: it's not a question of forgiveness any more. You've been forgiven many, many times already. All that's over and done with now, finished. I admit that in my anguish I blamed you. On one occasion I even told you to pack your things and leave, even though I broke down as I did it. Then I asked your forgiveness for my destructive grief, and it was you who finally made up your mind to leave me. I'd asked the same questions too many times, the same questions as the police had asked. Why did you leave Sonja alone? Why hadn't you applied the handbrake? Why hadn't you at least put the car in gear? And why was it so vital to take the slippers with you? Yes, why in God's name did you want those slippers?

And then there was something else. You'd gone there straight from the end-of-year celebration at the Institute where you'd had three or four glasses of champagne, and when you drove off you were over the limit. You weren't prosecuted. The reason the police gave was that you'd suffered too much already. Those were their exact words, you'd suffered too much already. So the police were more humane in their pursuit than your nearest and dearest. If you still blame yourself for what happened, for the moment's distraction when you forgot to apply the handbrake, let me tell you that you have more reason to blame me for continually pouring salt into your open wound. That *was* intentional, that was sometimes wholly premeditated.

But what I'm trying to say is that in a sense we'd worked through all that, and eventually we were reconciled. It wasn't because I hadn't forgiven you that you left for Barcelona. I even said that it could as easily have been me who'd been careless, as surely anyone may be in a rash moment, and your performance had given such pleasure at the Institute. It's one of those things that sometimes happen. A terrible misfortune strikes a small family as randomly as a bolt of lightning.

We were completely reconciled, Vera, so it wasn't because you felt unforgiven that you eventually packed your bags and left. It was my grief you were leaving, it was that you couldn't live with, you found it difficult enough to live with your own. For you bore the same sorrow yourself, though that wasn't so easy to flee from. You couldn't separate my continued unhappiness from the old recriminations. But I wasn't too clever during those weeks either, and had I been able to return to a family in another country, I might have done so. And for me it was also opportune that my long trip to Oceania was in the offing. There was too much sadness in the house, too much sadness under the same roof, and you chose to split our sorrow in two.

We stood on the ancient bridge looking down into the swift current, and when you'd finished telling me about the time Sonja came home clutching a hundred-kroner note she'd found in the coat pocket of one of the play-school assistants, I was on the brink of breaking the solemn promise we'd made to each other in the hotel. We needn't talk about it now, I was going to say, but some time we must both ask ourselves if we weren't at least going to try to find some way back together again, a new way, of course. We needn't retread the old, painful paths.

We'd both viewed the events following Sonja's death as inevitable. But does every end and purpose point in one direction only? Can't some current incident point back in time and give completely new meaning to something that happened earlier? The questions I'm asking are daring ones, I know, but couldn't we see if we could do something together that would give Sonja's death a meaning?

The only thing I managed to ask about on the bridge was whether you had a friend. And you didn't even manage to reply, because just then I caught sight of two figures down by the river's edge. They were entwined in an embrace as they walked, like two figures melted into one, and the reason I could see them so clearly was that for a few moments they moved in front of the powerful lights that floodlit the bridge, casting huge shadows over us; but I could see that it was a woman in red and a man in black. I was convinced it was Ana and José. I'd seen them together before, and now it was almost like being back in the palm grove at the Maravu.

I laid a hand on your shoulder and pointed.

'That's Ana and José,' I said, almost whispering in my excitement. You looked up at me with a mischievous smile. I've wondered subsequently if that warm and impish smile was a reaction to the mention of names you'd never heard, or if its roots lay in the question I'd just asked.

Up to then I'd said almost nothing all evening, but now my turn had come, and I began gabbling away about the strange couple I'd met on Taveuni, and the more I said, the broader your smile grew, and the louder you laughed.

It was so lovely to hear your laughter again, it was something I hadn't experienced since that morning when you'd been so excited because you were going to take part in the Institute's summer review. But I told you about the aphorisms they'd gone about reciting to each other down there, I said I'd spied on them as they bathed naked under Bouma Falls, I mentioned that Ana was a famous flamenco dancer, and that she'd suddenly been taken ill, and I must have said a whole lot more. But I definitely told you that Ana and José were clairvoyant and that was why they always won at cards. Also, and most importantly of all, I told you I was convinced I'd come across Ana before, I just couldn't place her. But you just laughed and laughed, it was almost as if you'd bottled up your laughter for a long time and were just waiting for an excuse to let it out, you were convinced I was pulling your leg.

First you suggested that I pointed the couple out because I'd got cold feet after quizzing you about a possible friend, and didn't dare wait for a reply. Then you said I'd begun telling tall stories just to keep you down there by the river. A third theory was that I'd suddenly deflected attention to a couple of lovers as a convenient preamble to breaking a solemn promise. But you also had a fourth explanation, it was the one you liked best, and the one you clung to for the rest of the evening. You said I'd begun making up preposterous stories just to get you to laugh. And your own laughter – just to touch on that finally – your own laughter delighted you so much, it was as if you were radiant with happiness at regaining a treasure you thought was irretrievably lost. Perhaps, by the way, you'll notice that all your explanations had one thing in common. They were all equally coy.

I remember considering going after Ana and José, as they soon left the river-bank and moved off in the direction of the town. But I was with you, and you'd put your finger on something when you hinted that I wanted to keep you there by the Tormes as long as possible, beneath the mild night sky. It was our last evening together and I was about to embark on one of the most important conversations of my life, I was even about to break a vow. But there was something else, too. I refused to break in on the warm intimacy I'd witnessed once more. And also, if I'd suddenly gone sprinting off, you'd have been able to read at least four different motives into it, and presumably burst into another peal of laughter.

How you laughed, Vera. I must have been very confused, and looked terribly silly. But how you laughed!

Only once did I manage to break through that compact barrage of laughter. When Ana and José had disappeared into the town, and I earnestly repeated that I really had recognised them, you said, 'They were just a couple of gypsies, Frank.'

We began strolling back to the hotel, and now there were two subjects that were taboo. One was Ana and José. The other was Frank and Vera.

Next day you took the morning train to Madrid and on to Barcelona, but I'd mentioned that I might spend an extra night in

Salamanca. Still you didn't believe me, and you must have had your own ideas as to why I chose to stay longer than planned.

I escorted you to your door that last evening. It had only been a few short months since we'd shared the same bed, and now it felt so unbearably sad and meaningless that we were no longer in the same room. And so, in a way, we were greater strangers than if we'd never met.

Next day I slept in late. Then I set off into the town in search of Ana and José. At first I wandered the streets at random, enquiring in a couple of places if anyone knew an Ana and a José, probably a renowned flamenco dancer and a TV journalist respectively, but of course it was hopeless without surnames.

I hadn't managed to grab any breakfast, so I soon turned into a busy café on Plaza Mayor where we'd lunched together that day you said your piece about Gibbons' criticism of my talk. I ordered a tortilla and a beer, and fortune must have been smiling on me in a big way, for not long after I saw Ana rushing in. She didn't notice me, and when I turned round I saw that José was seated behind a pillar right at the back of the café and was waiting for her. Perhaps he hadn't spotted me, either.

I pricked up my ears and heard them whispering excitably at one another, but they were too far away for me to gather anything of what they said. I decided to finish my omelette, and go and say hello to them, after all it was an extraordinary coincidence that we should bump into each other so far from the Maravu. But, shortly after, flamenco music began to blare from the sound system, and I guessed it might be in honour of the dancer. At all events there was much husky singing about love and deceit, life and death, and I turned towards the back of the café to look. Ana's body almost seemed to be moving to the music, and I remember thinking that perhaps she had to restrain herself from jumping up and dancing to those passionate rhythms.

Then she rose, but it wasn't to dance. As quickly as she'd entered the place, she ran out again. She turned once to José with the heartfelt cry: 'I want to go home! D'you hear? I want to go home to Seville!'

If I was thinking that emotional outbursts happen in all the best families, I wasn't able to think it for long, because now it was José's turn to come dashing through the café. I jumped up in front of him.

'José?' I said.

'Frank!' he exclaimed.

He gave me a desperate glance and raised his arms as if to say 'What can I do!' or something to that effect. But he was in a rush, and all he said as he forged past was: 'We must have a talk, Frank! Are you ever in the Prado?'

That was all, Vera. I wandered about Salamanca for the rest of the day, but I didn't catch sight of Ana and José again.

'We must have a talk, Frank! Are you ever in the Prado?'

What did it mean? What was all this about the Prado? But I knew it rang a bell somewhere. Suddenly I recalled my final conversation with John at the Maravu Plantation Resort. His farewell, too, had contained an exhortation to look in at the Prado. But surely I needed no such encouragement, as I was the one who'd first told the English author that I was particularly fond of its collections.

But certain things could be taken as read. When I'd left the Maravu after Ana's sudden turn, John had promised to give my regards to her and José. He must have said something about my fondness for Spanish art — they would like to hear that, the Spaniards would want to know about such a predilection. But why the Prado? Why not the Thyssen or the Reina Sofía? And why the need to choose whom I liked best, Goya or Velázquez, El Greco or Bosch? I should try to make time to look carefully at all of them, John had said.

Early next day I took the morning train to Madrid. As the train climbed the plateau I sat gazing at all the stone walls. There was something about this place that put me in mind of the summer farms of the Norwegian mountains.

When I caught sight of the fairy-tale city walls of Ávila, my thoughts turned to St Teresa. And then back to Laura at the Maravu Plantation Resort, as my line of association ran from religious mysticism, to Laura's brown eye – although I must admit it was her green eye and the tenderness she'd shown me that lingered the longest. This sweet fantasy was all too soon dispelled by a memory I'd never been able to blot out. On my previous visit to Salamanca I'd taken in the convent chapel in Alba de Tormes where, in some macabre way, Teresa's earthly remains are preserved. I'd visited one of her arms behind a door to the left of the sacristy – and her heart behind a door to the right. In the cloister of the Teresa Centre I'd also studied the index finger of St John of the Cross, that other great Spanish mystic. They'd both had great thoughts and visions, and now they'd been laid to rest. 'Rest in pieces,' I thought.

When I arrived at Madrid's Chamartin Station, I jumped aboard a train to the Atocha terminus. From there I walked up to the Hotel Palace and booked in for an indefinite period. I felt I couldn't return to Norway until I'd collected myself. And it wasn't easy to leave Spain when I knew you were there in Barcelona, either. At home there was only me to think about: in other words, nothing.

Bellis perennis

I was an enigma to myself because, in the event, I didn't visit the Prado until nearly two weeks had passed. I felt that much too much had been made of a chance comment about the pleasure I got from touring its ample galleries whenever I was in Madrid, and I wasn't fond of being dictated to, let alone led by the nose. I did, however, visit both the Thyssen and the Reina Sofía during that fortnight. I hadn't been to either for years.

I'd brought along much of the background material for the talk I'd given in Salamanca, and at the Palace I continued work on the report that had already claimed several months of my time. I took the opportunity to look up various colleagues at Complutense University, spent some mornings reading in the National Library, and made my first visit to the zoo at Casa de Campo.

I visited two flamenco bars on different evenings, not with the idea of seeing Ana dance, but because I clung to the hope that I might spot her name on a poster or in a brochure. Sooner or later I'd have to try to meet them again, but somehow I didn't want to begin tracking them down, at least not yet; it was better just floating about Madrid. But then it was quite possible I might bump into a TV journalist one workaday morning beneath the dome of the Rotunda at the Palace.

A month's salary didn't go far at the Palace, and my reason for staying at that exclusive establishment wasn't just old habit, nor even because we both had very special memories of the place, but because it was the only hotel in the city where there was an outside chance you might enquire for me. I must admit I hoped you would try to phone me in Oslo, after what happened that last evening in Salamanca. Then, if nothing else, I made you laugh again. If you failed to get me at home, you might eventually call the Institute, in spite of the anguish that would cause you. They would tell you I was in Madrid for the time being. After the first week I'd made certain that the Institute's secretary had the name of my hotel as well.

Then, all at once, I awoke from what I now regard as a long torpor. Suddenly one morning it hit me how idiotic I'd been and how badly I'd let things slide. I'd been specifically urged to go to the Prado, not simply to wander aimlessly from room to room, but to search for something quite particular. From the Englishman it had been some kind of hint, from José it had been almost an entreaty. Naturally the Prado was a clue, and not merely an echo of my idle chat about the Prado being an opulent museum – in the bedroom we've got a Monet, and above our fireplace we've hung a baroque mirror . . .

This was on Tuesday, exactly two days ago at the time of writing. I stepped resolutely round the Plaza Canovas del Castillo, or 'Neptuno', as the square is called locally because of its fountain and sculpture of Neptune. As I made my way towards the entrance, I looked up at the statue of Goya framed by the sumptuousness of the Ritz in the background and then, just at that moment, I felt I was starting to get warm.

I began on the ground floor, taking my time, looking at the visitors amongst much else. Soon I began examining 'El Jardin de las Delicias' – or 'The Garden of Earthly Delights' – that kaleidoscopic work by Hieronymus Bosch. If I had to choose one painting that summed up my feelings about life and human status as a vertebrate, it would be this. In addition to over a hundred fascinating human figures, the painter has placed at least as many other vertebrates in his composition. If I was playing at word associations and was given the word 'fantasy', I would say Bosch straight away. If the word was 'Bosch', I would say 'The Garden of Earthly Delights'. If the cue was 'The Garden of Earthly Delights', I would counter with 'frail' – and if I was allowed to reply with a full sentence, or even a little causerie, I would touch on how marvellous and mysterious life is, but oh, how fragile and delicate.

I stood there before 'The Garden of Earthly Delights' for at least half an hour, and that was nothing – the painting deserved at least a week. I studied some of its minutest details, though sometimes I had to let others in to look. And then all at once, Vera, all at once I heard a familiar voice behind me.

'It takes billions of years to create a human being,' the voice said. 'And it only takes a few seconds to die.'

Turning slowly towards José, I sensed immediately that his words weren't meant as a commentary on a five-hundred-year-old picture, but as an announcement that Ana was dead.

Ana was dead, Ana who wouldn't reveal where I'd seen her before, Ana who wouldn't dance the flamenco, Ana who'd had that sudden turn at the breakfast table and Ana, Ana who only a few days previously had left the lunchtime café in Salamanca with a cry about wanting to go home to Seville.

It wasn't just the aphorism that told me. I was staring into a pale, worn face that had been far, far away and still hadn't really begun searching for a way back. A visual memory flashed through my mind: José, in Salamanca, throwing me a panic-stricken glance and exclaiming, 'We must have a talk, Frank! Are you ever in the Prado?' Now he examined the painting and pointed down to the left at a pair of lovers encased in a glass globe. With passion and anger he whispered, 'Happiness is as fragile as glass.'

Nothing more was said for a long time, but I was sure he knew I'd understood. We began to walk slowly through the galleries, and up to the first floor. At one point he said, 'We were inseparable.'

I couldn't bring myself to speak, but I saw his resigned expression, and I believe I shook my head alternately shocked and sympathetic. But all the while I felt I was getting warmer. Now José led me into the Goya collection, and suddenly we were standing before 'The Nude Maja' and 'The Clothed Maja'. I very nearly fainted. José must have noticed, because suddenly he took a firm grasp of my arm. It was Ana!

It was Ana, Vera! This was where I'd seen her before, and so many times, too. I'd wondered if I'd watched her in a film or met her in a dream. I'd even imagined I might have met her in another reality. But here she was. Here was Ana lying on a chaise-longue in Goya's studio, here she was hanging on the wall of the Prado, clothed and naked as inquisitive tourists milled around.

As José held my arm, I was transported back to the Bouma Falls on Taveuni where I'd sneaked a glimpse of the naked Ana. It was there I'd realised it was only her face I recognised, and now I understood why. Ana had been much slimmer than Goya's *maja*, and perhaps that was why I hadn't connected them, why I'd been led astray. But even when I'd seen the clothed Ana in her red dress I'd been struck by two thoughts simultaneously: one was the certainty I'd met her before, while the other spoke of something not being quite right.

Much had now fallen into place. John had mentioned something about the internet, and he would have had little difficulty in logging on to Goya's greatest masterpieces. Then he'd intimated that I should visit the Prado. But why hadn't he told me everything there and then?

Now José and I were standing before it, and we moved back a few paces. I was shocked, I was overcome, I was frightened. Had the paintings not been executed two centuries earlier, I would have sworn that Ana must have been the model, at least for the woman's face.

And there was more. Ana hadn't enjoyed being recognised, and José had definitely disliked it. 'There are lots of dark-haired women in Spain. It's just a fact, Frank. Even in Madrid.' His reply was imprinted on my mind. Now, as I stood here, I could imagine just how annoying constant recognition must have been for Ana. It must have been tough being hailed as a woman who'd lived in Spain two hundred years ago.

Things can't have been helped when John Spooke put his finger on Ana's forehead and said, 'And this spirit's name is Maya!' He had been thinking of the Vedanta philosophy, of the mirage, the illusion and sensual deception, but perhaps he'd had Goya's *maja* in mind too, because hadn't he also described Ana as a 'masterpiece'? In truth, I stood there in the Prado witnessing the greatest delusion ever practised on me.

I was struck by a horrible notion. Why had Ana had that sudden attack at the Maravu? And why did she die a few months later? Could there be a link between her similarity to Goya's *maja* and the fact she died so young?

'She's absolutely identical.'

José shook his head.

'It *is* her,' he said.

'But that's quite impossible.'

'Of course it's impossible. But it is Ana.'

We stood for a long while at the back of the room talking quietly.

'Do you know the history of the paintings?' he asked.

'No,' I said.

I think I was still suffering from shock. He went on.

'Neither does anyone else really, not properly, but a little is known.'

I was impatient.

'And what's that?'

'"La Maja Desnuda" is first mentioned by Agustín Ceán Bermúdez and the engraver Pedro Gonzáles de Sepúlveda, who described the painting in 1800 when it was hung in a private cabinet in Manuel Godoy's palace, together with certain classical studies of nudes, namely Velázquez' "Venus and Cupid" together with a sixteenth-century Italian Venus. Both these paintings were gifts to Godoy from the Duchess of Alba.'

'Godoy had a particular penchant for nudes?'

'You could say that. In this same cabinet he had a copy of a Venus by Titian. At this time, however, paintings of undressed women were proscribed, though the more idealised studies of mythical figures – such as Venus – were marginally more acceptable than "The Naked Maja".'

'Why?'

'As you can see, Goya's *maja* is nothing like a mythical figure. She's very much a living woman of flesh and blood, and of course, painted from life. As such the painting was more suggestive – or decadent, if you like – than a Venus by Titian or Velázquez for example. It was considered pornographic.'

'I see.'

'Both Carlos III and Carlos IV contemplated destroying all such paintings in the royal art collection, though Godoy must have been granted the special privilege of keeping his pictures, but only in his own private apartments.'

'Did he also have "The Clothed Maja"?'

He nodded.

'"La Maja Vestida" was most probably painted after "La Maja Desnuda", because the work is first mentioned in a catalogue of 1808, a catalogue drawn up by the French painter, Frédéric Quilliet, who was José Bonaparte's agent. Here, for the first time "La Maja Vestida" is named in conjunction with "La Maja Desnuda".'

At this point he had to lower his voice to avoid being overheard by passers-by.

'Do you know what a *maja* is? Goya painted a number of them.'

'A village woman?' I suggested.

'Or a young peasant girl, a charming and gaily dressed woman. The male equivalent is a *majo*.'

'Could Ana have been called a *maja*?'

He shook his head emphatically.

'Ana was a gypsy, a *gitana*. Anyway, it's doubtful if "Maja" was Goya's title. When Ferdinand VII confiscated Godoy's property in 1813, a catalogue described the subjects of the two paintings as "Gitanas", gypsy women, and that's rather different from a *maja*. In 1808, too, the woman in the pictures was described as a gypsy. At this point we shouldn't forget that it had only been a few years since the works had been painted, the artist himself was very much alive, and it was to be many years before he virtually had to flee from Spain to France. The woman was referred to as a *maja* for the first time in 1815, a title that has followed both portraits ever since.'

José paused for a moment, but I motioned him to continue. I couldn't see the great significance in whether the woman in the paintings was a *maja* or a *gitana*. It wouldn't alter the fact that Goya had actually painted a face fully two centuries before it had seen the light of day.

'In March 1815,' he went on, 'Goya was summoned before the Inquisition to account for the two pictures. He was asked if he'd painted them, his motive in so doing, on whose commission, and for what purpose. The questions were never answered, and to this day no one knows for certain who commissioned the paintings.'

The crowd around the *majas* had thinned, and I went up to take another close look.

'It's not hard to see why you've studied the history of these pictures so carefully . . .'

'As I mentioned, there's good reason to believe that the naked version was done first. Both paintings were hanging in Godoy's palace, and he was, after all, not completely immune from the Inquisition. Possibly the clothed *maja* was painted to hang over the picture of the naked one. There's a fair amount of evidence to suggest that the pictures were arranged as a practical joke, showing the clothed version first, and then, using some mechanism, bringing the naked woman into view. Undressing women is a very old sport indeed.'

Again I was back at the Bouma Falls. I had peeked quite intentionally through the fingers that covered my eyes.

He went on.

'From 1836 to 1901 the pictures were hung in the San Fernando Academy, though the naked one was never on view. Since 1901 they have been in the Prado, but even here "The Naked Maja" was first displayed in a separate room with restricted admission.'

I was impatient to know more, for though I'd listened to everything he said, I could only think of Ana.

'Do we know who could have been the model for the pictures?' I asked.

He raised his eyebrows.

'Or models,' he said.

I looked at the two paintings again.

'They're exactly the same.'

'Go a bit closer and examine them carefully before you pass judgement.'

I did as he said. Possibly 'The Clothed Maja' had been executed more hastily and with less care than the naked one, the subject looked more arrogant and painted than her naked sister. If 'The Naked Maja' had been committed to canvas first, perhaps Goya had quickly produced a clothed version to cover the naked one. But they were the same woman, and both were Ana, even if only Ana's head, only Ana's face and hair. And there was the nub, of course. Now I could clearly see how Goya had first painted the naked body of a woman, and then added a different woman's face to the nude. With a little patience anyone could see that the female figure was in two parts, a body and a head, and this was particularly apparent in the naked woman.

It was Ana's head I was looking at, but not Ana's body. It was as if Ana's head had been grafted on to the naked figure.

I walked back to José.

'He used two models,' I said. 'One for the body and one for the head.'

He nodded, but without smiling. This was no game to José.

'The nude model was presumably a respectable woman,' he said, 'so obviously Goya couldn't paint her face.'

So he painted Ana's face instead, I thought.

'And do we know anything about this respectable woman?' I enquired.

'There are several theories. One popular one is that the painting was commissioned by Godoy, who was the queen's favourite, and that the model – the nude model – was his mistress, Pepita Tudó. If such was the case it would have been all the more important to conceal her identity. But there's also another theory.'

'Go on!'

'We know that the Duchess of Alba had a close relationship with Goya for some time, and that from 1796 to 1797, at the time "The Naked Maja" was painted, Goya was living at her country seat at Sanlúcar de Barrameda near the Guadalquivir estuary. From the very first years of the nineteenth century there was a persistent rumour that the Duchess of Alba had been the model for "La Maja Desnuda". This rumour may have spring from first-hand knowledge, and the older a rumour is, the more reason there is to have faith in its accuracy.'

'I see,' I said. 'I see!'

'If one examines Goya's other paintings of the duchess, like the well-known portrait dated 1797, or the drawing of the duchess arranging her hair, also from 1796 or 1797, there is nothing in the duchess's figure that would have precluded her sitting as a model for "La Maja Desnuda".'

'Was their liaison an erotic one?'

'That isn't known, although there is much to suggest that Goya would have had nothing against it. In a letter written in 1795 he speaks of the duchess visiting him in his studio to have her make-up applied. And he adds: "This gave me more pleasure than painting her on canvas." In the oil portrait of her at Sanlúcar he painted her in black with a mantilla, and she is wearing two rings bearing the inscriptions "Alba-Goya". And furthermore, the painting depicts the duchess pointing firmly and authoritatively down at the sand where the words "Solo Goya" have been inscribed. The Duchess of Alba was undoubtedly a beautiful and attractive woman, and she was widowed when the Duke of Alba, considerably her senior, died in Seville on the ninth of June, 1796.'

'So why shouldn't they have had an erotic affair?'

'The painting of the duchess was in Goya's personal possession, and so its motif may be rather more a matter of fantasy and wishful thinking than fact. Although the duchess was extremely liberal, I assume she wouldn't have liked such a haughty portrait of herself. And besides, how likely was it that a relative beauty of thirty-four would fall for a rather decrepit man of fifty, who was stone deaf into the bargain?'

'Yes, he had this disease . . .'

'Even so, nothing precludes the possibility that the duchess might have been the model for "La Maja Desnuda". The fact that he drew her so often would suggest that Goya was almost totally at liberty to come and go as he pleased within her private sphere. But the exact nature of the relationship Goya and the duchess shared will never be known, and it's no longer of any relevance. For a time they were remarkably good friends.'

During the intervening minutes I had done nothing but stare at the woman's face. I couldn't get Ana out of my mind.

'Up to now we've only talked about who was the original for the body,' I said. 'We haven't said anything about who might have been the model for the face.'

I can't be sure if I caught a tiny glimmer of a smile as he said, 'That's a much longer story, and more complicated too. But, more than that, it's a lot harder to comprehend. Shall we go?'

I nodded.

'You've seen enough?'

I walked up to the two paintings one last time. I looked into Ana's face. It was exactly the expression I'd seen so often on Taveuni – with those thin, pursed lips and the dark eyes that looked askance at me.

I accompanied José out of the Goya collection, down the stairs to the ground floor and out into the Plaza de Murillo. He walked purposefully across the square towards the entrance to the Botanical Gardens. He fished out 200 pesetas and bought a ticket, and I did the same. I simply tagged along behind him.

We began strolling through the Botanical Gardens and were assaulted by a symphony of scents from the plants and trees that now, at the beginning of May, were in full bloom. The birds, too, were at their busiest, it was almost impossible to tell one birdsong from another.

At first José walked a couple of paces ahead, but after a while he let me catch up.

'Ana loved this oasis,' he said without turning to look at me. 'Each time we were in Madrid, she insisted on walking here with me, at least once a day, regardless of the season. If I had a meeting, she might spend half the day here by herself, and if my meeting began at ten o'clock, it might be hours before I came to pick her up for lunch. She would always have discovered something new.

Searching for her in the Botanical Gardens was a kind of game we played. Where would I find her today? How long would I have to hunt? And more importantly: what news would she have for me? If she spotted me first she sometimes amused herself by hiding from me and even tailing me as I went about looking for her. One by one, she learnt the names of the trees and shrubs, and in the end she knew precisely which trees all the different birds nested in.'

'But you were based mainly in Seville?'

He nodded, then shook his head and said, 'Seven or eight years ago I began work on a television series about the history of the gypsies in Andalucía. I wanted to try to dig up something new about the evolution of flamenco culture in that ancient melting-pot of Iberian, Greek, Roman, Celtic, Moorish, Jewish and, of course, Christian traditions. That was how I met Ana in Seville; she was an oustanding flamenco dancer and had been a respected *bailaora* from the age of sixteen. After only a few weeks we were inseparable, and since then we'd never spent a night apart.'

I was still so spellbound by the extraordinary similarity between Ana and Goya's *maja* that I had difficulty in taking in what he was saying. But he went on without looking up at me.

'Her name was Ana María. That was what was on the billboards, and that was what everyone in her family called her. I call her Ana just to give her my own personal pet-name really.'

'And she had a surname too, of course?'

He nodded emphatically, as if he'd been waiting for the question.

'Maya,' he said.

'What did you say?'

'Her full name was Ana María Maya.'

I was completely speechless. Not only was Ana like Goya's *maja* in every detail, but she was also called Maya. Yet again I found myself back on Taveuni where John Spooke had placed a finger on Ana's brow, declaring in his inimitable way that he'd succeeded in discovering that Ana's name was Maya. José hadn't taken kindly to that.

'It can't be true,' I said.

He nodded once more.

'The name's not so very uncommon among Andalucían flamenco artists. Best known, of course, is the *bailaor* Mario Maya. But his daughter, Belén Maya, also has a reputation, as does his nephew, Juan Andrés Maya. Their flamenco dynasty is often called "Los Maya". Ana belonged to another Maya family, or at least another branch of it.'

'Does it have a meaning?'

'*Maya* is the name of a herb of the *Compositae* family, the daisy or *Bellis perennis*. I don't know exactly how that pretty flower came by the name *maya* in Spanish, but perhaps it's a corruption of the month of *mayo*, in some countries the daisy is also known as the "mayflower". Its Latin name must be a reference to the way it flowers almost all year round. Furthermore, the Spanish word *maya* can also mean a young girl, a May-queen or a costumed or masked woman.'

'Almost the same as the other word,' I pointed out. 'Virtually the same meaning as *maja*.'

'Exactly. And both words have the same Indo-European origin. You find the same root in the word for the month May or for the Roman goddess Maia, in all derivations of the Latin *magnus* or *maior*, as in Plaza Mayor, in derivations from the Greek *mégas*, in a number of Indo-European words for *much*, like the Sanskrit word *maha* for example.'

'Like *mahatman*, the world soul?'

He nodded.

'That was what Laura went on about so much at the Maravu,' I remarked. 'She talked about *Gaia* and *maya*, and here in Spain it's *Goya* and *maja*. It almost seems like there's some sort of connection.'

'Everything is connected,' José said, and when he spoke it was as if I was hearing Laura's voice again.

He still hadn't looked at me. As we rounded one of the marble fountains he said, 'Ana María was the youngest daughter of a venerable gypsy family that had lived in the Triana district of Seville since the early nineteenth century; and her poor parents live there still, as do two of her grandparents. One branch of her family is supposedly descended from the legendary *cante jondo* singer, El Planeta, the founder of what was to become the Triana School's special singing style. He was a native of Cádiz and lived from about 1785 to 1860. He probably got his name from the fact that he supposedly believed in the influence of the stars and planets; there are certainly lots of allusions to celestial bodies in his songs. His name may also be a reference to his being a "wanderer" or a "wandering star". He arrived in Seville early in the nineteenth century and worked in the forges of Triana, a very common employment for gypsies at the time. According to the family, he was Ana's great-great-great-great-grandfather, although I've been unable to find any proof of that outside the family's own esoteric tradition. But after seven generations, he must by now have several hundred descendants, perhaps several thousand, and why shouldn't Ana be one of them?'

'Go on!'

'In only a few weeks we became deeply attached to one another, very deeply you understand, unusually so. And she introduced me to a family tradition that not only entertained me enormously, but which I also thought I could make use of in the television series I'd begun work on. That never came to fruition, by the way.'

'Why not?'

'I became an Andalucían gypsy myself. At any rate an *aficionado*, a devoted lover of – and initiate into – the mysteries of flamenco culture. I felt I'd been adopted as a son-in-law by that traditionally minded family, and I couldn't make a television series about my own family. I'd begun to know too much because, as I've hinted, there were confidential aspects to these family traditions too. If there's one thing the gypsies of Andalucía have done, that they made certain they've preserved for more than five hundred years, it's their secrets. Over long periods they've had to hide from the Inquisition. Now, Ana's family had one special story that had been handed down over many generations, an incredible tale that reached right back to El Planeta and was also connected with the death of Ana's great-grandfather after a fight in 1894. The question is whether this gypsy story – call it a legend if you will – can throw any light on what happened to Ana. It certainly cast a long shadow over her while she lived.'

'This is really fascinating.'

He halted on the gravel path and looked me right in the eyes.

'First I should tell you what happened.'

We began walking again.

'A couple of years after I met Ana, she was diagnosed as having a heart defect. They couldn't easily operate, at least not without considerable risk, but it was a problem that she could live with for the rest of her life without even adjusting her normal routine. Over the next few years, however, her circulation occasionally got so bad that she'd lose colour in her face, although this rarely lasted more than a minute or two, and, according to the doctors, wasn't particularly alarming in itself. But it was enough to scare Ana, and me as well. Her first real setback came less than a year ago when she collapsed on stage and had to be taken to hospital. The doctors continued to reassure us, though now they said she'd have to give up flamenco. It's a dance that demands a great deal of stamina, you know, a great deal of stamina. At the same time – and I don't know which was the greater blow – they had to advise Ana not to have children.'

'How did she take all this?'

He gave a contemptuous snort.

'Badly. Flamenco was Ana's soul. And she wanted children, she would sometimes even buy baby clothes if she saw something she really liked.'

'And so you went to Fiji?'

He left the question hanging.

'Then you and I bumped into each other in Salamanca,' he said. 'Ana and I were now living in Madrid, but we'd spent a few days in Salamanca visiting my family. Flamenco music suddenly began playing in the café on the Plaza Mayor, it was a group Ana had worked with in Seville some years before. I could see how the music was beginning to take hold of her body. She began drumming her hands on the table-top and snapping her fingers, and finally I told her to stop, I said she shouldn't torture herself needlessly. That was when she suddenly leapt up and said she wanted to go home to Seville. I was worried that I wouldn't be able to prevent her from dancing, but we did make a visit to Seville and stayed a few days with Ana's parents in Triana. We hadn't been there for six months, and for a couple of days we took long walks in the María Luísa Park, the Plaza de España, the Alcázar gardens and the old Jewish quarter of Santa Cruz. But she wouldn't come wth me to the Plaza Santa Cruz itself, the place where she'd danced every night for the past few years, and from where she'd been picked up by ambulance the last time she performed. She said not a word about that now, nothing about her heart problem or flamenco, but each time we got near the square with its old, wrought-iron cross marking the spot where a tradition-steeped church had once stood, she would pull me into an alley that led a different way.'

We had arrived at the lower end of the Botanical Gardens where a cultivated escarpment formed the boundary with Claudio Moyano and its long row of second-hand book shops at one of which, a few years ago, you bought an old translation of Hamsun's *Victoria*. José seated himself on the marble fountain, and I did the same.

'We both loved the Alcázar gardens,' he resumed. 'And I was the one who introduced Ana to them, because even though she'd grown up in Seville, she'd never set foot in them before I took her there. From then on they became Ana's special refuge in Seville, and at times we would stroll through them at least twice a week. Well, then. On the third day of our visit to Seville, we were making a tour of the gardens as we'd so often done before. We felt that the enclosed garden complex was like a world of its own, and on that day we joked that we could lock ourselves inside the Alcázar gardens and spend the rest of our lives there. Perhaps we shouldn't have said that. We shouldn't have said that!'

'And then,' I said. 'What then?'

'We were sitting on a bench over by the café when suddenly Ana caught sight of a dwarf. First she pointed towards the Puerta de Marchena and said she'd seen the dwarf poke his head out from the Galería del Grutesco. "He took a photo of me," she said, as if that was a mortal insult in itself. The next moment we both saw the small figure peering down at us from one of the openings in the long wall that divides the Alcázar gardens in two, the old part and the new. He was clicking away at us again. "It's him!" Ana exclaimed. "It's the dwarf with the jingling bells!"'

'But who was it?' I interrupted. 'What dwarf?'

He made no answer, just continued his narrative.

'Ana leapt up from her seat and made off after the dwarf. By now we'd caught another glimpse of him under the Puerta de Marchena. I tried to hold her back, I think, but even I eventually got caught up in the chase because I'd heard Ana mention a particular dwarf ever since I'd known her. First she chased the dwarf round to the left, through the wrought-iron gate and past the pool with the statue of Mercury, then down the steps into the Garden of the Dance and on down into the Garden of the Ladies, past the Neptune fountain, through the large gateway and round Carlos V's pavilion, into the Labyrinth with all its three-foot hedges, and out of it again, up along the Galería del Grutesco, over to the right through the Puerta del Privilegio and finally down into the Garden of the Poets. Both Ana and the dwarf were running faster than me, and in addition I was held up by the remonstrances of various passers-by, who thought Ana was persecuting some poor dwarf, although really it was the opposite – it was only to put an end to his molestations that she'd set off after him. In the Garden of the Poets she sank down over the hedge surrounding the lower pool, a mere stone's throw from Plaza Santa Cruz in fact, because now only a high wall separated her from the flamenco-*tablao* "Los Gallos" where for so long she'd been the great *bailaora*. A whole crowd had gathered around her before I managed to get there. She was conscious, but almost blue in the face and gasping horribly for breath. I lifted her up to the big marble fountain between the two pools, and laid her in the water for a few minutes to cool her feverish body. I managed to shout out that she had a heart disease, and some time later the ambulance attendants came with a stretcher.'

José sat for a long moment just gazing out over Madrid's Botanical Gardens. No one else was in sight, but we heard the birds singing, and so loudly now that they almost drowned out the traffic from the Paseo del Prado. It was as if the birds, too, had something to sing about their dead friend.

'But what of the dwarf?' I asked.

'No one gave him a thought. It was as if the earth had swallowed him up.'

'And Ana?'

'At the hospital they gave her some injections, and over the next few hours she rallied a little, but she never got out of bed again. The doctors said they would try to operate once her pulse had returned to normal, but she didn't get that far. It's barely a week since she died, and on Friday we're having a requiem mass at the church of Santa Ana in Triana.'

He glanced up at me.

'It would be good if you could spare the time to come,' he said.

'Of course I'll come.'

'Fine!'

'But what did Ana say while she was in hospital? Was she conscious the whole time?'

'She was sharper than ever. She told me a lot I'd never heard before about the dwarf and El Planeta and the great-grandfather who died after that fateful fight, plus a whole lot about the secrets of flamenco. The last thing she said before her heart finally stopped beating was: "It takes billions of years to create a human being. And it only takes a few seconds to die." They were my words, an expression of my own sentiments about life, but sentiments that had influenced her just as I'd become a flamenco *aficionado*. These very last words Ana spoke were both a farewell and a declaration of love.'

I didn't get the chance to ask what he meant by that, as he rose hurriedly and began walking back up the Botanical Gardens. I followed at his heels.

While I'd heard him talk about Ana, my mind's eye couldn't help viewing those two paintings in the Prado. Was there a link between what he'd told me about the dwarf Ana had chased in the Alcázar gardens and the extraordinary likeness she shared with Goya's *maja*?

'When you first met Ana all those years ago . . .'

But he'd realised where I was heading, for he pre-empted me.

'No, I wasn't thinking about Goya. I think my reaction was identical to yours. I was sure I'd met Ana before, but that sensation might have been nothing more than a manifestation of my passionate love for her.'

'Perhaps we have some kind of defence mechanism that prevents us linking a person we meet in real life with someone who lived two hundred years ago.'

He merely shrugged his shoulders.

'And what do you think now?' I asked.

His expression assumed a particular intensity.

'They weren't just alike,' he said. 'They gradually became identical. From the time Ana was a teenager she had, more and more, to live with her strange handicap, and in Seville she eventually got the nickname "La Niña del Prado".'

'You said "more and more"?'

'She grew more and more like Goya's *gitana*.'

I put my hand over my mouth, and José continued:

'And she died as soon as she'd become identical to the artist's model. Then the work was completed, and she didn't live to be a day older.'

'But how do you explain the odd likeness?'

'There are several likely explanations. Or more accurately: one can point to various explanations, though all are equally unlikely.'

'I want to hear every one.'

He turned right, towards the Pavilion, as he said:

'Ana's great-great-great-great-grandmother might have sat for the face painted on to the nude . . .'

'Really?'

'But what's the probability of her being so similar to one of her descendants? Or the reverse of course: what's the likelihood of a woman being identical to her great-great-great-great-grandmother? You're the biologist. Is it even possible?'

I shook my head.

'Not over seven generations. If Ana's father had also been descended from the same great-great-great-great-grandmother – which is not improbable – there might be a chance that a degree of similarity could still be found in certain specific features. But identical? There's a greater likelihood of winning the main prize in the Lottery seven times in a row. And that sort of thing doesn't happen.'

'So it must have been one huge coincidence,' he remarked. 'Ana and Goya's *gitana* simply were identical. Their similarity was a fact, as we know.'

Once more I shook my head in disbelief.

'There's no such thing as two completely identical individuals. We've already dismissed that idea. Have you got any other theories?'

'Yes, lots of others, and I've thought them all through carefully.'

I couldn't imagine what possibilities remained, but then he said, 'The simplest theory of all is that it was Ana herself who posed for the painting you examined so carefully in the museum.'

'But it's two centuries old.'

'That's what they say.'

He hesitated a moment, then added:

'I've had to force myself to weigh up every conceivable and inconceivable possibility. So there's always the chance that Ana really was that old when she died.'

I looked into the pale face. Had it not been for the fact that I'd met Ana a mere fortnight before, I would have suspected José of being seriously mentally unbalanced, or at least of having severely impaired judgement.

'This isn't a joke,' I said.

'I'm not joking. Though I won't deny I feel myself on rather shaky ground, shakier than you could possibly understand. I was the only one who sat with Ana on that bench in the Alcázar gardens the day she became identical to Goya's *gitana*. That morning she'd even done her hair like the woman in the painting, even her make-up was the same. Do you understand?'

'I think so.'

'Experience tells us it is inconceivable that Ana was the Old Master's model, but logically it's not impossible.'

'With premises as liberal as these, you must have other theories?'

He touched his forehead and cleared his throat a couple of times before answering.

'If Goya's *gitana* was painted at the close of the eighteenth century, it might be possible that Ana was somehow formed in the model's image,' he said.

'How "formed"?'

'I'm just marshalling my thoughts. You know the story of Pygmalion of course?'

'Ovid's "Metamorphoses",' I replied. 'Pygmalion fell in love with the statue of a beautiful woman that he'd made himself. Then Aphrodite took pity on him and brought the statue to life. Other theories?'

He halted for an instant and gazed at me with a far-away look.

'They were so similar in appearance that they might have passed for identical twins.'

'Most certainly,' I said, although I still didn't quite see what he was driving at.

'Would you say,' he added, 'that it's totally impossible to conceive of a man living in two hundred years' time from now who's identical to me, even down to the fingerprints and all that sort of thing?'

'No,' I said. 'It isn't impossible. Just give me a few live cells and a decent freezer, and we should be able to make a clone of you in a couple of centuries. I ought just to point out that you'd have little joy of that "re-birth" yourself.'

I didn't glimpse the significance of my own remark.

'So it's feasible that a tissue sample was taken from Goya's model, and that this tissue – in some extraordinary way – was preserved for nearly two centuries before the genetic material from one of its cells was introduced into an egg cell without genes at some point about thirty years ago.'

I felt a cold shiver pass through my body, much as it had done when Ana and José came walking through the palm grove talking about the creation of man and Adam's lack of astonishment.

'I know what you mean,' I said. 'And, of course, it is a possibility. But a lot has happened in microbiology and fertility treatment during the past thirty years.'

'Therefore most unlikely,' he concluded.

'Most unlikely, yes. We'd do best to stick to the idea of total coincidence, though that in itself is vexatious enough. It implies something I would have renounced: that nature finds several parallel routes to precisely the same end. But nature doesn't work like that. It doesn't take sudden leaps, nor is it purposeful.'

'We've discussed this before.'

'What have we discussed?'

'The extent to which nature has a purpose, something it must achieve, something it wishes to show or display. We also discussed whether something that happens now can in some way be seen as causal to an event way back in the past.'

That had been at the 'tropical summit' organised by John Spooke. A lot had happened since then, and now I was struck by something else.

'Maybe we're making a mistake in assuming that Goya used a real model for the face at all. He only had to paint a face on the nude to conceal the model's identity, a pure camouflage job.'

José smiled doggedly, because he'd considered that too, of course.

'And so?'

'And so it might be coincidence that centuries later a woman appears who's exactly like the artist's mental picture.'

He shook his head despairingly.

'We'd practically be back with Pygmalion. One day God breathed life into Goya's mental image.'

'I expressly said it had to be coincidence. Though a very extraordinary one, I grant you.'

'So "coincidence" is a possibility. But what if Goya was capable of glimpsing the divine plan itself? I mean, could a visionary artist like that have been a tiny bit clairvoyant?'

We had arrived at the bust of Carolus Linnaeus.

'Any more theories?' I asked. 'Or is that the lot?'

He gave a sad nod of submission.

'Yes, that's the lot,' he admitted. 'I'm bankrupt.'

He paused for a few moments before adding, 'But then there is a completely different explanation, one that both Ana and her family swore by. They've been gypsies for generations, after all. I've only been one for a few years.'

He took a quick look at the clock, and just as I was about to hear Ana's own thoughts about her flawless resemblance to a woman who lived on this planet two hundred years ago, he said, 'Unfortunately, I've got to go now. I'm already quarter of an hour late for an important appointment.'

I felt cheated, and he must have read my feelings because, as he turned, he placed a hand on my shoulder and said, 'There's a lot that needs organising just now. Some of my duties are heavy ones, but others are pleasant. Scouring the Prado for you has been one of my pleasant tasks. But I have others to think about.'

With that he hurried off towards the exit.

Such a lot was left unanswered. I'd not found out who the dwarf in Seville was. I hadn't heard Ana's own views about her strange portrait double. I hadn't learnt any more about El Planeta – or about Ana's great-grandfather. I also needed enlightenment about all those odd aphorisms that Ana and José had gone about quoting on Taveuni. We hadn't even arranged another meeting. Or had he gathered I was staying at the Palace? Had I mentioned that?

The only thing I could rely on was a requiem in Seville that coming Friday, in the church of Santa Ana. There once more was that almost irritating similarity of name.

Suddenly, as I stood feeling so bereft, I had the idea that perhaps I could ask you to accompany me to Seville this weekend. I felt you owed me that, after your uproarious hooting when I recognised Ana and José down by the Tormes. If nothing else, you could do me the favour of being with me at a requiem it seemed important for me to attend.

How you laughed, Vera. But it's a short road from laughter to tears, because happiness is as brittle as glass. If anyone knows that, it must be we two.

I glanced up at Linnaeus. Perhaps he'd christened the daisy *Bellis perennis*. At least he'd tried to understand a bit more about this extraordinary world through which each one of us makes our fleeting journey.

On my way back to the hotel I returned to the Prado and the Goya collection. Again I had to study just what Ana María Maya looked like the day she'd chased a dwarf in the Alcázar gardens. 'La Niña del Prado' hadn't altered much in the months since I'd met her on Taveuni. I'd only caught a glimpse of her in Salamanca as she darted out of the café. But the dwarf, the dwarf had actually taken a picture of Ana from the Galería del Grutesco.

What did he want with it?

I had some food in a bar and wandered the streets before returning to my hotel. When at last I reached my room, I walked to the window, looked down at the Neptuno, over to the Ritz and to the Prado building on the opposite side of the Paseo del Prado. Two paintings of Ana María Maya hung within it.

It was then I decided to do everything in my power to get you to come to Seville. To be sure of it, I first had to narrate this whole, long history that I've been working on now for more than forty-eight hours, tapping it into the memory of my laptop here in the hotel.

I sat down at the desk, switched on the machine, noted that it was Tuesday 5 May 1998, and began, paragraph by paragraph, to work on the text. The first thing I did was to give a rough outline of what I'd seen and experienced in Oceania from November to January; I wrote about the flight from Nadi to Matei, I gave a brief portrait of Taveuni and the Maravu Plantation Resort, and I described my first meeting with Ana and José. I began my letter the day before I met José in the Retiro Park, before I'd heard what befell El Planeta in Marseilles in the summer of 1842 and before I'd discovered what happened on the quayside in Cádiz one winter's day in 1790.

As I write now it's Thursday 7 May, the time is 4 p.m., and it won't be long before I'm on the train to Seville. I've a bundle of photographs in front of me, and the most striking thing about these photographs is not their subjects, but what Ana has written on the back of each one. I also have a grotesque account of why Ana was so like a portrait that's two hundred years old.

Two days have elapsed since I returned to my hotel room after strolling with José in the Botanical Gardens, and in the intervening period it's become even more vital for me to send you this epistle. I can't risk it not finding you now, because you must, you simply must come with me to Seville tomorrow, and hopefully, by the time you get to read this, you'll already have made up your mind to travel. I've decided to phone you right this moment, and so this long letter will also record my attempt to get in touch with you, before I e-mail all I've written. You'll have to choose your words with care. In a few hours' time they'll be popping up again on your computer screen.

I'm sitting at my desk, picking up the phone and dialling your number in Barcelona . . .

Of course I can't remember every word that passed between us, but this is my recollection of how the conversation went.

'Vera.'

'It's me.'

'Frank?'

'Ana is dead.'

'I know.'

'What did you say?'

'I know that Ana's dead.'

'But you didn't know Ana, did you?'

'No, exactly! I never knew her.'

'But you know she's dead?'

'What is all this, Frank?'

'How do you know she's dead?'

'I don't understand you. I really don't know why you set all this up.'

'I don't either . . . I mean, I don't know what you mean by "all this".'

'Come on!'

'I am alone in a hotel room, I've been here for almost two weeks. I just wanted someone to talk to. I needed to tell someone that Ana is dead.'

'Didn't you give him my phone number?'

'Which him?'

'He called himself José.'

'What?'

'A man just phoned saying he'd met you in the Retiro Park. And that he'd given you a present we were to share.'

'He said that?'

'And then he said that Ana was dead.'

'He said that to you?'

'Didn't you know he'd rung?'

'No!'

'What about this "present", then?'

'It's true he said something to that effect. That it was for both of us.'

'Look, I'm going to ring off . . .'

'Hello?'

'I'm going to ring off if you don't tell me what he meant by this "present".'

'I don't know why you're being so aggressive.'

'I'm not being aggressive.'

'Excitable, then.'

'I'm not being that either. I just asked what this "present" was.'

'It's some photographs. And then there's a sort of manifesto.'

'A what?'

'A manifesto.'

'Fine. Well, you just hang on to it, Frank.'

'I really didn't know he'd called you.'

'At least you must know if you gave him my phone number.'

'I haven't given him anything at all.'

'Well, did you give him my name?'

'That's quite possible.'

'A "manifesto"?'

'But that wasn't why I rang.'

'So why did you ring? I do have things to do, you know.'

'Do you remember how you laughed? . . . You're not saying anything.'

'It *was* a lovely evening, Frank. Look, I'm sorry that I was a little irritable. Just now, I mean. I naturally thought it was you who got him to ring. About a present for the pair of us. Do you see? And then, half an hour later, you phone.'

'I had no idea he'd called you.'

'I remember laughing. Of course I thought you'd invented the whole thing. They're both typical of you.'

'Both?'

'Making up stories and then getting acquaintances like that to ring me up about a present.'

'We've dispensed with that second notion. If not *I'll* ring off . . .'

'Hello?'

'I've been sitting here day and night writing to you.'

'About us?'

'About Ana and José.'

'Send it to me. I'll read it of course.'

'But there isn't much time, you see. Will you be logging on tonight? I need a few hours more.'

'I certainly will.'

'In this long letter, I'll be begging a favour of you. Even if it's the very last thing you do for me.'

'What's so important?'

'If I tell you now, you'll only say no.'

'Just tell me what it is.'

'I want to ask you to come with me to Ana's requiem mass tomorrow evening. It's in Seville.'

'You've already asked me about that.'

'Have I?'

'The man who rang did. I feel that's practically the same thing.'

'Did he ask if you'd come to Seville?'

'Are you saying you didn't know about this?'

'No! I mean, yes. I didn't know a thing. He must have rung Directory Enquiries.'

'I said it was rather inconvenient this Friday. I didn't know her, Frank.'

'You know me.'

'Well, fortunately it's not you who's dead.'

'I seem to remember there were lots of people at Sonja's funeral who'd never seen her.'

'That's totally different.'

'Not if I tell you that Ana was a close friend of mine.'

'I realise that. But we're not living together any more.'

'Will you turn up at my mother's funeral?'

'Now I think you're being macabre.'

'We needn't argue about which of us is being more macabre.'

'I'm not arguing, really. I'm through with all that. We've said goodbye to each other, Frank. When will you realise that?'

'Have you got another man?'

'You asked about that on the bridge. And then you began telling all those mad stories.'

'Have you got a man?'

'I don't see what right you've got to ask that.'

'Now you're just cheapening yourself. I'm only asking if you've got a lover.'

'No.'

'What?'

'I'm not going to marry again.'

'How can you be so sure of that?'

'But I've lots of good friends. And I hope you have, too.'

'Not so many here in Spain. That's why it would mean a lot to me if you came to Seville. Of course I'll pay all the expenses.'

'I don't know, Frank. I really don't know.'

'Well, we'll let the question rest for the moment. But promise you'll read what I'm sending you tonight?'

'I've already said I will. I'll make time for it.'

'Fine. Then we'll see if you change your mind.'

'What is all this you're writing about? What you were telling me on the bridge?'

'Partly, but I knew almost nothing then.'

'You're making me curious. Can't you give me a potted version?'

'No, it's quite impossible. I want you to have the whole thing at once, all or nothing.'

'Then I'll wait till this evening.'

'You can have a riddle. So you've got something to chew over.'

'A riddle?'

'How can a person living today be identical to someone who lived two hundred years ago?'

'I don't know. Anyway, nobody really knows exactly what people who lived two hundred years ago looked like.'

'There's lots of portraits.'

'But no two people are exactly alike, Frank. I thought you'd studied genetics?'

'I said it was a riddle.'

'Have you been drinking?'

'Don't start all that hysterical stuff again.'

'I don't think alcohol agrees with you all that much.'

'D'you know who you remind me of?'

'I asked if you'd been drinking.'

'You remind me of a gecko.'

'Oh, do stop!'

'I mean a very specific gecko.'

'Are you suffering from nervous problems at the moment?'

'Do you believe in dwarfs?'

'Do I *believe* in dwarfs?'

'Forget it. The requiem is in Triana, at the church of Santa Ana, at seven p.m.'

'We'll see. But I'll read what you've written.'

'I'm at the Palace.'

'You're mad. I'm glad we don't have a joint account any more.'

'I wouldn't have written or rung if I didn't still care about you.'

'And I wouldn't have let such an absurd phone call go on so long if the feeling wasn't mutual to some extent.'

'Goodbye, Vera.'

'Goodbye. You're a real crackpot, you know. But then you always were.'

The dwarf and the magic picture

On Wednesday morning I was in the Prado a little after nine, just a few minutes after the gallery had opened. I went in the hope of finding José again, as we hadn't arranged any other meeting place. The next opportunity would be the church of Santa Ana in Seville, but there would undoubtedly be lots of other people about then.

Once more I passed 'The Garden of Earthly Delights', and waited there a while, as it was where I'd met José the previous day. I went up to the first floor and was soon standing before the two *majas*. I stood staring into Ana's eyes for a long time, and it was almost eerie how unblinkingly she stared back. It wouldn't have surprised me if she'd given me a wink.

After an hour I left the gallery and walked up Calle de Felipe IV, across the bustling Calle Alfonso XII and into the Retiro Park. All the lawns in the park were covered with maya-flowers in yellow, white and red, with daisies, with *Bellis perennis*. I spent some time sauntering about the spacious park watching all the childen in their school uniforms, the student couples, the pensioners and the host of grandparents with toddlers, many of whom had brought along bags of food for the squirrels. There was such a contrast between the real wondrousness of everyday life, and the banality with which it was treated by those involved. I remembered something that Ana or José had said on Taveuni: 'The elves are in the fairy-tale now, but they are blind to it. Would the fairy-tale be a real fairy-tale if it could see itself? Would everyday life be a miracle if it went round constantly explaining itself?'

I made up my mind to go back to the Prado again, but first I sat down on a bench above El Parterre with its many formal beds and pieces of topiary. All at once José was standing before me. It was as if someone had tipped him off about my daily rounds of the Retiro Park.

He sat down beside me on the bench, and there we remained for a couple of hours. He was clutching a newspaper and a large yellow envelope. He said he was catching the midday train to Seville, and again I assured him I'd be attending the requiem on Friday. I definitely didn't mention anything about my secret hope that you might come as well. But I may have let your name drop in Fiji, and if I hadn't mentioned your surname to him, I certainly had to the Englishman, who stayed on at the Maravu after I left.

José sat there for a couple of minutes without speaking. Not only was his face wan, but his whole being had suddenly taken on an almost spectral aspect. I remember my thoughts turning to Orpheus who'd returned from the underworld without Eurydice.

I was the one who finally broke the silence.

'These must be hard days for you,' I said.

He clutched what he had in his hands tightly.

'I've been thinking some more about the amazing resemblance between Ana and the woman in Goya's picture,' I went on. 'I'm trying to come to terms with the idea that it's simply one extraordinary coincidence.'

He nodded hastily. It was as if he was trying to marshal his thoughts for an answer.

'But you told me, didn't you, that Ana and her family had a very different explanation?'

Again he nodded.

'It was something to do with an old story, little more than an old yarn, if you ask me. It all began with something that happened to El Planeta himself in France.'

'Go on,' I said. 'Please go on!'

'In the spring of 1842 he is said to have set out on a pilgrimage from Cádiz to the shrine of Les-Saintes-Maries-de-la-Mer on the Île de la Carmargue between the two estuaries of the Rhône. On the twenty-sixth of May that same year he reportedly arrived in Marseilles where he took a job as a dock-hand for a short while, just to earn money for the return journey. A few weeks later he experienced something that has since been handed down from generation to generation, right down to the present day. It's a story, by the way, that I was told when I first became acquainted with Ana and her family. And I might as well make it clear from the start that the story I'm about to tell has a large number of variants, even within the Maya family itself. We're dealing with an oral tradition, an entire cycle of myths, almost. I've never been able to find any written documentation concerning this Andalucían tradition, not even material from more recent years. But there's said to be an entirely unrelated Swiss tradition that's supposedly just as old as the Andalucían one. I'll try to tell it briefly, so I'll stick to the basic facts.'

'Carry on!'

'Late one afternoon at the beginning of June 1842, El Planeta was on the dockside in Marseilles waiting to board a schooner that had tied up to discharge her cargo. The schooner, which by the way was supposed to be a Norwegian vessel, bore clear signs of having experienced heavy weather. Even before they'd fixed up the gangway, a little man had climbed over the rail and jumped ashore. He ran between some dockside sheds and vanished.'

'A little man?'

'He was a dwarf, and a dwarf who was literally dressed as a *bufón* or court jester. The costume in which he was figged out was described as violet and he had a green and red cap with ass's ears attached to it. Both cap and costume were covered with small sleigh-bells that tinkled loudly as he darted in between the sheds to hide. He disappeared quite quickly, therefore. Lots of people on the quay had seen him, and now some enquiries were made of the seamen aboard the schooner as to his identity.'

'What did they say?'

'The schooner had come from the Gulf of Mexico, and somewhere south of Bermuda they had picked up the dwarf and a German sailor in an open boat. The sailor said they'd been on the full-rigger *María*, which had capsized several days earlier, and that presumably they'd been the only survivors of the wreck.'

'He didn't say any more?'

'The German sailor was pretty taciturn, and they were having serious communication problems on the quayside at Marseilles that afternoon because the German couldn't speak French or Spanish, and soon he too had vanished just like the dwarf. One story has it that he subsequently set up as a baker in a Swiss mountain village.'

'Were either of them seen again?'

'The dwarf, yes. El Planeta was living rough between the warehouses on the quay, all he wanted was to head back to his native Cádiz as soon as he'd earned enough money. When the schooner's cargo had been discharged, he went off to get some sleep, but soon became aware of someone hiding amongst some empty wine barrels, someone who was weeping bitterly. El Planeta moved in closer, and there he found the unhappy dwarf.'

'What had he to say?'

'He could speak nothing but German, and the language was as incomprehensible to the gypsy from Cádiz as Spanish was to the little man. But at least one of the stories about El Planeta's meeting with the dwarf indicates that he tried to conceal something.'

'Conceal what?'

'His clown's costume. It seems to have been as vital for the dwarf to conceal that as it would have been for an escaped convict to hide his prison uniform. He didn't want to be recognised, not as a jester. El Planeta reportedly lent him a short coat, and after that all trace of the dwarf in Marseilles is lost.'

'El Planeta never saw him again?'

'Tradition is divided on that point. Some say that El Planeta and the dwarf lived together for several days amongst the quayside shacks of Marseilles. And that one evening the dwarf tried to tell his story using sign language and some drawings he'd made.'

'Drawings?'

'He drew a pack of cards, a pack of the French type with hearts, diamonds, clubs and spades. Then – though still in German – he's supposed to have recited a short verse for each of the fifty-two cards in the pack. El Planeta managed to memorise a few of these verses, even though they were in a language he couldn't understand. In the only surviving portrait of El Planeta, a copperplate engraving by D. F. Lameyer, many people believe he's emulating a joker, or a court jester. What is certain, however, is that he took the tale of the enigmatic dwarf to Seville, and the story was still well known when a strange fate befell Ana's great-grandfather exactly fifty-two years later, in June 1894.'

'A hundred and four years ago,' I said.

'A hundred and four years ago, that's right. Ana's great-grandfather's name was Manuel and, like his own great-grandfather, he was a respected *cantaor* who lived in Triana or, as the district also gradually became known, *el barrio gitano*. Manuel lived in what is called the golden age of flamenco with the growth of *los cafés cantantes* in Seville. He, too, has become a myth-enshrouded figure in the family, and was nicknamed "El Solitario", or Manuel el Solitario. Perhaps he got the name because he was regarded as a loner, an outside or muser, and possibly also as a very lonely person. Many of his songs were about man's loneliness. It's said he was also a good card-player, and was fond of playing solitaire. He was an all-round entertainer, who was skilled at fortune-telling with cards. And perhaps it was the thing about cards that . . .'

José stopped short all of a sudden as if there was something important he'd left out.

'What was it about cards?' I asked, trying to move him on.

'Perhaps it's better to begin at another point.'

'It doesn't matter where you begin, provided it all comes together in the end,' I said.

'One summer's evening in 1894 Manuel el Solitario walked down to the banks of the Guadalquivir. It was nothing unusual: he used to stroll through that part of Seville every evening after singing at Silverio Franconetti's *café cantante*. Silverio's mother came of good gypsy stock, though Silverio himself was considered a non-Romany or *payo* by the gypsies of Seville, and the fact that *payos* had begun singing *cante gitano* was something completely new . . .'

'One summer's evening in 1894 Manuel went down to the banks of the Guadalquivir,' I repeated.

'And that evening they say he saw a strange figure moving about in the dark down by the river's edge, on the Triana side, between the Puente de Triana and Puente San Telmo bridges, only a stone's throw from the church of Santa Ana. Perhaps I'll get the chance to show you the exact spot some time over the weekend, as Betis is still a place that's worth an afternoon's stroll, with its fine views across the river to the bull-ring, the Torre del Oro and La Giralda. But anyway, the figure in the dark was reputedly a dwarf.'

'Another one?' I exclaimed.

'Now, you must remember that Manuel was well acquainted with the old story of El Planeta's meeting with the dwarf in Marseilles . . .'

'Though obviously it couldn't have been the same dwarf.'

José sat there a moment just staring down over El Parterre. Then he said softly – perhaps as much to himself as to me – 'No, obviously it couldn't have been the same dwarf.'

'He would have been very old by then.'

José shook his head.

'He wasn't. But Manuel stood there looking at him because, according to Ana's grandmother, he began thinking about El Planeta's visit to Marseilles. Just then the dwarf beckoned to him with his left forefinger – exactly the way El Planeta is beckoning in the old copperplate. He went down to the dwarf, who was dressed in the simple costume common amongst *payos* of the time. "So, you're taking the air," said the dwarf, and thus began a lively conversation between the dwarf and Manuel el Solitario.'

'This dwarf did speak Spanish?'

'He even spoke it with an Andalucían accent, but in a manner that clearly revealed that he hadn't been born in Seville, Andalucía or anywhere else in the Iberian Peninsula.'

'And what did they talk about?'

'Don't expect too much, now, remember this is something that took place more than a century ago, and I should emphasise that I've heard many different versions of the conversation. Though "conversation" is hardly the right word. What I mean is the dwarf's account of his origins. I've heard this story told by Ana's cousins and second cousins, but so far I've never heard exactly the same story twice.'

'Then choose one! Or tell them all.'

'I'll combine them. My potted version will only include the points all the different accounts agree on. We haven't got all the time in the world, anyway.'

I naturally wanted to hear as much as possible, and was already worried that he might get caught out for time, just as he had in the Botanical Gardens. The pale Spaniard with his fair hair and blue eyes was becoming more and more of an enigma, and I wasn't quite sure how far I could trust him. If he was trying to fool me, I wanted to stop him in his tracks before he turned me into a laughing-stock.

'Carry on!' I said.

'The dwarf made himself out to be the same one who'd been given El Planeta's coat fifty-two years earlier, and from the first he's supposed to have known he was speaking to El Planeta's great-grandson. Furthermore, he opened a sack, from which he pulled a very old coat which he proceeded to give Manuel, presumably as a pledge of his sincerity. As he opened his sack, Manuel could hear the muffled sound of bells.'

'But this dwarf wasn't old!'

José shook his head.

'He was in the prime of life.'

'I'm beginning to see how this story touches on Ana. But what did the dwarf have to say?'

'The schooner that brought him to Marseilles had indeed picked him up from an open boat in the huge expanse of ocean south of Bermuda, and the boat had also contained a German sailor. But they hadn't been plucked from the sea after a shipwreck.'

'Why else should anyone be sitting in an open boat in the middle of an ocean?'

'The dwarf's origin was a volcanic island that had suddenly become submerged. The German sailor had only been on the island a few days, after the wreck of his ship, the full-rigger *Maria*.'

'And the dwarf?'

'The dwarf had arrived on the island with another sailor after a shipwreck way back in 1790. There he'd remained for a full fifty-two years before rowing away from the island, which by then had fissures opening up in it and finally sank beneath the waves.'

At that point I gave a sarcastic laugh.

'I see, so the dwarf had come to an island in the Atlantic fully one hundred and four years before he met Manuel in Seville. And he was still in the prime of life!'

But José didn't display even the ghost of a smile, quite the opposite really, because he went on:

'Another fifty-two years after that, on a June night in 1946, he was again seen, this time in the Plaza Virgen de los Reyes outside the cathedral in Seville. Ana's great-uncle swore he saw him there. On account of La Giralda and the high walls surrounding the Alcázar, the Plaza Virgen de los Reyes has a particularly good echo, and he heard a frenzied tinkling of bells as the tiny jester raced across the square in the direction of Archivo de Indias and Puerta de Jerez.'

He was still in deadly earnest, but for an instant I thought I'd been fooled. Perhaps José was deranged, or at least full of humbug, and it might therefore be possible that Ana wasn't really dead at all.

'Now perhaps you're going to tell me this was the same dwarf that Ana chased in the Alcázar gardens?'

He lifted his right forefinger to his mouth and shook his head.

'But Ana thought so, she was convinced of it. The first thing she said when I reached her in the Garden of the Poets was: "I heard the bells!" That was something she repeated many times before she died. It's now 1998, exactly fifty-two years since 1946.'

I did my sums. There had been a story about this dwarf every fifty-two years.

'So we'll have to wait and see what happens in 2050,' I said blithely. 'But of course you don't believe in these stories yourself?'

As if he was unwilling to give me a direct answer, he would only repeat, 'Ana believed every word of it. All her life she'd been anticipating what might happen in Seville this year.'

'You said that Manuel died after a fight?'

'A couple of years after he'd met the dwarf in Seville, he was playing cards with some friends, and Manuel kept winning every game. He liked to make out he was some kind of sorcerer with special gifts that made it an easy matter for him to win at cards, and he proceeded to narrate all the tales about the dwarf from the time the island sank, to the meeting with El Planeta himself, and of his own encounter with the dwarf down by the banks of the Guadalquivir.'

'Did he say more than you've already done?'

'He mentioned the dwarf's genesis as well . . .'

'Oh?'

'. . . and it was that part of his narrative that unleashed the ill-fated fight in Triana. The police have verified that a certain Manuel was beaten to death in Triana at that time, so we're dealing with historical fact, at least as regards the fight.'

'Go on!'

'I told you that the dwarf had come to the island after a shipwreck in 1790. That's only partially correct.'

I laughed.

'One either comes to an island in 1790 or one doesn't. One can't come or go *partially*.'

'Calm down. I'm only trying to tell an old story, the story that the dwarf gave to Manuel el Solitario. After a shipwreck in 1790, a lone seaman arrived on the island. He was German too, and the only thing he had in his shirt pocket when he crawled ashore was a pack of cards. He lived completely alone on the island for fifty-two long years, and with no company other than his pack of cards. It was an exquisitely made pack, each card illustrated with a figure in full-length, but it was almost as if they were fairy-tale characters, for each was short, and looked something like the elves you hear about in fairy stories.'

'Perhaps they resembled the people in "The Garden of Earthly Delights",' I suggested.

'What did you say?'

I repeated the suggestion, to which he replied:

'It's possible, though in Bosch's painting the people are naked. The elves on the cards were dressed in the finest costumes of the French Enlightenment. And the dwarf was supposedly decked out in a violet suit and a cap with ass's ears. His garb had small bells attached that would have given away the jester's slightest movement.'

'I don't know if . . .'

'The shipwrecked seaman filled his long days by playing solitaire, just like Napoleon did in his exile on St Helena. After a while he took to dreaming of the characters on the cards; they were after all his only company throughout many long years. So vividly did he dream of the humanoid elves on the playing cards that he imagined he could see them during the day as well. It was as if they floated about him like ethereal beings. In this way he could hold long conversations with them, though in reality, of course, it was only the lonely seaman talking to himself. But then one day . . .'

'Yes?'

'. . . one day the elves managed to find a way out of the seaman's imagination and into the real world of a deserted Caribbean island where he'd fetched up after a shipwreck. They had managed to force the portal between the creative space within the seaman's consciousness and the created space beneath the heavens. So they popped out, one by one, it was as if they leapt out from the seaman's brow, and after a few months the entire pack was complete. The last to arrive was the Joker, he was what's often known as an afterthought. The seaman was no longer alone, soon he was living in a village surrounded by fifty-two large-as-life elves, as well as the little jester.'

'He was hallucinating. Years of loneliness on the island had turned his brain. I don't think that's so hard to understand.'

'He asked himself this same question, about whether he was hallucinating. But then, in 1842, the young seaman arrived on the island after the *María* went down. The odd thing was that he too could see the fifty-two elves on the island. He noticed, though, that they seemed to have no notion of who they were or where they'd come from. They simply were there on the island, and for them the world they lived in was as unremarkable a thing as it is for the majority of peasants. The exception was Joker. He wasn't quite like the other elves, you see. He'd managed to penetrate the veil of illusion and finally came to understand who he was and where he'd come from. He realised that he'd come into a world in some marvellous way and that he was part of an inexplicable adventure. Existence was one huge miracle to Joker. Or to put it in his own words, as reported by Manuel el Solitario: "Suddenly you were in a world, and you saw a heaven and an earth." For the other elves took both these things for granted once they were here. But Joker was different, he was the outsider who saw what all the others were blind to. Or as he put it himself: "Joker slinks restlessly amongst the elves like a spy in the fairy-tale. He reaches his conclusions, but has no one to report to. Only Joker is what he sees. Only Joker sees what he is." '

'Then you said something about the island sinking into the sea?'

José looked at me with his blue eyes, and I had to dismiss any notion that this was something he'd simply made up.

'The old seaman and every one of the fifty-two elves went down with it. Only the young seaman and Joker managed to get off the island in a rowing boat. But there's still something else you must know if you're to understand what happened later on.'

I glanced at the clock.

'Tell me,' I said. 'Tell me what it is!'

But several moments passed before he said, 'Neither Joker nor the elves changed in the least during all the years they lived with the seaman. The seaman himself got older and older, but none of the elves had so much as a wrinkle or a dirty mark on their bright costumes. That was because they were spirits. They weren't flesh and blood like us ordinary mortals.'

'And the fight?'

'Manuel el Solitario always won at cards, and when he was asked why, he said that he'd learnt a few tricks from the same dwarf that El Planeta had met in Marseilles. This was enough to make one of the players, who'd lost heavily and had also got completely drunk on manzanilla, lay into Manuel with his fists, and several days later he died of the injuries he'd received. He left a wife and two young children, a boy and a girl. Some people believe he only acquired his sobriquet after he'd told the story of the seaman and the magic pack of cards. *Solitario* doesn't just mean "lonely". It also means "hermit". And *Solitario* is the Spanish word for "solitaire", as when we say *hacer un solitario.*'

'I don't know whether to clap or just say "and they all lived happily ever after".'

'You needn't do either. But you said yourself how amazed you were at Ana's similarity to Goya's *maja.*'

I'd forgotten that everything he'd narrated was to do with Ana and, as I now realised, with the tiny piece of mystery I'd witnessed myself too, in a way.

'You were going to tell me what Ana's, and her family's, own explanation of the resemblance was,' I said.

'But now that you've heard about the little jester who weaves in and out of the story, perhaps you can guess the connection between the two. You've heard how only a few days ago the dwarf took a picture of Ana in the Alcázar gardens . . . I'll have to go for my train soon.'

'Wait a bit,' I said. 'So the dwarf went to Marseilles in 1842, he met Manuel in Triana in 1894, and he ran across Plaza Virgen de los Reyes in 1946. And Ana believed that was the same dwarf who turned up again in the Alcázar gardens in 1998.'

'So the stories go, yes.'

'But the dwarf couldn't have met Goya anyway. The painter died long before El Planeta came to Marseilles.'

'Goya died in 1828.'

'And even if the dwarf had managed to meet Goya, he didn't see Ana until long after the great man painted his naked and clothed *maja.*'

'We should take things one at a time.'

'Well, let's then! You promised me all the loose ends would be tied up.'

'The seaman who brought the magic playing cards to the island that vanished under the sea sailed from Cádiz early in the year 1790. It was a Spanish brig called the *Ana*, a relatively common name for a vessel in those days. The *Ana* sailed first to Veracruz in Mexico, and it was on the return journey to Cádiz that the ship foundered with a large cargo of silver. All the facts tally, I've checked old records and ships' registers.'

'You've checked that a brig called the *Ana* really did sink with a large consignment of silver in 1790, and that it was bound for Cádiz?'

'I have, although the vessel is said to have gone down with all hands, and there were no rumours of any survivors.'

'Well in a way there weren't any, since the seaman went down again with the desert island fifty-two years later, and didn't return to civilisation.'

'I'm glad you're following it all so carefully. But when he sailed from Cádiz in 1790, he had with him a pack of cards. I don't know if I need go into the tradition associated with this strange pack of cards, or more properly how the seaman came by it.'

'Oh yes,' I urged. 'I must hear that too.'

'Before they sailed from Cádiz in 1790, the brig tied up at the quay for a while, having just sailed down from Sanlúcar de Barrameda, and on the quayside was the usual gaggle of gypsies selling everything from oranges and olives to cigars, tinderboxes and playing cards to the sailors who were about to cross the ocean. Our seaman is said to have purchased the strange pack of cards from a five- or six-year-old gypsy boy called Antonio who much later was to become known as the legendary *cantaor* El Planeta.'

'Was he really that old then?'

'El Planeta was born at Cádiz in about 1785. You can check that in an encyclopedia.'

'It's still rather a tall story,' I exclaimed. 'They're certainly an inventive bunch, these gypsies.'

'There was also a dwarf on the quayside at the time, not so very remarkable in itself, but tradition is firm on the point that under his ordinary clothes he wore some tinkling bells, just like a *bufón* or jester.'

I gazed searchingly into his pallid face.

'I think that last twist should be cut out of the story,' I said.

'Why?'

'He was *in* the pack of cards! He was in the seaman's pocket. He couldn't stand on the dockside watching the ship cast off. And besides . . .'

Suddenly it was if I'd been pole-axed, and I stopped short.

'And besides?' echoed José.

'Even if I were willing to accept that this dwarf from the magic pack of cards didn't age like other mortals because he was a spirit and not flesh and blood . . .'

'Yes?'

'He still couldn't move backwards in time. He didn't arrive in Europe until 1842.'

There was a spark in the blue eyes.

'Can't something ethereal move backwards in time?' he asked.

'Yes, in the mind the spiritual can move back and forth in time.'

José nodded with an appreciative expression.

'You're getting nearer the point. But there's still a little twist, you see, call it an epic epicycle if you will. These stories maintain that the dwarf was a sort of fantasy, and the fantastic doesn't age as we do. That was why the dwarf could be so old. It's also been pointed out that the dwarf can move backwards in time, but no further back than his own conception. Hence, there are no stories about either the Little Prince or Alice in Wonderland before Saint-Exupéry and Lewis Carroll wrote of them, although there have been masses of references and cross-references to them ever since.'

'I thought the dwarf was "conceived" by a seaman on the other side of the ocean, or at least after the sailing ship *Ana* had put to sea.'

He'd reckoned with this objection:

'Joker came from a pack of cards made in France at the end of the 1780s. From then on there's always been at least one person in the Old World who's had sight of him, and that's exactly how far he can move back in time. In addition . . .'

'Go on, go on!'

'People say they saw him down in the docks in Cádiz on that winter's day in 1790, but all traces stop there. There are no references pre-dating that sighting. There isn't a trace of him before that.'

'And Ana really believed in all this?'

José shook his head at that.

'She knew all the stories concerning El Planeta, Manuel el Solitario and her great-uncle, who died a few years ago, and I won't say she believed all of them, she could even manifest a certain embarrassment about the "Romany tales" she took in with her mother's milk, because gypsies are almost synonymous with trickery and cheating. But she was convinced she was chasing the dwarf with the jingling bells in the Alcázar gardens. "I heard the bells," she said. That was why she made off after him. It was as if she'd rescued her family honour.'

'And Goya's *maja*?'

'We're coming to that now. As Joker stood on the dock at Cádiz watching the *Ana* set sail, he had something strange in his coat pocket, something he was said to have used on several occasions to protect himself from drunken youths who mobbed him because he was a dwarf.'

'What might that have been?'

'It was a small picture of a young woman.'

'Oh?'

'It was a miniature, painted using a wholly unknown technique. It wasn't a copperplate, nor any kind of oil painting, and its surface was as smooth as silk. Above all, this extraordinary portrait was so true to life that the dwarf was considered an artistic genius with supernatural powers. The picture he displayed was as realistic as something you could see with the naked eye.'

I was back in the Prado where there were two paintings of a woman who'd been sitting on a bench in the Alcázar gardens just a few hours before she died. Then a dwarf had arrived and taken a photograph of her . . .

'I know which picture you're talking about. But that picture is only a few days old.'

'Yes, for us. For the people on the quayside at Cádiz it was even newer.'

'What do you mean?'

'It belonged to a distant future. That's why they saw it as magic. It had to be the devil's work, they said.'

'And there really are old tales about a dwarf who had just such a perfect portrait of a beautiful woman?'

'Yarns, yes, tall stories, gypsy fancies. Few such anecdotes were believed. But the legends have had their lustre all the same. The tale about "The dwarf and the magic picture" is just such a legend. Though it's only now we realise just how remarkable the old myth about the dwarf and the magic picture really is, because the story itself is a lot older than the art of photography.'

'And Goya?'

'Goya's great idol was the seventeenth-century painter Velázquez, who came from Seville and later was made court painter to Philip IV. The old master painted many dwarfs and *bufóns*, they were all around him in those days, for in Velázquez' time it was common for royal households to retain the services of such people.'

'Really?'

'So when Goya chanced on the diminutive jester in Sanlúcar de Barrameda in the spring of 1797, he tried to manhandle him into his studio by force so that he could paint him.'

'But the dwarf objected?'

'He shouted and screamed and tried to resist as best he could, but the great artist was stone deaf, of course, and couldn't hear what the dwarf was saying. Only when he pulled out the mysterious picture of Ana María Maya did the artist let go, for he'd never seen anything like it before. He had almost finished painting "La Maja Desnuda", and now he added Ana's face to the nude in order to hide the model's real identity.'

We were sitting on a double bench with a back-support running down the middle of it, and an elderly man had now arrived and had seated himself on the other side. José waited a while before saying any more, and then in hushed tones he continued: 'Ana never found it easy being identified with the woman in the painting, and sometimes the burden could be a heavy one. But I'm sure you can imagine that it would have been no easier for a model living in Goya's time. A gypsy woman who'd let herself be painted naked in those days might have been risking her life.'

I sat there for a few moments deep in thought. Then I asked, 'Are there really gypsy traditions that mention all this about Goya and the dwarf and the mysterious picture?'

José looked at me, and for the first time with the glimmerings of a smile. Almost imperceptibly he shook his head.

'The stories only say that the dwarf with the jingling bells stood on the quayside at Cádiz as the *Ana* sailed away — and that he showed a picture of a woman so detailed and true to life that the people on the dock were amazed. One of them was little Antonio, who was to become Ana's great-great-great-great-grandfather. And so there's reason to suppose that the picture of Ana has been in Andalucía since 1790, and therefore several years before Goya painted his naked *gitana* or *maja*. I think that's enough.'

Just then he looked at the clock and said he'd have to start for the railway station. I suggested I could walk with him through the Retiro Park.

We moved slowly up Paseo Paraguay to Plaza Honduras in the centre of the great park, José firmly clutching his newspaper and yellow envelope. It never occurred to me that anything he'd brought along could be for me. As I walked I thought through everything he'd told me about the two shipwrecks, El Planeta, Manuel el Solitario and the diminutive jester who popped up everywhere.

So, a dwarf stands on the quayside in Cádiz in 1790 waving farewell to a brig bound for Mexico. In his pocket he has a miniature of a young gypsy woman. It looks as if the artist has managed to paint the woman exactly as his eyes saw her in some large garden or patio, because the colours and detail in the picture are clearer than the finest silk Gobelin. But what sort of technique did the artist use, for the paper is only a millimetre thick? It's certainly not a watercolour, nor an oil, and it can't be any kind of coloured copperplate. Perhaps the most surprising thing about the little picture is its completely shiny surface, as though it has been sealed with wax or resin. Running about on the quayside, too, is a small gypsy boy of about five or six. He is the great-great-great-great-grandfather of the woman in the picture, and it is he who, many years later, will bring the flamenco singing style to Seville. Also, in just over fifty years he will again meet the dwarf in Marseilles. He won't then recall that he's seen that same dwarf before, but perhaps the dwarf will. And there on the ship's deck the crew has begun to hoist the sails, but then one of the sailors turns and waves back at the dwarf and the gypsy boy. He has bought a pack of cards from the little boy, and on one of the cards is a miniature of the same dwarf who's standing on the quayside. When the sailor opens the pack several weeks later, after a shipwreck, he will look at that picture, and in the ensuing years he'll study it over and over again. But will he ever realise it's the same dwarf that stood on the jetty as he sailed out of Cádiz?

José said, 'Ever since she was small, Ana had heard these legends about the dwarf on the quay in Cádiz, the dwarf that clambered down off a boat in Marseilles, the dwarf who met Manuel el Solitario in Triana and the one who ran across Plaza Virgen de los Reyes so fast that the bells on his costume sounded like a one-man band.'

'She hadn't, of course, heard any legend concerning the same dwarf in the Alcázar gardens?'

He shook his head thoughtfully.

'But of recent years she'd become very concerned about what might happen in 1998. Of all the stories, Ana's favourite had always been the one about the dwarf who saves his skin by showing a magic picture of a young woman. From the way the picture was described in the old tales, Ana had imagined it must be a photograph, even though the episode on the dock happened long before photography existed. Then there was something else, something quite different . . .'

'Yes?'

'Ever since her teens Ana María had been hearing that she

looked like one of Goya's paintings. She was proud of this, as a young girl she took it as a compliment, even though she was sometimes embarrassed that it was a nude she resembled. But she just went on getting more and more like the gypsy woman in the painting, until it didn't matter how she made herself up or did her hair. She'd become "La Niña del Prado", and the one could no longer be distinguished from the other.'

'Hang on a moment,' I said. 'There's an important detail you've rather glossed over.'

'What's that?'

'If Ana had managed to make herself look any different, by changing her make-up or hairstyle, her appearance still wouldn't have deviated one iota from the face in Goya's painting.'

'And why not?'

'Because then Goya's painting would have looked different.'

He thought for a second, then said, 'You're right, of course. Fate won't allow itself to be retouched. It's merely a shadow of reality. And maybe I should add . . . Oh, I don't know.'

'Why are you hesitating?'

'That morning Ana chased the dwarf in the Alcázar gardens, that was the only morning in all the time I knew her that she used some rouge, which she kept for very occasional use when dancing.'

I halted instantly. Then I said, 'That was all that was missing! She didn't have red roses in her cheeks.'

He sent me an almost petrified look, and I added, 'If Ana had used rouge in Fiji, I would have hit on Goya's painting right away.'

We began walking again.

'But why did she use rouge that day?' he said. 'Can you understand it? It made her even more like the woman in the old portrait, in fact, it made her identical.'

'There's something called "in the fullness of time",' I remarked. 'And anyway, the question you're posing is like asking which came first, the chicken or the egg.'

'And there's something called "courting one's destiny".'

'Did Ana never associate her likeness to Goya's *maja* with the stories from Cádiz about the dwarf and the magic picture?'

'In time, yes. One of her uncles was the first to interpret the legends about the dwarf's perfect painting as being what he believed was a modern colour photograph. But, in that case, it had to be a photograph of someone who'd lived long after the dwarf showed off the magic picture on the quayside at Cádiz. A photograph can't lie, it always has a living subject. And from then on, that element became part of the story itself. If there was one thing the family already knew, it was that the dwarf didn't age like us ordinary mortals. But that he could also travel back in time was something quite novel. In recent years there was even speculation as to which of the daughters of El Planeta's numerous descendants might be the woman in the picture, and it was hinted that perhaps the photograph would be taken during 1998. People again began to watch out for dwarfs.'

'And when Ana grew up to be so like the Goya portrait . . .'

He nodded emphatically. 'Yes, some of them believed that the ring had been closed, and some totally new stories grew up about how the dwarf had sold his strange picture to the great artist. One of these stories maintains that Goya's real model had been beheaded by her family because she'd let herself be painted naked. Her severed head, according to this tradition, was placed on a pike as an object of public ridicule. All this was never talked of openly, and certainly not when Ana was about.'

'But she had her suspicions?'

'She brushed it off. She could laugh at the whole thing. But yes, she had her suspicions. In any case, it didn't make it any easier to be so like Goya's famous model. Sometimes it was hard to get her to go out. Not so much in Seville, perhaps, but in Madrid people would stop and point at her, some even seemed shocked. I don't know, but maybe that was part of the reason she liked being in the Botanical Gardens so much. She could hide there. Ana was stigmatised. It was as if she went about with a large birthmark on her face.'

'Not to mention a mark of doom,' I said.

Just then a passionate twitch contorted the pale face.

'There's more to come. For over half a century it's been

predicted that the girl in the magic picture would die as soon as she reached the same age as Goya's *maja*, but . . .'

He hesitated, and I motioned him to continue.

'It would only happen if she gave herself to a man. It was the punishment for so shamelessly allowing herself to be painted naked. She'd already given herself to many men, it was said, she was no longer a respectable woman, and so fate would chastise her if she tried to enjoy a love life as well.'

I turned to him.

'That was a most unreasonable notion. Not to mention unfair. It wasn't the woman in the photograph who'd let herself be painted naked. Wasn't it Goya who'd just painted her head on to another woman's bare body?'

He tilted his head from side to side as if considering my remark.

'Fate is neither just nor unjust,' he declared. 'It's simply unavoidable. It is as it is. That's why it's always right as well.'

Once again my thoughts turned to Ana's heart problem.

'You've suggested that Ana died because she'd become just like the woman in Goya's painting, because then the thing was accomplished. Couldn't we equally say that Goya's woman was Ana's double at the time because that picture of her just happened to be taken a few hours before she died?'

'It comes to exactly the same thing. That, too, is like the chicken and the egg, a riddle that can never be solved no matter which end one begins with. But when the dwarf took that fateful snap of Ana, the story of the dwarf's picture and the story of Ana's resemblance to Goya's *maja* came together. The ring was closed. In a way, that whole amazing knot of myths about the dwarf began in the Alcázar gardens. And there it ended as well.'

I had another go.

'I haven't said I believe these stories, and you probably don't yourself . . .'

He motioned me to continue.

'Ask away,' he said.

'Ana was suffering from a heart problem. She wasn't supposed to dance or have childen. But she chased a dwarf through the

Alcázar gardens. And that was what killed her. Over-exertion. Wasn't the pursuit through the gardens every bit as strenuous as flamenco dancing?'

'It was her dance of death. But *why* did she chase the dwarf? Because he took a photo of her. No one but Ana would have set off after a dwarf just because he'd clicked a camera. But the photo he'd taken had already hounded Ana all her life. It was something she'd grown up with.'

We'd halted practically every other step since leaving the bench at El Parterre, and each time we passed strollers in the park, José had taken care to lower his voice. Now we walked on a while before either of us said any more. I was the first to speak.

'You said that in Marseilles the dwarf sketched a pack of cards for El Planeta and also recited a little verse for each card in the pack.'

He'd begun walking a little faster.

'El Planeta memorised some of these verses even though they were in a language he didn't understand, and he wrote them down phonetically on a piece of paper. This piece of paper was still said to be in the family's possession in Manuel's time.'

'Yes?'

'And when the dwarf met Manuel in Triana, he pulled out an old coat loaned him by El Planeta, and also some sheets of paper on which he'd written out all fifty-two verses, this time in Spanish. Later, Manuel el Solitario is supposed to have discovered that the German verses El Planeta had scribbled down were identical to some of the verses he'd now been given in Spanish.'

'But none of the verses have survived?'

José nodded secretively.

'Now,' he said, 'our paths are beginning to cross.'

At first I didn't see what he meant. But then my mind went back to Taveuni. I was sitting on the veranda in front of my hut at the Maravu, when I heard voices from the palm grove. I said, ' "The mere experience of being created is as nothing compared to the overwhelming sensation of conjuring oneself out of zilch and standing completely on one's own two feet." '

His eyes widened.

'Bravo!' he cried. 'Not only is your memory impressive, but you speak tolerable Spanish, too.'

I bit my lip. Just then it dawned on me that we'd been speaking Spanish the whole time, as we'd done when we bumped into each other in Salamanca.

'You both saw through me?' I asked.

He laughed.

'Almost from the word go. But again, let me begin from a different angle. Those fifty-two verses presented to Manuel by the dwarf in Triana before he vanished again have been in the family's possession ever since. Over the years, some phrases have even found their way into flamenco lyrics and are sung all over Spain. Ana was familiar with these texts from childhood.'

'Was it those texts you . . .'

He cut me short.

'Each verse went with a special card in the pack. And Ana and I quite often played cards with friends. We were always partners, and once I'd mastered the old texts too, we had a secret language linked to each card's identity.'

'You cheated at the auction?'

'Sometimes, yes. By mumbling a couple of non-sequiturs during the game we could quickly let each other know what cards we were holding.'

'That's the most despicable thing I've ever heard. So the Italian was right?'

'Not entirely. Mario had a more occult explanation for our repeated victories. He said we were clairvoyant.'

'But really it was all done with smoke and mirrors?'

He made no answer to that.

'We would often sit far into the night playing cards with friends, particularly after Ana was forbidden to dance any more. She took a childish delight in winning games, and, well — now that dancing was out, I felt that she deserved to win. I couldn't deny her that small pleasure, though I got quite carried away with the game myself. We had no children, but we shared a childish sport. We had a secret language that only she and I could understand.'

'You weren't found out?'

'We had to change things all the time, so we couldn't use the same code words for lengthy periods. This, and something else, meant that we were always either embroidering the old verses or inventing completely new ones.'

'What was the something else?'

'Even from the time the heart problem was first diagnosed, we both became very attuned to the realities of life. Every single second we had together was a gift. When later she was told not to dance the flamenco, and also advised not to have children, it became a matter of defining the very meaning of life.'

'Did Ana find a new meaning?'

'She didn't take up knitting, if that's what you mean; by nature she was just too impetuous for that. But we still had one another, and we shared a particularly intense feeling for life. The doctors had tried to reassure us, but when a renowned *bailaora* is suddenly told not to dance any more, you might as well say she's already on the periphery of existence. And Ana María was – we both were – but with one important difference: Ana was convinced that this life was not the only one. She firmly believed in an after-life as well. What we shared was a heightened feeling for the wonder of life, and we made a game out of finding new words and expressions for what we were thinking and experiencing. So we extended the old sayings that were connected with each card in the pack. We kept some of the dwarf's formulations, and we rejected others. That's how we created our own little manifesto of life. And perhaps I should add that we wanted to create something together that might live on after us. The manifesto was also to be our spiritual testament.'

'So you were inventing those aphorisms all the time?'

'Yes, all the time, and every day. Our "manifesto" was in constant flux, it was an eruptive process. Right to the very end we were creating new aphorisms and using them to replace some of the old ones.'

'That's almost a bit . . . mad.'

He shook his head.

'Far from it. And it's not as unusual as it might sound. The gypsies of Andalucía have always picked up small maxims about life and death and love. Ever since El Planeta's time flamenco songs have come about that way.'

I recited: ' "If there is a God, he is not only a wizard at leaving clues behind. More than anything, he's a master of concealment. And the world is not something that gives itself away. The heavens still keep their secrets. There is little gossip amongst the stars . . ." '

I had to stop there, since I couldn't remember any more of what Ana and José had said in the Maravu palm grove on that first evening. But José chimed in and finished it off:

' "But no one has forgotten the Big Bang yet. Since then, silence has reigned supreme, and everything there is moving away. One can still come across a moon. Or a comet. Just don't expect friendly greetings. No visiting cards are printed in space." '

I gave him a little silent applause, then asked, 'Presumably that bit about "the Big Bang" doesn't derive from the dwarf who met El Planeta in Marseilles?'

'Why not?'

'Both the term and the theory came about long after the middle of the nineteenth century.'

He gave a knowing smile now.

'I believe that crafty rogue can smuggle a bit of anything up and down the centuries. To me, he stands for man's constant striving to understand more of what the world is all about. I think it's a consolation to know that we have a representative like him who can travel the centuries with messages and information.'

I merely stared open-mouthed, and he quickly added, 'But you're right. In the dwarf's own manifesto we only find the first sentences: "If there is a God, he's not only brilliant at leaving clues behind him. More than anything, he's a master of con-cealment." '

We had passed Plaza Honduras and were moving down Paseo de la Republica de Cuba.

'Perhaps it's time to sum up,' I said.

'Go ahead!'

'When I arrived on Taveuni that day in January, the first thing I did was sit out on the veranda. Suddenly an intimate couple walked down the palm grove, stopping on the path to recite some weird texts to each other in Spanish. I pricked up my ears. You didn't know that I was on the veranda, did you?'

He grinned.

'John tipped us off that a newly arrived Norwegian guest might make a good bridge partner. A Dutchman had left the island that day, and he and Mario had played against us over the past few days. John told us which hut you were in and also that he'd noticed you on the veranda.'

'But you couldn't have known that I spoke Spanish?'

'Not then, no. But it's hardly a minority language. Half the world speaks Spanish.'

'That's a slight exaggeration. Half the world's art is Spanish, I might go that far, but no further.'

For a few moments it seemed as if an amused expression played on the pasty mask of his face.

'Then I met you both down on the beach.'

'And you explained a bit about what brought you to that part of the world. You aroused our curiosity, and as we were always composing new aphorisms for out manifesto, it occurred to us that we might borrow some existential perspectives from an evolutionary biologist. This was all the more enticing because you chose to talk to us in English the whole time, although you obviously spoke Spanish too.'

'Obviously?'

'The most important thing for an actor is to stay in character.'

'And I didn't?'

'You gave yourself away before you'd got off the beach. Neither Ana nor I had watches, but Ana still asked what the time was, in

Spanish. You immediately looked at your own watch and said it was quarter past twelve.'

I was dumbstruck.

'Of course, that on its own wasn't enough to convince us you understood Spanish. But many similar examples of poor concentration were to follow. There's a maxim that says a liar needs a good memory. You have to remember that Ana and I were inveterate card players, as well as experts at make-believe.'

'Why didn't you call my bluff?'

'Ana thought it was exciting to have a . . . well.'

'A what?'

'An audience, shall I say? We were proud of the manifesto we'd put together. Or rather, the one we were constantly honing. We enjoyed seeming a bit mysterious.'

'Well, you managed it.'

'And then we wanted to pump you about your theory of evolution. For that we had to make ourselves seem interesting. We had to put out some bait . . .'

'The theory of evolution isn't mine.'

'Exactly so. Ana and I agreed that natural science might turn out to have a total blind spot.'

'I realised that. And what is its blind spot in your opinion?'

'We've already gone into that. It's blind to all context. To the meanings of life, in every direction. The Big Bang was no random occurrence.'

'I'm sorry, but I haven't a clue what you're trying to say.'

'That's because you can't see that the world is a mystery.'

'Oh yes, I know that only too well. But all I can see is that we're speaking of a riddle, a riddle neither of us is in a position to solve.'

'It's possible to see a meaning in something one can't understand.'

'But aren't you also attributing a motive where there isn't one?'

With a glint in his eye he said, 'Go back to the Devonian period. What do you see?'

My mind was in such poor shape after everything I'd heard that I fell right into the trap. 'I see the first amphibians,' I said.

He nodded.

'Only now can we see the significance of what happened then. Had we been witnessing life on earth four hundred million years ago, we would have experienced what we saw as a monstrous exhibition of meaninglessness. But the mystery also has a time axis, and with the advent of human consciousness, life in the Devonian period is shot through with meaning. It was the prelude to us – it was the prelude to the very notion of life in the Devonian period. Were it not for the tadpoles, there would never have been any consciousness of life on earth, now or later. One should not only honour one's parents. One must also honour one's children.'

'So man is the measure of all things?'

'I didn't say that. But now it's our consciousness that decides what's meaningful for our intellect. The creation of a solar system seemed a contemptible process when it took place. But it was just a prelude.'

'A prelude?'

'Yes, a prelude. And the paradox is that we're capable of appreciating this prelude even though we didn't appear until long, long afterwards. Thus the history of the solar system bites its own tail.'

'Like the story of Goya's *maja*? That began in the Alcázar gardens only a few days ago – and ended there as well.'

'But the same can be said of the entire universe. The applause for the Big Bang was heard only fifteen billion years after the explosion.'

I walked along shaking my head.

'It's a strange way of looking at things.'

'But we two – who didn't turn up until fifteen billion years afterwards – we actually "remember" what happened fifteen billion years before. So the universe has finally, and very tardily, woken to a consciousness of itself, and in much the same sort of way as the noise from a distant bolt of lightning doesn't reach us until long after the flash has flickered across the sky.'

I tried to laugh, but it caught in my throat.

'You're being wise after the event,' I remarked.

He peered into my eyes with an almost radiant look.

'Even hindsight is a kind of wisdom. It can be wise to look back. After all, we're our own past more than we are our future.'

'I can understand the concept that something happening here and now only acquires meaning in the light of future events.'

'If there is a "before" and "after" at all, that is. What we can see far out in space – and therefore billions of years back in the history of the universe – is also the cause of current events. The universe is both chicken and egg, and both of them at once.'

'Like Ana,' I commented. 'Or the picture the dwarf took of her.'

He didn't reply to that, but said, 'We don't know where we are going. We only know we've set out on a long journey. Only when we're at our way's end will we discover why we made that great journey, even though it may have stretched over many generations. So we always find ourselves in an embryonic state. Much that we can see no meaning in today may show its purpose at the next crossroads. Even the most meaningless event may prove itself to have been essential. I mean, who would have bothered about a gypsy boy selling a pack of cards to a young sailor?'

I stopped suddenly, sensing for the first time that there was something fishy in all of this. Weren't these precisely the same sentiments the Englishman had expressed on Taveuni? Wasn't it he who had described the Devonian period as "reason's embryonic state"? Could José still be in contact with him? Had they enjoyed an extensive collusion, not just in Fiji, but afterwards as well? I was no longer able to distinguish the thoughts of the one from the other.

We had arrived in Calle de Alfonso XII, and we both glanced up at the clock. It was a quarter to twelve.

I walked with him all the way to the station.

'In the end you were both lost to us,' I remarked. 'You withdrew completely.'

'Once people began talking about who Ana resembled, yes.

When they also began pressing her to dance the flamenco, we did retreat. I don't think you realise just how much she wanted to perform.'

'Then she collapsed at breakfast, and you just gave her a slap?'

He cleared his throat a couple of times before answering.

'It always made me so dreadfully scared.'

'I can well imagine.'

We were right by the entrance for the AVE train, and yet again I assured him we'd see each other in Seville in a couple of days' time. It was then that he handed me the yellow envelope.

'This is for you and Vera.'

'For Vera?'

'For both of you, yes.'

So he *had* been talking to John. There could be no doubt now. I hadn't spoken to anyone about you in detail except John.

'But what could be in this envelope for Vera?'

He looked me resolutely in the eyes.

'Haven't you understood yet?' he said, and now he was genuinely astonished.

I could only shake my head.

'It's a gift, but it's also a burden. It's something that must be shared by two people. It's something that isn't healthy for a man of your age to shoulder completely alone.'

He glanced at the clock again. And then ran for his train.

I opened the packet as I walked back to the hotel. Inside the yellow envelope was a formidable collection of photographs that Ana had taken on Taveuni. Only when I got back to my room did I turn the photos over and discover that something had been written on the back of each. It was the manifesto, Vera. That was what had to be shared by two people. It was the manifesto that wasn't healthy for a man of my age to bear alone.

Logic is far too lacking in ambivalence

That's how the letter to Vera ends. It was sent as e-mail late on the evening of Thursday 7 May 1998, and it was to be a full year before I managed to secure a copy for myself.

I promised to append a comprehensive postscript, and that's coming, but first we must find out how Vera reacted to Frank's letter. This we can do, because Frank sent another e-mail to Vera after she'd read his long letter and had finally rung him in his hotel room.

As I sit here on this summer evening in Croydon with a lengthy epistle on my desk in front of me, it would be inexcusably negligent if I didn't mention that I actually met Frank at the Hotel Palace in November that same year, just six months after he'd sat in that very hotel writing to Vera. I recalled vividly how pent up he'd been about his chances of meeting her in Salamanca, and when I bumped into him in November, I had no inkling if they really had met, or, if they had, how it had turned out. I'd had no contact with the Norwegian since we'd said our farewells in Fiji.

Was it possible that Frank and Vera had found their way back together again? Or was Frank simply on a flying visit to Madrid that had no connection with Vera whatsoever?

I sat beneath the dome of the Rotunda drinking tea, munching biscuits and listening to the seductive strains of Tchaikovsky's *Sleeping Beauty* on the harp, just as Frank had done on a previous occasion. From my table just outside the bar, I suddenly spotted the Norwegian making his way into the Rotunda. I felt a frisson run through me, for what a remarkable coincidence it was that I should meet him here at the Palace – and so far from either Fiji or London. Oslo would have been a more likely spot to chance on him, and I'd actually been there on a short visit only a few weeks before.

I thought Oslo a charming city, and what I found specially delightful was that Frank's home town was a modern European capital and yet he was only a few hundred yards from unspoilt countryside. I'd taken a long walk up to an idyllic forest hut called Ullevålseter and from there on to Frognerseter, meeting hardly a soul on the way.

Seeing Frank at the Palace felt a bit like being caught in the act, and I was so taken aback that I didn't immediately jump up to greet him, and besides, it was obvious he was looking for someone in the Rotunda. He soon noticed me however, and made his way over to my table.

'John!' he cried. 'What a surprise.'

He sat down for a few minutes until he was located by the woman he'd come to meet. I felt sure she wasn't Vera, but it was another hour before I could be certain of the fact. By then, and for particular reasons, I'd formed a clear picture of Vera, without having seen a hair of her head. This may sound a little cryptic, but I'll explain it all in detail in the postscript.

Frank had said he was staying at the hotel for a few days, and we agreed to meet for a beer in the evening.

'We must have a little chat,' he said. 'Such times are all too easily forgotten.'

As soon as he'd gone into the restaurant, something about this remark began to work inside me, and soon I'd laid a crafty plan. All I had to do was make a couple of strategic telephone calls, one more brazen than the other. The question was, could I really manage it, and even more tricky, would it be possible to tempt Frank along? I was painfully aware that I might cause an awful mess, and not just for myself, but also for the others who'd inevitably get sucked in too.

I won't say chance encounters like these are the 'work' of fate or of any kind of transcendental consciousness, but this was an opportunity I would only get once, and I couldn't let it pass. I was in a tricky situation, but I should make it clear right away that I wouldn't have Frank's letter before me now if I'd turned down the opportunity that suddenly presented itself that afternoon in Madrid.

Well, the floor is yours, Frank. You penned yet another greeting to Vera, and after that only the last act remains. After this final missive there won't be any more correspondence. All the same, one of us will have to describe what happened in Seville. I think I'd better take care of that, in the postscript.

Dear Vera,

After my long letter, yet another greeting from me.

When I left the railway station – clutching a large yellow envelope – and got back to my hotel room early on Wednesday afternoon, my head was buzzing with all the things I had to tell you. I made up my mind not to leave my room before I'd committed it all to paper, because I needed every minute from then until Thursday evening if you were to have enough time to read through all I'd written before, hopefully, preparing to travel to Seville.

I switched on my PC, but before I sat down at the desk, I again opened the envelope with all the pictures of Fiji. There were thirteen pictures from Prince Charles Beach, thirteen from the date line, thirteen from Bouma Falls and thirteen from the palm grove at the Maravu. I think it must have been the obvious symmetry of the numbers that made me turn one of the photographs over.

Under the heading *NINE OF HEARTS* was the following: *Aeons after the sun has turned into a red giant, occasional radio signals can still be intercepted in the stellar haze. Have you put your shirt on, Antonio? Come to mamma this minute! Now there's only four weeks left to Christmas.*

I turned over the next picture in the pile, and this was *THREE OF CLUBS*: *Here and now the voice is articulated by the heirs of the amphibians. It is coughed up by the nephews of terrestrial lizards in the asphalt jungle. The question posed by the heirs of the furry vertebrates is whether there is any reason beyond this shameless cocoon which grows and grows in every direction.*

My pulse was racing. On the back of the third photograph it said *FIVE OF SPADES*, and here I read: *Joker awakes inside an organic hard disk on the pillow. He feels himself trying to crawl on to the shore of a new day from a hot current of half-digested hallucinations. What nuclear power sets the elves' brains on fire? What makes the fireworks of consciousness fizz? What atomic force binds the brain cells of the soul together?*

I went on to turn all fifty-two pictures over. It was the manifesto, Vera, I had the entire manifesto in my hands. It was for both of us, and so I sat down right away and carried on writing that long letter to you. I wrote and wrote, and I didn't tear myself away from my desk except for a few hours' sleep, a hasty cup of tea under the dome and a quick march to the Retiro Park when room service came to clean the room. Then I sent the whole thing to you as an e-mail on Thursday evening. I included a copy of the manifesto and said I'd decided to arrange the texts in four columns representing the pack's four suits, and in the order clubs, diamonds, hearts and spades. However, after sending you my lengthy missive, I've thought of another way of organising the manifesto, which is far preferable, but that's something we can come back to when we see each other.

In a brief covering note I asked you to phone me at the hotel as soon as you'd read the whole thing, but not before. And you rang me in the middle of the night.

I hadn't gone to bed, but I'd kept to my room all evening despite the fact that after being cooped up constantly for thirty-six hours a visit to the bar wouldn't have gone amiss. I paced back and forth between bathroom and bedroom, and, to be honest, by the time you eventually rang, both miniatures of gin had gone from the fridge, and so too had the miniatures of vodka.

The first thing you said was:

'You're a devil, Frank. D'you know that?'

'Have you read it all?' I asked.

'Yes, every single word. You're a devil.'

'Why so?'

'Who *are* "Ana" and "José"?'

'You think I've invented them?'

244

'No, not exactly. I think you're colluding.'

'Colluding? How?'

'There was something I didn't tell you in Salamanca.'

'I think there was a great deal we didn't tell each other in Salamanca.'

'Like what?'

'No, you first.'

'Why?'

'You were the first to say there was something you didn't tell me in Salamanca.'

'I'm just not quite sure if you were in on it.'

'I don't know what you're getting at. I'm going to a requiem mass tomorrow, Vera. Are you coming?'

'*Yes*, Frank. I'm coming to Seville. And heaven help you if you don't turn up. My plane leaves at ten thirty.'

'I'm really pleased to hear that.'

'But I feel as if I'm being bamboozled.'

'What do you mean?'

'He's rung again.'

'Who?'

'That "José".'

'Oh, that's ridiculous. I agree that's ridiculous. What did he say?'

'The same as you. He always says exactly the same as you. That's the whole point. He asked if I'd come to this requiem again. And this time he was certain you'd be coming as well.'

'He also said the manifesto was for both of us. He's clearly got some reason for that.'

'A reason?'

'Oh, I don't know, Vera. I just don't know.'

'It's not you who's asking him to phone?'

'Do you really think that?'

'But you were in on it at Salamanca?'

'I haven't the foggiest idea what you're talking about.'

'You didn't understand why I was laughing. Let's begin there.'

'I'm getting curious.'

'Oh, I really don't know . . .'

'Go on, spit it out. I'm so looking forward to seeing you.'

'I'd met Ana and José before . . . Frank? Are you there?'

'*You'd* met them before?'

'And you didn't realise?'

'But the last time we spoke, you said you wouldn't go to the requiem because you didn't know Ana.'

'I believe you, Frank. I believe you.'

'*You* believe *me?*'

'They asked me to keep it to myself. You weren't to know that I'd spoken to them on any account.'

'When, for Christ's sake? Where?'

'In Salamanca. Just hold on a bit. It was the same evening we walked down to the river . . . They came to the hotel late that afternoon. They simply walked into reception, and asked me if I was Vera.'

'How could they know that?'

'Ah well, Frank. Ah, well.'

'What sort of answer is that?'

'You and I had eaten lunch in that café on Plaza Mayor – the same place you met them the following day. They'd seen us there, and they came to the hotel to find out if I was Vera.'

'That's what they were like in Fiji, too. An odd couple, almost scheming in a way . . . Just think, that was only a few days before she died.'

'I am thinking – constantly.'

'And you said you were Vera?'

'At which point they said they'd been with you in Fiji. And then they asked me to do them a little favour . . . Are you there?'

'I'm just waiting for you to go on.'

'They thought it was really bizarre finding you in Salamanca, and they said they wanted to play a practical joke on you. I was to take you for an evening stroll down to the river, and they would appear in the background so that you'd catch sight of them. But I had to promise not to breathe a word about them speaking to me. It seemed things could go badly wrong if you got to hear of it. So I kept my promise . . .'

'That's about the worst thing I've ever heard.'

'You didn't know anything?'

'Not a thing, no.'

'They were very sweet, by the way. There was something else too. When they came to the reception desk, the first thing I thought was that she was incredibly like Goya's *maja*.'

'But you didn't say anything to me about it?'

'No.'

'So you've been mulling it over all the time without saying anything?'

'I'd made a promise.'

'And down by the river I couldn't get a word in edgeways. I couldn't tell you anything.'

'I just had to laugh. I was almost splitting my sides. And I couldn't say anything.'

'You said you thought I was making up stories to keep hold of you.'

'And you got totally desperate. You talked non-stop. But maybe it was a good thing I didn't listen to you.'

'Why?'

'You wouldn't have written it down.'

'And what's your verdict?'

'Astonishing . . . But I don't give it any credence, Frank. I'm as unmoved now as I was in Salamanca.'

'What don't you believe?'

'I agree that she resembled "La Maja Desnuda". But I don't believe in these jesters cavorting up and down the ages. And neither do you.'

'I believe she died in Seville at any rate.'

'You do?'

'Don't you?'

'I was going to let tomorrow decide that.'

'I saw the attack she had on Taveuni. I saw how excitable she

247

was in Salamanca. I saw how crushed José was when I met him in the Prado. I mean, you don't lie about your wife's death.'

'No, perhaps you don't . . .'

'No, you don't.'

'I wasn't very impressed with the Australian she-primate. You might have spared yourself that, Frank.'

'I was so utterly alone. That was what I was trying to say. I *am* so utterly alone.'

'I didn't mean like that.'

'Like what?'

'I haven't any moral scruples, if that's what you're thinking. I'm just saying that I didn't care for that "Laura".'

'Don't let her worry you.'

'Didn't you find her incredibly childish?'

'Certainly. Sometimes I feel like a child myself.'

'But I didn't like her. I felt that she was really rather unpleasant.'

'I have registered that.'

'I can't understand why you had to write about her. Were you trying to make me jealous?'

'Not really. I miss you.'

'But I liked the manifesto.'

'It's for both of us.'

'I've got it here. Wait a tick . . . This is one I'm very fond of: *The cobweb of family secrets has stretched from the micropuzzle in the primeval soup to clairvoyant lobed-finned fish and advanced amphibians. Carefully, the baton has been carried on by warm-blooded reptiles, acrobatic prosimians and gloomy anthropoid apes. Did some latent self-perception lurk deep in the reptilian brain? Did no eccentric anthropoid ever get a soporific inkling of the master plan itself?'*

'Oh yes, they filched like a pair of magpies.'

'Don't be so pompous . . . Or what about this: *In the eyeball there is a clash between creation and reflection. The two-way globes of sight are magical revolving doors where the creative spirit meets itself in the created spirit. The eye that surveys the universe is the universe's own eye.'*

248

'I'd forgotten that one.'

'They must be extraordinary people.'

'That's what I thought from the very first moment I set eyes on them.'

'But, of course, I don't subscribe to these ideas.'

'Are you thinking of anything in particular?'

'You haven't forgotten that you have certain professional responsibilities, Frank? I mean, in terms of scientific theory it's mostly rubbish.'

'I'm not so certain any more.'

'You don't believe that something which happens today can have an effect on events of long ago? Or have you turned to the occult?'

'Certainly not. But I do now feel that life has a meaning.'

'You surprise me.'

'If someone alive today is exactly like someone who lived long ago, it's far from certain that it's pure "chance".'

'As I said, you surprise me.'

'Nothing is more surprising than that there's a world at all. We're alive, Vera! It's unbelievable!'

'I agree about that, naturally.'

'But haven't we actually been countenancing the basic dogma that the very existence of the universe is really one monstrous accident? And that it certainly has no "meaning"?'

'You're getting rather lofty now.'

'I think the universe is intentional.'

'Have you turned religious?'

'You could say that. But with no specific confession, other than that I've begun to be aware of an intention both for my own life and the world around me.'

'That's quite a lot in itself. But can you define this "intention" more closely?'

'I'm not joking, Vera. We know how life has evolved over billions of years, though the natural science establishment never tires of labelling this incalculable work of creation as a long series of blind, random and basically quite meaningless physical and biochemical processes. I just don't see it that way any more.'

'Then you'll have to re-train as a clergyman or a quack.'

'Well, listen to this then: the human being is a complex biochemical process, which at best lasts eighty to ninety years, and at root is nothing but a deceptive frame in which certain macromolecules battle to reproduce themselves. The only object that can be attributed to human life is the one that is played out in each individual cell, i.e. the genes' mass reproduction of themselves. A "human being" is thus nothing more than a survival machine for genes. The actual object is the individual gene – and not the organism. The aim of existence is the survival of the genes, and not what the genes control. The object is the egg and not the chicken, because the chicken is merely the product of the egg. It is no more than the egg's sex cell. So, we might as well shove you into a coop!'

'I think you're a little overwrought, but I'll let that pass as an acceptable précis.'

'You shouldn't. In fifty years most people will ridicule that sort of idea of the world. We belong to a generation of biologists who are almost corporately guilty of *reductio ad absurdum*.'

'And what is the meaning of existence?'

'As I've said, I don't know. I simply say that the universe isn't without meaning. The evolution of life has been a more spectacular proces than even the most way-out creation myth could possibly describe.'

'You're weird. You're absolutely weird.'

'Would you agree that you have a soul?'

'I don't know. I don't know if I'd use that word.'

'But you'd agree you have a consciousness?'

'Certainly. It would be a contradiction in terms to say I hadn't.'

'You therefore have consciousness of this universe . . .'

'And of myself. *Cogito, ergo sum.*'

'We can certainly go back that far, to Descartes, I mean, because that was where the whole process began to go off the rails. There is matter, and there is a consciousness of matter. I believe that consciousness is such an essential part of the very nature of the universe that it can't just be an accidental by-product.'

'But matter came first.'

'That may well be.'

'I've yet to see a consciousness manifest itself materially, but I've seen the opposite.'

'Wait a minute. You've yet to see a consciousness manifest itself materially?'

'Yes.'

'What about the world, Vera, what about the world?'

'You have a point there. But you're not speaking as a scientist any more.'

'In which case, maybe it's important to speak about something other than science. For me consciousness is a more essential part of the nature of the universe than all the stars and comets put together.'

'But matter comes before consciousness. That's an overriding principle in discussions like these.'

'That may be so, as I've said. But it's become clearer and clearer to me that cosmic matter has become pregnant with consciousness. Consciousness is no less a universal aspect of reality than nuclear reactions in the stars.'

'I really don't know. You've obviously thought a lot more about this than me,' said Vera.

'Blood comes before love.'

'What was that you said?'

'Blood must flow in the veins before we are able to love one another. That doesn't mean that blood is more important than love.'

'Perhaps that too is a chicken-and-egg situation.'

'How?'

'If it weren't for blood, there'd be no love. And if it weren't for love, there'd be no blood.'

'Yes, that was what I meant.'

'But we can talk more about this in Seville. It's almost three a.m.'

'I only wanted to say that I'm through with the over-egged

reductionism that has ridden this century like an incubus. It's about time for a new millennium,' I said.

'And I'm just saying you're being far too vague. We have nothing to base natural science on apart from the forces of nature.'

'Hah! We draw conclusions far in excess of those indicated by the four elemental forces.'

'Have you an example?'

'The sun isn't merely a star, the earth isn't merely a planet, a human being isn't merely an animal, an animal isn't merely dust, dust isn't merely lava, and Ana isn't dead.'

'What was that last bit?'

'I don't know. I just blurted it out, it fitted the sentence so well.'

'Just for the rhythm, eh?'

'Yes, just for the rhythm.'

'And I also like this one: *Joker is only half there in the elves' world. He knows he will go, so he's paid his dues. He knows he's going, so he's already half gone. He's come from all that exists and he's going nowhere. Once he arrives, he won't even be able to dream of returning. He's bound for the land where even sleep doesn't exist,*' Vera said.

'So you're quite sure this Nothingness Land really exists?'

'Unfortunately, yes. To the extent that "nothing" can be said to exist.'

'Then it's even more important for us to meet. Our lives are so short.'

'I wouldn't disagree there.'

'I think that's just what the manifesto's all about.'

'For me it's saying that we're part of something huge.'

'I'll see you at Seville airport.'

'Have you booked any hotel rooms?'

'I've booked in at the Doña María. It's on the Plaza Virgen de los Reyes which is in front of La Giralda and the cathedral.'

'You've booked for me as well?'

'Yes. I reckoned you'd come when I laid it on so unctuously.'

'Unctuously?'

'Perhaps I should have said thickly. Have you printed it out?'

'I made a copy straight away. I hate reading from a screen.'

'Me too.'

'Now I know why you said I reminded you of a gecko. I was fond of Gordon.'

'I can imagine that.'

'You need someone to take you to task.'

'But it's not you who resembles Gordon. Gordon was the one who was like you. Cause and effect, Vera!'

'Very amusing . . . So you've booked two rooms?'

'I've booked both.'

'What does that mean?'

'I've booked one room and two rooms . . . Hello?'

'I'm speechless.'

'Why so?'

'You're so hare-brained. And you've become far too slack about logical principles.'

'Can you clarify that?'

'It's not possible to book one room and two rooms. You've booked *two* in that case.'

'Logic is far too lacking in ambivalence. That's why it isn't much use in conflict resolution, or processes in general. It's as dead as a doornail, Vera.'

'But that's almost the same as not being able to arrive "partially" on a desert island. Coming or going is something one does fully. You ought to think about that. You ought to think about that, Frank.'

'I don't know if I'm so sure now. In one sense the dwarf did come to the island with the seaman. In another sense, he didn't turn up until later.'

'I think we're talking at cross purposes. I am the desert island.'

'Vera?'

'But we'll see each other tomorrow.'

'And we'll soon find out how we see each other.'

'Was that a profundity?'

'Perhaps there's another sky above this one.'

'And was that even deeper?'

'I've no idea. I haven't a clue what I'm saying any more. It's as if someone's putting words into my mouth.'

'It's called disclaiming responsibility.'

'But I was suddenly thinking of something Ana said in Fiji.'

'What was that?'

'She said, "There's something beyond this."'

'God, yes, that's right. Wait a sec . . .'

'What are you doing?'

'Wait, I said, I'm leafing through . . . "You'll all think you're at a funeral," she said, "but in reality you'll be witnessing a new birth." D'you think she was clairvoyant?'

'I said I didn't know. All I know is that I'm taking the AVE train at eight a.m.'

'You know – I've studied that Goya painting again. She really made me jump when I saw her in Salamanca.'

'That might have done you some good.'

'What might?'

'To jump a bit.'

'Bye for now.'

'See you!'

POSTSCRIPT
by John Spooke

It often gives me a start when I catch sight of the large colour photo of Sheila that hangs, framed in black, above my writing desk. It's been there ever since I took it some years ago, in front of Croydon's old town hall. She must have looked straight into the lens just as I clicked the shutter, because she seems to be staring down at me. Sometimes it feels as if that's how she planned to keep an eye on me if she was ever snatched away.

I've always found looking at sharp colour portraits of the departed particularly disturbing. Imagine what a shock it must have been two hundred years ago for Andalucían peasants to be confronted with the dwarf's photograph of the beautiful gypsy woman in the Alcázar gardens.

Even after three years I still can't believe I won't see Sheila again. Though why am I so sure we'll never be reunited? I feel pretty certain, but not one hundred per cent. By its very existence, the world has already breached the bounds of improbability. If this world exists, why shouldn't there be another one afterwards?

Frank might have said: because we're flesh and blood like frogs and bats. Well, yes, I agree about that, and if there's one thing that ails me it's my circulation. I'm an ageing primate. But am I not a spiritual being too?

I've never been able to come to terms with the idea that a human soul is nothing more than a surreal, protein-based phenomenon like a giraffe's neck or an elephant's trunk. My consciousness enables me to plumb the entire universe. I'm no longer convinced that the soul is merely a biochemical secretion.

We know there are other galaxies. Perhaps, as many astronomers think, there are other universes as well. So why should a progression from one level of reality to another be less likely than a progression in time and space? Or put another way: why should a progression from plane to meta-plane be so unthinkable? It's possible to wake from a dream.

We don't know what this world is. I imagine it's easy to be

tricked by the limitations of the level of reality one finds oneself in at the moment. And Ana wasn't dead.

When I arrived on Taveuni to take part in that television programme on the future of man, I hadn't written a novel for years. I found it impossible to write while Sheila was ill, and I wasn't able to begin anything new in the years immediately following her death. I've never been any good at having more than one thought in my head at once. It's strange how attached a man of my age can be to a woman. And almost terrifying how loss can reduce one's vitality.

I needed to meet new people in order to start writing again, and in Taveuni I came across many who were quite different from anyone back home in Croydon. I needed the stimulus of new ideas and concepts. Perhaps that was why I invited the guests at the Maravu to a tropical summit.

I'd often based my novels on real-life situations. I've certainly never been short of imagination, but I've frequently had to struggle to conjure up living fictional characters.

Even before I met Frank, I'd singled out Ana and José for the next novel I would write. Ana was a striking woman in her late twenties. She was almost half a head taller than José, had long dark hair, black eyes and moved like a goddess. He was older than she was, with blue eyes, and rather fair skin for a Spaniard. They'd presented themselves as television journalists, but José once mentioned that Ana was a well-known flamenco dancer. As for me, I'd been sent to the island by the BBC to stand on the date line and spout some well-chosen words about global ethics and the earth's future. The Spanish couple were apparently there to make a similar documentary for a Spanish television channel, and we happened to bump into each other a couple of times on the 180° meridian. There'd already been a swarm of TV crews on the island, although the actual celebration wouldn't be for another two years.

There were several reasons why I'd latched on to the Spanish couple. When they were alone, or rather when they affected to be alone, they would regularly quote strange formulae at one another. They reminded me of people who go about talking to themselves – even though there were two of them – because there was little to indicate that one partner said anything the other wasn't already familiar with. Though I didn't speak Spanish, I recall noting their curious mutterings with great interest, before Frank came to be struck by the same thing. The difference between Frank and me was that Frank understood what they said. That was an essential distinction. It was the form I had reacted to and not the content. Even on Frank's first day I could already see him eavesdropping on the two Spaniards at dinner. When he asked if he could borrow a pen, the pleasure was all mine. I imagined I'd already enthused him in a way, without his being in a position to realise it.

There was something else, too, and it was this that really caused me to react to, if not pursue, the Spanish couple: from the very first I had a strong feeling I'd met Ana before. Then Frank arrived on the island. When he also said he felt Ana was intensely familiar, I made some enquiries of my own, and I won't deny that it was quite a shock when I eventually made the connection. I was startled, and from then on I regarded Ana in a totally new light.

I decided to do nothing hasty. I wouldn't say anything to Frank, either, it would only confuse him even more. I contented myself with giving him a little clue to follow as he checked out of the Maravu. Then I would wait and see. This was something I wanted to take home with me.

I've never liked talking about what I'm working on, and certainly not before I've begun the actual process of writing. I feared that the whole thing might get talked to death if it became a topic of dinner-time chat on that Fijian island.

When Frank arrived on Taveuni, he'd been in the South Pacific for a full two months. I learnt almost everything I know about that part of the world from him. The more I got to know him, the clearer it became to me that Frank must be the narrator in the novel I wanted to write. I thought we set each other off well, in spite of a considerable difference in age. I might point out here that the dream Frank told Gordon about was, in fact, borrowed from me. It was I who had a nightmarish dream one night at the Maravu. I dreamt I couldn't remember if I was eighteen or twenty-eight. Then I awoke, and far from being a frightening forty like Frank, I was a shocking sixty-five. I got right out of bed and stood before the large bedroom mirror. It was I who was the ageing primate.

No two people are alike, and of course, there is a vast flora of human characteristics. Though as far as I'm concerned, there are really only two types of people. One category, the vast majority, is made up of those who are content to live seventy or eighty or ninety years. The reasons given for this are various. Some point out that after eighty or ninety years they would have had a long and eventful life and, by then, they'd be looking forward to turning belly up and dying full of years. Others say they have no desire to be old and dependent and thus a burden on others. Others again stress that wanting more than eighty or ninety years of life wouldn't be sensible given that we aren't naturally designed to live longer. Then there are those – possibly the largest sub-group – who, if things were so arranged that they could inhabit the planet for hundreds or thousands of years, would find it awful to contemplate. Well, fair enough! Good, and perfectly in harmony with nature. But there's a completely different caste of people: a small number of individuals who want to live for ever. They suffer from being unable to grasp how a world can continue after they've gone. Frank was one of them, and that was why I conceived such an interest in him from the very first moment. Anyway, it was a necessary prerequisite to making him the novel's narrator.

I've never felt much kinship with the faint-hearted who retreat from the thought of everlasting life on earth. When I was younger, it was one of the first things I would try to elicit when meeting people for the first time. If you had the choice, I'd ask, would you choose to live for ever? Or are you resigned to the fact that one day you'll be no more? I took a sort of informal poll that way. The result I came to is that the vast majority want to die. Well, fine! It's good that nature's so sensibly attuned.

But it's not always those who relish life the most who are the least willing to renounce it. Quite the opposite: those who enjoy themselves most often show scant regard for the fact that life will end one day. This may seem like a paradox, but on closer inspection it isn't. People who refuse to surrender to life's finality already find themselves in a no-man's-land. They realise they'll soon be completely gone, so they're already half gone. It's immaterial whether they've five or fifty years of life in front of them. It's here they differ from all the people who accept the condition of mortality – provided it doesn't happen right away. Those who want to live for ever are not the first to elbow their way out on to the dance-floor. They're not the ones we call 'hard livers'. The kings of the dance-floor are so engrossed in the dance of life itself that they won't allow themselves to be distracted by the thought that some day their dance will end.

In his letter to Vera, Frank tells of his short flight from Viti Levu to Taveuni. I think it's obvious even here which type he belongs to. It was to be some time before I could read about the thoughts he was grappling with that first morning on the island. But I believe even then I had an inkling of the compass of his mind, and more was to fall into place in the days that followed. Frank was one of a rare breed of people. He was the kind who feel themselves oppressed by the grief that lack of existential spirit and permanence brings.

Frank concludes his description of the flight from Nadi by claiming that 'it had provoked an inalienable sense of being merely a frail vertebrate in the noonday of life'. Well might he say that, I thought, and not because I had any difficulty recognising myself in him. The difference, and to me it seemed considerable, lay in the fact that I was almost thirty years older than him, and therefore of an age with the pilot. As I sit crouched over my desk here in Croydon, I'm racked from time to time by a capricious sciatica. So I hardly need to be an expert on vertebrates to know that I'm the possessor of an ailing skeleton. I'm also receiving treatment for angina pains and I realise that every moment more I have in this world must be regarded as a bonus. It's like living with a pistol at your head. It's as if all the remainder of my time in the Milky Way were to be spent in a matchbox-plane with dickey instruments. I haven't even got a girlfriend with me to help me read the map on the final leg.

It's been three years since Sheila died, and even longer since she was able to cross the room and lay a soothing hand on my neck. When Sheila went, we'd known each other for more than forty years. I'm wallowing in these private matters simply to emphasise why I acted as resolutely as I did when I met Frank in Madrid almost a year later.

When the Spaniards appeared at breakfast on the morning I'd fetched Frank from the airport, I mentioned that a Norwegian had arrived by the morning plane, and that most Norwegians are reckoned to be good card players. This of course, as I pointed out, is to do with their long winters. I'd gathered that it was mainly for Ana's sake that they'd sat on playing cards the previous evening. At all events she'd been the keenest to scrape together some opponents. A Dutchman they'd played against had just left the island that morning, and who was to fill his place at the bridge table? Not me, at any rate, for I could not play cards, nor did I have the slightest desire to learn.

Packs of cards are things I associate with Sheila. She could spend whole evenings playing solitaire while I was in the attic working. She was always so pleased when I came down to the living-room after my work was finished. To massage her feeling of self-esteem I'd have to sit and watch her finish her game, and if she felt like teasing me, I'd have to shuffle the cards for her to play another. Only then would she look up at me.

I'd noted which hut Frank had been shown to on his arrival. And then, in the unmanned reception, I took the opportunity to note down his home address, his date of birth and the fact that his passport had been issued in Oslo. A bit later on I told the Spaniards which *bure* the Norwegian was staying in and also that I'd seen him sitting out on his veranda. I think he's feeling a bit lonely, I said. It was kindly meant.

I'm trying to indicate in a general way that some of what

occurred at the Maravu on those January days didn't happen completely unaided. I'm not saying I was playing some kind of amusing game. But I did rather stage-manage certain things. I helped advance the odd social process that otherwise might have taken a whole week.

I was the one who tipped off Ana and José that Frank might be willing to take over the card-playing from the Dutchman. That was the first thing, and that was mainly for Ana's sake. It was I who, after breakfast, pointed out the hut that the Norwegian had just moved into – that was the second thing. The third was my suggestion to the Spaniards that later on in the evening we might try to pump an evolutionary biologist about where his science was now, nearly 150 years after Darwin's *Origin*. I thought the opportunity was too good to miss. The previous evening, José and I had agreed over a clever theory about how modern man is much too lacking in what we chose to call 'cognitive imagination'.

If the letter to Vera – including its appended postscript – really does end up in a time-capsule on the International Date Line, I'll find myself arraigned for such tricks in a thousand years' time, and the place of execution is already being erected. But all indictments would be time-barred by then, even those relating to my doings in Seville almost a year later. Because the story of Ana and José is still not complete, nor is the tale of Frank and Vera.

I can take some comfort from the fact that, no matter what we get up to, it's all soon forgotten. To you who read this in a thousand years' time, I only make this plea: that Ana's story should not be drowned in the euphoria of entering another new millennium.

I read about the 'Millennium Monument' which was planned for Taveuni some time ago in the *Daily Telegraph*. For five hundred dollars anyone who wants to can pen a greeting to the fourth millennium and put it in a glass capsule. The capsule is placed in a cavity inside a brick, which is then sealed and used to build the monument. During the coming millennium a foundation will look after the wall and also guarantee that your own individual time-capsule will be opened in the year 3000.

A thousand years will pass, and then the story of Ana María Maya will be read out where the 180° meridian crosses Taveuni. Whenever I try to form some mental picture of the people standing on the date line in a thousand years' time, I always imagine a dwarf sitting atop the monument reading these lines.

The letter to Vera opens with Frank painting a detailed picture of the island he'd come to, and I can't quite understand how he found time to do that. I mean, he's sitting in a hotel room in Madrid with only a couple of days to tell Vera about Ana and José, and he spends time expounding on frogs and bats! I don't know how much room there is in these capsules one can buy for five hundred dollars, I only know they fit inside a hole in a brick. If my own message-in-a-bottle to the future won't hold all Frank has written, I'll have to tear out the odd page here and there. On the other hand, when the letter to Vera is read out on Taveuni on 1 January 3000 – and all my energies are being used to ensure it will be – our descendants will get a comprehensive idea of how things looked on 'the Garden Island' a thousand years before. Poor fools! Perhaps they'll begin to hate us. I doubt if the orange dove will still be making its morning flight over Lake Tagimaucia. I doubt if there'll be much left of the luxuriant rain forest. That's the reason I haven't yet torn out all the pages Frank has written on the natural life of Taveuni. If the worst comes to the worst, I'll have to make do with placing a diskette in the sealed brick. But there's the problem of how compatible it would be in a thousand years' time. For safety's sake I'll also make sure to insert a print-out of the manifesto itself. That won't take up much room.

Now and then, on the rare occasions when I confront myself with what might have happened if Vera really had received that letter from Frank, I get a tingle down my spine. Once I've added the postscript, though, I'll make certain Vera reads it some time. It may give her a better understanding of what happened in Seville. If she does insist that other people get the chance to read Ana's story, I may have to give up the time-capsule idea. There's no point in putting a piece of writing in a time-capsule for a thousand years if it's already been doing the rounds. It's a matter for the world at large to decide what is handed down to posterity and what is simply forgotten. The footsteps of man are always filled with the sound of many voices, far too many. If we also heard the voices of all previous generations in one great, verbal backdrop, the situation would be intolerable. Either one should be able to keep a secret for a thousand years, or not at all.

I was the one who began talking to Frank about geckoes, as I assumed my aversion to them, at least as regards physical contact – while asleep for instance – had to be greater than his. I'd imagined that Frank, who presented himself as a kind of expert on such creatures, might have a few consoling words about the tranquil co-existence of reptile and man, even with a grouchy Englishman like me, but I rather got the impression that he would have liked his room cleared of geckoes too, though he didn't say why. He mentioned that he'd only seen one gecko so far, but he'd been careful not to keep the door open and let mosquitoes into the room, something I hadn't bothered with at all. This was the gecko who took the name Gordon, christened after a celebrated London fire-water that's always been dear to my heart, so dear that Sheila was forever going on about it. When I take the cap off the stuff – particularly a new bottle – I still get the feeling that Sheila's watching me.

Frank was not simply a man who felt himself oppressed by the grief that lack of existential spirit and permanence brings. He was one of those who constantly hears voices in his head.

I, too, have had voices in my head, particularly since Sheila died. This enables me to hold long conversations with her even now, and I'm not always sure how much is conducted aloud, or if it's all something going on inside me. I know I talk out loud sometimes, and she answers me in my thoughts.

Even when she was alive, Sheila's conversation was transparent. If I expressed an opinion about anything, I always knew what she was going to say, and not just what she thought about this or that, but word for word. We knew each other terribly well.

I believe everyone has their own speech patterns and perhaps we're especially idiosyncratic in our choice of everyday words and phrases like 'there you are', 'just about', 'put it this way', 'if you know what I mean', 'I've always thought that', 'can't you see how stupid that is' – and so on. When I'm with people, shards of sentences that belonged to Sheila frequently lodge in my mind and keep her close to me in some way.

Often when I get worked up over something Sheila says, I reply out loud. This happens even when I know in advance that she'll say something that will cause me agitation. My life hasn't altered dramatically on this level. It might sound strange at my age, but I miss her body. Much of the rest of our life together is largely intact, not just because we still talk, but because of all the memories we share. Sheila has a central place in those, of course. I sometimes even miss her asking me to shuffle her cards.

Sheila had always played solitaire, and when she was young it was one of those little traits that made me fall so head over heels in love with her. In later years I could hate her for precisely the same thing. I could hate the way she spent hours in front of the fire frittering away a whole evening playing solitaire. I remember saying to her once that playing solitaire was considered a fatuous pastime. It wounded and hurt her terribly. Sometimes I even got annoyed if I caught her fiddling the cards to make her game come out. And yet now – now that she's gone – I miss her because of the very same things I used to hate her for. So it's come full circle, and it's not a vicious one. It's easier to love someone who's always out of reach than someone it's impossible to escape.

I've got a neighbour who's accused me of talking to myself a couple of times. He's easily fooled. So far I'm glad he's never heard what Sheila says. But there'll come a day when I won't be able to keep Sheila's words to myself. I know I'm beginning to get old. It may be far too early, but I've already acquired a smidgen of what I might call verbal incontinence. It may burgeon.

So long as the voices remain inside my head I've nothing to be ashamed of. I've never felt guilty about Sheila just because I go on talking to her. That would be turning things round the wrong way. She was the one who left so much resonance in her wake. 'It's tea-time, John. Are you coming soon?' 'Surely you're not going to wear that suit? I told you to take it to the cleaners two months ago.' 'I thought we might invite Jeremy and Margaret one evening. They haven't been over for ages!'

I won't comment in too much depth on Frank's description of the tropical summit I so shamelessly stage-managed. In general, I think he paints an adequate picture of the way our conversation went. There is only one important point on which it may be apposite to colour Frank's summary.

Frank writes that Ana summed up her concept of reality in three remarks. First she said: 'There is a reality beyond this one. When I die, I won't die. You'll all believe I'm dead, but I won't be. Soon we'll meet again in another place.' Then she said: 'You'll all think you're at a funeral, but in reality you're witnessing a new birth.' And lastly: 'There is something beyond this. Here we are merely fleeting spirits in transition.'

Something of the sort was indeed said, I'm not disputing that, though of course it's impossible to recall the exact words as spoken more than a year ago. Circumstances have made it incumbent on me to point out that good old Frank goes a little too far in stressing that Ana pinned her dualistic view of the world on her *own* life and her *own* death and interment. She was speaking in far more general terms when she expressed her belief in a reality beyond this one and an existence after our present life. I remember her linking up with something Laura and I had touched on, because I definitely recall her saying: 'Perhaps we'll meet again in another place and remember this as a dream.'

Had I not met Frank in Madrid some months later, the letter to Vera needn't have been subjected to my quibbles. But Ana's exact words were to have a far greater importance than any of us could have guessed. I also believe – in common with Frank – that she went so far as to compare a funeral with a birth. Apart from that, I can only emphasise that José really did shed a tear while Ana was speaking, and I don't think it was because he had something in his eye, either. Later I wondered if there could be any connection between these tears and Ana's sudden attack a day and a half later.

Frank is right in saying that I withdrew shortly after the Spanish couple walked off into the palm grove, and therefore have no idea how long Frank remained there. I have reason to think, though, that he let himself be seduced by Laura's natural mysticism; that seems to be apparent from his nocturnal conversation with Gordon. It seems to me that he was fighting an inner battle to free himself from an over-mechanistic view of the world. As such, maybe the dulcet perspectives peddled by the young woman with the dark plaits and singular eyes were a welcome temptation.

In his letter Frank relates how he took his leave on that final evening before his departure. I remember following Frank and Laura with my eyes right until they'd seated themselves on the veranda. And to keep the record straight I ought, perhaps, to make it clear that I've no clue as to what happened later that night, other than what is apparent from Frank's letter to Vera.

I travelled home to London the day after Frank, but unlike him I journeyed westwards to Sydney and on to Singapore and Bangkok. These long flights afforded me the first opportunity to put what I'd seen at the Maravu into perspective.

And there was another occasion, after the Norwegian had left, when Ana suddenly fainted. It was in the palm grove in front of the swimming pool, just after I'd passed on Frank's greetings. The attack lasted a couple of minutes, and again José's reaction was one of panic. He pinched her arm, shouted her name several times and tried to prop her legs up on one of the palm trunks. The trunk bore a notice clearly warning people to beware of falling coconuts.

I'd conveyed Frank's concern about Ana and said that he'd asked me to wish her a speedy recovery. I'd also said a few words about how he loved Spanish painting and that he'd described the Prado as one of the greatest art collections in the world. I may conceivably have added a brief comment about Goya being the Norwegian's favourite amongst Spanish masters. But I didn't get the reaction I'd anticipated, José simply became annoyed. He said: 'I see. But would you mind just leaving us in peace for a while?'

Ana seemed more reconciled to the fact that I took the initiative in talking about Goya, even though it was she who sank on to the grass by the pool a quarter of an hour later. During dinner I merely nodded to them a couple of times, as by now several new guests had arrived.

Frank doesn't say what he did in Oslo in the period up to the end of April. If he was still living in Sognsveien, it must have been hard for him to walk up that last, steep hill on his way home from the university. And if he used a car, he would have had to pass the very spot where the accident occurred, maybe several times a day. If I'd been in his shoes, I think I might have moved house, just for that reason alone. In Croydon, I often make long detours to avoid walking past the hospital where Sheila spent her last days.

Frank and I shared some of the same sense of resignation about life. But I felt almost offended by the fact that he and Vera couldn't talk. They had lost a child, but they'd also once had that child together. Sheila and I tried for many years, but we never had children. She had her solitaire. And I had my novels.

I have now explained that much of what Frank describes in Fiji is based on real events.

If I possess a literary philosophy, it's this: I always build on real events when I can. But one can't dig up data about everything, and it's in these grey areas that imagination finds a degree of free rein. As for historical matters – like Goya's models, Manuel Godoy's art collections or the pioneers of flamenco – there is a limit to what's available to historical research. On the other hand, I feel I must add that it's also possible for a novelist to turn up a source which until then has been hidden from professional historians. And not only that. The author may even be lucky enough to gain access to some almost pristine sources which really can throw new light on historical events. On this occasion I experienced several such strokes of luck, and I emphasise the fact in order to make the point that much of what is narrated from Fiji and Spain is authentic enough.

I found it baffling how similar Ana was to Goya's *maja*, and in the Prado's official Goya guide it says of 'The Naked Maja' that 'this image, whose riddle has yet to be solved, is an exercise in confidential painting'. It says 'yet to be solved'. It doesn't say 'never to be solved'. But it uses the word 'confidential'. It's exactly two centuries since the painting was finished, and there are still plenty of old drawers in Spain, in Sanlúcar de Barrameda, for example, where something might turn up.

What created such a disturbing hiatus in my work on this occasion was that I met Frank in Madrid. Right in the middle of my novel, the main character himself turned up at the Palace – on location in fact. I was only staying at that exclusive establishment because I'd pictured Frank sitting here writing his long letter to Vera.

The week before I'd been rash enough to travel down to Seville. That was a mistake. There, too, something had happened that was a trifle inopportune for my novel.

I was forced to steer clear of the requiem itself, and that hadn't been my original intention, on the contrary, now that Ana María Maya had died after chasing a dwarf who'd taken a picture of her, I'd been looking forward to describing a grieving band of gypsies.

So what took place in Seville?

It sometimes happens that our lives, in all their monotonousness, are so extraordinary that no work of fiction can surpass them.

When I got down to the bar in the Palace, Frank was already sitting there with a beer. It was the middle of November and almost a year after we'd met in Fiji. Still fresh in my mind was the picture I'd formed of him as the rather subdued man I picked up at the tiny airport, together with the two Americans.

Now almost six months had passed since he'd sat in the Hotel Palace writing his long letter to Vera. Or, to make things quite clear, since I'd imagined Frank sitting in an hotel room in Madrid writing a long letter to Vera, after meeting her at a conference in Salamanca. It's becoming important to separate the two stories. By November '98 I was already well on the way to writing the letter, but it still wasn't perfect.

I hadn't even considered the possibility of meeting Frank at the same hotel. I knew he lived in Oslo, and even though he'd had

Spanish connections earlier in his life, the likelihood of meeting him in Madrid had to be remote. It wasn't Frank who'd given me the tip about the Palace. That had come from Chris Batt at the new library back in Croydon.

As I sat down, the Norwegian smiled expectantly and pulled out a black 'Pilot' drawing pen from his inner pocket.

'I forgot to return your pen,' he said. 'So, here it is!'

I laughed, but my laughter was double-edged, because in reality I was the one who should have been thanking him.

'I said you could hang on to it,' I responded, but took it all the same. I felt it had assumed a certain sentimental value.

'How did your report go?' I asked.

'Fine. It's almost ready. And what about your novel?'

'I could say the same.'

'You're on holiday in Spain?'

Naturally this was a question I was expecting.

'Not really.'

'Doing research perhaps?'

'In a way, yes.'

'Writing about things Spanish?'

I put a finger to my lips.

'I never talk about what I'm writing. And you?'

'I don't mind talking about my report.'

'I mean why you're in Madrid.'

When he didn't answer immediately, I added, 'Are you visiting Vera?'

'She lives in Barcelona.'

'Oh yes, I remember you mentioned that. Did you meet her at that conference in Salamanca?'

He gave a quick nod.

'But you don't have much contact?'

'We'll see,' was all he said.

'Yes, we'll see,' I repeated. 'She wasn't the one you had lunch with this afternoon, was she?'

He shook his head. It was obvious he was turning over what we were talking about in his mind.

'She was an old friend from university days. I studied for a time in Madrid.'

'And now you're here for a short break?'

He'd begun to squirm in his chair, but then he said, 'On a spur-of-the-moment long weekend. I spent several years here as a boy. My father was a newspaper correspondent here for four years. There's always something to draw me back.'

'Vera as well, maybe? Will you get in touch with her?'

He'd come with me thus far, but no further. Now he smiled and said, 'This is getting to be a bit of an interrogation, isn't it?'

Ah yes, it had begun to be a bit of an interrogation. But I had to try to find out roughly how the land lay. Also, if I could, I had to try to tease out of him if he had any days free. I took a roundabout route.

'You've been to the Prado and that kind of thing?'

He lit up now, and I don't think just because I'd changed the subject.

'I'd actually been thinking of going tomorrow,' he said. 'We could go together, if you've got the time. You know, there are a couple of pictures I would very much enjoy showing you.'

I see, I pondered, a couple of pictures.

'Goya or Velázquez?'

He looked secretive.

'Goya,' he said.

'And which pictures are you thinking of in particular?'

He looked me straight in the eye. I could see his pupils dilating with excitement.

'You must see them,' he said. 'I really think I'll enjoy watching your face when you discover them.'

He adopted an expression of something approaching pride, as if part of the honour for what he was going to reveal was his. Then, suddenly, he was on his guard.

'Or do you know what I'm referring to?'

Of course I had an inkling which pictures he wanted to show me in the Prado. While we were on Taveuni, I'd gained an advantage. I'd been able to borrow a laptop computer and modem from

Jochen Kiess, and it was the work of minutes to find some clear images of Goya's best-known works. When they began to appear, I was so astonished to see them that I was on the point of throwing open the door on to the palm grove – wearing nothing but my underclothes – and yelling 'Eureka!' But I'd contained myself and instead searched the web pages for information about flamenco in Seville. It hadn't taken long to discover that Ana was a well-known flamenco dancer and that her name was Ana María Maya. After that, things began to gather their own momentum. Wasn't it odd that Laura began to talk about the ancient Indian concept of *maya* on the very day I discovered it was Ana's surname? Then I succumbed to the temptation of putting my forefinger on her forehead and calling her by her proper name. I even went so far as to describe her as a 'masterpiece'. And the result was exactly as Frank describes in his letter to Vera. Ana was so like Goya's *maja* that she must have been thoroughly fed up with the constant exposure to it, and perhaps that was why José reacted so hotly when I found out her surname. From then on they kept more and more to themselves. Then Ana had her sudden turn, and yet another one after Frank left. I'd begun to wonder if she could be seriously ill.

'There are a great many of Goya's works in the Prado,' I said.

So I'd not understood what he was talking about. He breathed a sigh of relief.

'I think you'll be amazed,' he said.

The conversation continued a while. We beat about the bush, and not even the same bush, either. I decided to go directly to it.

'I'm going to Seville tomorrow,' I said. 'I got back from there a week ago, as a matter of fact, but I'm going down again for the weekend before heading back to England.'

'You must send my love. Send my love to the orange trees.'

'I will, I promise.'

I didn't know if he'd ever been there himself, but now he said, 'It must be lovely in Andalucía at this time of year.'

There, I thought. Now!

I looked into his brown eyes.

273

'You don't want to come along, then?'

He looked at me in mild confusion. It was as if he was thinking: what's all this *about*?

'There's something I'd really like to show you there.'

He laughed loudly.

'And what might that be?' he asked.

I put my finger to my lips again.

'You must see it for yourself, Frank.'

So as far as wanting to show each other things was concerned, it was one all. Frank looked at the clock and shifted uneasily in his chair again.

'I think perhaps not,' he said. 'Both for reasons of time and money.'

I felt I'd got him hooked now.

'I'll take care of the expenses,' I said. 'That won't be a problem.'

'To tell you the truth,' he said, 'I'd really been planning to travel home via Barcelona. I've just got to ring first, and you know how it is . . . I've left it all to the last moment.'

'You can do both,' I assured him. 'First a day or two in Seville, and then you can fly to Oslo via Barcelona. You might get a becoming tan in Seville. People notice that kind of thing.'

The Norwegian ordered another beer and sat weighing it up. While he was thus engaged, I tossed in a casual, 'I think I can promise you won't be disappointed. I think you'll be amazed.'

The set of his features took on a quizzical expression due, doubtless, to my mimicry.

'Or do you know what I'm planning?'

He grinned, but shook his head. I went on, 'It's a really impressive sight. I'll be surprised if it doesn't rank as one of the finest sights of your life.'

He shrugged his shoulders, and now, now he'd nearly made up his mind.

'When were you thinking of going?'

'Tomorrow morning. The AVE trains leave almost every hour. So we can have lunch on board.'

He hemmed and hawed.

'It's not a bad idea. I've never actually been to Seville. But of course, I couldn't allow you to pay for me.'

'Of course you can. It won't just be a pleasure; it may easily prove to be invaluable research.'

He gave another of those typically boisterous Scandinavian laughs.

'I hope you're not saying that I'm the object of research.'

I lit a cigarette.

'Don't say that. We might have a bit of a chat about reptiles and that kind of thing, or endangered species in Oceania. There's a lot I need to brush up on.'

'Of course. Just ask away.'

We stayed in the bar until late that night, and we even managed to burrow a little way into evolutionary biology. I also heard the full story of the tragic accident that had cost his daughter her life.

A few hours later we were aboard a train to Seville. I felt I was playing for high stakes, and I must be honest and admit that I felt somewhat caught up in my own web. But now the wheels were in motion.

When the train stopped at Córdoba, he suddenly raised his head and clapped a hand to his brow, as if there was something he'd forgotten.

'I never showed you the paintings!' he exclaimed.

But he refused to tell me which paintings they were. He only repeated that I had to see them with my own eyes.

I had booked three rooms at the Hotel Doña María, and Frank remarked on the fact, but I explained that one room was for a friend of mine who'd be turning up during the course of the evening. I wasn't wholly certain that the third room would be needed. I told him he'd have to wait until the evening for his unforgettable experience. In the interim we'd plenty of time to look round.

I took him to see the cathedral and Patio de los Naranjos, and as we strolled along the neat lines of orange trees all now laden with ripe fruit, Frank told me that Laura had sent him a photograph she'd taken on Taveuni of the rare dove with the orange-coloured breast. This amused me, because he had no idea what I'd written about their little romance on the Fijian island.

We went to the top of La Giralda, which was originally a minaret before it was added to and turned into a belfry. From here we had a tremendous view over the white city on both banks of the River Guadalquivir. We crossed Plaza Virgen de los Reyes with its long line of horse-drawn taxis and made our way to the cooling ponds and fountains of the Alcázar gardens. Palm trees grew everywhere, and it was strange to think Frank and I were once again sauntering through a grove of palms. It was almost like being back at the Maravu.

After we'd explored the oldest part of the gardens, we walked through the Puerta del Privilegio and looked down across the romantic Jardín de los Poetas with its two pools surrounded by three-foot hedges. Frank stopped abruptly and exclaimed with a gasp:

'It's so . . . beautiful here.'

I noticed tears welling up in his eyes and laid a hand on his shoulder. Perhaps he couldn't believe the beauty of it, I thought, because he immediately rubbed his eyes. Perhaps by way of covering his emotional reaction he said, 'I think I had a déjà vu experience.'

We went up on to the wall with its covered viewing platform and then sat on a bench in the gravelled square in front of the Puerta de Marchena. It was extremely hot, and I went to the café and got us something to drink.

Not long after, something odd occurred, and in one way it was here everything began – although in other ways it began outside a nursery school in Oslo, in the little airport on the Fijian island of Taveuni, by the bridge over the Tormes, between some squalid dockside sheds in Marseilles, in Barrio Triana on the west bank of the Río Guadalquivir, in Cádiz harbour more than a century before that, or at the Duquesa de Alba's country seat in Sanlúcar de Barrameda – not to mention what was to unfold later that evening in Seville. For a greater – and for me paramount – perspective, it was even necessary to travel right back to the Devonian period when the first amphibians crawled on to dry land on their four primitive, but oh, so advanced feet. But why not go right back to the Big Bang fifteen billion years ago when time and space were created? Once, the genesis of all stories was contained in a compact nucleus of undetonated creative power.

What happened was as follows. A dwarf suddenly came trotting in through the Puerta de Marchena. The strange costume he was wearing made him look as if he'd come straight from a carnival. After that, he resolutely took up position before us, and fixed us with a determined look. A moment later he brought out a camera and took several snapshots of us, first me and then Frank.

'Did you see that?' cried Frank.

The dwarf turned on his heel and half a minute later was staring down at us from an opening in the viewing platform. Once more, he pointed his camera at us and took a picture or two.

'What a strange guy,' Frank said.

'Strange behaviour, certainly,' I remarked.

But the Norwegian wasn't satisfied with that. He jumped up from the bench and set off purposefully after the dwarf. I could see him through the openings in the wall running over the Puerta del Privilegio, and when he returned several minutes later, he could only open his arms wide and say, 'He's vanished into thin air.'

It was half past four, and the Alcázar was about to close. We walked out into Plaza Virgen de los Reyes once more and into the narrow alleyways of the old Jewish quarter of Santa Cruz, peering into cool courtyards and up at an extravaganza of wrought-iron grilles and balconies. I'd been there only the week before and was able to tell Frank that the wrought-iron bars protecting all the windows and courtyards had served a double function. One had been to promote both outlook and insight, to curb crime by fostering a more transparent society, but on the other hand the grilles were always kept locked, and consequently provided security. In former times young maidens could sit behind the grilles, while their suitors stood outside for hours whispering honeyed words, but if infatuation should take a more serious turn, the suitor had to 'eat iron'. I explained that in the warmer half of the year, life is still largely lived in the courtyard, and when the sun is hot, an awning is often drawn right over it.

We had a beer in the Plaza de la Alianza and gazed up at a luxuriant bougainvillea that was climbing up one of its façades. Behind the façade grew a proud palm, and behind that again we glimpsed La Giralda. Like all other squares in the old Jewish quarter, it was lined with orange trees.

An hour later we moved on to Plaza Doña Elvira and its elegant ceramic benches, and from here I took Frank into the narrow alley called 'Susona'. I said I'd show him the secret of Santa Cruz. We emerged into a small square, originally an internal courtyard, and here I pointed up to a ceramic tile with a picture of a skull on it. The tile was in the wall above a window, and under the skull was the word SUSONA.

'Is that the secret of Santa Cruz?' the Norwegian asked.

I nodded.

'Susona was a Jewish girl who lived in the fifteenth century,' I explained. 'She was secretly in love with a young Christian, but then Susona heard that her own family were planning a bloody insurrection against the leading Christians of the city. Amongst those to be put to death was Susona's lover, and so she went to him and warned him of the plot. The result was that her own father was sentenced to death, and Susona herself was later jilted by her lover. When, after a miserable life, she finally died, she gave instructions in her will that her head should be severed from her body and displayed outside her house, as a warning to others. Her skull hung there right to the end of the eighteenth century, and later the ceramic tile was fixed on the same spot.'

There were a couple of orange trees in the square, and Frank asked me if I knew how to tell if a tree had sweet or bitter oranges. When I said I didn't, he broke a leaf from one of the trees and showed me that under the leaf proper was a narrow leaf on the same stalk, so this tree bore bitter fruit.

We walked up to Plaza de los Venerables where once there'd

been a hospital for retired priests. There were two restaurants in the square, and two orange trees. We sat down at one of the tables outside and had a glass of manzanilla before ordering dinner. We started on the subject of the evolution of life again; I think it was Frank who began the conversation, perhaps to give me value for the money I'd invested in this trip to Seville. A lot of what we discussed that evening I've made good use of since. It was here he told me about the tuatara in New Zealand.

So far, I thought, my chance meeting with Frank in Madrid had been nothing but a pure, unalloyed pleasure. But the decisive moment was approaching, for it was almost nine o'clock. After paying the bill I guided Frank through the narrow alleys and out into the Plaza Santa Cruz. I showed him how close we were to the high wall that divided us from the Alcázar gardens, and the Jardín de los Poetas in particular.

'I think you must have scales in front of your eyes,' I said.

He didn't know what I meant, so I told him to take a good look around. He pointed to the great iron cross in the middle of the square, and I told him how the French had burnt down the old church which had once stood there and had, in its time, given both the square and the district its name. We did one and a half circuits of the square that surrounded the baroque cross. Then he suddenly caught sight of something. He looked at me with a glint in his eye and disappeared into the flamenco *tablao*, Los Gallos.

'My mind's been full of those Goya paintings,' he exclaimed as he slapped his forehead. 'I'd quite forgotten she was one of Seville's famous flamenco dancers!'

I punched him playfully on the shoulder.

'This is going to be fun!' he said, but I wasn't so sure he mightn't eat his words later on.

Apart from a group of Japanese tourists, the flamenco bar wasn't very full, and we sat at a table I'd reserved right up by the stage. We each ordered a glass of brandy, and Frank said nothing, merely raised his glass to me expectantly.

Soon the show began. First, three men in black trousers and

white shirts came trooping down the stairs from a gallery at the other end of the room. They made their way through the audience and took up their positions on the stage. One of them carried a guitar, the two others had no instruments other than their soulful voices and their own pentadactyl rhythm. The guitarist began to play, while his two companions clapped and snapped their fingers.

Then she appeared, as gracious and grand as a goddess. Ana descended to the stage by means of a circular staircase, to rapturous applause from the Japanese, who clearly recognised her – it was largely because of her that they'd travelled all the way from Tokyo, Kyoto and Osaka. Ana was wearing a red dress, a rose-coloured shawl and bright red shoes. Her dark hair was tied up in a pony-tail, and decorated with a rose.

'Ana!' Frank whispered as she stepped on to the stage.

I nodded. 'Ana María Maya.'

'Is that her name?'

I nodded once more.

'Maya?'

'Shhh!'

Ana began to dance. Her dance was energetic, and more elaborate than I'd seen the previous week. I noticed a sharp contrast between the rigid, concentrated facial expression and the fluid arm movements, not to mention the elegant finger-play reminiscent of the Indian temple dance I'd once witnessed at Orissa.

Other numbers followed, with other dancers, but it was Ana María Maya who was the evening's biggest star. Ana danced with her arms and hands, feet and fingers, belly and hips. She was proud, she was severe, she was flirtatious and she was meek. It was Ana that I most wanted to show Frank in Seville. I wanted to show him the profligate celebration of the post-animal vertebrate's elastic limbs. The original amphibian should be witnessing this, I thought – the great-grandchildren dancing flamenco in Seville – using every extremity of the tetrapod, every muscle and vertebra, every coordinating synapse of the brain. But little did those first amphibians know what they were heading towards when, in

Devonian semi-darkness, they padded all unsuspecting through ferns and club moss en route to their periodic love trysts by overgrown puddles and tarns. It was a proud, erect and flamboyant victory dance we saw, and Proto Amphibia and Proto Amphibius would have had good reason to rejoice in all the tadpoles that would soon fill Fern Lake and Reedy Tarn, because their oats had not been sown in vain. It wasn't only a victory dance we were watching, but also the death throes of the transient vertebrate, because soon a song – deep, hoarse and compelling – began, a song about love and death, deceit and oppression.

Then there was an interval. After the applause, Ana followed the rest of the ensemble up into the gallery, but just at that moment José made his way to the table where we were sitting. He was carrying a tiny baby in his arms, and Frank's eyes opened wide in amazement. The child was only two or three months old. Before greeting José properly, Frank looked at the infant and then up at José.

'Is it . . . yours?' he asked.

José nodded proudly and grinned.

'This is Manuel,' he said and seated himself at the table.

Soon Ana arrived and joined us.

'How lovely to see you, Frank! This is a surprise.'

Frank sat there stony-faced.

'How old is he?' he asked. His question seemed directed at himself just as much as to the delighted parents.

'Ten weeks,' Ana replied.

The biologist began counting on his fingers. 'Did you know about this on Taveuni?'

His question hung in the air because just at that moment an elegant woman with a large shoulder bag entered the place and made for our table. It was Vera. A swollen stomach quite clearly spoke of a pregnancy that only had a couple of months left to run.

'Vera?'

For the second time that day Frank rubbed his head and looked non-plussed. Maybe he'd had another déjà vu experience, for it wasn't the first time he'd seen Vera with a round stomach.

Vera leant across and gave him a reunion hug. I said, 'Her name's been in my book ever since I got back from Fiji. Then I rang her a couple of times from Madrid after we both met yesterday afternoon. I thought the five of us should meet. Or the six of us. Or seven. It was only last night I invited her to Seville.'

I knew Frank hadn't seen Vera since they'd met in Salamanca. His glance now lighted intermittently on her pregnant stomach, and when he looked away from Vera I could read deep sorrow on his face. He struggled hard to maintain his social aplomb as he turned to Vera and nodded at her condition.

'Congratulations,' he said wanly.

A few moments later he'd turned to me and was looking into my eyes with a reproachful air. I couldn't rightly tell if this was because I'd invited the expectant mother to Seville, or that I'd kept it secret from him.

Vera smiled uncomfortably. That pained me a bit since it was my fault she found herself there. She didn't even get the chance to respond to Frank's congratulations, as the guitarist and the two erect *cantaores* were once more coming down from the gallery, making their way through the locale and up on to the stage. Only when they had settled themselves did the flamenco queen herself step on to the stage. She walked down the winding stairs like a diva ex machina.

Vera was seated between Frank and me and looked at each of us before whispering, 'I think I must have met her before.'

Despite his obvious mental trauma, Frank couldn't help smiling. He looked across at me, both of us no doubt recalling how we had, quite separately, gone about at the Maravu trying to remember where we'd seen Ana before.

He looked at Vera, and now, only now, said, 'Think of the Prado.'

'Of the Prado?'

'Of Goya, then.'

Vera's eyes grew large. Then, in a voice so loud I was afraid she might be heard right up on stage, she said, '"La Maja Desnuda"!'

Both Frank and I nodded proudly, as if we'd been responsible for reincarnating Goya's myth-enshrouded model. So now he didn't need to take me to the Prado after all.

'She's absolutely identical!' whispered Vera.

'Shhh!' I said, and the dance began again.

When the performance ended one and a half hours later, it was one thirty in the morning. Now a long table was laid with tapas and manzanilla down in the bar. Ana and José kept in the background while Frank, Vera and I had an opportunity to take sorely needed stock of the situation. I felt a responsibility for what I'd set in motion and also reckoned they might need a chairman.

'Now don't feel shy on my account,' I said. 'In any case, I'm the only person who knows the background to it all from both sides. That's often the case when two grown-up people can't talk to one another.'

They were both equally nervous, like schoolchildren hauled up before a stern headmaster. I won't hide the fact that I took some enjoyment from the situation I found myself in.

'Perhaps you're right about that,' Frank commented.

Again he nodded at Vera's stomach.

'It's only a few weeks since we last spoke on the phone, and a very nice conversation it was, too. I think you might have told me you were pregnant.'

At this she turned very solemn.

'I was too much of a coward,' she admitted. 'I didn't dare.'

He glanced at me before turning his gaze on her once more.

'I assume the child has a father.'

'Frank . . .'

'But anyway our period of separation's over. So it's fine by me. You're free to marry again.'

She stared at me baffled, but I didn't want to help her any more; they'd have to manage on their own. I just nodded sternly back.

She took Frank's hand, and he was quick to withdraw it, but her eyes pleaded for understanding as she looked at him. 'It's your child, Frank.'

For a few moments his face took on a hue that reminded me of

Ana's, before she collapsed over the breakfast table on Taveuni. Then his cheeks flamed and he breathed a bit more heavily. It was as if I could hear his blood pressure rising, and for a moment I was worried he'd slap her. Then he said firmly, 'That's quite impossible.'

She shook her head.

'Can't you count?' she said.

'But . . . you're joking!'

It was somewhere around this point that I motioned to the waiter and got Frank another glass of brandy. He needed calming down.

Now Vera began to get down to business.

'Surely you haven't forgotten that we spent that night together in Salamanca. You hadn't had that much wine.'

He turned to me. 'Do you really want to listen to all this?'

'Yes,' was all I said.

She went on, 'No, I didn't dare tell you, Frank. We'd made a solemn vow not to get together again. And then – we found ourselves just standing around outside the door of my hotel room. Either you had to go to your own room, or come in with me. You remember? We were in full agreement that what we termed an intermezzo wouldn't form the start of a reconciliation. Because we *had* completely finished with each other.'

'That's what we said, at least,' Frank conceded.

'Then I reassured you there'd be no contraception problem that night. It was just about the safest day of the month for me. When, against all the odds, I became pregnant, I naturally thought of Sonja. I wanted the baby, I was sure of that. I was prepared to be a single mother, and of course I was going to let you know immediately after the birth. But I had to wait, things could go wrong again, I mean . . . I was going to leave it up to you to decide just how much contact you wanted to have with the child, and that's something, something I still intend to do.'

Frank didn't try to hide the fact that he was crying.

'Go on,' he said.

'Then a John Spooke phoned, and he said he'd been with you in

Fiji and that he'd met you quite unexpectedly again in Madrid. He said you'd probably be spending this weekend in Seville, and he invited me down to what he called "the flamenco show of the century". And he wasn't exaggerating, she's quite fantastic. I thought it might give me the chance to explain everything. That was yesterday afternoon, but then he rang again in the middle of the night, just to confirm that you really were on your way to Seville. He'd ordered an air ticket which I could collect at Barcelona Airport. He also said that he thought you still loved me. Then he gave me a thorough dressing down about the way we'd both behaved after the accident in Oslo.'

When he didn't reply at once, she said, 'Can you forgive me, Frank? My pregnancy hasn't any strings attached, not for you, anyway. But can you forgive me?'

'How long are you staying?' he asked.

'I don't know. My return ticket is for three thirty on Sunday. And you?'

'I don't know. Till Monday maybe.'

So they did still need an intercessor after all.

'You must both stay exactly the same length of time, and then you must decide if you're returning to Oslo or Barcelona. If not, I want all my expenses returned.'

We weren't able to discuss it further, because just then we were called over to the large table laden with plates and glasses, tapas and manzanilla. I noticed, though, that Frank placed the flat of his right hand on Vera's round stomach and that she laid her hand on top of his.

It put me in mind of something Ana had said in the car from the date line to Maravu, according to Frank's letter: 'In the darkness of swelling stomachs there always swim a few million cocoons of brand-new world consciousness. Helpless elves are squeezed out in turn as they become ripe and ready to breathe. As yet they can take no food other than the sweet elfin milk that flows from a pair of soft buds of elf-flesh.'

Another thought occurred to me. When we'd been sitting in the palm grove at the Maravu and everyone had been airing their beliefs, Ana had expressed her faith in a reality beyond this one. 'Perhape we'll meet again in another place and remember this as a dream,' she'd said. So maybe I could allow myself the literary licence of allowing Frank to embroider her statement into his long letter to Vera. Because here we were, all assembled, and Ana wasn't dead.

We drank a lot of manzanilla that night, and blew new life into many a memory from Fiji. We now had someone who hadn't been there, and Vera wanted to hear what everyone had to say. She was highly amused when we explained about Bill and Laura, but I refrained from telling her how Frank and Laura had set off for his hut with a bottle of wine they'd pinched from the party.

Ana and José had travelled to Taveuni to make a documentary about the twenty-first century, and one of the clips was to be shot at the date line on the island. The programme had long been made and broadcast, and José gave Frank a video copy. Ana proudly added that the Fiji sequence included a short interview with Frank in which he talked about biodiversity and the threat to the traditional habitats of Oceania.

Frank and I explained that we'd both shared a strong feeling that we'd seen Ana before we met her on Taveuni.

'Oh, please don't!' Ana laughed.

She hid her face in her hands and said, 'You've no idea how often I get told that.'

I explained how I'd logged on to the internet and in the space of a few minutes had found some crystal-clear images of Goya's *maja*. I'd also dug out some material on the famous *bailaora* Ana María Maya.

'Then you put your finger on Ana's forehead and let it be known in an indirect way that you'd found an internet article about her,' José commented. 'I linked this to the way you'd both begun to talk – quite excessively – of having seen her before, and I knew how much Ana would hate being recognised, either as the *bailaora* from Seville or as Goya's *maja*. I think you even began to describe Ana as a "masterpiece"? But we were in Fiji, in Fiji for God's sake! Even the internet can be abused.'

'Did you know Ana was pregnant?' Frank asked again.

They both shook their heads.

'But maybe that was why you passed out at the breakfast table?'

It was José who answered.

'Yes, we realised that later. I was petrified when she had that attack. I thought Ana was in anaphylactic shock, since she's always been allergic to insect bites. I wasn't thinking all that rationally, but I felt a sharp slap might get her adrenaline going.'

So the conversation flowed back and forth, and the bottles on the table were constantly being replenished. Frank was even taxed with peeping at Ana through his fingers while she was bathing naked at the Bouma Falls.

'That was when I realised it was only your face I recognised,' he declared. 'I'm not normally a peeping Tom.'

Ana laughed.

'I looked more like Goya's *maja* a few weeks later.'

The party broke up at about four in the morning, and I had to shepherd Frank and Vera back through the narrow alleys to the Hotel Doña María. When we met the night porter, he observed that no one had turned up to claim the third room that I'd booked. Frank and Vera looked at one another for a few moments; perhaps they were thinking about how they'd faced a similar problem outside an hotel room in Salamanca three quarters of a pregnancy earlier. Then they both burst out laughing.

'I think we're well supplied with rooms,' I said. 'But perhaps you could find me a wife?'

The last thing I said to Frank and Vera before we turned in was that I had a dog-eared picture postcard with a view of La Sagrada Familia lying on my desk at home in Croydon, and that I'd have to remember to return it some time.

The sun was high over the city when, as one big family, we set out on a long stroll next morning. Ana and José met us at the Doña María with Manuel in a red-and-black-striped pram, and soon we were walking across Plaza Virgen de los Reyes, past the Archivo de Indias to Puerta Jerez and on down to Paseo de las Delicias which followed the Guadalquivir for a while before taking us into the María Luisa Park, the largest of Seville's many green oases. The park had originally been donated to the city by Princess María Luisa in 1893 and was later made the setting for the great Ibero-American exhibition of 1929. With its labyrinth of walks and paths, summerhouses and pavilions, grottoes and artificial hills, flowers and shrubs, shady groves and innumerable trees, the María Luisa is now one of the lushest of Europe's parks.

Of the pavilions, the Maya-inspired Mexican one particularly drew our attention. José explained that it had been used as a maternity clinic after the World Fair, and the new mother and the mother-to-be noted the fact with keen interest. Frank pointed out that 'maya' was a word used by both American and Asian Indians, though of course there wasn't any linguistic relationship. José said Frank's statement was somewhat crass and riposted that the Spanish word 'flamenco' also meant flamingo, without there being any etymological connection. Ana and José told of a pilgrimage they'd once been on to Saintes Maries-de-la-Mer where Ana had danced the flamenco at a large convention of gypsies from all over Europe. In the Carmargue they had also managed to see the flamingoes of the Rhône delta.

We walked to the Plaza de America in front of the Archaeological Museum. The entire space was full of white doves, and Ana bought a bag of bird seed. Soon she was lost in one flapping cloud of white dinosaur progeny, and Frank again mentioned the photo Laura had managed to take of the endemic orange-breasted dove.

From the Plaza de America we went into the park itself. Ana and José took turns pushing the pram, while Frank and Vera were showing more interest in one another than either was in a position to realise, as Frank always looked at Vera when she'd turned her head away, and Vera almost invariably stole a sidelong glance at him when it was his turn to peer into the pram or turn to Ana and José. The only thing they avoided was looking straight into each other's eyes.

It was I who got Ana and José to tell us a bit about the roots of flamenco in Andalucía. They explained about El Planeta and the famous *aficionado* Serafín Estébanez Calderón, nicknamed El Solitario, 'the loner'. In the book *Andalucían Stories* dating from the middle of the last century he had penned a number of lively sketches from the flamenco milieu of contemporary Seville, and not least in the tale *Un baile en Triana*, or 'A Celebration in Triana'. El Solitario could justly be called the first flamencologist.

'El Planeta and El Solitario?' Frank repeated.

Ana nodded knowingly, but Frank was clearly brilliant at spotting associations.

'It reminds me of Laura,' he said. 'She was always reading "Lonely Planet".'

'Impressive,' José admitted, as he got the connection.

We stood looking at a placard that listed all the park's resident birds, and I think it was here that Frank mentioned the strange dwarf we'd seen in the Alcázar gardens.

Ana grinned.

'He lives there,' she said.

'Lives there?'

'Well, that's what people say at any rate. He runs round the gardens taking Polaroid snapshots of tourists, and then sells them for an arm and a leg at the exit. They say he lives in the Galería del Grutesco. He's worked the gardens for as long as I can remember, and no one knows how old he is.'

We emerged into the Plaza de España which was built for the great Ibero-American exhibition. The sickle-shaped plaza was surrounded by canals with Venetian-inspired bridges and a large crescent of a palace built to house Spanish industry and crafts at the World Fair. This majestic building, which faces the sun and the Guadalquivir, is separated from the plaza by four colonnades, each with thirteen double pillars.

We crossed one of the bridges, and Ana and José steered us towards the colonnade on the left. They pointed out that beneath the balustrades were detailed ceramic mosaics illustrating the most important historical events of each of the Spanish provinces together with a map of the province and its coat of arms. José informed us that Spain has fifty provinces in addition to the two autonomous Spanish cities of Ceuta and Melilla in Morocco.

'That's fifty-two,' Frank said. 'The same as the number of constituencies in the Fijian House of Representatives.'

This association game between Frank and José had turned into a sport, and José retorted:

'Or the number of cards in a pack. We beat you hollow.'

I had my own reasons for finding all this talk of *maya* and now the number fifty-two particularly amusing. And I felt I capped the lot of them when I said:

'Or in the ancient Maya calendar. The astronomical year had 365 days, but they also had a ritual year of 260 days. So, for the numbers to work out, their calendar had a cycle of fifty-two years.'

Ana looked at me, and once again it felt as if I had eye-contact with Goya's *maja*.

'You're kidding, aren't you?' she said.

But I shook my head.

'Fifty-two astronomical years equal 18,980 days, and if you divide that by the 260 days of the festival calendar, you get seventy-three ritual years. The 260 days were also divided into thirteen months.'

Now that we were on the subject of calendars and time calculations, and as I held the floor, I went on, 'You remember how they started planning for the new millennium in Fiji?'

'That's why we were there,' José remarked. 'Apart from the Antarctic and a small patch of Siberia, Fiji is the only piece of land bisected by the 180° meridian. It's the only place on earth where you can cross from one day to another without using snow-boots.'

I nodded patiently.

'But have you heard the latest?'

José shook his head, and I said: 'Because of the intricacies of date lines, summer times and sunrise times, fierce competition has developed between several Pacific islands as to which will be the first to enter the year 2000. In fact, only Taveuni and a couple of other Fijian islands actually lie on the 180° meridian, but just to beat Tonga and diminutive Little Pitt Island, from this year put their clocks forward an hour for the first time. But that's not all . . .'

'Well, go on!' said Frank. 'I hope you're not going to say that they've built a luxury hotel on the date line?'

'No, not quite. But they're going to erect a "Millennium Monument" on the 180° meridian – just where Ana interviewed Frank about endangered animal species in Oceania. Anyone who wants to can put a time capsule inside it, which won't be opened for a thousand years. You write a greeting to the fourth millennium and place it inside a glass container. The container fits into a cavity inside a brick, which is then sealed and laid to form part of the monument. The whole thing only costs five hundred dollars per time capsule, and there's an organisation which will look after the wall for the next thousand years. They also guarantee that the time capsules will be opened with due ceremony on New Year's Day, 3000.'

'I don't know if I've got anything to say,' said José. 'It's such a long way off. What about you?'

'I've thought about depositing a manifesto from the twentieth century,' I said.

'A manifesto?' José asked. 'A political manifesto?'

I shook my head.

'I've composed a kind of abstract of the tropical summit we organised at the Maravu Plantation Resort. Don't you all think we owe it to Fiji to leave a brief résumé behind us?'

They laughed.

Ana explained that the Spanish provinces were displayed alphabetically from Álava to Zaragoza, and as we drew near to the colonnade, she pointed down at the balustrade and reeled off: 'Álava, Albacete, Alicante, Almería, Ávila . . .'

She was interrupted by Vera.

'I was conceived in Almería,' she cried, 'in a small town called Vera. That's why I was named after the town.'

Then she hurried towards the map of Almería and pointed to the town called Vera.

As we stood in front of the piece about Álava, Ana looked at José and said, 'Can I tell them a secret?'

It was reminiscent of the way José had continually prevented her from answering some of our questions when we were with them on Taveuni. Now all he did was shrug his shoulders as a sign that she was no longer gagged.

'We walk here almost every Sunday,' she said. 'And, over the years, we've made up a little story for each Spanish province. When we're on our travels, we try to remember all the stories in the right order. Or we make up completely new ones.'

Frank and I exchanged knowing looks. Even the eternal mumblings of two Spaniards had at last found its explanation. I hadn't understood what they'd said, of course, that was one very good reason why I'd needed Frank as interpreter and go-between, a function he still remained blissfully unaware he'd fulfilled.

We started walking slowly past the Spanish provinces. Ana and José pointed at the mosaics and narrated a little fairy tale, legend or anecdote for each province.

Now Frank and Vera began to take turns pushing Manuel's pram. I ruminated that had it not been for a meteorite striking the earth sixty-five million years ago, they might well have been pushing an egg pram, as the dinosaurs, too, would have invented the wheel in the end.

By the time we arrived at Zamora on exactly the opposite side of the plaza, they were both wheeling it, but it was only when we stood in front of Zaragoza and José was speaking of the beautiful cathedral of Nuestra Señora del Pilar with all its Goya frescoes that they took the plunge. As they returned the pram to Ana, they joined hands and looked resolutely into one another's eyes. Now one half of the circle was complete. The other half was Frank's letter to Vera. It had never been my intention to put both halves together to make a whole. I'd not reckoned on meeting Frank in the Rotunda at the Hotel Palace. Once it had happened, it caused me a lot of headaches, but also gave me lots of new ideas.

At one point José asked me how I was doing with the book I'd begun making notes for when we met in Fiji, and again I raised a finger to my lips and declared that I never talked about my current work.

'I only asked how it was going,' José reiterated.

Now that everyone's eyes were on me, I realised how unreasonable it was that, while they'd all opened up to each other, I was the only one who'd added nothing new since our last meeting. The others had even managed to produce two new world citizens.

'It's a real story, as well as being a work of fiction. But I don't know which of the two is the more fantastic. Perhaps that's because, in a sense, they're both interdependent. They're like the chicken and the egg. Without the authentic story, the made-up one would never have existed, and without the invented one the true story would have been unthinkable. Also, it's impossible to say where the two stories begin and where they end. It's not only the beginning that defines the end. The end defines the beginning as well. This is something we've already talked about. The applause for the Big Bang was heard only fifteen billion years after the explosion.'

'But what are these two stories about?' Vera wanted to know.

I thought hard.

'They're about vertebrates.'

Frank's eyes widened.

'Vertebrates?'

I nodded.

'They're about synapsids, and especially that final bud on the twig, by which I mean post-animal primates. I'm one of these extraordinary creatures myself, and I've lived to see sixty-five. So it's odd to think that I'm descended from a small shrew that lived here sixty-five million years ago, or, for that matter, from an amphibian that lived here 365 million years ago. Well fine, good! But we might still only have reached the chrysalis stage.'

And then I bowed, first to the pram containing Manuel, and then to Vera's stomach.

'This immense, lineal relay race still hasn't been run. The pursuit will continue, my friends, it will pull away from us, and will travel on. Just where this long journey is taking us, it's much too early to say.'

Ana nodded mutely, and I had the feeling she would not be rushing out and devouring my book when it was published. But that might be just as well.

Frank's letter to Vera had been accompanied by four lots of thirteen photographs from Taveuni, and on the back of each Ana had written out the manifesto they'd gone round reciting. As we went from one end of the Plaza de España to the other – and all the way from Álava to Zaragoza – I attempted to recite what I remembered of the manifesto to myself, with one aphorism for each of the Spanish provinces. It struck me that José would have to remember to indicate that the manifesto was written to be shared by two lifelong companions, as the very perspective it opens up is almost unendurable for anyone without a hand to grasp.

Frank was no longer as dejected as he'd been when we talked in the palm grove at the Maravu Plantation Resort. I imagined he might now be finding it a mite easier to bear the idea of a lost eternity. At least he wasn't heading for cosmic night all on his own any more. Now he had someone to tread that weary road with him. He was still an angel in despair, but necessity teaches wingless angels to love.

At the Plaza de España we went our separate ways. Ana and José went home with Manuel, while Frank and Vera confessed that they needed the rest of the weekend in Seville to themselves.

So, I found myself on my own once more. I felt an attachment to each and every one of my young friends, a far greater one than any of them could know.

Before I took the AVE train back to Madrid and then the plane home to Gatwick, I strolled down the Guadalquivir, crossed by the Puente San Telmo and all at once found myself standing before the church of Santa Ana in Triana. The doors of the church were open, and suddenly, it was I who was having an intense feeling of déjà vu.

As I stood in the square before the ochre-yellow parish church, a crowd of people dressed in black slowly gathered. I took it that a requiem mass was about to be said, and when they began trooping into the church, I followed. I understood little of what the priest said, but it was obvious that the deceased was a young woman, because I could clearly distinguish her parents and husband.

Silently, as the priest officiated, I began asking myself who this was that had been snatched away, why she'd been taken – and if what had happened could be my fault in any way.

As we rose and left the church, I caught sight of the dwarf from the Alcázar gardens. As I passed through the church door, he looked up at me and winked. Perhaps he recognised me from the previous day, I thought, and though I can't remember if I winked back, he beckoned me with his finger and drew me aside from the rest of the crowd. He thrust his hand into the inside pocket of his coat, flipped through a little pile of colour photographs and then handed me one. It was a picture of me sitting in the square in front of the Puerta de Marchena in the Alcázar gardens. I rooted frantically through my pockets for some change, but the dwarf refused with a 'De nada, de nada!' I thanked him profusely, but before I could take a proper look at him, both he and all the others were gone.

I stood a long while in the square before the church of Santa Ana, gazing at my picture. I saw only what I already knew, and what I had known all along. I saw a grieving primate, and I could find no reconciliation in the desolate gaze that stared out at me. So at last I came to realise that the novel I'd started writing wasn't really about Frank and Vera or Ana and José. It was about Sheila and her solitaire. And it was about me.

Almost out of instinct I turned over the photograph I'd just been given – and on the back the dwarf had written something in red ink. It ran: *Man is possibly the only living creature in the entire universe who has a universal consciousness. So conserving the living environment of this planet isn't just a global responsibility. It is a cosmic responsibility. Darkness may descend again one day. And this time the spirit of God won't move upon the face of the waters.*

THE MANIFESTO

♣ 1

There exists a world. In terms of probability this borders on the impossible. It would have been far more likely if, by chance, there was nothing at all. Then, at least, no one would have begun asking why there was nothing.

♣ 2

To the impartial eye, the world not only seems an unlikely one-off phenomenon, but a constant strain on reason. If reason exists, that is, if a neutral reason exists. So speaks the voice from within. So speaks Joker's voice.

♣ 3

Here and now the voice is articulated by the heirs of the amphibians. It is coughed up by the nephews of terrestrial lizards in the asphalt jungle. The question posed by the heirs of the furry vertebrates is whether there is any reason beyond this shameless cocoon which grows and grows in every direction.

♣ 4

One asks: what is the chance of something coming into existence out of nothing? Or the opposite, of course: how great are the odds that something can have existed for ever? And either way: is it possible to calculate the odds of cosmic material suddenly one morning rubbing the sleep of ages out of its eyes and waking up to consciousness of itself?

♣ 5

If there is a god, he is not only a wizard at leaving clues behind. More than anything, he's a master of concealment. And the world is not something that gives itself away. The heavens still keep their secrets. There is little gossip amongst the stars. But no one has forgotten the Big Bang yet. Since then, silence has reigned supreme, and everything there is moving away. One can still come across a moon. Or a comet. Just don't expect friendly greetings. No visiting cards are printed in space.

♣ 6

In the beginning was the Big Bang, and that was a very long time ago. This is just a reminder of this evening's extra performance. You can still grab a ticket. In brief, the encore revolves around the creation of the performance's audience. And in any case, without an audience to applaud it would be unreasonable to describe the event as a performance. Seats are still available.

♣ 7

Who could enjoy the cosmic fireworks display when the rows of seats in the heavens were filled with nothing but ice and fire? Who could have guessed that the first bold amphibian was not only crawling one small step up the shore, but also taking a giant leap on the long road to the point where the primates could see a panorama of their proud evolution from the start of that selfsame road? The applause for the Big Bang was heard only fifteen billion years after the explosion.

♣ 8

There can be no denying that creating an entire world is a highly commendable achievement. Though even more respect must be due to an entire world capable of creating itself. And vice versa: the mere experience of being created is as nothing compared to the overwhelming sensation of conjuring oneself out of zilch and standing completely on one's own two feet.

♣ *9*

Joker feels himself growing, he feels it in his arms and legs, he feels that he isn't just something he's imagining. He feels his anthropomorphic animal's mouth sprouting enamel and victory. He feels the lightness of the primate's ribs under his dressing gown, feels the steady pulse that beats and beats, pumping the warm fluid into his body now.

♣ *10*

There's nothing odd about the fact that the Creator is supposed to have recoiled a pace or two after moulding man from dust and breathing life into his nostrils, and turning him into a living being. The surprising thing about the event was Adam's lack of astonishment.

♣ *11*

Joker moves amongst the elves in a primate's guise. He peers down at a pair of strange hands, strokes a cheek he doesn't know, clasps his brow and knows that within lies the haunting riddle of the self, the soul's plasma, the jelly of cognition. Closer to the essence of things he will never come. He has a vague notion that he must be a transplanted brain. Therefore he is no longer himself.

♣ *12*

A longing pervades the world. The bigger and mightier a thing is, the keener its lack of redemption is felt. Who listens to the sand grain's suffering? Who lends an ear to the louse's longing? If nothing existed, no one would yearn for anything at all.

♣ *13*

We bear and are borne by a soul we do not know. When the riddle raises itself on two legs without being solved, it is our turn. When the dream picture pinches its own arm without waking, it is us. For we are the riddle no one guesses. We are the fairy-tale trapped in its own image. We are what moves on and on without arriving at understanding.

♦ *1*

Something cocks an ear and opens an eye: up from the tongues of flame, up from the thick primeval soup, up through the caves, and up, up above the horizon of the steppes.

♦ *2*

The secret path doesn't wind inward, it winds outward, not into the labyrinths but out of the labyrinths. Up from hydrogen vapour, rotating whorls and exploding supernovas, the secret path has passed. The final leg has been a web of self-made macromolecules.

♦ *3*

The cobweb of family secrets has stretched from the micropuzzle in the primeval soup to clairoyant lobed-finned fish and advanced amphibians. Carefully, the baton has been carried on by warm-blooded reptiles, acrobatic prosimians and gloomy anthropoid apes. Did some latent self-perception lurk deep in the reptilian brain? Did no eccentric anthropoid ever get a soporific inkling of the master plan itself?

♦ *4*

Like enchanted mist the panorama rises, through the mist, above the mist. The Neanderthal's lionised half-brother clasps his brow knowing that behind his primate's forehead swims the soft cerebral matter, evolution's auto-pilot, the protein festival's airbag between mind and matter.

♦ *5*

The breakthrough comes in the tetrapod's cerebral circus ring. This is where the newest triumphs of the species are announced. In the warm vertebrate's nerve cells the first champagne corks fly.

Post-modern primates finally achieve the great overview. And are not afraid: the universe is viewing itself in wide-angle.

♦ 6

The vertebrate suddenly looks back and sees the enigmatic tail of its kin in the retrospective reflection of the light-years' night. Only now has the secret path reached its end, and that end was the consciousness of the long journey towards the end itself. All one can do is clap one's hands, extremities one places on deposit for the heirs of the species.

♦ 7

The elephant is naturally embarrassed at how its ancestors suddenly turned down an endless blind alley. More honour to the prosimian. It may have looked ludicrous, but at least there was nothing wrong with its sense of direction. Not all roads lead to Joker.

♦ 8

From fish and reptiles and small, sugar-sweet shrews, the chic primate has inherited a pair of becoming eyes with binocular vision. The distant heirs of the lobed-finned fish study the flight of the galaxies through space, knowing it's taken a few billion years to perfect their sight. The lenses are polished by macromolecules. The gaze is focused by hyperintegrated proteins and amino acids.

♦ 9

In the eyeball there is a clash between creation and reflection. The two-way globes of sight are magical revolving doors where the creative spirit meets itself in the created spirit. The eye that surveys the universe is the universe's own eye.

♦ 10

The elves are not virtual, but vertebrate. They are fish roe, frogspawn, mutant reptilian progeny. The elves are pentadactyl vertebrates, legitimate heirs of the primeval shrew, tailless primates shinning down from the trees, representing the dull echo of the primeval kettledrum.

♦ 11

The elves don't come from outside, but from within. They are the micro-inspired cobweb of frisky DNA spiders. The elves are not shadow figures on a cave wall. They are hyper-differentiated cell colonies. They aren't fantasy. But they are fairy-tale, pure fairy-tale.

♦ 12

The living planet is currently administered by a few billion hyperindividual master-mammals. They all originate from the same gulf, and from the belly of the very same lobed-finned fish. Never have two of them been identical. Never have two elves landed on precisely the same planet.

♦ 13

Joker stands at the end of the secret path. He knows he bears an ancient baggage, not in packs and sacks, but in each and every cell of his body. He sees how the earth continues to expand its elaborate DNA sculptures following inner, micro-inspired measurements. Who is this year's elephant? Where is this year's ostrich? Who, right now, is the world's most famous primate?

♥ 1

The elves are in the fairy-tale now, but they are blind to it. Would the fairy-tale be a real fairy-tale if it could see itself? Would everyday life be a miracle if it went round constantly explaining itself?

♥ 2

The elves are always more vital than sane, more fantastic than reliable, more mysterious than they can conceive with their slight understanding. Like dizzy bumble-bees buzzing from flower to flower on sleepy August afternoons, the season's elves stick to their urban habitats in the heavens. Only Joker has pulled himself free.

♥ 3

The elves turn their radio telescopes towards distant mists on the periphery of the introverted fairy-tale. But the wonder cannot be understood from the inside, and the elves are insiders. The elves live in their own world. They are encapsulated by the ontological gravity of this riddle. They are what is, and for that there is no understanding, only extension and continuation.

♥ 4

At forty thousand feet, the fifth cousins of the fishes sit well back, peering down at the lights from all the Hansel and Gretel houses. Even if the power failed, there would be comings and goings down there in the semi-darkness. Even if all the light-bulbs blew, an aura would still arise from the ground.

♥ 5

It's early morning in Elfland, and still almost dark, though a hundred thousand inner lights are burning on low flames before the electric bulbs are lit. The elves have begun to shake themselves out of their sluggish dreams, but still their brain cells run films to one another. The film is sitting in the cinema watching itself on screen.

♥ 6

The elves try to think some thoughts that are so hard to think that they can't think them. But they can't. The on-screen images don't leap out into the cinema and attack the projector. Only Joker finds his way down to the rows of seats.

♥ 7

The elves play their wildly improvised parts in the magic theatre of civilisation. They all get so carried away by their roles that the production never has any audience. There are no outsiders, there are no dispassionate views. Only Joker takes a step backwards.

♥ 8

Mother elf stands before the mirror inspecting the blonde hair that cascades down over her slender shoulders. She thinks she's the world's loveliest she-primate. The elfin children crawl about the floor, their hands full of small, brightly coloured plastic blocks. Father elf is lying on the sofa, his head hidden under a pink newspaper. He thinks everyday life is solid.

♥ 9

Aeons after the sun has turned into a red giant, occasional radio signals can still be intercepted in the stellar haze. Have you put your shirt on, Antonio? Come to mamma this minute! Now there's only four weeks left to Christmas.

♥ 10

In the darkness of swelling stomachs there always swim a few million cocoons of brand-new world consciousness. Helpless elves are squeezed out in turns as they become ripe and ready to breathe. As yet they can take no food other than the sweet elfin milk that flows from a pair of soft buds of elf-flesh.

♥ 11

The candy-toddler in his blue rompers looks good enough to eat. Mother elf watches him rock to and fro on a plank tied to two stout ropes and fixed to a branch of the big pear tree. Thus she keeps tabs on this afternoon's sparks from that vast, miraculous bonfire. She surveys everything in the small garden, but she's blind to the sparkling light that binds all gardens together.

♥ *12*

The Queen of Hearts is her own flower. When she wants to decorate her living-room or meet her lover, she picks herself. It's really rather a feat, she knows she's a rare strain. The tulips are bursting to do the same. The daisies look up at her enviously. The lilies nod deferentially.

♥ *13*

When we die – as when the scenes have been fixed on to celluloid and the scenery is pulled down and burnt – we are phantoms in the memories of our descendants. Then we are ghosts, my dear, then we are myths. But still we are together, still we are the past together, we are a distant past. Beneath a dome of the mysterious past I still hear your voice.

♠ *1*

Joker slinks restlessly amongst the elves like a spy in the fairy-tale. He reaches his conclusions, but has no one to report to. Only Joker is what he sees. Only Joker sees what he is.

♠ *2*

What do the elves think as they are released from the secret of sleep and arrive fully formed at a brand-new day? What do the statistics say? It is Joker asking. He gives the same start of amazement each time the small miracle occurs. He is caught out by it just like one of his own pieces of hocus-pocus. This is how he celebrates the dawn of creation. This is how he greets the creation of today's dawn.

♠ *3*

Joker awakes from unfettered dreams to skin and bone. He hurries to pluck the berries of the night before the day over-ripens them. It's now or never. It's now, or never again. Joker realises that he can never get out of the same bed twice.

♠ 4

Joker is a mechanical doll that falls to pieces every night. When he wakes, he gathers arms and legs and reassembles them so the doll is like it was yesterday. How many arms were there? How many legs? And then there is the head, with a couple of eyes and ears, before he can get up.

♠ 5

Joker awakes inside an organic hard disk on the pillow. He feels himself trying to crawl on to the shore of a new day from a hot current of half-digested hallucinations. What nuclear power sets the elves' brains on fire? What makes the fireworks of consciousness fizz? What atomic force binds the brain cells of the soul together?

♠ 6

He feels that he's floating in empty space. Can't go on like this. Doesn't one deserve to move one step on? Joker makes some defiant gestures in the bedroom mirror, tries to wring a perspicacious glance from his soul's doppel-ganger. But everything is as it was. He clenches his teeth, pinches himself in the miracle.

♠ 7

Suddenly he's sitting in the saddle on a doomed ride from alpha to omega. He can't remember mounting, but now he feels the wild stallion of existence galloping under him and is raised by mysterious forces to a headlong stop.

♠ 8

Joker is so rich in assumptions that for one dizzy moment he feels intensely robust. How many generations can he reckon since that first cell-division? How many births can he tot up since the first mammal? It's time for the big numbers. Wasn't he well on the way to preparing this morning's reflection when the first lung-fish broke the surface of the waters? Then, all at once, the little jester feels mortally giddy. He's rich in background. But he has no future. He's rich in past. But he is nothing afterwards.

♠ *9*

Joker is an angel in distress. It was a fatal misunderstanding that led him to assume a body of flesh and blood. He only wanted to share the primate's lot for a few cosmic seconds, but he pulled down the celestial ladder behind him. If no one fetches him now, the biological clock will tick faster and faster, and it will be too late to return to heaven.

♠ *10*

The door out of the fairy-tale stands wide open. Someone ought to report it, of course, but there's no one in charge to report to. Joker is dragged inexorably towards the cold draught of everything that is not there outside. He dabs at a tear, no, he's really crying now. And so the nimble jester takes his sad farewell. He knows he can't haggle. He knows that the world will never return.

♠ *11*

Joker is only half there in the elves' world. He knows he will go, so he's paid his dues. He knows he's going, so he's already half gone. He's come from all that exists and he's going nowhere. Once he arrives, he won't even be able to dream of returning. He's bound for the land where even sleep doesn't exist.

♠ *12*

The closer Joker comes to eternal annihilation, the clearer he sees the animal that meets him in the mirror when he awakes to a new day. He finds no reconciliation in the inconsolable gaze of a grieving primate. He sees a bewitched fish, a metamorphosed frog, a deformed lizard. This is the end of the world, he thinks. This is where the long journey of evolution comes to an abrupt end.

♠ *13*

It takes billions of years to create a human being. And it takes only a few seconds to die.